# A GIRL
## Divided

# A GIRL Divided

ELLEN LINDSETH

LAKE UNION
PUBLISHING

Text copyright © 2018 by Ellen S. Lindseth
All rights reserved.

No part of this book may be reproduced, or stored in a retrieval system, or transmitted in any form or by any means, electronic, mechanical, photocopying, recording, or otherwise, without express written permission of the publisher.

Published by Lake Union, Seattle

www.apub.com

Amazon, the Amazon logo, and Lake Union are trademarks of Amazon.com, Inc., or its affiliates.

ISBN-13: 9781503903876
ISBN-10: 1503903877

Cover design by PEPE *nymi*

Printed in the United States of America

*Dedicated to Heather—*
*Your fearlessness and thirst for*
*adventure inspire me to this day*

*Let all hesitation and discouragement*
*burn away.*
*Let the mild breeze*
*turn into a roaring wind.*
*Awaken in me*
*impossible, improbable dreams.*

—Rabindranath Tagore (from *Gitanjali*, translated
by Brother James Talarovic)

# Chapter 1

The damp, cedar-tinged air of the Chinese mountains lingered on Genie's tongue, spicy and familiar, as she turned her face to catch the mist falling from the gray January sky. She closed her eyes in pleasure, the tiny droplets cooling her flushed skin as she waited on the steep footpath. A deep magical hush blanketed the valley this morning, one interrupted only by the faint shushing of the river far below and the occasional bird twitter. Except for the crunch of footsteps behind her, she might be all alone, an adventurer exploring an unknown mystical world, far, far from the modern twentieth century, with all its revolutions and wars.

Her father would be horrified if he knew Genie secretly hoped that the enchanted creatures from Zhenzhu's stories were real, that if she ventured far enough she would find them—talking monkeys and tigers, virtuous princesses and evil demons—between the jagged limestone peaks, still waging their elemental battles of good versus evil.

The footsteps stopped beside her. "It's not fair," a musical feminine voice said in Chinese between gasps. "You spend as much time inside as I do, and yet you aren't even breathing hard."

Genie laughed as she opened her eyes. Li Ming was glaring at her, her delicate heart-shaped face flushed from exertion. If her best friend weren't so averse to hugs, Genie would have given her one.

"It's because I'm so much taller than you," Genie answered in the same language. "But don't despair. Which trait makes for a more valuable wife: Long legs, or the ability to weave the most beautiful patterns in China?"

Her friend flushed more deeply, this time with pleasure. "Perhaps not all of China."

"That's not what my father says. Wherever he goes, he says your fabric is the first to sell, for which he is most thankful, since it helps pay his expenses."

"As it should, since he's a man of the cloth," her friend said drily, but her dark eyes twinkled.

Genie joined in her friend's amusement, then looked out over the valley and sighed in deep appreciation. "Sometimes I wonder that he ever leaves here at all. It's so beautiful."

"It looks rather ordinary to me," Li Ming said doubtfully, her breathing almost back to normal.

"Oh, not at all." Genie ran her gaze down the steep terraced hillsides as they cascaded like irregular stair steps to the valley floor. They were gold and brown now, fallow with the season like the narrow patchwork of fields flanking the river that divided the valley. But come summer, the landscape would become a deep verdant green, like the most precious of gems.

With practiced ease, she found her tiny house on the edge of the village and smiled. Home. Smoke from Zhenzhu's cooking fire lazily wended its way from the small hut behind the dark-timbered house. Reinforced with river stone, the construction was the same as every other building, the methods unchanged from the century before.

She hadn't been sure, when her father had decided to move to this valley ten years ago, whether she would ever adjust to this raw, primitive land. Having been raised in cities like Peking and Hankow, she had found the silence that came with the endless open air, and the utter lack of commotion, with no carts or cars or ceaseless crowds, terrifying and strange. Now this forgotten corner of Kweichow Province in south-western China was as close to heaven as she could imagine.

Li Ming touched Genie's sleeve. "We should keep going."

Steeling herself for another steep climb, Genie tightened her grip on the soup pot she was carrying and started up the narrow path once more. Soon her own gasps for breath filled her ears, so loud she almost didn't hear the faint rumble of far-off thunder. Except it wasn't the season for storms, and the sound didn't fade. Instead it grew louder and more distinct. Genie's heart stuttered as she froze, her gaze flying to the sky, the covered dish in her hands forgotten. Li Ming likewise stiffened.

"What is it?" her friend whispered, her dark eyes darting around the clearing. The otherworldly growl seemed to come from everywhere and nowhere.

"An airplane, I think." Frantically Genie searched the low clouds for movement. There was no mistaking the sound now, though she had heard it only once before, back in Hankow, before her father had moved them here.

"You mean the flying machine your father was telling the village about? The ones we should be on the lookout for?"

"Yes. But I can't tell if it's one of ours or not." Her father had taught her the symbols to look for, to tell whether a pilot was friend or foe, in case of such an emergency. But that would only work if she could actually see the plane.

In theory it shouldn't matter, since she and Li Ming were unarmed civilians. Yet there wasn't a soul in China who didn't know about the massacre four years before, after the Japanese had overrun Nanking.

Wild stories of fifty thousand dead had snaked along the trade routes and over the radio waves. A hundred thousand. Even hundreds of thousands. And not just men but women, children, the elderly, infirm . . . all slaughtered for no reason. Genie's father had privately thought the numbers inflated until he had journeyed north on one of his missionary rounds. He had come home grim and unusually silent about the trip and with a keener interest in the spreading war.

Overhead, the growl faded and then intensified in a maddening tease, like a giant deadly wasp lurking out of sight. Genie turned around, careful not to lose her footing on the steep path, trying to catch the direction of the plane's flight. Was it headed west toward the high mountains? Or east toward the sea and the Japanese?

Li Ming grabbed her arm. "We should go back. Wu Fang can eat later."

"No. We're so close." Shaking her friend off, she thought of the elderly man who waited for them higher up the mountain, next to his shortwave radio. He would be just as exposed as they were. "I refuse to behave like a rabbit, afraid of its own shadow. Besides, the pilot could be Chinese. He could be defending us!"

Li Ming looked at her askance. "Or he could be a Japanese rabbit hunter looking for a few stubborn, foolish does to kill."

"He can't shoot what he can't see. See all those clouds? He would have to be a fool to try to descend through them. He'd hit a mountain for sure." Or at least she hoped the overcast sky would serve as a worthy deterrent.

"What if he were one of your countrymen—the ones Wu Fang was telling us about? Would such a one be foolhardy enough to try?"

"Just because someone volunteers to defend a country not their own doesn't mean they want to die," she said firmly, though she sometimes did wonder why the handful of American pilots had volunteered to come here to defend China in her hour of need. Even more surprising was that they had done so months before Japan had attacked Pearl Harbor.

Her chest tightened as she thought of that morning, two months before, when her father had rushed into the courtyard. She and Zhenzhu had been dipping candles in preparation for the Christmas service. His face had been ashen as he told them the news, and she remembered feeling curiously light-headed. It wasn't until the next day—when Wu Fang had told the assembled village that the US had officially declared war on Japan—that she had started to cry. Yes, her beloved Chinese friends would finally have help against the Japanese, but it also meant her relatives in the US would be in danger.

Peace on earth, indeed.

She shoved the gloomy thought aside. "In any case, as long as we are back in the village before the mist burns off, we should be safe enough."

"Perhaps we will be, but there are so many others," Li Ming said softly.

Genie glanced at the slender woman next to her. "You're thinking of Xiao."

Li Ming pulled her fur-lined jacket tighter to her throat, though the movement had little to do with the cold and everything to do with her fiancé, a soldier in the Chinese National Army. "One cannot fight one's destiny. If he was a good man in his last life, he will be safe in this one."

"Actually, destiny is in the Lord's hands," Genie corrected gently as she searched the sky again.

"So your esteemed father is always telling us. Speaking of whom, are you sure he won't object to you coming to the festival today?"

"For the hundredth time, I'm sure." At least she hoped he wouldn't mind. She couldn't actually ask him, since he was gone on another of his mission trips into the Chinese countryside. This one had taken him north, deeper into the mountains. A secret part of her wished she could have tagged along, but his "no" had been so adamant the one time she had asked, she knew better than to inquire again.

The sound of the plane had faded, leaving only the gentle shush of dried grass and the delicate twittering of tiny birds. Relieved, she started up the trail again, the magic of the morning lightening her heart. As they passed through a stand of fir trees, the spicy fragrance of the dried needles being crushed beneath their feet filled the air. The path became more exposed, hugging the base of a limestone cliff, and a cool breeze pulled at her wide-legged trousers and tunic. Suppressing a shiver as the sweat dried on the nape of her neck, she picked her way over the loose rocks, careful not to trip. Keeping Wu Fang fed so he could man his radio was the responsibility of the village women. Genie had begged to be included. If she failed and spilled the soup, it would be blamed on her being *guai lo*, or non-Chinese, a distinction she fought hard to erase.

Wu Fang sat on the ground, dozing in the shelter of a small cave. A tattered blanket was draped around his shoulders, and small wood-and-metal headphones covered his ears. Next to him sat a large rectangular box of brown-painted steel, bristling with antennas and dials. It hummed faintly, indicating it was on. Gingerly, she stepped over the cables that connected the radio to the chemical battery, which was placed a safe distance away.

When Wu Fang had accompanied her father home seven years before, seeking refuge from the civil war raging between the Communists and the Kuomintang Nationalists, he had used the radio as an inducement to let him stay. At first the device had been an amusing curiosity. Now the radio was the village's one fragile tie to the rest of the world.

On a clear, cool night, the old Communist could snare broadcasts out of the air from as far away as Peking. It was over these airways that the village had learned of the rare Chinese victories against the Japanese at Changsha and Guangxi. It was also how Wu Fang monitored the slow advance of the Japanese across the lowlands.

"Wu Fang." Li Ming crouched near the old man and set her covered bowl on the mist-dampened ground. When he didn't stir, she hesitantly touched his thin hand. A faint flutter pulsed beneath the thin papery skin of his neck, so at least he wasn't dead. Relief rushed through Genie.

"Wu Fang," her friend said again, louder this time, pulling her hand back.

His eyelids twitched. "Mei?" The name was little more than a dry husk of sound. Genie bit her lip. Mei was the name of his long-dead wife.

"No, Honorable One. It is only two worthless girls from the village, Li Ming and Yu Jie," Li Ming said, switching to a more formal address out of respect for his age. She had also used Genie's Chinese name instead of her English one, Eugenia, which was difficult for the villagers to pronounce. Genie actually rather liked the Chinese version, since it meant "beautiful jade."

"We have brought you soup and rice rolls. If it pleases, we will serve you."

He struggled to a more upright position and then removed his headset. Without comment, he reached for Genie's soup bowl with his left hand, his right arm having been amputated years ago. Genie removed the cover for him.

"Are there any new reports on the war?" Li Ming asked as she unfolded a plain cloth napkin and held it out to him.

He grunted around a mouthful of soup. The girls waited politely, knowing it would do no good to press. As young unmarried women, they were so far below him in social status, he could answer them or not as he pleased.

"Where's Jianyu?" he asked Genie abruptly, using her father's Chinese name.

She hesitated, tempted to ignore his question the same way he had ignored Li Ming's. Then ingrained respect for her elders won out. "My honored father is due back before the new year." Which was only a month away, by the Chinese calendar.

Wu Fang finished the soup and then handed the empty bowl back to her. Ignoring the napkin, he wiped his hand on his worn linen trousers and then pulled a battered feather from his pocket. Its ragged surface bore the distinctive cream-and-brown striping of a hawk's. He handed it to her. "For Jianyu. No one else."

She took it from him, puzzled by the gift. "As you wish."

He glanced up at her, and the bleakness in his black eyes chilled her to her core. The feather seemed to burn under her fingertips, and she was seized by the sudden desire to fling it back at him. Except to do so would be rude.

Looking away, he settled the headphones back over his ears.

Realizing she had been dismissed, she stood, her fingertips still tingling as she tucked the feather into her robe. He had asked that she give it to her father, and so she would, no matter her misgivings.

# Chapter 2

"Stop fidgeting," Li Ming whispered later that afternoon as they sat together on a wooden bench with the rest of her friend's family, watching the annual Laba Festival play. Genie stilled, embarrassed to be caught tapping her foot yet again. Onstage, villagers in elaborate costumes and wooden masks were acting out scenes from Buddha's life. On any other day she would have been fascinated, but she couldn't shake the sensation that something awful was about to happen. Wu Fang's feather had unnerved her, to be sure, but worse was the possibility that her father wouldn't, in fact, approve of her being here. Ever since Li Ming's comment, Genie had racked her memory and couldn't recall a single instance of him attending a Buddhist festival.

Perhaps her father would never find out, since Nathan, her father's irritating clerical assistant, wasn't around to tattle on her. She had arrived back at her house to find a note saying he had been called to a neighboring valley to pray over a sick child and wouldn't be back until late. While she felt sorry for the child, she couldn't help but be relieved by this stroke of luck. As unpleasant as Nathan could be, he never refused a call for help.

Stifling an urge to search the clouds for any sign of an airplane, she distracted herself by running her fingertips over the intricate embroidery that decorated the red silk robe loaned to her by Li Ming's mother. The artistry and the patience it must have taken to create such beauty—

"You're doing it again," her friend hissed.

Li Ming's little brother snickered as Genie promptly sat on her hands and redirected her attention to the stage. Perhaps because she was unfamiliar with the story line, having learned very little about Buddha's life from her father's schooling, she was soon lost, and her thoughts began to drift again. A hawk was a hunter, so perhaps the feather meant the enemy was getting closer.

She shivered. It wasn't out of the question. Her father and Nathan had been discussing such a possibility for months now, whenever they thought she was out of earshot.

Li Ming stiffened beside her. Puzzled, Genie glanced at her friend and then past her as she divined the problem instantly. A lean man was striding toward the gathered villagers. His Western-style trousers and a collared shirt briefly brought her father to mind, but it wasn't him. It was his assistant.

Guessing he would be upset—and not trusting Nathan to keep his voice down while he told her as much—Genie quietly excused herself and went to meet him.

She forced herself to smile. "Nathan, I thought you'd be gone until this evening."

"I prefer you speak to me in English," Nathan said, startling her slightly. She hadn't even realized she had spoken to him in Chinese. She also noted he hadn't smiled back. He gestured back toward the village. "Let's go."

Aware of the curious glances directed their way, she kept her smile in place even as she refused to budge. "Are you sure you wouldn't like to stay?" she asked, careful to use English this time. "The play isn't over yet. And I thought I'd like to stay for the actual ceremony, since I helped Li Ming prepare her family's *congee*."

Especially since it had taken them nearly twenty-four hours to make the special rice porridge, too, because no mistakes could be made. Apparently, offering a less-than-perfect *congee* to one's ancestors was tantamount to asking for a bad harvest and even worse fortune.

"Don't be ridiculous, Eugenia." Nathan took her arm and pulled her away from the assembly. "Do you know how worried I was when I returned and found you gone? It never even crossed my mind you would be so thoughtless as to attend a non-Christian rite."

"It's a harmless festival. And you could have asked Zhenzhu where I was."

"I did. She pretended not to understand me."

Genie wasn't surprised. Likely her father's Chinese housekeeper had hoped to give Genie as much time as possible at the festival.

"Just so you know," he went on, his fingers tightening on her elbow as he guided her between the stone and timber houses, "when you are my wife, I won't tolerate such disrespect of our Lord's teachings."

"Wife?" She laughed in utter disbelief. "Don't you think you should propose first?"

He swung her around to face him. "Do you really not care how this affects your father's standing in the village? That you are threatening a lifetime of work? Endangering your soul, even?"

"Don't exaggerate." She yanked her arm free of his grip. "Sharing in the joy of friends is hardly damning. What better way is there to reach the hearts of the people you seek to save?"

"Your father would say by personally living and sharing the Good Word, not by participating in pagan festivals."

She rubbed her elbow where his fingers had dug in, as guilt niggled at her again. "Not necessarily, and Buddhists aren't pagans."

"Don't quibble with me, Eugenia. Your father and I talked before he left, and I told him I was worried about your growing affinity for the Chinese. Though it can only be expected, surrounded as you are day in and day out by natives, without having a proper Christian woman to serve as a role model."

Outrage at his barely concealed insult blazed through her. "If by proper Christian woman you mean white, know that I could ask for no better mother figure than Zhenzhu."

"No one doubts your loyalty to your housekeeper."

"And does Father know your true feelings toward those he hopes to save?" she asked, refusing to be placated.

"He understands the importance of remembering who you are—both a Christian and an American—even if you do not."

"I know exactly who I am," she said hotly. "I've been a Christian my whole life and am unlikely to forget it."

"And American?"

Conflicting loyalties caught the words in her throat. She had met only a handful of her American countrymen, and then only as a child. Yet could she truly call herself Chinese, when even the villagers she had lived with for almost a decade still considered her *guai lo*?

"It's not your fault." Nathan's voice turned gentle, as if he sensed her disquiet. "With no mother to guide you, isolated from your own kind—"

Outrage surged to the fore again. "Own kind? Are we not all the Lord's children?"

"Don't twist my words, Eugenia." Nathan's hands closed on her shoulders.

She tensed at his unwanted touch. "Nathan, I—"

"Let me take you away from here." His gray eyes searched hers, the expression on his narrow face becoming almost tender. He pulled her closer, and her stomach knotted. "Let me give you the life you were supposed to have. Your father has meant well in keeping you here, but you deserve so much more. Friends, children, a husband who loves you—"

"I have friends." She twisted out of his embrace. "And you don't love me. To pretend otherwise would be a sinful lie."

"I esteem and admire you. What better foundation is there for love?"

"Respect. Affection."

"I do respect you," Nathan protested.

Genie bit her lip, aware of what he didn't say.

"A spirit as bright and as warm as yours shouldn't be buried away in her father's study," he continued earnestly. "Your gifts are wasted here. Together we can travel the world and reach so many more souls. Children adore you. We could have several of our own."

"I'm not ready for that."

"Of course you are. The Good Lord created women to be wives and mothers, and in your heart you know this."

What she knew in her heart was that she wanted to be anywhere but here, having this conversation. "What about the war?"

"All the more reason to act now, before we are trapped here by the Japanese. Once we are married I can petition the Society for a transfer—"

"I'm not leaving my father behind." The very thought chilled her.

"Just because he wishes to stay doesn't mean you must. His calling is not yours."

"Nor is yours mine. If you want to see more of the world, go ahead. I'm staying here."

His jaw tightened. "It's not safe."

"This is my home, Nathan. Whatever danger my father faces, I'll face by his side. Besides, who would take care of my father if I left?"

"Zhenzhu. The same way she has for the past twenty years."

"And his work? Zhenzhu is illiterate. Without me, who will assist him with his dream of translating the Bible into all the different dialects of Chinese?"

He took her arm again. "It's clear you're in one of your moods, so we will speak no more of this. But know I've already asked your father for his blessing."

"And did he give it?" Dismay strangled the words in her throat.

Nathan hesitated. "He said he wished to talk to you first."

*Thank the Lord.* Genie sucked in a deep breath as she turned away, wanting to hide the wave of relief at having her faith in her father restored. Not that Nathan was a bad man. Nor was he bad-looking, though she wasn't so naive as to think marriage should be based on something as fickle as physical attractiveness. Yet she envied the spark in Li Ming's eyes when her friend spoke of her fiancé, Xiao, and the shy pink blossom of color in her cheeks when Genie had asked her if they had kissed yet.

She drew a deep breath, unsettled by a sudden pang of longing.

"You don't need to make a decision now," Nathan said gently. "All I ask is you think on it. I truly believe we could be happy together."

She glanced up at the steep limestone hills that defined the landscape in this part of China. Like the exposed tips of dragons' teeth, they scraped the sky, forbidding and fierce, the bones of an enormous bestial guardian she wished would awaken and drive away the Japanese so she might stay forever.

But was that what she really wanted? She had never been asked, her role as a missionary's daughter having been defined from the day she was born. *We can travel the world . . .* Part of her liked the sound of that, but to be Nathan's wife? An ache started behind her eyes. She massaged her temples. "Thank you for the offer, Nathan, but my answer is no. I won't leave my father."

# Chapter 3

"Yu Jie! Come quick." Zhenzhu stood in the doorway, her black eyes bright with excitement. Even more interesting was that she had spoken in English.

Genie hesitated, torn between finishing her work and obeying. She glanced down at the half-finished page of Chinese calligraphy in front of her. It had taken her most of the day, but she was almost done with translating Psalm 46. Another three lines . . .

"One moment, Zhenzhu."

*He maketh wars to cease unto the end of the earth.*

She carefully made the first character.

"No 'one moment.' Your father is home," the older woman said, switching to rapid Chinese, her agitation palpable across the room. "And he has brought a man with him. A stranger."

*A stranger?* That decided it. Genie rinsed off the brush and laid it to the side. Her heartbeat quickened. She couldn't remember the last time they'd had a visitor to the village, let alone someone unknown. As she scooted the chair back from her father's desk, a curious kind of excitement warmed her blood. One that made her fluttery and restless, as if she had drunk too many cups of strong tea.

"Where is he now?"

"Close by." Zhenzhu frowned. "You can't meet him looking like that, Beautiful Jade. You must change."

She glanced down at the ink-smeared overshirt. "What makes you think I wouldn't?"

"I meant the dress. You look like a farmer's wife in that old rag. Come." Zhenzhu backed into the hallway and beckoned for Genie to follow her.

"It's not that old." Though the hem was a little frayed . . .

"This afternoon you will do what I say." Zhenzhu took Genie's arm and firmly guided her toward the ladder going up to the sleeping rooms. "No arguments."

"I don't understand—"

"Psht. Hurry. Soon all will be clear. Wear the green dress, I think. And brush your hair."

Spurred on by the older woman's gentle push, Genie ascended the ladder. Whoever the visitor was, he must be of high rank to have Zhenzhu in such a tizzy.

The second floor of the house was a large open room partitioned into separate, more private spaces by heavy embroidered blankets. When she had lived in Hankow, their house had been much more traditionally Western, with painted walls and bright hand-sewn curtains. Her bedroom had been white and blue, with little yellow daisies embroidered on her quilt—a gift from the wives of the other missionaries. Worried about her survival with only a father to care for her, they had taken it upon themselves to provide as normal an upbringing for her as they could. That Genie had had Zhenzhu to care for her hadn't even registered with them.

Perhaps the other missionaries hadn't believed it, but Genie was convinced Providence had smiled the day Zhenzhu appeared in her and her father's lives. Her father rarely talked about the dark period after Genie's mother died, or about his decision to hire a domestic servant to care for his colicky infant daughter, but he did tell her Zhenzhu had come to a service one Sunday seeking alms. The young Chinese woman had been cast out by her village, having been doubly shamed by being both a widow and barren—the latter condition the most damning—and was on the verge of starvation. Considering it a sign from the Good Lord, he had brought Zhenzhu home, told her this was now her home, too, and then handed his screaming daughter to her.

That had been nearly twenty years ago. Now Zhenzhu was less a housekeeper than surrogate mother, confidante, and heart of their little family.

Unfortunately, as Zhenzhu's importance to the household had increased, so had the whispered accusations of impropriety and even indecency in the missionary community. Finally her father had felt compelled by the unending gossip to move his family far away to this little village so he could focus on his work unencumbered by petty minds.

The echo of excited shouts reached through the spaces in the rafters, announcing the arrival of her father. Genie yanked off the stained overshirt and shimmied off her work dress. Downstairs, the heavy front door scraped open, allowing in a flood of masculine voices. Hurriedly, she flipped open the big steamer trunk where she kept her clothes and dug out the moss-green dress she wore for company. It had been her mother's and so was at least twenty years out of date. But it was still in good repair, covered enough of her to meet all standards of decency, and was a pretty color. Her father would never have allowed it to be turned into rags. He treasured everything that had been her mother's.

Genie slipped the garment over her head. The fine cotton lawn slid down her angular, boyish figure with a wistful-sounding swish, as if longing for the more feminine curves of its former owner. *No hope of fixing that,* she thought as she buttoned up the front. Mice had long ago chewed the lace collar that had originally adorned the dress, which was a pity. With no jewelry—her father didn't believe in such vanity—she had only ginger hair and green eyes to work with, both inherited from her mother.

She fastened the cuffs on the long sleeves—which were a half inch too short—in quick, sharp movements. Normally she tried not to think too much about her appearance, vanity being a symptom of pride, which was one of the seven deadly sins. Zhenzhu had done this, with her talk of strangers and the need to impress. At the last second, she remembered her hair and quickly brushed out her normal braid and twisted it up, jabbing a score of pins into the mass to hold it secure.

Shivering beneath the thin fabric, she paused and looked longingly at the padded silk tunic still in the trunk.

"Eugenia?" Her father's voice boomed up from below.

"Coming." She closed the trunk lid with a sigh. It wouldn't kill her to be a little cold, and Zhenzhu had specifically told her to wear the green dress instead of a more Chinese-looking outfit.

The entry was empty by the time she reached the bottom of the ladder. As she followed the cacophony of voices to her father's study, her heart swelled with pride as she heard him, his preacher's voice carrying easily over the rest. Then, to her surprise, he was cut off by a different voice, an unfamiliar one marked by impatience and even a touch of arrogance. One that was also speaking English, with a decidedly American accent.

"Reverend Baker," the man was saying as she entered the room, "not to complain, but might we get on with finding that Wu Fang character? I've got to radio in ASAP and tell the commander I'm all right."

"In a moment, my good man. As soon as I tell my daughter I'm home," her father said in his usual unflappable style. "Which shouldn't take—"

"I'm here, Father," Genie called out. As she had guessed, her father's study was crowded with men from the village, his homecoming always an event, since he brought news from the surrounding provinces. As luck would have it, the men parted like the Red Sea to let her pass, so she didn't have to fight her way through. Or maybe it was for Nathan, who appeared right on her heels.

"Sorry I'm late." Nathan pushed past her, breathing hard as if he had run a long way. "I just heard the news."

Genie shot him an annoyed glance, but it bounced harmlessly off his back.

"Another English speaker. Thank the Lord," the unfamiliar voice drawled. "You wouldn't be the fellow with the radio?"

The owner of the voice moved into Genie's view, and her heart skittered a few beats. The visitor her father had brought home was no middle-aged explorer. He was younger, for one thing—close to her own age—with long-lashed, dark-brown eyes that stole her breath the moment they met hers. Canted up ever so slightly at the corners, like a fox's, they regarded her with frank curiosity, even as she took in his fiercely angular jaw and wide unsmiling mouth.

The blue-and-white sun emblem of the Chinese air force blazed brightly on the chest of his fleece-lined leather jacket, but he wasn't Chinese. On that she would stake a great deal, though he might be half. He did have glossy black hair, like almost every other man in the room save her father and Nathan, but his had a definite wave to it. And his skin tone was more bronze than gold.

Nathan moved, cutting off her view. "No. I'm Nathan Sterling. Wu Fang is the one with the radio."

"Lieutenant Ted Younan, AVG." As the two men shook hands, the newcomer's intensity charged the air. "Any idea where Wu Fang might be?"

Nathan's brow furrowed. "I imagine he's up on Temple Mountain."

"He's not." Reverend Baker turned to Genie. "Eugenia, do you know where Wu Fang is? Zhenzhu said you visited him recently. Did he mention going anywhere?"

The lieutenant's attention shifted to her, and she felt her cheeks flush. "No, but he did give me something. I put it in your desk, by Aunt Hazel's letters. Here . . ."

Edging past Hua and Te, two of the village men, she went to her father's desk. She quickly opened the top drawer, careful not to disturb her still-wet calligraphy on the desktop. After pulling out the hawk feather, she handed it to her father. He pulled a pair of glasses from his pocket and examined it. The room fell silent as everyone from farmer to foreigner waited. After a minute or so, her father handed the feather back to her. His expression didn't change, but there was a new tension in his shoulders.

She held her breath, fervently praying the news wasn't what she feared.

He removed his wire spectacles and glanced around, his clear blue eyes giving nothing away. "Did Wu Fang say anything else when he gave this to you?"

"Only to give it to no one but you." She hesitated. "And I think I might know where he is. Before we arrived he had been sleeping, and when he awoke, he confused me with Mei."

"You think he's at the cemetery, then?"

"Who's Mei?" the lieutenant asked before she could answer. His intent gaze flicked from Genie to her father and back again.

"His wife," Nathan said drily, "who died nearly a decade ago, in a different province, and yet he still insists on visiting her grave up on the hill at least twice a week, even though she isn't actually buried there."

"You know that doesn't matter," Genie said, irritated by his flippant dismissal of what she considered a touching gesture of true love. "Part of her spirit is linked to the grave marker, no matter where her body is."

"All of her spirit is in heaven, Genie," Nathan corrected her.

"Or hell," she shot back, "since she wasn't saved. Or so you told him last month. And you wonder why he doesn't come to Sunday services?"

Nathan flushed a dull red, his jaw hard.

"Eugenia, please." Her father raised his hand to cut off whatever Nathan had been about to say next. "We have guests."

"And I've forgotten my manners." Lieutenant Younan held out his hand to her. "I'm Lieutenant Ted Younan."

Startled at being addressed directly, she hesitated before taking the lieutenant's hand. "Eugenia Baker. It's nice to meet you."

"Likewise. An unexpected pleasure in an otherwise rotten situation." His lips curved into a wry smile, and her nerves fluttered uncertainly. She pulled her hand from his grasp, her skin tingling wherever his strong fingers had touched her.

"I understand your plane crashed not too many miles from here," Nathan said, moving closer to her. Unexpectedly, she found his hand settling on the small of her back, and she stiffened in surprise.

The lieutenant's eyebrows lifted slightly. "News travels fast."

Nathan shrugged, his palm still uncomfortably warm through her clothes even after she edged away. "I overheard the reverend talking to the village elders."

Genie glanced at her father, who was indeed in deep conversation, seemingly oblivious to the liberties Nathan was taking with his only daughter.

"Speaking of forgotten manners." She shifted farther to the side. This time, to her relief, Nathan's hand fell away. "May I offer you some tea, Lieutenant?"

"You got anything stronger?" Despite the hopeful, teasing note in Lieutenant Younan's voice, the shadows in his eyes told a different story.

She shook her head. "I'm sorry. Liquor leads to sin, in my father's opinion, so we don't have any."

"Then tea will do."

"Have Zhenzhu prepare a plate of *nem* rolls as well," Nathan said as she turned to leave. "Your father is likely hungry after his journey."

The reminder was, of course, entirely unnecessary, but she could feel the lieutenant's gaze on her, so she held her tongue.

Zhenzhu met her in the small courtyard behind the house. "Well?"

"Well, what?" Genie said breezily as she continued on to the small kitchen building, hoping her shaky knees wouldn't give her away.

Zhenzhu trotted impatiently alongside her. "The young man. Did he see you?"

"Of course. He has eyes." Wonderfully dark ones that made her never want to look away . . .

Giving herself a mental shake, she entered the kitchen and reached for the ceramic tea service. Her jitteriness around Lieutenant Younan was likely nothing more than inexperience in conversing with men her age. The ones in the village usually avoided her because she was white—the taboo against interracial marriage being as strong in the Chinese community as it was in the missionary one—and any missionary men who visited the valley were always more interested in talking to her father. And Nathan didn't count, as he never listened to her no matter what she said.

Zhenzhu studied her shrewdly. "Bah! It's because you wore green. Tonight you wear red. For luck. Then he'll more than just see you."

Genie sighed as she hung a kettle over the already-started fire. "I'm not changing again, not even for you."

The older woman took her arm, her fingers digging in sharply. "You must! He must take you with him, even if I have to buy enchantment powder to sprinkle on his food."

"Hush!" Genie started with alarm. "You know how Father feels about such things."

"I also know how he feels about you." Zhenzhu let go of Genie's arm to begin assembling what she would need to make the small spring rolls. "He worries that the Japanese are getting closer every day and thinks you would be safer elsewhere."

Genie hesitated as she measured the tea into a strainer, her brow puckered with doubt. "He's never said as much to me."

Zhenzhu made an impatient sound. "Are you sure? Or is it you haven't listened?"

"No, I'm sure." Genie took a deep breath to calm herself. Zhenzhu was mistaken about her father. She had to be. It was bad enough that Nathan, and now Zhenzhu, wanted to tear her away from everything she knew and loved. Surely her father would never be so cruel as to send her away. Yet if he did, as a good daughter she would be expected to obey, whether she wanted to or not.

The awful thought almost made her drop the tea canister.

*Concentrate, Genie! Good daughters also have to be good hostesses,* she reminded herself. Carefully, she finished preparing the tea service while the water heated. Once it was hot, she filled the teapot, took up the heavy tray, and left Zhenzhu to her work. As she reentered the house, the din of male voices became louder. A renewed rush of nervousness made her skin prickle.

If only Lieutenant Younan would act like all the other men in the room, maybe she wouldn't be so unsettled. Instead he had looked right at her, not through her, had introduced himself and shaken her hand as if she were his equal, and hadn't been the least bit cowed by her father. Of course, that he was also good-looking and of her age, with an intriguing American accent, didn't help any.

*Don't be a fool, Genie. Be yourself. Pretend this is like any other afternoon when your father is home and the village elders have come to call.* Drawing a deep breath, she breezed into her father's study. The lieutenant's gaze met hers as she entered, and her heart immediately skipped a beat. Hurrying on to her father's desk, she prayed her cheeks weren't as bright red as she feared. Then, turning her back to the room, she set the lacquered tray down.

As she poured the tea, she couldn't help but overhear the recently arrived Wu Fang arguing with Nathan in emphatic Chinese that his information was completely reliable—a statement that made Nathan snort in disbelief. As put out as she was with Nathan, his skepticism wasn't entirely unfounded, since Wu Fang had been known, on occasion, to exaggerate and even embellish his tales.

Picking up one of the freshly poured cups, she turned around. Lieutenant Younan stood off to the side, his hands in his pockets, looking from one speaker to another, clearly not understanding a word of Chinese. Since it might be a while before someone remembered to translate for him, she walked over and held the cup out to him. "Tea?"

"Thanks." He took a sip and then jerked, nearly spilling the contents. "Ow!"

"Be careful; it's hot."

While he sipped more carefully, she used the moment to study his face in more detail. In the filtered light coming through the study window, she could make out the slightly lighter skin stretching from temple to temple and surrounding both his eyes, like a reverse mask. Or a pair of goggles.

"You're one of the volunteer pilots," she said suddenly, the pieces all coming together. "That's why you don't look Chinese and don't understand the language."

Startled, he glanced at her. "Pardon?"

"One of the Americans who volunteered to come fight for us. I should have guessed right away. But these . . ." She drew invisible circles around both her eyes with her finger. "They were the final giveaway."

"Ah, my unfortunate suntan lines." The laughter in his voice turned it rich and warm. She could listen to it all day. "And here I thought it was *this* that gave me away," he said, turning to expose the back of his jacket.

Her eyes widened. Large conjoined Chinese and US flags were embroidered on the leather, with a section of Chinese writing sewn on below. She moved closer, curiosity overwhelming any lingering shyness. "What on earth?"

"They're called blood chits, and they were on the back of all of our flight jackets when we got here. More than that, your guess is as good as mine, though your father says it tells whoever finds me to give me aid." He somehow managed to sound both intrigued and doubtful, which made her smile.

"Well, my father doesn't lie, but give me a moment, and I can tell you for sure."

"You can read Chinese?" The incredulity in his voice widened her smile.

"Depending on the dialect and script, usually." She finished reading the first line. "Luckily this is written in the traditional style."

"That you can read any kind is impressive, at least in my book."

Her skin warmed with the unexpected praise. She smoothed her fingers over the silk embroidery, unable to stop herself. "And I'm impressed you came all this way to help us."

"'Us'? You're not an American, then?" He looked at her curiously over his shoulder.

"No, I am. Or at least both my parents were . . . are. My mother is deceased. But I was born here, in China, so I'm not always sure."

"I see. And my condolences on your mother." He turned around again so she could continue translating the patch. "As I was saying, the Chinese air force needed experienced pilots to fight the Japanese, but the US couldn't send them. Not officially, at least. Not before last month. So Uncle Sam rounded up a bunch of 'volunteers' to come over. Of course the AVG—sorry, that would be the 'All Volunteer Group'—is bankrolled by the US, even though we fly for the Chinese. Though that'll likely change now America is at war with Japan, too."

"Of course." A curious emotion gripped her chest at his almost casual reminder.

"Not that I would mind flying for the US again, as long as we could keep our planes painted the same. And our nickname: the Flying Tigers. Maybe you've heard of us? The Chinese press gave it to us not long ago, and we kinda liked it. Anyway, I was told that patch you're looking at would guarantee me safe passage back to Kunming if I crashed."

"Well, it does say the Chinese government promises a substantial reward for your safe return."

He turned to face her, one black eyebrow raised. "No kidding? Then why was your father the first person willing to help me?"

"They probably didn't know what to make of you, a *guai lo* wearing a Chinese uniform." She smiled wryly. "Rather than grousing about your cool reception, I'd say you were lucky they didn't shoot you on sight."

"But the blood chit—"

"Probably isn't that much of a help, since most of the people around here—unless they are administrators of some sort—are illiterate."

He laughed once in disbelief. "I guess I should thank my lucky stars your father showed up when he did, then."

"Or thank the Lord." She glanced up to find him watching her, his dark gaze intent . . . mesmerizing. For a moment she forgot to breathe.

"Lieutenant." Her father's voice cut through the din, and Genie jumped back, full awareness of the crowded room returning with heart-thumping speed.

"We will ask the lieutenant's opinion," her father continued in English.

Lieutenant Younan turned around. "On what?"

Genie hurried over to the desk, ostensibly to pour the rest of the tea. What she really wanted was a moment alone to regain her composure.

"What do you know of the current Japanese troop position?" her father asked. "Is the situation as dire as Wu Fang is making it out to be?"

"It depends on what he's told you," the lieutenant answered. "But I would say 'dire' about sums it up at the moment. We're losing ground in Burma, the Philippines—throughout the region. Most of the East Indies will be under Japanese control soon, if it isn't already."

"But the Americans are in the war now," Nathan pointed out.

"As are the Australians, the Brits, and the Dutch." The lieutenant dragged his fingers through his hair in helpless frustration. "We're trying, all right? But Hirohito got a head start."

"How long until China falls?" her father asked.

Genie flinched, and tea sloshed over the edge of her cup.

"It won't, as long as we can keep the enemy occupied elsewhere. Which is why I've got to radio in ASAP. The sooner I can get back to my unit, the sooner I can return to the fight."

"Wu Fang, is it possible to radio the Kuomintang base in Kunming?" her father asked the old man in Chinese.

At the mention of the Chinese Nationalist government, Wu Fang's face puckered in distaste, and Genie was afraid the old man might actually spit on the polished wood floors. "Why would I want to talk to those pigs?"

Her father sighed before responding in Chinese. "Because this young defender of the Chinese needs to return to his people, taking Yu Jie with him. You are right; it is time my little flower left the garden. Even if China doesn't fall, the storm still approaches."

Genie stiffened. Her heart slammed against her ribs as her gaze flew from the implacable determination of her father to the uncertainty reflected in Wu Fang's eyes. An impassioned avowal to not leave burned on her tongue, but she couldn't get the words out. To gainsay her father in public would be an unforgivable act.

The lines around the elderly man's mouth deepened. "It is possible," he said finally.

"So you agree to send a message?" her father pressed.

"Fine. I'll try tonight. When the heavens are clear and the signal will travel like a well-feathered arrow. A flaming arrow, though. Or the enemy will track its flight, bringing danger."

"Understood," her father said, even as Genie's world crumbled. He turned to Lieutenant Younan and said in English, "Wu Fang will try to contact Kunming tonight, after sunset. In the meantime, write out your message, and I'll have Eugenia translate it."

"It'd be easier if I talked to them directly."

"Wu Fang has only a field transmitter, and unless you're well versed in Chinese telegraphic code, you'll have a tough go of it."

"Why not use Morse code? That I do know. Every pilot does," the lieutenant said, clearly not understanding.

"First, the Chinese language doesn't have an alphabet, so Morse won't work." Nathan's tone was derisive. "And second, with the Japanese listening, nothing would arouse suspicions like picking up a transmission in Morse code. You might as well broadcast 'downed American pilot' to the entire countryside."

The lieutenant exhaled in frustration. "Fine. Your point is valid. But fair warning—if your idea doesn't work, I'm making that radio call my way, risky or not."

"Even if it endangers everyone in this valley? Miss Baker included?" Nathan gestured at her, and she wanted to sink into the ground.

"You got a better idea?" the lieutenant said sharply. "Because I'm not sticking around, coolin' my heels while there's a war going on."

A tense silence fell over the study, one broken only by the faint barking of dogs in the fields.

"Eugenia," her father said after a moment, "if you're done pouring the tea, you may leave us."

# Chapter 4

Genie crossed the courtyard in a daze, her thoughts circling in panic. There had to be a way to change her father's mind. Maybe if she translated faster to show her worth. Or slower so he would want to keep her around. Or if she were more attentive, more loving. The familiar haze of spice and cooking oil engulfed her as she entered the kitchen, but it offered no comfort. Instead it made her stomach lurch. Swallowing hard, she set the tray next to the wash bucket.

"Well?" Zhenzhu's gaze stayed on the rice paper as she rolled it out. The stone cylinder struck the low wooden table with a steady rhythmic thump that mocked the frantic beating of Genie's heart.

Her fingers trembled as she dunked the teapot in the water. "You were right. I'm to be sent away."

"Good."

"How can you say that?" Genie cried as she whirled to face the woman she had always regarded as her stepmother, if not more than that. Her voice broke as she continued, "Don't you love me?"

Zhenzhu sighed and set the stone aside. "Beautiful Jade, only a fool shuns the truth."

"How is it foolish to not want to leave my family, my home?"

"Would you rather be raped by the Japanese? Or killed?" she asked sharply.

"If the alternative was never seeing you or Father again? Yes."

Zhenzhu made a dismissive sound as she sprinkled diced cabbage and leeks over the rice-paper squares. "Then you're a bigger fool than I took you for. Preferring death over bringing peace to your father's heart. Huh."

Genie's gaze dropped to the dirt floor under the sting of Zhenzhu's words. She knew Zhenzhu was right: Father would worry if she stayed, but wouldn't he also worry if she left? Leaving the dishes to soak, she went outside, but there were no answers to be found there, either. Only ancient stone walls that couldn't keep out a modern enemy, and barren patches on the ground where vegetables would grow come spring . . . if anyone was left to plant them.

Tears blurred her vision as the unfairness of it all squeezed her chest. She needed to think . . . plan . . . something. She wasn't going to be sent away. She wasn't. To ask her obedience in this matter was too much. If she could just find the right words to convince him.

She sucked in a deep breath as inspiration hit her: Li Ming would know what to say. Hadn't she somehow convinced her own father to accept Xiao's proposal, even though he thought the young man not good enough?

Hope gave her feet wings as she bolted through the front entryway. She tried not to listen as the men discussed in both English and Chinese distances and travel times, but she wasn't fast enough to miss hearing the lieutenant's distinctive drawl cut through the hubbub, his tone sharp with anger.

"I don't care what you say. I'm not taking her with me."

Renewed panic had her fumbling with the latch. Finally, the heavy cherrywood door opened with a loud scrape, and she slipped outside. If she was in luck, Li Ming would be at her loom. As if demons were chasing her, Genie flew down the narrow alley that ran between the stone buildings, past a neighbor's chickens—which darted into a nearby doorway in a clucking flurry of brown-and-gold feathers—and toward Li Ming's house. Her wool slippers were nearly silent on the hard-packed dirt.

"Yu Jie." Li Ming's voice came from behind her. "Stop. Wait for me!"

Genie stumbled to a halt and then spun around, gasping for air. "Li Ming, my sister. I need your help."

Her friend hurried toward her, a bundle of wool in her arms, her face pinched with concern. "Of course. What's wrong? You run as if a tiger is chasing you."

"A tiger . . ." She gave a strangled laugh. "Yes, exactly. I was thinking a fox, but no. Tiger is better, except one who flies."

"What nonsense is this?" Li Ming put her hand on Genie's arm. "Is it that stray dog your father brought home? The one you call a fox? My uncle says he's a harbinger of evil."

Genie shook her head, not surprised that her friend had already heard the news of their guest. Gossip flowed through the village faster than a spring flood. "The lieutenant's not an evil spirit. He's . . ."

"He's what?"

*Fearless and handsome, with eyes I could fall into.* Her chest squeezed with misery as she remembered his angry refusal of her father's request. Fresh tears filled her eyes. "Li Ming—my father wants to send me away, out of China."

Li Ming was quiet for a moment as she absorbed the news. Then she gestured toward the river. "Let us walk while you tell me everything. We both know you cannot disobey your father, but perhaps there's a way to change his mind."

Beyond relieved, Genie impulsively hugged her friend. "I was hoping you would say that. Whatever would I do without you?"

"Live your life as always?" Li Ming said as she awkwardly embraced Genie in return, the wool still tucked under one arm. "Though to be honest, Yu Jie, you know you weren't meant to stay here forever."

Genie released her, her newborn hopes plummeting. "But this is my home."

"No, this is your father's home," Li Ming corrected, not unkindly. "Your home will be elsewhere, with your husband after you marry."

"Unless I can find someone who wants to stay here. Maybe I could convince Nathan . . ."

Her friend waved a dismissive hand. "Bah! Better to marry a stray dog than that pig."

"Lieutenant Younan is not a stray dog," Genie said with a shaky laugh. "He's far too healthy and well fed."

"Then a successful dog." Her friend pursed her lips in thought and then nodded. "He has possibilities."

Genie rolled her eyes. "I'm not marrying the lieutenant, nor is it likely he would want to marry me."

"Then what's the problem?" Confusion puckered Li Ming's brow.

"My father has asked him to take me west, to Kunming."

"Why? Do you have family there?"

"No, but I have an aunt in the United States, and my father believes the Americans in Kunming will help me get to her, though I don't know how. It's nowhere near the coast."

"Huh. And you are to travel alone with this lieutenant without first being made a proper wife?"

"I guess my father trusts him."

"More the fool, your father. I cannot imagine going on so long a journey with a strange man and no one to defend my virtue."

"I doubt the lieutenant is going all the way to America with me."

"Still, a journey to Kunming is more than a few days. Plenty of time for trouble." Li Ming drew her to a stop. "You need to talk to your father, Yu Jie. Do not presume to know his mind."

"I heard him tell Wu Fang that I am leaving. How else should I take that?"

Li Ming thought for a moment. "What if the lieutenant refused to take you?"

Genie snorted. "When has my father ever lost an argument?"

"Good point." Li Ming tapped her jaw thoughtfully. "But what if he were dead?"

"My father?" Genie stared at her friend in shock.

"No, no!" Li Ming waved her hand impatiently. "The lieutenant. If he ate something that didn't agree with him and then happened to die, he wouldn't be able to take you anywhere."

"Killing people is a sin, Li Ming!"

"I was only joking. But it would solve your problem."

"We are not poisoning anyone," she said firmly, as much to convince herself as her friend.

"Then your only option is to tell your father what you want, Yu Jie. Yes, we must listen to our esteemed parents and do what they ask, but that doesn't mean we must remain silent. Sometimes even the weakest of trees must push back against the wind if it wishes to survive."

Genie made a face. "I am not a weak tree."

"Have you ever stood up to your father, even once? Be more like our dear lady Guan Yin. Stand up for what you believe in."

Genie rolled her eyes. Like any child of China, native or adopted, she had grown up with tales of Guan Yin, the Buddhist goddess of mercy and compassion who had been an imperial princess granted immortality for her loyalty and unfailing kindness. In many ways, the goddess served a similar role to her worshippers as the Virgin Mary, except with a couple of key differences. "You do remember that Guan Yin was executed by her father for disobeying him."

"Not true," Li Ming corrected sternly. "He may have ordered it, but she didn't die. The Celestial Tiger came down from the sky and saved her."

"By carrying her to hell, which I can't see as an improvement!"

Li Ming waved Genie's rebuttal away. "Far better to suffer and be alive than be dead. Nor did the Tiger leave her there. In fact—"

"Eugenia!" Nathan's voice echoed down the alley in English, cutting her friend short. "Your father wishes to see you immediately."

"I've got to go," Genie said, letting her friend know the gist of Nathan's command. She hugged her friend again, afraid as she had never been in her life.

"The wind blows, Beautiful Jade," Li Ming whispered before pulling back. "Be brave, sister. Speak."

Genie nodded, though she wondered if that would even be possible. A lifetime of holding her tongue, of always trying to please, had bound her as tightly as the sturdiest cords.

"Eugenia!" Nathan called again, impatience lacing his voice.

Drawing a deep breath, she turned away from Li Ming. Nathan waited for her, his hands in his pockets, his light-brown hair uncharacteristically tousled as if he had run agitated fingers through it. An odd expression had hardened over his narrow face like a *nuo* opera mask.

Her sense of foreboding increased.

The house was silent when she and Nathan reentered, empty of men and activity. Leaving Nathan in the front entry, she peeked into the study. Her father stood at his desk, her most recent translation in his hand.

Straightening her spine, she walked into the room. "You wished to see me?"

"Yes." The still-damp ink winked in the afternoon sunlight as he set the paper back on the desk. "Your calligraphy is beautiful, Eugenia. Truly the finest I have seen."

"Then let me stay so I may continue."

His gaze remained on his desk as he lifted another of her pages. In the harsh afternoon light, new, deeper lines creased his chapped, sunburned cheeks. And there was a new gauntness to his already-spare frame.

She suddenly felt very small. *"Baba?"*

He glanced at her, a faint smile twisting his weary, beloved face. "You haven't called me Daddy in a long time."

"Why are you doing this? Don't you love me?"

"More than life itself." He inhaled as if to say more, then seemed to change his mind and looked down at the desktop.

"If it's no longer safe, perhaps we should leave together," she said hesitantly.

"Have I ever told you how much you look like your mother?" He looked up, his blue eyes clear and calm. "China took her from me, but it won't take you. Oh, I know you'll say I'm being fanciful, but it's true. I should have sent her home when I learned she was with child, but she so loved China, she wouldn't hear of leaving."

"More likely it was you she wouldn't leave."

A small, sad smile crossed his lips. "I fear she loved this country more than she loved me, and not without cause. I was not a very good husband."

She shook her head. "I cannot believe that."

"Nevertheless, what I failed to do then, I will not fail to do now. My resolve is firm. You will go to Kunming with Lieutenant Younan."

"And you'll come, too, yes?" she asked, daring to press.

"My life is here in these mountains with Zhenzhu. If I leave, where would she go, with no family, no one to take her in?"

"Then bring her with us."

"No, Eugenia." He pulled her into his arms, and his familiar scent of wool, sweat, and road dust cocooned her in comfort. "But don't worry. Your aunt Hazel is waiting for you in America. We agreed shortly after your birth that if anything should ever happen to me, she would take you in without hesitation."

Fear gripped her. "Are you saying you are ill?"

He sighed. "No, I'm fine. However, the country is not, and it is no longer safe here. I wish it were otherwise, but apparently the Almighty has other plans for you. So bowing to His will, I talked to Mr. Sterling. He has agreed to accompany you as far as your aunt's."

Genie stiffened. "*Baba*, no."

"He's a good man, Eugenia. Decent, upright, and of good moral character. You need not fear for your virtue in his company. And he has traveled enough times with me that I know he is capable of providing and protecting you, no matter what hardships the journey may bring."

"But—" She tried to push back from him so she could look him in the eye.

"I've made my decision. There will be no discussion," he said sharply, and she stilled. Then he relaxed and kissed her on the forehead. "Your reluctance warms my heart, but in the dark days ahead, to know my precious daughter at least is safe will be of great comfort to me."

"Fine." The word was barely intelligible for the tears clogging her throat.

"Wu Fang wishes to leave at first light tomorrow, so pack your things tonight. He has agreed to guide you all as far as the Kunming highway. Lieutenant Younan will lead the rest of the way and has promised to make arrangements for you and Mr. Sterling once you reach the city."

Feeling as if the ground were falling away beneath her feet, she could barely comprehend her father's words. It was all too much, too fast. She knew her chance to do what Li Ming had counseled was slipping away. She should tell him she wouldn't go. Except she couldn't make herself say the words. She was too afraid that he would stop loving her if she did.

He gave her a gentle push toward the door. "Go. Zhenzhu is preparing an early dinner so you'll have plenty of time to say goodbye to Li Ming."

"And to you, too, I hope." Every second with him was beyond precious now.

"I'll be with Wu Fang after dark, helping set up the transmitter. Which reminds me." He reached over to his desk and picked up a sheet of paper. "I translated the lieutenant's message while you were out, but your Chinese is better than mine. I wonder if you could please check it."

She took the paper from him. It actually contained two messages. One was the original English version, scrawled boldly in all capital letters, and then under it, in more delicate strokes, was the same message in Han Chinese. Or rather, something approximating the original message.

Her lips quirked a little as she read her father's attempt at translation. She couldn't help it. "Does the lieutenant know he is a tiger found in the stone forest without his wings?"

"My hope is that it will describe the situation in a slightly safer manner than the lieutenant's version."

She had to agree, as Lieutenant Younan had written what amounted to a military situation report. Frowning slightly, she reread her father's version, checking the characters for accuracy. "Will it really take six days for us to get there?"

"That is merely an estimate. It usually takes me at least three days to get to the highway. My hope is that you'll be able to catch a ride on a passing truck, which will shorten your journey considerably. But with the war . . ." His voice trailed off as he glanced at her. The sorrow in his gaze tore at her. The image would haunt her for the rest of her life, she knew.

She handed the paper back to him, her resolve to resist dissipating like winter mist before a breeze. Her father worried so about everyone. It would be selfish of her to add to his burden. "Wu Fang should have no trouble with the translation. And I'll be ready to go tomorrow. Don't worry, *Baba*."

# Chapter 5

The morning dawned clear and cold. Genie shivered as she waited for her father to finish talking with Wu Fang about the journey. They stood in a small group not far from the trailhead that led west, following the river up into the mountains and then beyond. Nathan hovered near her father, as did a silent, subdued Zhenzhu. Lieutenant Younan stood off to the side, alone, his gaze on the mountains. The sunrise was just touching the tips, turning the usually white rock to gold.

Huddling deeper within her many coats, the varying heights of the collars turned up against the winter chill, she gazed out over the valley, steeped in deep-purple shadow. The familiar contours, the frosted slopes that had contained, all these many years, everything that was precious to her, brought tears to her eyes. How could she bear to leave this place, not knowing when or if she might return? Her one hope that her father would relent had faded the night before, when he had donated a pair of his old trousers for her to use on the journey. He had been concerned her long skirts would endanger her on the trail, and he wasn't about to sacrifice her safety for modesty. And her father's willingness to abandon modesty spoke volumes about his resolve.

Of course the garment needed to be altered to fit Genie's shorter, slighter frame, a task Zhenzhu had worked late into the night to finish.

Genie had been torn between gratitude and resentment at the older woman's eagerness to help. If anyone could have changed Father's mind about today's departure, at least anyone female, it would have been Zhenzhu. Yet she had ignored Genie's frantic pleas to talk to him, and with single-minded determination, she had continued fixing the trousers and reinforcing Genie's coat with a heavier lining.

Genie's anger hadn't lasted, though. Especially after, in the small hours of the morning, long before sunrise, she had been awakened by the older woman's muffled sobs, the only outward evidence of a sorrow so deep it could no longer be contained by correct behavior.

Biting her lip, Genie dropped her gaze to the frozen ground, the memory bringing her despair too close to the surface. She scuffed the path with the toe of her leather boot, her mood as bleak as the dead grass caught beneath the coating of frost. How could her father stand it, knowing his decision was causing such pain to the two women he loved most? Her own heart felt like it was tearing in half.

Or maybe into thirds, since she was leaving Li Ming, too. Genie wished she could hug her friend one last time but knew better than to hope. Li Ming, for all her loyalty and kindness, had no patience with sentimentality. So Genie hadn't been surprised when Li Ming had said she wouldn't come this morning. Sad, yes. Li Ming had been her confidante and closest friend since Genie had moved to the valley ten years ago. But maybe it was for the best. She didn't want to see the change in her friend's eyes when she became nothing more than an inconvenient ghost, a painful memory that couldn't leave fast enough.

*Stop it.* Desperate for a distraction, she glanced at Lieutenant Younan. With his unshaven cheeks already bluish-black from beard stubble and an impatient scowl tightening the sharp planes of his face, he looked unnervingly fierce, dangerous even. He shifted from one foot to the other as if impatient to get going, his intense gaze alternating between Wu Fang and the mountains.

Perhaps it was a good thing Nathan was coming along to protect her. She wasn't at all certain the lieutenant wouldn't push her over a cliff just to be rid of her.

As if summoned, Nathan appeared beside her. "Ready?"

"No." The word slipped out before she could stop it.

Nathan took her mittened hand. "It's all right, Eugenia. Your desire to stay does you credit. But it's also right and proper to submit to what cannot be changed."

"Says who?" the lieutenant interjected sharply, startling her. She glanced over to find his dark gaze watching her with an almost ferocious intensity. She swallowed nervously. "If you don't want to go, Miss Baker," he continued, "don't. In my book, no one should force a child to leave a parent behind if she doesn't want to."

"Forgive me, Theodore," her father said, temporarily abandoning his conversation with Wu Fang. "Eugenia and I have already discussed the situation, and a child's greatest gift to a parent is obedience."

Lieutenant Younan's focus didn't waver. "Miss Baker?"

Her skin flushed hotly as everyone's attention turned to her. The lieutenant was serious; she could tell by the set of his jaw and the tension in his posture. All she had to do was say the words, say she wanted to stay—be the tree that stood against the wind—and he would leave without her, her father's wishes be damned.

Of course, the lieutenant had also made no bones about the fact he didn't want her on the trip, so it would be in both their interests for her to speak up.

She wiped her palms on her trousers, searching for the courage to say what she felt, that every fiber of her being ached with the need to stay. That she was terrified not just of leaving her family and her home but of becoming alone in the world. That at the ripe old age of twenty-two, she had never been apart from Zhenzhu for more than a night or slept in any bed other than her own. Though her father traveled extensively, she hadn't set foot outside this valley in years.

The reality of what her father was asking of her hit Genie like a landslide. She could scarcely breathe for the rising panic. He might as well have asked her to jump off a cliff and fly. She wasn't ready to leave everything she knew.

*Come on, Genie. Don't shame your father. You're not a coward, nor will the war last forever. You'll be home before you know it.*

Calling on a strength she didn't know she had, she squared her shoulders and handed the unexpected gift back to the lieutenant. "Thank you, but I will do as my father asks."

The lieutenant's expression didn't change, but something like disappointment flickered in his tilted cat eyes.

Nathan patted her approvingly on the shoulder. "Good girl."

A sudden, most uncharitable urge to yell at Nathan seized her. Instead she spun around and hugged Zhenzhu. She buried her face in the older woman's soft neck, breathing in her familiar scent, wishing she would never have to let go.

"Goodbye, Mama," she managed to choke through unshed tears. "I'll come back. I promise."

Zhenzhu stiffened and then hugged Genie fiercely back. "Good luck and good fortune, my Beautiful Jade. My little daughter."

Forcing herself to let go, Genie turned to her father. Despair clogged her throat as she gave him a final silent hug—a bittersweet one that she wanted to remember forever. It nearly broke her, but she managed not to cry as he kissed her on the cheek. Then, with no one left to say goodbye to, she bent to pick up her pack.

Nathan reached it first. "Here, I'll carry that for you."

"Nope." Lieutenant Younan stepped on one of the straps, pinning it to the ground. "She carries her own pack. We're going to be covering a lot of ground in the next few days and can't afford being slowed down because you're doing double duty."

"Then we'll divide her things between us. There's no reason to abandon chivalry because you're in a hurry."

"Look, the longer we're on the trail, the more dangerous it is for all of us. Either she carries what she's got or she repacks. But we carry our own gear."

"I'm fine, Nathan." With deliberate nonchalance she slung the backpack onto her shoulders. Like her father, she was tall and athletic and also relatively strong for a woman, which would have made Nathan's concerns laughable if they weren't so predictable. Sometimes she wondered if he thought her capable of anything.

Wu Fang studied her while the others buckled on their own backpacks. He had donned his own pack earlier with surprising ease, considering he was missing most of his right arm. The only concession he had made to his infirmity was to knot his jacket sleeve at the base of the stump to keep out the morning chill. Once everyone had their packs on and their straps adjusted, Wu Fang turned silently toward the path that led northwest away from the village and its fields and along the river as it cascaded down between the steep hills.

The lieutenant followed next, then Genie, and Nathan brought up the rear. The valley's early-morning silence was broken only by the twitter of birds, the sibilant slide of water over the rocks as they walked. Except for an occasional crunch of stones under the lieutenant's boots and the clunk of a metal canteen on the side of a pack, their passage was silent.

The path began to climb, and the dense foliage of the hills began to crowd closer, signaling the end of the valley. Genie slowed, all too aware that the village she had called home for the past ten years was about to disappear from sight. Throat tight with unshed tears, she stopped and started to turn.

"Don't look," Nathan said softly from behind her. "Be not like Lot's wife, pining for the past. Better to remember a place with your heart than your eyes."

She hesitated, wondering if Nathan was right. But what if the image wasn't impressed firmly enough for her to remember the rest of her life?

"For heaven's sake, if she wants to look, let her."

Genie looked up at the lieutenant, who had stopped a few feet in front of her.

"No god will smite her for wanting to catch a glimpse of her family one last time," he went on, sounding exasperated.

Her heart skipped with sudden, sharp longing. "Do you think they are still there?" she asked him.

The lieutenant's stern expression seemed to soften a little. "Maybe, maybe not. But I think you'll feel better for checking."

Still she hesitated, torn, afraid that Nathan was right and that it would only bring her a fresh wave of pain.

"I was in your shoes once," the lieutenant said, his voice turning surprisingly gentle. "And I didn't look back, because of my pride, because I wanted to look brave. It's something I've regretted ever since."

Convinced, she whirled around.

The valley was spread out beneath her, a patchwork of small fields and open pastures, beautiful even in its winter raiment. Smoke curled lazily from a dozen chimneys as the morning meals were prepared, the ancient stone walls surrounding the village keeping all threats at bay. And there, where the path separated, with one heading up to Temple Mountain and the other down to the river that wound like a narrow, dark ribbon toward the far end of the valley, stood a lone figure. Not her father. Not Zhenzhu. But Li Ming.

Genie's heart constricted painfully. She raised her arm in farewell. Amazingly, Li Ming must have seen the gesture, because she raised her arm, too. Then her friend turned and made her way slowly back to the village. Genie stifled a small sob.

Nathan's hands settled gently on her shoulders, offering silent compassion as his attention locked on the man behind her, his narrow face tight with anger. "Satisfied?"

"There's no avoiding the pain," the lieutenant said evenly. "Only the opportunity to trade a greater regret for a smaller one."

"He's right, Nathan," Genie said, wiping her eyes as she moved back, away from her father's assistant. "Nothing can make me like leaving, but at least I got one last look."

"What did Tiger say?" Wu Fang asked in Chinese as she and the two men rejoined him.

Genie rapidly translated the conversation into Chinese, her heart catching with fresh pain as she remembered Li Ming's wave.

Wu Fang's mouth became a flat line. "Tiger is right." He looked up at the sky and then the mountaintops. "Come. We're wasting time we don't have."

Genie frowned slightly as Wu Fang made his way stiffly up the path. If she hadn't been mistaken, his eyes had been suspiciously moist as he had turned away. But then, he, too, was leaving someone beloved behind, except his wife was no longer alive. She wondered if a second parting would hurt less than the first. She let the contemplation of loss and regret distract her from her own grief as the trail grew steeper and less traveled, and the passing minutes turned into an hour or more. Wu Fang had lost his beloved Mei while fighting with the Communists. Her father had lost her mother. Zhenzhu had lost her family to a cholera epidemic. And the lieutenant had hinted at a loss of his own. So much parting and heartbreak. Maybe that was the true nature of life, more than happiness and contentment.

The sun was high in the sky when Wu Fang veered off the trail. They followed him out onto a broad rocky ledge that overlooked the narrow river valley. Genie shivered as she shrugged off her pack, the wind cold on her perspiration-streaked skin. At least the sunshine was warm. Next to her, Nathan took off his pack with a grateful sigh and laid it next to hers. The lieutenant was last and reluctantly shrugged his off only after Wu Fang pantomimed vigorously that he should do so.

The lieutenant eased himself onto a rock, and Wu Fang shot him an inquisitive look.

"I'm fine." Then he sucked in a sharp breath as he gingerly extended one leg and then the other.

"Yu Jie, come here," Wu Fang ordered as he dug into his pack. He pulled out an old shirt and ripped it into two. "Climb down to the river and soak these. Do not wring them out before coming back."

Perplexed, she took the ruined shirt strips and started toward the edge of the precipice.

"What are you doing?" the lieutenant asked sharply, and she realized Wu Fang had spoken in Chinese. So used to being addressed in that language, she hadn't even noticed. But she would have to start. Someone needed to translate for the lieutenant so as to keep him in the conversation.

"Going down to the river. Wu Fang wants these wet." She held up the cloths.

"I'll do it." He started to get up but then grimaced as if in pain.

"Stay," she said quickly, a little surprised that a mere half-day hike would have him in such a state. What would he be like in three days? Or even five? "It's not that far, and I'm used to these cliffs."

Sensing Wu Fang's impatience, she clambered off the rock shelf and then half climbed, half skidded down the hillside to the snow-fed river that rushed through the narrow canyon. Crouching at the edge of the icy torrent, she dunked the shirt strips several times to soak them through, gritting her teeth against the sting of the cold water. As soon as she was satisfied, she left the stream and made the arduous ascent back up to the ledge.

The lieutenant still sat where she had left him, but he had bunched his trousers up to expose well-muscled calves . . . and severely bruised knees.

Wu Fang took the dripping cloths from her numb fingers and draped them across one of the lieutenant's knees. The lieutenant inhaled sharply, and then was still as Wu Fang did the same for the other knee.

Genie winced. She could only imagine how much they hurt. The dark purple color as well as the swelling told her the injuries were recent.

"Hit them on the instrument panel when I landed," the lieutenant said in answer to her silent question. "The nose kinda crumpled on me."

"When you crashed, you mean?"

His eyes narrowed. "I didn't crash. It was a perfectly executed forced landing, at least until the landing gear hit a rock."

"So you meant to land in . . . wherever it was you landed?" she asked curiously. She had never heard of anyone choosing to land anywhere but at an aerodrome.

He flexed his right knee and winced. "Given that the alternative was hitting the side of a mountain, yes, I thought the rice paddy looked like a better option. Though I was kind of hoping to make it back to Kunming."

"Yu Jie," Wu Fang interrupted. "Dinner."

Genie, not yet done with her questions, nodded and dragged her pack over beside the lieutenant. It wasn't every day she got to talk to a pilot, even if he was surly from pain.

"Why risk a forced landing at all?" she asked as she began removing what she needed to prepare a meal.

"The engine quit. That's when I noticed both gauges were on empty. If I had to guess, I'd say a bullet punctured one of the fuel lines. Funny thing about airplanes—they don't fly well without gas."

Nathan snorted from his perch on the ledge. "You were lucky you didn't explode."

The lieutenant glanced at the other man. "True. But as my CO always says, 'Better lucky than good.'"

"Were you injured elsewhere?" she asked, trying not to think about him caught in an explosion. Not long after she had moved to the village, a small boy had caught fire standing too close to a bonfire. The memory of his horrific screams still shook her.

"Wrenched my back pretty good, but it seems okay now. And hit my head on the control panel." He pushed back his hair to reveal a thin, inch-long scab along the hairline. "Knocked me out for a bit. If there'd been a fire, I would've been a goner."

Genie's hand stilled as an unbidden image appeared before her eyes. The plane in flames with the lieutenant slumped behind the controls . . .

"Hey." The lieutenant's warm fingers touched her hand, his dark eyes round with contrition. "I didn't mean to upset you. As I said, I'm fine. Nothing caught on fire—which only supports my fuel-line hypothesis." He sat back and laughed without much humor. "Be thankful for the small things, I guess."

She busied herself with emptying the pack, hoping he wouldn't notice her hands shaking. "Not so small, in my opinion. Thank God you're all right."

"Yeah, well"—the lieutenant began massaging his thigh—"you can thank who you want, but God and I are kind of on the outs with each other at the moment, so he may not have had much to do with it."

Shocked by his irreverence, she stared at him. "Of course he did. God watches over us all, a loving Father to each and every one of His children."

"Really?" A muscle in his jaw flexed as he worked on his leg. "Was he watching over my friend whose plane *did* slam into a mountain? Was he watching over the three Japanese pilots I shot down? Was he there in Burma when the Japanese bombed civilian targets? Seems to me if there is a God, I shouldn't even be here. Nor should there be a war forcing you from your home."

"Man's actions have been his own ever since the Garden of Eden," Nathan interjected calmly. "You can't blame our heavenly Father for this war. We have no one to blame but ourselves and our own sinful pride and greed. God is the one showing us the way out of conflict."

"Your god, maybe. But Japan's god is currently urging them on."

"There is only one true God. Their mistake is from our failure to spread our message."

"Then should I hold you accountable?"

"No more," Wu Fang said in his heavily accented English, glaring at the two men. "We eat now."

Genie handed out the food Zhenzhu had prepared, as eager as Wu Fang to be done with the conversation. She had been around unbelievers all her life and had listened to her father argue with them since she was a child. Still, it was unsettling and a little shocking to hear Lieutenant Younan be so blatantly blasphemous. If her father had been here, she wondered if he would have been still so eager to send her with the American pilot.

The lieutenant sniffed the unwrapped doughy bundle.

"It's *char siu bao*," she said. "Steamed pork buns. Or I have some cold egg rolls, if you would prefer. I was going to save them for tomorrow, but it doesn't matter."

The lieutenant took a tentative bite while she handed a cloth napkin to each man. He made an appreciative sound and then took another bite.

"Did you cook this?" he asked between mouthfuls.

Nathan snorted. "If you knew Eugenia better, you wouldn't ask. Her cooking is awful. One meal in particular had us violently ill for days."

Embarrassed heat climbed up her neck. "That wasn't my fault. How was I to know oyster sauce goes bad? Fish sauce doesn't."

"You can make a sauce out of oysters?" the lieutenant asked with a lift of his eyebrows. "I've only had them steamed or raw."

"It's a delicacy of sorts. My father brought a bottle back from one of his trips to the coast." She picked at the pork bun on her napkin. "For Zhenzhu, who's the real cook in our family."

"I'm sure you're just fine at it," the lieutenant said, the gentleness in his tone surprising her. "All it takes is a little practice."

"Yes, well . . ." Nathan coughed and wiped his lips. "She'll have plenty of time to practice once we're married."

Genie turned to stare at Nathan in disbelief. *Married?*

The lieutenant stilled, his expression alert. "You two are engaged?"

"No, we're not." She swung her attention back to her father's assistant. "What in heaven's name—"

"I'm sorry, Eugenia." Nathan shot her a warning look as he folded his napkin and handed it to her. "I know you wanted to wait until we reached your aunt to announce our engagement. But with our traveling arrangements, I didn't want the lieutenant getting the wrong idea."

"Wrong idea?" she asked furiously, outrage building at his audacity.

"Now is not the time to discuss this." Nathan's tone brooked no argument. His gray eyes bored into hers, a silent, almost desperate plea for forbearance in the wintry depths.

Confused and uncertain, she bit back her protest. Appetite gone, she silently gathered up the remains of lunch. As much as she wanted to set the record straight, she couldn't entirely discount the possibility that Nathan had a good reason to lie. One that she would definitely ask about later, in private, as seemed to be his request.

While she cleaned up, Lieutenant Younan gingerly removed the wet cloths from his knees and rolled his trousers down. Nathan took the now-useless rags from him and then extended his hand. With a grateful look, the lieutenant accepted Nathan's help and staggered to his feet.

"Thanks," he said, once he had caught his balance.

Wu Fang tapped Nathan on the shoulder and said in Chinese, "Tell him if he needs to stop and rest, he must speak up. I'm not a nursemaid."

Nathan relayed the message. The lieutenant's jaw tightened. "Tell him not to worry. I've survived much worse."

A small smile touched Wu Fang's lips, though whether he understood the words or only the tone, Genie didn't know. With no further comment, the old man slung his pack over his shoulder and disappeared into the thick foliage at the forest's edge. Nathan scrambled to get his own pack on, and Genie hurriedly stuffed everything back into hers. By the time she was finished, both men were ready and watching her, the lieutenant with his habitual impatience, Nathan with . . . well, she wasn't exactly sure.

She hurriedly shrugged on her pack. "No need to wait. I can catch up."

The lieutenant hesitated and then, apparently taking her at her word, he headed off into the brush after Wu Fang. Once she was ready, Nathan gestured for her to proceed in front of him, saying nothing as she passed him and plunged into the forest.

# Chapter 6

Six hours later, Genie shifted her pack on her shoulders and then stifled a sharp gasp as it landed on a sore spot. Hungry and tired, with every new step setting off a wave of pain, she wanted nothing more than to ask Wu Fang to slow down. But she didn't. If the lieutenant could keep going despite his damaged knees, she could ignore her own discomfort. Her pride demanded it. Already she had been forced to ask the men to stop so she could relieve her bladder. They, of course, had only to step off the trail to take care of their needs, barely breaking stride. If only she were so lucky. Clearly the Good Lord had been distracted when he had made Eve. How else to explain all the inconveniences that came with being female?

In front of her, the lieutenant and Wu Fang disappeared behind an outcropping of rock. Biting back a groan, she picked up her pace so they wouldn't get too far ahead. The sun was starting to set, leaving the forest steeped in shadows and making the path harder to see.

"Watch it." Nathan, who had been following close behind, reached past her. He brushed aside a tangle of naked vines dangling from the canopy above, vines that she had noticed just fine on her own. Nor did it help her mood that Nathan was happily humming behind her, seemingly unfazed by the strenuous hike.

Irritated with Nathan for being Nathan, with herself for being in pain, with her father for forcing her on this trip—with the whole world in general—she quickened her steps, her attention fastened on the trail. Roots and more vines snaked with regularity across the path, ready to trip the unwary. With the deepening shade of twilight, she was finding it harder and harder to pick her way with confidence. Somewhere beyond the tall, fragrant cedars and thick bamboo stands, the sun was disappearing behind the high peaks to the west, taking with it what little warmth remained in the air.

Several rapid curse words followed by a thud came from the trail above her. All irritation forgotten, she broke into a painful run, Nathan right behind her. Lieutenant Younan sat sprawled by the side of the trail, massaging his knees, a half-buried vine not far from where he fell. His jaw was clenched in either anger or pain. Genie guessed both. She winced as she noticed the deep impressions in the rich soil where he had landed.

A whisper of movement came from under the fern behind him. Her pulse leaped with fear.

Darting forward, she shrugged off her pack and tossed it onto the fern. Before she could catch herself, her momentum slammed her into the lieutenant, who was getting to his feet. The ground and sky traded places in a dizzying rush as they collided and rolled. What little breath she had left was knocked out of her as she landed on her back, the lieutenant on top of her. The leafy canopy high above her spun sickeningly for a moment as she tried to reinflate her lungs. Adrenaline prickled all over her body, like tiny needles, hot and cold at the same time.

The lieutenant sprang up and off her, finally allowing her a chance to breathe.

"What the . . . ," he began and then stopped abruptly.

Nathan stood over her, a knife in his hands. But his gaze was on the ground, a detail Genie's brain registered a split second before the lieutenant's not insubstantial weight slammed on top of her a second time. Pinned to the ground, she could only listen as Nathan's blade sank into the dirt with a soft thud, mere inches from where her pack had fallen.

After a brief moment of silence, Nathan straightened and gave a shaky exhale. "Well, that was close."

Genie licked her dry lips. Her pulse raced, but not just from adrenaline. A new, different kind of awareness slid through her veins as her body registered the oddly appealing sensation of a man lying on top of her. She had trouble breathing under his weight, but it didn't alarm her. It was . . . exciting, and she found herself wanting to arch up and press herself more firmly against him. Against all that strength and warmth.

As if suddenly electrified, the lieutenant leaped up and off her, and Genie's mind cleared in a snap. What in heaven's name? Horrified by the lustful direction of her thoughts, she quickly sat up to find Nathan staring at her. Not able to hold his gaze, she glanced over at Wu Fang, whose attention—to her relief—appeared wholly on the snake. At least one person had missed her immodest reaction.

The lieutenant ran his fingers through his hair, looking everywhere but at her, his suntanned skin flushed. "Sorry for flattening you. I thought Sterling had lost his mind for a moment. I didn't see the snake." He took a deep breath and glanced at Nathan. "Thanks."

"You're welcome." Nathan toed the dead krait free of the fern with his boot, revealing the snake's characteristic bands of bright yellow and black. "Though likely you weren't in any real peril. It's still early in the season, so it was probably sound asleep before you roused it, and likely still sluggish. But better safe than sorry. Their bite can be fatal."

"All the more reason to thank you."

Nathan retrieved his knife. "Thank Eugenia, since she saw it first. Though catching her after she threw herself at you like that was probably thanks enough."

The lieutenant glanced at her uneasily, and Genie flushed. Despite Nathan's calm, matter-of-fact tone, there was no missing the censure in his words. Already on edge, she felt even more tense.

Wu Fang picked up the dead snake and examined it with a critical eye. "Too bad we don't have any wine," he said in Chinese. "Krait makes a powerful tonic, one I could sell for good money."

"If you can find anyone foolish enough to buy it." Nathan wiped the knife blade clean on his trouser leg.

Wu Fang scoffed and then said in Chinese, "You're the fool. One drink can make old men young again. And give dried-up young ones more fire. Maybe you need a whole bottle?"

Nathan shot the old man a hard look. "Watch it."

Genie bit her lip, carefully hiding her amusement as Nathan brushed past her to pick up the fallen backpack. As little as she liked the man, she knew she needed to tread carefully. Not that she worried about him hurting her, but he could make the rest of the journey unpleasant all the same.

"What did the old fellow say?" Lieutenant Younan asked her in a low voice.

Genie cleared her throat and sought the best—least embarrassing—way to translate the exchange. "Wu Fang wanted to pickle the snake, but we don't have any wine with us."

He made a face. "You're kidding. He'd waste good alcohol on that?"

"The Chinese would hardly think it a waste," she said with a laugh. "Snake wine is considered an extremely useful tonic."

"For what? Killing off your enemies?"

"No." Then, realizing she would have to give more of an explanation, she flushed and her gaze slid away. "It's for . . . um . . . for improving a man's performance. With women."

"I see." His soft laughter stole through her like sunlight, chasing away her embarrassment. "Let me guess—Wu Fang suggested Sterling might benefit from it."

"Wu Fang has a strange sense of humor," Nathan said coolly as he rejoined them with Genie's pack.

Wu Fang laughed, and Genie wondered again how much English the old man actually understood. Then, with a sigh, he flung the snake into the underbrush and said in Chinese, "No more chatter. Let's go."

Nathan held her pack while she shrugged it on. By the time Genie had the buckles fastened, Wu Fang had already started up the trail. Though "trail" might be stretching it a bit, as she had seen deer paths more obvious than whatever it was Wu Fang was following. Or perhaps he was only being economical, taking the shortest line between two points, no matter how steep or treacherous.

By the time Genie had her pack resettled onto a less tender part of her shoulder, the lieutenant had already disappeared into the dense vegetation, along with Wu Fang.

"A word, if you please, Eugenia." Nathan grabbed her arm when she would have turned away. He continued softly. "You should be more careful in your dealings with the lieutenant."

"I could hardly let the man be bitten by a krait."

"You could have trusted me to handle it." Nathan plucked an errant leaf from her hair and then brushed a fallen strand out of her eyes. "You must know I would never let anything happen to my future wife."

She batted his hand away, alarm icing her stomach. "I thought we agreed we were incompatible?"

"You suggested it; I never agreed. And don't argue. For the rest of the trip, you will act like my fiancée, whether in truth or not. Your father and I both decided it would be safer."

"He didn't tell me as much."

"There was no time. But we can discuss it later." He glanced over his shoulder. "When we're not in danger of getting lost. Though from all the noise the lieutenant's making, there seems little danger of that. I've heard angry boars thrash about more quietly."

"Only because he's injured," she snapped back before she could stop herself.

Nathan stiffened, his grip tightening. "Stay away from him, Eugenia. I won't tell you again."

Clamping her lips shut, she whirled away, a hundred imprudent comments burning to be let out. But Nathan was right: it was getting dark, and she really didn't want to spend the night lost in the forest because she had wasted time pointlessly arguing with him. Following her ears and the shadowy trail of broken branches, she was able to track Wu Fang and the lieutenant. She and Nathan caught up just as the trail opened out onto a wide rock ledge that jutted out from the hill. The view was beautiful, at least what she could see of it in the deep twilight. The ledge looked out over a cleft in the hills cut by the river that rushed not too far below. Farther out, she caught glimpses of other peaks half-hidden by the dense forest.

Fairly sure this was where they were going to spend the night, Genie shrugged her pack off her aching shoulders.

"How does the old fellow do it?" the lieutenant muttered as he looked around.

She understood his surprise. She hadn't seen any signs in the forest indicating that this clearing was here. Yet here it was, big enough to fit all their bedrolls as well as set up a fire without fear of it spreading.

She started unbuckling her pack. "Perhaps it's because he was a soldier for many years?"

The lieutenant made a noncommittal sound as he walked over to the edge of the rock shelf, where Wu Fang sat expectantly, with the confidence of a king ready to be served.

Nathan dropped his pack onto the ground next to hers, kicking up a small cloud of dirt in the process. "Here, hand me a pot, and I'll go find water for supper before it gets any darker."

She flipped open the top of her pack. "Give me a moment . . ."

"Do you want me to start a fire?" the lieutenant asked, coming back to stand right behind her. His soft drawl sent shivers up and down her spine. "The air's already got a definite nip to it."

Keeping her eyes safely on the pan as she pulled it from the pack, Genie tried to slow her suddenly racing heartbeat. He was standing so close, she could almost feel the heat rolling off his body, reminding her how warm he had felt lying on top of her in the forest . . . how wonderfully heavy.

"Oh, I'm sure Eugenia can handle it," Nathan said, taking the pot from her. "You should rest your knees."

*Knees, yes.* The lieutenant was injured. Best to focus on that and not how her body had tingled with . . .

She jumped to her feet before her thoughts could go any further and grabbed the pot back from Nathan. "I'll be right back."

Nathan might have protested, but she wasn't sure. She was over the edge of the hill and halfway down the slope before she allowed herself to breathe again.

After setting the pot on the small stones littering the edge of the stream, she plunged her hands into the icy stream, welcoming the painful bite. Water streamed through her fingers as she lifted her palms to her overly warm cheeks. A small, despairing sob escaped her.

*What is wrong with me?*

She had never reacted to a man this way. Her father would be horrified if he knew how utterly the lieutenant's presence was affecting her. And the lieutenant would be as well. No one must find out. This weakness was hers and hers alone. Maybe, with help from the Lord, she could make it through the next few days with no one the wiser. *Oh, please, Lord. Help me.*

Hastily blotting her face on her sleeve, she pulled herself together and then filled the pot with water. When she returned to the ledge, Nathan was gone. The lieutenant was arranging some kindling to start a fire, while Wu Fang was gazing off into the distance, a lit cigarette dangling from his one hand.

"Where's Nathan?" she asked, carefully setting down the full pot. She had purposely filled it with more water than she needed for dinner so she'd have enough to soak a couple of cloths for the lieutenant's knees.

"Looking for more wood." The lieutenant tilted his head toward Wu Fang. "What's the story with the old fellow? Is he going to help out?"

"Not if he doesn't want to." Genie knelt by Wu Fang's pack and looked for the rags they had used earlier.

"Because he only has one arm? Can't say it slowed him down much on the trail."

She glanced up, startled. "No, it isn't that. It's because he's an elder and therefore has earned the right to relax, as a sign of respect and an acknowledgment of his longevity and wisdom. Is that not the custom in America?"

"Not really." He watched her as she dipped the cloths in the pot and wrung them out. She willed herself not to blush under his steady gaze.

"Here, roll up your pants. Your knees have to be killing you. Especially after your fall."

He hesitated, a protest on his lips, but something in her look must have changed his mind. With a sigh, he sat back and did as she asked. New welts of red and purple blossomed under his skin. Swallowing hard, she laid the first cold cloth on his knee. He jerked and then held still.

"You know," he said as she placed the second cloth, "unlike Wu Fang, I don't expect to be waited on. If you want any help cooking dinner, just ask."

"Thank you, but despite what Nathan said at lunch, I'm not that bad a cook." She returned to her pack and began removing the rest of her cooking supplies. She was glad to see that throwing the pack at the snake hadn't damaged anything.

"I never said you were. However, four hands could make the work go faster. And . . ." He hesitated briefly. "I wanted to apologize. I know I had made it kinda clear I didn't want you tagging along. I thought that you, being a woman and all, would slow us down, but it hasn't turned out that way. And if you hadn't been there this evening, I might've been a goner." He drew a deep breath. "So as a peace offering, I'd like to help with dinner."

"And what were you thinking of doing?" She selected two sweet potatoes and then unsheathed a cooking knife to pare them. She kept her gaze on her work, afraid if she looked up that he would see how greatly his words had shocked her. She could probably count on one hand how many times a man had apologized to her. Ever. Even including her father.

"I could peel, chop, slice. Anything you want. Since my father worked late most nights when I was growing up, it was either learn my way around a kitchen or starve."

Her hands stilled. "Your mother . . . ?" She didn't know quite how to finish the question.

"Passed away when I was seven, along with my sister." His tone was neutral, but she sensed the undertow of emotion lurking beneath the words.

Her heart squeezed in sympathy as she stared sightlessly at the potato in her hand. "I'm sorry. I never had a sister or a brother. But my mother died, too. When I was an infant."

"I'm sorry for your loss."

She shrugged and put the potato down. "I don't remember her. I was too young."

"I sometimes wished my father had remarried like yours did," the lieutenant said. "Other times I was glad it was just him and me."

"What makes you think my father remarried?" She pulled out a small carved board given to her by Zhenzhu, ostensibly as a gift for Aunt Hazel, but Genie doubted she would mind if it was slightly used by the time it reached her.

"Well, the woman who greeted us? Isn't she your stepmother?"

"That was our housekeeper, Zhenzhu. My father hired her to take care of me after my mother died so he could resume his travels."

"So fifteen years ago. That's a long time for a man and woman to live under the same roof."

"Actually more like twenty. I'm not that young." She pushed the chopped potatoes aside and then frowned. "And what exactly are you implying?"

"Nothing. Forget it." He gestured at the onions on the ground next to her. "Are you going to cut those?"

"There is nothing improper going on, if that's your point." Her fingers tightened on the knife as old hateful memories stirred in the back of her mind. The whispers and innuendos . . . "Zhenzhu was starving when my father took her in all those years ago. Her husband had died from cholera, and since there were no children, his family kicked her out, and her own family wouldn't take her back. Should he have turned her away, too?"

"It's fine. You don't have to explain."

"And yes, maybe she has grown fond of us over the years, as we have of her. But that doesn't mean she, or my father . . . that they . . ." To her dismay, her voice broke. She pressed the back of her hand against her lips. The chopping board became a blur as she remembered how the missionary wives would whisper whenever she and Zhenzhu passed by, their suspicions and disapproval clear in their pinched expressions.

"Hey." He crouched beside her, close enough that she could feel the warmth radiating off him, smell the musk of his clothes and the sharper scent of sweat. Every inch of her skin tightened. "I meant no disrespect. Your father is a man of the cloth. Of course he is kind to those in need."

The gentleness in the lieutenant's tone only added to her emotional turmoil. Loss, despair, and anger all buffeted her broken heart in turn, and underneath it all were the new torments of desire and the shame that realization brought with it.

"Here, I'd better chop the onions. But don't go anywhere. You'll need a plausible excuse for those tears when Sterling gets back. Otherwise, he'll probably punch me, thinking I made you cry. And then we'd both be crying."

She gave a short watery laugh, then sniffed and wiped her eyes on her sleeve. She really should move away from him, away from the almost magnetic pull exerted by his body. Except he had asked to stay close, even if it was for a very different reason, and she, for purely selfish reasons, wanted to obey.

He peeled the skin off the onions and then began slicing them. His movements were expert and sure, as if he'd done the task a hundred times. "I'm guessing from your reaction that it's taboo for a white man to fall in love with a local woman?"

"Not exactly, but one would run the risk of being a social pariah. And in my father's case, such an alliance would cost him his sponsorship, which is why we left Hankow, though my father has always said it was because of Communist unrest. Rumors were starting to spread among the other missionaries. Unfounded ones, mind you. Still, by moving us south, we not only escaped the gossip but the need to dismiss Zhenzhu merely because the wives didn't like her."

"Smart man."

Wu Fang ground out his cigarette and stood. Genie watched as he bent to throw another branch on the fire. Since he was keeping his back to her and Lieutenant Younan, she guessed he didn't want any help.

She pulled out a packet of salted fish and unwrapped it. "It's sad, really. That people can't love whomever they want."

"Sad, and also common. In California, for instance, miscegenation— the intermarriage of races—isn't just frowned on; it's illegal. And in several other states, too, as I recall."

"But not in every state?"

"No." He slid the onions next to the chopped potatoes. "Despite what it says in the Declaration of Independence, all men are not created equal—at least not in the eyes of the American government. Or its society, for that matter."

"You sound very sure of that."

"I am. Hand me a carrot," he said. She did, and he resumed chopping. "My family landed in New York when I was five. We came from Turkey, from a university town that was the equal of any in Europe. My father was an engineer, and my mother was from a well-to-do family on the coast. And yet neither mattered after they arrived. They were shunned and spat upon. The only work my father could find was on the docks. I think it was despair that killed my mother, although my father says otherwise. No matter how hard she tried, she never found a way to fit in."

"But you did." It wasn't a question. The truth of the statement was sitting in front of her, looking and sounding like every other American she had met.

"Children are more adaptable." He handed the knife back, the carrots all sliced.

"And if one isn't a child? If someone my age is shipped off to America?"

"I suppose it's all in how willing you are to let go of the past and everything familiar in order to fit in."

Her throat tightened as she considered his words. To let go of her father, Zhenzhu, Li Ming . . . could she do it? It seemed an impossible task. They were woven into the fabric of her soul, her very existence.

"Younan. I need your help," Nathan called out, standing by the unlit fire, his arms full of scavenged branches and brush. The lieutenant's knees almost folded under him as he staggered to his feet, and she flinched at his grunt of pain. From under her lashes, she watched as he and Nathan started the fire and then rigged a sling to hold the cooking pot over it.

Loneliness crept over her spirits again, and sorrow. How she wished Li Ming were here. She wanted someone to talk to, someone to tell all about her adventures of the day. Someone who might also have an explanation for why she hoped the lieutenant would come back and sit by her, why the sound of his voice seemed to resonate somewhere deep in her belly. She glanced up, unable to stop herself. He was looking at her from across the clearing. Her skin flushed hot, then cold.

She dropped her gaze to the rice scoop in her hands, praying that the twilight was deep enough to hide her flaming cheeks. Why, oh why did she have to be so aware of him? It felt all wrong. She barely knew the lieutenant.

No wonder Li Ming had been so worried for her: only it wasn't the lieutenant leading her astray but her own body. How she was supposed to get through five more days in the lieutenant's presence, she had no idea. Of the three men traveling with her, the lieutenant was the most pleasant. The most fascinating . . . And yet she was supposed to pretend to be affianced to Nathan.

*Oh, Lord help me. None of this would be happening if I were safe at home.*

*So go home, then,* a small voice whispered in her head. *Father won't send you away again; this time he'll listen to reason. He might be angry, but you know he would give in and let you stay.*

Her breath caught on a sudden wave of possibilities. She *could* go home. The path back, having been recently traveled, should be easy enough to find. She could sneak away while the men were asleep, find somewhere safe to stay the night, and then continue home in the daylight. Then she could stay in China, in her village, under her father's roof, translating the Bible into Chinese, safe from distracting men. And after the Bible was finished, she could . . . She racked her brain for another potentially fulfilling task.

The sound of laughter pulled her back to the clearing. The fire burned briskly now, and the three men sat around it, looking relaxed.

Her gaze fell on the lieutenant. He was holding his right hand in front of him, pinkie and thumb splayed like airplane wings as he spoke. His words were lost beneath the crackle of the fire, but his tone was animated as he leaned one way and then the other. Nathan snorted with laughter, and even Wu Fang seemed captivated.

A different kind of emotion pulled on her. A part of her wished she could sit by the fire, too, listening and laughing at the lieutenant's story, sharing in the men's easy camaraderie. It was a fool's wish, though. She had been raised to be a proper wife and mother whose place was here, preparing food and waiting on the pleasure of others.

A rebellious spark flared up within her, but she squashed it ruthlessly, along with the foolish thought of returning home. That she was even considering disobeying her father showed how tired she was. Tomorrow she would see the world, and likely the lieutenant, differently. Rationally. She would once more know her place and be comforted by it. Holding on to that thought like a buoy even as she drowned in sorrow, wishing she were home, she gathered up the ingredients for dinner and carried them to the cooking pot.

# Chapter 7

Genie awoke in darkness. Somewhere in the distance a bird chirped sleepily, breaking the fitful silence of predawn. A cool breeze rustled the tree branches, a quiet counterpart to the steady rushing of the river beneath the ledge. She rolled onto her back and snuggled deeper into the wool blankets. Overhead, a thousand tiny specks of light glittered like silver dust scattered over a swath of violet-black silk. Soon their ethereal beauty would be erased by the sun, but not yet.

Letting the last vestiges of the night and quiet soothe her, she picked out with practiced ease the various constellations that comprised the seven celestial houses spanning the heavens. Zhenzhu would be proud of her. And then she found her favorite one: the White Tiger of the West, guardian of the winter sky.

Oh, she knew there were other names for the star groupings. Western ones. Ones that were probably more appropriate for her American heritage. Her father had given her an astronomy book for her sixteenth birthday that cataloged them all. But the names felt as foreign to her as the Greek myths that defined them. She preferred the Chinese tales, with their melodramatic plots and cunning twists. Like the one Li Ming had mentioned, where the White Tiger had left his post in the sky to rescue Guan Yin when she had still been an imperial princess and not yet a goddess . . .

A twig snapped in the woods not far away, jolting her fully awake. Hardly daring to breathe, she strained her ears. Was it a leopard? A boar? A thief? A slight movement at the edge of the clearing caught her eye, and then a tall figure materialized. A scream clogged her throat as her heart rate accelerated. She was about to elbow Nathan, who was sleeping next to her, when she noticed the empty bedroll on the other side of him—the side where Lieutenant Younan had been sleeping. The knot in her chest eased as the shadowy form took on the familiar outline of the lieutenant. Sighing out her fear in a shaky exhale, she watched curiously as he skirted the clearing and then sat beneath a tree overlooking the valley.

A small flash and then a whiff of cigarette smoke reached her on a stray breeze.

The rational part of her brain told her to go back to sleep. She was still tired, and today's journey was likely to be no easier than yesterday's. Except she wasn't sleepy anymore. Not after fearing for her life moments before. And what better time to test her newfound resolve to not let the lieutenant disturb her equanimity than now, before the others were awake?

She shimmied out of her warm blanket cocoon and almost gasped at the bite of the frosty air. Rubbing her arms to chase away the morning chill, she eased across the campsite. Her muscles were still stiff and sore, so she gratefully sank onto the ground under the tree next to the lieutenant. Without speaking, he scooted over to make more room for her.

At first she felt awkward in the silence, painfully aware of every drag he took from his cigarette, every flick of his fingers as he got rid of the ash. Then, as the dusky blue-gray sky slowly separated from the mountains to the east, the view was so spectacular she almost forgot he was there. High clouds of peach and pink streaked the heavens as the background turned from slate to lavender to pale gray. Genie blinked back tears as the sun at last breached the peaks in a brilliant orb of light. All around was beauty so perfect, from the gilded treetops to the glittering frost in the valleys. The air so crisp and pure. And she might never experience it again . . .

A hand unexpectedly settled on her shoulder, and the spell broke. She held perfectly still, her attention centered on the slight pressure of his fingers. Should she pull away? Say something? All her confusion of last night rushed back.

Then he released her, and the crushing of her heart began to ease. Hugging her knees, she let the unspoken empathy of his gesture erase any question of what was right and proper. It was enough to be understood. Because the lieutenant surely did, having had to leave the land of his birth as well.

To have a travel companion whose past so closely mirrored hers was truly a gift, one that seemed divinely ordained.

More birds began to sing in the forest, their clear calls coaxing the day out of hiding.

"Penny for your thoughts." His voice was low, likely so as not to disturb the sleepers.

She considered the different things she might say and then discarded them all as too embarrassing or too revealing. "They're not that interesting."

"Try me."

She stifled a sigh. "All right. I was wishing time would stop, so I wouldn't have to leave China."

He stubbed his cigarette out on the hard ground and then laughed softly. "And here I am counting the minutes until I can get back to the base."

"So you can get back to the war?" she asked, recalling his words of two days before, when he said he'd be damned before he'd sit out the fight in their small village.

"Hardly. No one with a lick of sense looks forward to that part." He settled back against the tree, his gaze on the far-off hills. "It's the being grounded I've had enough of. I want to get back in the air."

"Even though your last flight ended in a crash?" she asked a little incredulously.

"For the last time, it wasn't a crash. And yeah, I know it's hard to understand. But see that?" He gestured toward the lightening horizon. "Pretty as that is from here, it's a hundred times better at five thousand feet. It's like watching the world being born. A bird's-eye view of creation."

She considered for a moment. "Like watching the sunrise from a mountain peak? I did that once; it was beautiful."

"That's close, but . . ." He made a frustrated sound as he tucked his unfinished cigarette into his shirt pocket. "I don't know how to explain it."

"If you don't like wars, why are you here? Couldn't you fly in the States?"

"I could, and I did. But I also happen to believe one country shouldn't be allowed to invade another just because it wants to."

"So you do want to fight," she said slowly, still not quite understanding.

"Like I said, only a crazy man *wants* to fight. Though you lose enough friends in battle that any man can become crazy. Still, some things are worth fighting for." He inhaled and massaged the bridge of his nose. "Look, if you don't mind . . . can we talk about something else?"

"Oh, sorry." She turned back to the sunrise and rested her chin on her knees. For all his protests that he didn't like the war, she remembered the way he had acted out air battles for Wu Fang and Nathan the day before with a little boy's enthusiasm. Or maybe it was only the flying part he liked . . . and the rest he endured because he felt it was the right thing to do.

If she'd had a brother, would he have volunteered to fight for another man's country? It was a choice she would never have to face, being a woman, but if she had been born a man? She would like to think she would have been brave enough.

More and more birds began singing, and Wu Fang began to stir. Genie reluctantly stood. The men would want breakfast soon. She turned to pick up the cooking pot and then froze. Nathan was sitting up on his bedroll, staring at her. His light-gray eyes were as icy as the frost on the ground, and a chill slid through her veins. How long had he been awake? Not that she had done anything wrong by sitting with the lieutenant, or that his touching her had been anything but innocent. Drawing a deep breath, she stared right back, daring him to say anything. After a long, tense moment, he turned his face away, but his censure hung in the air.

For the next ten or twelve hours, she did her best to avoid both the lieutenant and Nathan. She didn't have the energy to examine her reaction to the one or suppress her irritation with the other. The forest became thinner the higher they went, the stream they were following becoming little more than a trickle of spring water.

By the time Wu Fang signaled a stop, the sun was hanging low in the west. Genie groaned as she set her pack down, pretty sure every square inch of her feet was covered with blisters. At least they had stopped next to a small pool so they could refill their water pouches. Hers had run empty hours ago, but she hadn't dared say anything. The mood of the little group had become grimmer as the clouds overhead began congregating in ever thicker layers.

"We'll eat here while there's still light." Wu Fang set his pack down. "But no wasting time. We still have farther to go."

Nathan's pack hit the ground with a weary thud. "Why? Are we falling behind schedule?" he asked tersely in Chinese. Genie could sympathize. Her own eagerness to keep walking was severely lacking.

Wu Fang dug around in the underbrush and removed a long stick, tested it in his hand for balance, and then tossed it aside. "I want to listen on the radio tonight, which means we go high."

The lieutenant glanced from one man to the other. "What's going on?"

"Wu Fang wants to keep going after supper," she said, almost too tired to translate. "So be sure you refill your canteen, since this may be your last chance for a while."

The lieutenant unslung his backpack with enviable grace and set it on the ground. "All right. Did he say why?"

"He wants to use the radio."

"Which means we need to get somewhere with good reception." The lieutenant looked up and squinted at the sky. "And after sunset is probably a good move."

"Why?" she asked, genuinely curious.

"Because we're getting closer to Kunming, our odds of attracting unwanted attention are also increasing. From Jap fighter planes," he added, dispelling her confusion. "I was in the process of chasing off a pair that day I was forced to land."

"I only heard one plane. I didn't know . . ." Fear erased her exhaustion as she pictured Li Ming and the other villagers going about their daily lives, out in the open, exposed. "I knew there was a possibility we could be shot at from the air, but I didn't think . . ."

"Don't listen to him, Eugenia." Nathan shot Lieutenant Younan a dark look as he joined them. She stiffened as he casually draped his arm over her shoulders. "The lieutenant is exaggerating the level of danger. There's nothing to worry about."

"The hell there isn't," the lieutenant said coldly. "Those eight-millimeter machine guns the Japs got up front aren't just for firing on other aircraft. They can make hamburger out of a man in a matter of seconds."

Genie sucked in a breath, and spots swam in front of her eyes as images of raw, shredded meat filled her head . . .

"That's enough, Lieutenant." Nathan tightened his grip on her, holding her upright. "There's no point frightening her."

"Yeah, well . . . keeping her in the dark isn't doing her any favors, either," the lieutenant said. "She has a right to know the score, just like the rest of us."

She wanted to double over and vomit as the bloody images took on faces, became her friends, her family, her father. "We've got to go back and warn the others."

"Eugenia, no."

"But they're in danger. They could die."

Nathan turned her to face him. His hands gripped her shoulders firmly, refusing to let her turn away. "They already know. It's why your father wanted me to take you away, to keep you safe."

"What of the others?"

"They can make their own decision on whether to leave or stay."

"But not me." Anger burned beneath her skin.

"Your heart is too soft to make such an important decision. You would have been swayed by emotion instead of reason, which is why your father and I decided for you. You should feel honored that you are so well cared for and loved."

Except she didn't feel any of those things. She felt helpless and sick. Everyone around her seemed to have a say in her future except for her, and she was tired of it. She wasn't an infant. This had to stop. Her family was in danger.

"I'm going back." She snatched her pack from the ground and threw it over her shoulders. Her muscles screamed in protest, but she ignored them.

Lieutenant Younan reached out and snagged her by the strap as she brushed past. "No, you're not."

"Why not?" she demanded, her fear for her family making her bold.

His dark eyes were filled with sorrow when his gaze met hers. "You don't have enough experience to find the trail on your own. You'd never make it."

"Then come with me."

"I'm sorry; I can't. I have to get back to base."

She turned to the others. "Nathan? Wu Fang?"

From the way the old Communist was shaking his head, she knew he had followed enough of the conversation to know what she was asking.

"Many years ago," he said slowly in Chinese, his face grave, "when your father persuaded the village to take me in, when I was ill and would have died, I told him I would someday pay back this favor. And so I am. Once I have delivered you safely to the Kuomintang, my blood debt will be repaid, and I can return to my comrades in the north."

"So no one will help. No one cares if I ever see my family again." She looked at the three men, from one to the other, traitors all.

Nathan reached his hand out to her. "Don't be distressed, Eugenia. Remember Ephesians six: 'Children, obey your parents in the Lord, for this is right.' And this is what your father wanted. For you to be here with me."

A scathing retort rose in her throat, only to be choked off by truth: this *was* what her father wanted. And that betrayal was the bitterest of all.

"Do you need help preparing dinner?" Nathan asked gently. His offer surprised her, but then maybe he could tell how close she was to breaking.

She shook her head, afraid she might scream if she opened her mouth. The worst part was that she understood why they had refused her. Well, at least why the lieutenant and Wu Fang had turned her down. A blood oath was sacrosanct in China, and she knew of the lieutenant's commitment to return to the war. But Nathan . . . he could have helped her yet had refused. And she would never forgive him. Not for as long as they both lived.

# Chapter 8

She kept to her promise all the next morning, despite the punishing pace set by Wu Fang. Not once did she ask to slow down, even though her thighs now burned as if stabbed by red-hot pokers. The air was growing thinner, and each new breath scalded her lungs. She might be a woman, but she was not lesser. She did not need to be coddled like a rare orchid. She was that strong tree pushing back against the wind, just like Li Ming had told her to be. She would make her friend proud. And more important, she wouldn't give the lieutenant a reason to reverse his good opinion of her.

She stepped on a stone and almost blasphemed as her ankle twisted. Ahead of her the backs of Wu Fang and Lieutenant Younan were slowly receding. She was falling behind. Again. Redoubling her efforts, she pushed on through the knee-high grass, sweat running down her back.

Two days down, four to go. *No, three and a half.* She wanted to cry at the thought, except she didn't have the energy.

Hitching up her pack to relieve the ache of her shoulders, she focused on taking her next step. Even though the afternoon sun was hidden behind a thickening layer of clouds, its heat was still palpable through the brisk mountain air. Her heart pounded, crying for oxygen that wasn't there.

Suddenly she was pitching forward, her foot tangled in something. She tried to catch her balance, but her reflexes were too slow, her muscles too starved for air. The ground rushed up, and then pain exploded from her knees, hips, shoulder, and palms. A flash of light as more pain registered. Then . . .

"Eugenia." Nathan's voice seemed to come from far away.

She cracked her eyes open. A long second later, her lungs expanded in a gasp. A sharp whistle made her flinch. The grass was oddly prickly and sharp beneath her cheek, and her nostrils were filled with the musty scent of dirt and dead vegetation. Muffled thumps shook the ground as she flexed her fingers and then her toes. She needed to get up.

"What happened?" Wu Fang asked in clipped Chinese.

Embarrassment washed through her. Shaking and chilled, she began to push herself up and got as far as her knees before the ground started to spin. A muttered expletive close to her ear startled her. A pair of strong hands grabbed her shoulders, shoving her back down.

"Don't move." The lieutenant's voice.

Calloused fingers lifted her chin, and she blinked to clear her vision. The lieutenant's fierce expression swam into focus. His taut, angry gaze scanned her face, though she had no idea what he was looking for.

"Are you all right?" he asked.

"Yes." With an effort she tried but failed to push herself off the ground. Her legs were shaking too badly.

A water canteen appeared in front of her, the cap unscrewed and dangling from its chain.

"Here, drink. You'll feel better," Lieutenant Younan said.

Her hands trembled as she took the metal tin from his hands. Her own water pouch had run out a while back, but true to her new resolve, she hadn't said anything. If the men could keep going, so could she.

"We should slow down," Nathan said as she took another swallow. "Eugenia is clearly exhausted, which is why she fell."

It wasn't true, but her throat was too parched at the moment for her to argue. Besides, she wasn't opposed to the idea of slowing down, as long as it wasn't she who had to ask.

The lieutenant made a frustrated sound and glanced at the sky, reminding her of the danger they were in. If there had been a hole to crawl into, she would have done so.

"Ask Wu Fang what our options are," he said.

The older man's answer made Genie choke. Horrified, she recapped the canteen and staggered to her feet, the weight of her pack nearly pulling her down to the ground again. Nathan reached out to steady her, but she brushed him off.

"We can keep going. I'm fine."

"Is that so?" The lieutenant's dark eyes reflected his doubt. Maybe because she was swaying like a reed in a high wind, but it couldn't be helped. "Sterling, what did Wu Fang say?"

"That we either need to reach the highway by sunset, if we hope to catch a ride, or we turn back to find better shelter for the night, since it's going to rain."

Not waiting to hear more, Genie spotted the path of bent and broken grass left behind by Wu Fang's recent return and headed for it. Every step was torture, but she would crawl before she would make them turn back.

"Hold on there." Lieutenant Younan snagged ahold of her arm, and she staggered, almost falling over. "How 'bout we get a plan first?"

"We have one. We walk."

"Not without making a few changes first." He started sliding the pack off her shoulders. She struggled and then gave up. He dropped the pack on the ground and unfastened it.

"What are you doing?"

"Redistributing the weight. Sterling, come over here and help me out."

"No." She grabbed one of the straps and tried to pull it back. "You said everyone carried his own pack."

"I changed my mind," he said, easily reclaiming her pack from her.

Nathan slung his pack down next to hers and then knelt. "Give me the heaviest items."

"Don't insult me." Lieutenant Younan began pulling things out of Genie's bag: cooking supplies, foodstuffs, the copper pan. "Here, open up, Sterling. We'll split it."

"That's enough." She leaned down and yanked her pack from his hands when he started pulling out undergarments. "The rest are clothes."

"Are you sure? I've got plenty of room in my pack." Amusement glimmered in the lieutenant's dark eyes as he watched her shove the intimate items back down and out of sight.

"No, thank you. I can manage." Her fingers fumbled on the buckles, but at last she managed to fasten them securely.

Wu Fang glanced at the sky. "We go?"

She eased the pack onto her sore shoulders and stood, staggering only a little this time. "I'm ready."

Behind her Nathan muttered something to the lieutenant too quietly for her to hear.

"Relax," Lieutenant Younan said, sounding annoyed. "I know."

Wu Fang motioned toward the hill in front of them. "It's not far to the crest," he told her. "Maybe two thousand *bù*. And the highway is on the other side."

A quick conversion of *bù* to the English equivalent almost had her throwing up. Another two miles. She closed her eyes and silently prayed for strength.

Nathan was more verbal. "This is ridiculous. Eugenia is in no shape to continue. I vote we find shelter for the night and then press on tomorrow."

"And I say if Miss Baker can't walk, then one of us will carry her. I'm not missing our ride to Kunming. You want to talk about long walks?"

Wu Fang stepped between the two men and pushed them apart. "Enough. Nay-tan take Yu Jie," he said in heavily accented English, effectively silencing them all. "Tiger take packs."

"Why Sterling?" the lieutenant asked as Nathan shrugged out of his pack. "I've got a better chance of getting her up that hill."

"I'm not as weak as you think, and Eugenia is my responsibility. Not yours."

Genie bristled at having her independence stripped away yet again. "I'm not anyone's responsibility. I'm fine."

Wu Fang shot her a hard look, cutting off any further protest.

"This is stupid," the lieutenant muttered as he picked up Nathan's pack. Genie heartily agreed but recognized they were both going to lose this battle.

"Eugenia, come here." Nathan turned his back to her and squatted slightly.

She hesitated. Given a choice, she would much rather the lieutenant carry her, except it wouldn't be proper. She barely knew the man, whereas Nathan had been her bane for years. Reluctantly, she put her hands on his shoulders and let him toss her up onto his back. His grunt as she landed did nothing to improve her mood.

Nathan hitched her up higher to balance her weight, forcing her to cling to him. His shoulders were mostly bone under her arms, the sharp angles of his hips beneath her thighs unsettling. She fought the urge to jump back down, the consequences be damned. Then she caught the lieutenant's grimace of pain as he slung Nathan's pack up alongside his own.

Dismay washed through her. Because of her weakness, the lieutenant was now carrying double the weight. No, more than double, because Lieutenant Younan now carried most of her pack as well. On top of a wrenched back and damaged knees.

She looked away, unable to bear the sight any longer. Tears blurred her vision. If he had forgiven her presence on this trip before, surely he was regretting it now.

Wu Fang, apparently satisfied by the new arrangement, nodded and then started off toward the hill crest. The other two men took their usual places, with Lieutenant Younan second in line and Nathan bringing up the rear. Desperate to distract herself from her misery as well as from the unpleasant dampness of Nathan's shirt and its nausea-inducing scent of new sweat layered over old, she focused on the wild, raw beauty of the land. How would she ever survive anywhere else?

"Genie, stop strangling me," Nathan growled. "I'm having a hard enough time without you cutting off my air."

With a start, she relaxed her grip and then carefully slid her arms farther down around his chest. Then her attention drifted to the scenery again. Off in the distance, a bright ribbon of white water spilled through a notch in the high rocks, cascading down into a jade-green river far below.

"Nathan, you grew up in the US. Does it look like this?"

"Parts." He readjusted his hold on her, and this time she was careful to not let her arms creep up around his neck again. "Eastern Kentucky has the thick forests and steep hills, though the hills aren't as tall, and there's no bamboo."

She tried to place Kentucky in relation to the rest of the US. The effort made her head throb, so she gave up. "What about California, where Aunt Hazel lives?"

"Again it depends on what part. Where your aunt lives it's mostly farmland, but there are mountains and forests. And beaches along the coast."

"It sounds pretty."

"It can be." He was starting to sound increasingly winded.

"You don't miss it? America, I mean."

"No."

There was no hesitation his answer, which surprised her.

"What about China? Will you miss it?" She would. She had no doubt about that.

"Not a bit. It was never my first choice of ministries. And now, with the Society having cut off our funding—"

"Wait! The Society cut my father off?" Her heart squeezed. *Please don't let it be because of Zhenzhu . . .*

"Your father thinks the stipends were lost somewhere in the chaos of wartime. More likely they were siphoned off by corrupt bureaucrats, assuming they arrived at all. But your father, being who he is, refuses to believe that."

"Of course." Her father was the eternal optimist, though apparently not when it came to the Chinese army and its ability to protect them.

The unwelcome acid of anxiety and anger scorched its way through her veins again, knotting her stomach. Did her father not know how much his and Zhenzhu's safety meant to her? To be sent away, not knowing if she would ever see them again, to be rendered unable to defend what she loved most, was the worst punishment imaginable. Yet if she turned back, she would be putting her own selfish wants in front of his. And to what end? What good would she be, really, against the Japanese? She couldn't fire a gun or wield a sword.

Her gaze wandered to the lieutenant walking several yards ahead of them, the doubled-up packs on his shoulders bobbing with each step in a mesmerizing display of strength. *I bet he can do both.* Perhaps if she had been born a male, she would, too, though she had heard rumors that the Communists had allowed women into their army. She doubted those women would feel as useless as she did now, being hauled around on Nathan's back like a tired child. For a stolen, foolish moment, she imagined she was on the lieutenant's broad back instead, feeling the muscles of his body flex and contract.

She must have dozed, for the next thing she knew, Nathan had released her legs and she was sliding down his back. They had reached the crest, and far below, as Wu Fang had promised, wound a narrow ribbon of dirt cut into the side of the hills.

"Nice highway," the lieutenant observed sarcastically. "Let's hope the truck gets here before the rain turns all that dirt into mud. And does anyone else see that rockfall back by that curve?

"Looks from here like it's blocking the road, unless the truck, or whatever we're catching a ride on, can cut below it. But that slope has gotta be at least ten percent. Not much can handle that without sliding a ways down the valley, and likely rolling in the process."

Genie's heart sank as she and the three men sized up the situation. It looked like the slope above the road had partially given way.

Wu Fang squinted at the sun, which was sinking ever lower to the west. "There's not much time before the truck comes. And those rocks must go. Come." He started sideways down the steep hill, half walking, half sliding, as Nathan translated.

Lieutenant Younan swore softly, and Genie couldn't blame him. The situation was truly hellish.

Nathan sighed and held out his hand to the lieutenant. "Pack."

"What about Miss Baker?"

Indeed, what about her? Impulsively, she stepped over the side of the crest after Wu Fang.

"Eugenia, wait."

The soil was loose and slippery beneath the dead grass and low shrubs. It slid out from under her shoes, and she lost her balance. Adrenaline burned through her in an icy, white-hot rush, driving the exhaustion from her muscles as she scrambled to catch herself. Between luck and effort, she managed to keep her feet under her as she careened down the treacherous slope. Luckily the hill shallowed out the farther she got, and closer to the road, she was able to almost walk normally. Or would have been able to if her legs hadn't felt like aspic jelly.

By the time she reached the road, Wu Fang was already talking to Nathan. Apparently he had passed her on the way down, and she hadn't even noticed. Blaming it on the headache she'd been fighting ever since she'd fallen, she looked around for the lieutenant, wondering if he had passed her, too. Lord, she was tired.

The afternoon sunlight slanted into the valley, touching an enormous boulder crowding one edge of the road. The relatively flat surface on top, the result of its calving off the cliff above, seemed to beckon to her. She tried to tear her gaze away but couldn't. To lie down for a few seconds—surely that wouldn't be such a bad thing. She might even regain enough energy to help the men clear the road.

Exhausted from the scramble down the hill, she staggered to the rock. With the last of her strength, she shucked off her pack and clambered up. The stony surface was breath-stealingly cold against her skin as she stretched out, but she was so tired. She only had to bear it for a little bit, a minute at most, just long enough to rest. She closed her eyes. *Not too long . . .*

Someone nudged her shoulder. "Miss Baker?"

She opened her eyes and then blinked in confusion. The valley was completely swathed in shadows, the sun having disappeared behind the hills. She must have been asleep for over an hour. Startled, she sat up. Her gaze darted toward where the road had been blocked, only to find it completely cleared.

"Are you all right?" Lieutenant Younan asked.

She shivered as his soft American drawl slid along a sensitive nerve. She wished he would keep talking to her. Something about the long vowels and musical consonants appealed to her, warming her deep inside.

"You need to get out of this wind." The lieutenant shrugged out of his leather flight jacket, and before she could protest that she wasn't cold, he had it wrapped around her shoulders. As he tucked the garment around her, she turned her face into the shearling collar and breathed in, unable to resist the curious mix of scents: leather, cigarette smoke, aftershave. And the earthy musk of warm male that was individual to him. Her eyelids drifted shut.

"Stay with me, here." His tone was sharper this time, almost angry. "When did you last have something to drink?"

She shook her head, trying to clear the fog from her brain. "After I fell."

"That's what I thought. Come on. Bottoms up." A metal canteen found its way into her hands and then was guided up to her mouth.

The water was warm and metallic and yet tasted like heaven. Then she choked from trying to breathe and swallow at the same time. The canteen left her lips for a second, and she managed to push it farther away. "Stop. I'm fine."

"Sorry, but I don't believe you."

"I'm—" She stopped as his face finally came into focus. Her heart skittered, his expression was so fierce, and she forgot to breathe. With a wealth of dark stubble shading his jaw, and his eyebrows like two black slashes over intent, intelligent eyes, he looked more than intimidating. He looked . . .

*Tyger Tyger, burning bright* . . .

She shivered again as the words materialized in her head, so fitting. Too late she realized she had tilted the canteen too far, and water had sloshed onto his jacket. Clumsily brushing the water droplets off before they soaked in, she tried to recall the rest of William Blake's poem. It had been in a book of poetry given to her by father. And there had been something about azure skies and wings in it, too . . .

Something cool and slightly rough pressed against her forehead. She flinched without thought.

The lieutenant pulled his hand back. "Damn it. Were you going to tell anyone you're running a fever?"

Confused, she stared at him, letting his second use of profanity today go unremarked. "I'm what?"

"Feverish. You know, being hot when everything around you isn't? Chills. Disoriented."

"I'm not . . ." Another shiver hit her.

"Yeah, you are. So you can drop the martyr act. I like it better when people are straight with me, gals included."

Her right temple started to throb. "Whatever are you talking about?"

He didn't answer. Instead, he stepped back. "Sterling, we need you down here!" he called up the hillside, startling her.

She turned to see Nathan far above them, bounding down the slope.

Lieutenant Younan turned her face back to him. "Listen. I know fellas like your fiancé prefer their gals empty-headed so they can do all the thinking. But it isn't right. In fact it can be downright dangerous. Like this afternoon. You knew you were in trouble, and yet you didn't say a word."

She winced under his rebuke. "I thought I could make it."

"And what was the result? You can't change what is by wishing it otherwise."

What could she say? He was right. She had made a mistake. From the corner of her eye she saw Nathan reach the road and start jogging toward them. She envied his seemingly inexhaustible energy.

"My point is, while you were waiting for Sterling to think for you, he was busy thinking of something else, letting you exhaust yourself to the point of getting sick."

Swallowing painfully, she shook her head at the injustice of that claim. "You've got it all wrong. I wasn't waiting—"

Nathan joined them. "What's the matter?"

"I was just telling Miss Baker here she needs to take better care of herself. She's running a fever."

Nathan turned to stare at her. "Is that true, Genie?"

*Genie, not Eugenia,* she noted. For some reason the nickname released a wave of homesickness so deep, she couldn't breathe. Tears blurred her vision as she tried to deny anything was wrong with her, but the words caught in her swollen throat.

"Where's Wu Fang?" Lieutenant Younan asked, looking around.

"Farther down the highway. East of here."

No sooner had Nathan pointed down the road than she heard the faint growl of an engine. The lieutenant tensed, and for an awful second she imagined they were about to be captured by the Japanese, the exertions of the last three days rendered useless.

A canvas-topped truck rounded an outcropping several hundred yards away. The driver began honking wildly and waving at them from his open door. And then she saw the familiar blue-and-white sunburst of the Kuomintang painted on the hood.

Lieutenant Younan started jogging back to his pack.

Nathan held his hand out to her. "Looks like our ride has arrived."

The truck stopped, and Wu Fang hopped down from the back, his expression stony.

"Time to go," he said in English, gesturing toward the back of the truck, where at least twenty soldiers were already crammed. Nathan picked up Genie's pack and tossed it in along with his own.

"There's no room for us," she rasped, her head starting to throb viciously.

"You can sit on my lap." Nathan took her elbow and propelled her up into the truck.

The Chinese garrison leader yelled for them to hurry, and Genie was all but tossed inside. Nathan and Lieutenant Younan were right behind her. Room was made on one of the crowded bench seats for them. Thankfully, Genie didn't have to sit on Nathan's lap but was wedged between Nathan and the lieutenant. The truck lurched into gear just as raindrops began to tap on the canvas roof. Genie summoned her dwindling strength and leaned forward to peer out the back.

Wu Fang stood in the road, a lone figure growing smaller and smaller. Even though he had told them yesterday of his plan to rejoin his old compatriots, sorrow still squeezed her chest as the road curved and the old man disappeared. One more person from her old life . . . gone, likely forever.

She leaned back and surrendered to the dark exhaustion pulling her under. Vaguely, she remembered being resituated so her head had better support. Then time lost meaning as she sank under again until the cold roused her. Shivering, she burrowed closer to her only source of heat. But there was no escaping the pain. The bumping and swaying reached into her bones, crushing them. She hurt everywhere.

After what felt like an eternity, the motion stopped. Nathan tried to wake her, but she was so tired. It occurred to her that she was being held securely in someone's arms, but they weren't Nathan's. She cracked open her eyelids and gazed up into Lieutenant Younan's worried eyes.

"We just arrived at the hospital," he drawled softly, a thrilling gentleness in every syllable. "You'll be okay now. Don't you worry about a thing."

She wanted to touch his face, to reassure him, even though she was the one who felt like she was dying. But her throat was on fire, and she was just too tired. She closed her eyes and returned to the dark.

# Chapter 9

A siren wailed, waking Genie. With a groan, she buried her face into her pillow, trying to escape the insidious sound. It was too loud, too insistent, and it really seemed to her someone should shut it off. Even though her throat was feeling better, she still needed more sleep . . .

The *tak-a-tak* of the hospital window shade being pulled closed sent a jolt of surprise through her, and her eyes flew open.

An unfamiliar woman stood by the window. "Good, you're awake. We haven't much time."

The woman, a very pretty brunette in her early thirties, smiled pleasantly as Genie studied her, trying to determine whether they had ever met. She wasn't a nurse. Outside, in the bright winter sunshine, the siren wailed on.

"How are you feeling? Shall I fetch a wheeled chair?" the woman asked in her oddly accented English, adding to Genie's confusion. It wasn't like Lieutenant Younan's drawl or Nathan's more clipped New England accent. Perhaps she was European, another refugee of the war? Her dark eyes were assessing, cool. "It's unfortunate timing, but better safe than sorry."

Genie sat up and dragged her fingers through her snarled hair, her mind still foggy with sleep. "Who . . ." The word came out little better than a croak, so she cleared her throat, winced, and tried again. "Who are you?"

"Oh, I'm sorry. You sound like you could use some water." The woman poured her a glass from a pitcher on the bedside stand. "I'm Natasha. Natasha Greenlee. My husband, Harvey, works for the AVG. Here, drink this, and then we really should be going. The trucks are likely to be crowded, and we don't want to lose our seats."

Genie's hand shook as she took the glass. She forced herself to concentrate as she took a sip so as not to spill it. It was hard, though, with that horrid noise like a red-hot poker in her skull. Finishing the glass, she handed it back, more awake now.

"Why are we getting back in trucks?"

It had been four, no five days since Lieutenant Younan had lifted her out of the back of one and handed her over to the nurses. Not nearly long enough for her to forget how wretchedly uncomfortable the ride had been.

"Because we only have twenty minutes—maybe an hour if we're lucky—before the planes reach us." Natasha looked around and then hurried over to where a robe had been hung behind the door. "Put this on. Be glad the doctors decided you're no longer wildly contagious, or you'd have to tough it out on your own here."

Genie stiffened in horror as the pieces began to fall into place. "Is that what the siren is warning us about? That the Japanese are on their way?"

Natasha gave her an odd look. "I thought you knew. Though now I think about it, I should have guessed. When Harvey told me you'd been buried in the countryside, I only thought that meant you wouldn't have anything suitable to wear tonight. I should have realized . . . well, no matter. I can fill you in as we go. Do you think you can walk?"

"I'll try. Where are we going?" Genie swung her legs over the edge of the bed.

"Out of the city, if we can. That siren you hear is an air-raid warning. While our boys will do their best to defend us, there are no guarantees they'll be able to scatter the bombers in time. Though the success rate has gone up in the last few months, thanks to improvements in the Chinese air-warning system. In fact Ted mentioned you were traveling with one of the radio operators. It's too bad he didn't come with you to Kunming, so we could thank him for his work."

"Who? Wu Fang?" He was the only person Genie knew with a radio. And he did spend day after day up on the mountain, doing heaven only knew what. Apparently he had been helping track enemy aircraft. Had her father known?

Natasha glanced around the floor. "I have no idea. And hurry with that robe while I find your shoes."

"What about Nathan? The other man I traveled with." Genie's fingers fumbled with the robe's cloth belt. "He likely doesn't know what the siren means, either."

"I'm sure he's fine. He's been bunking with the pilots, who will tell him." Natasha handed Genie her shoes and then helped her put them on.

"And Lieutenant Younan?"

"Lieutenant . . . oh, you mean Ted!" Natasha helped Genie stand. "Well, if there's an available plane, I'm sure he's already up flying. He's one of our best pilots, though all the boys are excellent flyers. The AVG has the best kill rate in the Pacific."

Natasha gestured toward the door. Genie took a step and then staggered slightly. Natasha immediately slipped her arm around Genie's waist. "My, you are very thin. I hope the dresses I brought won't slide right off you."

"Dresses?"

Her legs caught on to walking again, which hurried their progress.

"Yes. That's the whole reason I'm here. You and Mr. Sterling have been invited to a dinner tonight hosted by General and Madame Chiang. They want to personally thank you for rescuing one of their borrowed pilots."

"You can't be serious." Her knees turned weak. She wasn't sure what frightened her more: meeting the de facto head of China or the prospect of enemy bombs.

Natasha opened the door leading into the hallway.

"I am. But don't worry. Once the all-clear is sounded, we can work on getting you ready. In fact . . ." Natasha cocked her head as the siren reversed pitch and then faded into an eerie silence. "There it is . . . huh, that was fast. It must have been a false alarm."

Out in the hallway, relieved shouts echoed down the corridor as Natasha helped Genie back into the hospital room. Happily, she reached the edge of her bed just as her legs gave out from under her.

Natasha gave her a sideways look. "When was the last time you ate? We've got a long afternoon ahead of us if you're to be ready in time."

Genie exhaled shakily. "How can you even think of food at a time like this? We might still be bombed." *Or shot at by enemy fighter planes with their awful machine guns.* She closed her eyes, willing herself not to throw up. Her father and Zhenzhu were out there, unprotected, along with all her friends.

"Oh, come on. You're not going to be one of those girls, are you?" Natasha's voice was laced with disdain.

Stung, Genie opened her eyes. "What do you mean?"

"You know . . . someone who refuses to get on with the business of living simply because there's a war going on. Because if you are, I have some news for you—if you put your life on hold now, you might as well end it."

Shocked into silence, Genie could only stare at the other woman.

Natasha made an impatient sound. "Don't look at me like that. You know it's true. Tomorrow is never guaranteed, so we might as well live while we can.

"And speaking of which, why don't you get cleaned up while I find you some lunch. The showers down the hall should be empty this time of day, but to be safe, drape the ribbon hanging next to the door over the door handle to tell the boys to stay out."

"All right." Genie rubbed her aching temples as Natasha left with enviable energy.

Following the woman's advice, she forced herself off the bed and down the hall. Fifteen minutes later, after having scrubbed off what felt like over a week's worth of grime and illness, she felt much better. Still weak, but more alert.

After re-donning her hospital pajamas—she should have thought to bring a change of clothes with her to the showers—she returned to her room. A young Chinese boy was setting a luncheon tray on the desk. His wary, worldly gaze assessed her in a way that broke her heart. He couldn't have been more than ten, far too young to be working, in her opinion, yet she understood how important his income was to his family.

As much as she loved her birth country, there was no ignoring the brutish poverty that racked so much of it—a situation the war wasn't helping one bit. Her father had once hoped to change things by tire- lessly preaching the twin Christian pillars of charity and love for one's neighbor, but the problem was proving nearly intractable. When she had asked Nathan about it, he had told her that it wasn't just China. Corruption and selfishness had poisoned societies everywhere.

Apparently deciding she represented neither threat nor opportu- nity, the boy slipped silently out on bare feet. At least the weather in Kunming was relatively mild even though it was February. In the mountains, it would have been a different story.

Her stomach growled at the smell of food, her appetite abruptly returning. She walked to the tray and lifted the napkin covering it. Except for the cup of tea, none of the other contents looked famil- iar. She picked up a spoon and poked uncertainly at an oddly shaped noodle mass in a yellow sauce.

"Oh, good. You're back," Natasha said as she breezed into the room with several dresses slung over her arm.

Genie picked up the bowl and tilted it toward Natasha. "Can you tell me what's in this bowl?"

The other woman gave her an odd look. "Macaroni and cheese. Why?"

"Oh." She debated whether to mention that she had no idea what either word meant, then decided against it. She held up a smaller bowl of diced fruit in liquid. "And this?"

"Canned peaches."

The tension in her temples eased. Peaches she knew she liked, though she'd never had them canned.

"Here, look at these while you eat up." Natasha slung the garments over the only chair in the room.

Still weak, Genie returned to her perch on the edge of her bed, the peach bowl in her hand. Natasha selected one of the dresses, a bright-blue satin. Then, holding it to her body, she turned around to show Genie. "What do you think?"

Genie almost choked. The hemline barely brushed Natasha's knees, and Genie was several inches taller than the woman. She didn't even want to think where the hemline would fall on her.

"Well?" Natasha prompted.

"It's very pretty, but also a little, um . . . revealing. Don't you think?"

Natasha glanced down at the dress, clearly puzzled. "How so?"

"Well . . ." And what could she say that wouldn't make her sound hopelessly provincial? It hadn't escaped her attention that all the women in the hospital wore knee-length dresses like the one Natasha was wearing. That is, if they weren't wearing trousers that fit their figures much more closely than she was accustomed to seeing.

"Do you have one that's a little longer?" she finally asked.

"I have one." Natasha turned back to the chair and pulled out a navy wool dress. "And you're thin enough, you won't even need a girdle with it. Which is a blessing, if you've never had the misfortune of wearing one."

Not knowing what a girdle was, and not sure she wanted to know, Genie bowed to the inevitable, put the peaches aside, and stood. Sternly telling herself she was not a Jezebel, she shed her hospital clothes and allowed Natasha to dress her like an American. The silk slip was cool on her skin, if a little tight. Natasha handed Genie a pair of garters and stockings to put on, and then it was time for the dress.

The wool floated down over her skin as soft as kitten fur, and when she turned around to check her appearance in the mirror on the wall, she did a double take. The gathered shoulders softened the angles of her jaw, while the deep blue color brought out the red in her hair and made her skin almost translucent. The effect was so startling she could almost forgive the war for bringing her here.

For the first time in her life she felt . . . pretty.

Natasha gave her a thorough once-over. "Very nice. A little make-up, some earrings, and a better hairstyle, and your Mr. Sterling will never know what hit him."

At the mention of Nathan, all her newfound confidence vanished. No doubt the change in appearance would leave him stunned—just not in a good way.

She started reaching for the zipper in the back. "Do you have anything else? Maybe a *chipao*?" The traditional one-piece Chinese dress might be as body-hugging, but it was also so widely worn, there was no way Nathan could object.

One perfectly drawn eyebrow lifted. "You want to dress like a Chinawoman?"

Genie stilled as a different voice echoed in her ears. A deeper one with a slight drawl. *You're not American, then?* The question had seemed unimportant in the safety of her father's study, but now that she was on her way to the US, where—at least if the lieutenant was to be believed—her success depended on her ability to fit in, it haunted her.

Which was she, Chinese or American?

She drew a deep breath. "No, you're right. The dress is perfect."

# Chapter 10

Surrounded by amiable laughing guests all waiting to be called to dinner, Genie knew she should be enjoying the moment. It wasn't every day that a daughter of a missionary was invited to meet heads of state, yet she could muster no excitement. She glanced around the crowded room at the men, women, and soldiers, all gleaming in their evening finery, their conversations, both in English and Chinese, animated and gay, her mood as unsettled as the gray sky outside.

Unlike the others tonight, she couldn't forget, despite the sea of laughter and smiles, the terror she had felt over the air-raid warning that morning. Nor could she forget the drive up to this hillside mansion that had taken her past charred, bombed-out buildings. Past whole Kunming neighborhoods reduced to ghostly drifts of stone and ashes that even the soft moonlight could not totally erase. Past remnants of lives and dreams cut short by the war.

A war that was much closer than she had ever imagined.

"Would you like a glass of punch?" Nathan asked quietly from beside her.

She eyed the glasses in the hands of the other guests. Part of her wanted to say yes, because the room had grown increasingly stuffy. Yet she was still furious over the way he had humiliated her earlier, demanding she go back to her room and change, and she didn't want to talk to him.

She hadn't changed, of course, but only because the other occupants of the car—Nurse Foster, her pilot husband, and another pilot—had overruled him, saying there was no time, and that she looked fine.

Ice clinked softly nearby, reminding her of his question. "Yes, please."

To her surprise, he hesitated. Then she glanced at the makeshift bar, with all the pilots clustered around it, and understood his indecision. As much as he didn't want to abandon her in a crowd of strangers, he also clearly didn't want her anywhere near the other men. She wanted to roll her eyes. She would have enjoyed listening to the pilots' conversations, which looked quite animated from where she was across the room, but she knew Nathan would never allow it. Tonight she was to play the part of fiancée, a part reinforced by his introducing her as such to everyone they met, and she was fine with it. Mostly.

The truth was she was too tired to fight about it.

"Don't go anywhere," he said finally.

"I won't."

Pressing the back of her fingers against her cheek with the vain hope of cooling them, she watched Nathan stride stiffly across the room, looking as out of sorts as she felt. Even in borrowed stockings, her calves felt uncomfortably exposed. On the other hand, she'd never had the experience of men stopping midsentence to examine her before, either. The attention hadn't lasted, of course. She had no illusions that she was a beauty, but that brief taste of masculine appreciation had been heady as well as a little unnerving.

If only Li Ming were here with her, she would be less nervous. Together they could have admired the beautiful silk *chipaos* worn by the wives of local businessmen, her friend critiquing the embroidered designs and craftsmanship while they waited for dinner to be served. Her friend would be equally interested in the young men, of course. Not for herself, but for Genie. She could almost hear Li Ming's wry, clear-eyed assessments of this pilot or that one.

A burst of masculine laughter pulled her from her thoughts, and she glanced toward the bar again. More pilots had arrived, and she wondered if still more were expected. Dinner had been delayed to give all the pilots a chance to get cleaned up. Two separate squadrons had gone up this afternoon, several hours apart, looking for the enemy aircraft that had been reported, some getting back later than others.

She had only learned that on the way over in the car. She had wanted to ask if Lieutenant Younan had flown, too, but had refrained with Nathan sitting beside her. She also had wondered if the lieutenant would even be here. She had also learned on the way over that Natasha had given a somewhat inaccurate description of the dinner tonight. Genie and Nathan were not the guests of honor. They were last-minute additions. Madame Chiang, as someone who liked to entertain, had planned the party weeks ago.

"He's not over there," Nathan murmured as he rejoined her, glass in hand.

"Who?" Her cheeks burned as she took the glass of punch from him. It bothered her that she hadn't seen him approach because her thoughts had been directed elsewhere.

"You know who. And it's embarrassing the way you throw yourself at him."

"The way I . . . ?" She turned to stare at Nathan. "When have I ever?"

"On the trail. Then again in the truck. You were practically in his lap the whole way." His jaw tightened fractionally as his gaze swept the room. "I know what you're trying to do, Eugenia, but it won't work. No matter how much you try to seduce him, he's not going to take you home. Rumor has it he's about to be shipped out anyway. So your little plan to defy your father won't work."

For a moment, she was too startled to respond. Then her bemusement turned into anger. "I'm not trying to seduce anyone. And when have I ever been anything but obedient to my father?"

"How about tonight? Do you really think he would have approved of . . . this?" He gestured at her dress, his expression tight.

"As a matter of fact, I do," she said, her temper sparking further. "It was always his belief that fitting in with one's surroundings was the key to success. Why else would he insist I learn as many dialects in Chinese as I could?"

"Learning the language is not the same as stooping to harlotry." He dropped his gaze to her lips. She fought the urge to wipe them. She would *not* be shamed for wearing lipstick, something plenty of other women were wearing tonight.

"Miss Baker. Mr. Sterling." The familiar drawl cut off whatever retort she would have made, and she stiffened. After Nathan's account of her behavior in the truck, something she didn't remember at all, she was suddenly afraid to turn around.

"Younan." Nathan nodded curtly at the man behind her.

Drawing a deep breath, she turned to greet the man she had supposedly thrown herself at. She forced her lips into what she hoped looked like a casual smile. "Hello, Lieutenant."

"Hello. How are you feeling this evening? Better?" To her relief, only friendly concern narrowed his beautiful eyes.

Her smile relaxed into something more real. "Much, thank you."

"Good." He grinned back. With his hair slicked back and shiny in the light, his cheeks smooth and freshly shaved, he looked entirely different from the last time she had seen him. Civilized, even. A whiff of his aftershave, something spicy and herbal, like mountain air after a rain, tickled her senses.

Then her eyes narrowed as she noticed the lack of insignia on the lieutenant's shirt collar. In fact, there was no military decoration at all on his impeccably pressed tan shirt.

"I don't know much about the Chinese air force, but shouldn't you have something here?" She touched her collarbone where a shirt collar would lay.

"Yes," Nathan said coolly. "But he's not really a lieutenant. Are you, Younan?"

A ghost of a smile touched Ted's lips. "Technically, no. We were all forced to give up our commissions to fly over here, so as not to violate American neutrality. Except for General Chennault, our commander, since his role is only 'advisory' in nature. The rest of us, being engaged in active combat, have to maintain civilian status. Or had to. All that has changed now that the US has entered the war."

"So how should I address you? Lieutenant or Mr. Younan?" she asked.

"Ted is fine." His smile deepened as their eyes met. Her heart skipped a beat.

"Reverend Baker will be disappointed to learn you lied to him," Nathan sneered.

Ted's jaw tightened as he turned to the other man. "I did *not* lie. I am indeed a lieutenant in the US Army Air Corps, a rank I worked hard to achieve and am damn proud of."

Genie eased between the two men, aware of the attention directed their way. "As you should be. I'm sure my father would understand."

Ted gave a slight nod, his expression relaxing. "Thank you. And before I get distracted again, the Generalissimo and his wife are ready to meet you now."

"Excellent." Nathan held out his arm. "Ready, Eugenia?"

Together, the three of them cut through the crush of people to the front of the room, where a well-dressed Chinese couple was holding court. The husband—a fit, handsome man with a closely shaved head and wire-rimmed glasses—sported a military tunic bedecked with all the medals and ribbons of his exalted rank as well as a pleasant, relaxed smile that wouldn't look out of place on a kindly uncle. She wasn't deceived, however, and guessed he had to be Generalissimo Chiang Kai-shek, leader of the Chinese Nationalist government.

Genie's attention turned to the woman who stood beside him. On the exterior, Madame Chiang was indeed as elegant and beautiful as a jade butterfly. Yet the woman was listening to the men gathered with such quiet intensity—her jet eyes missing nothing—Genie could well believe the rumors that she was the real power behind the throne.

"Even though I know you both speak Chinese fluently, I advise you to stick to English," Ted murmured as they approached. "Madame Chiang spent many years in Georgia, attending college with her sisters, and likes to show off her language ability."

"Of course," Nathan replied just as softly.

"Does the Generalissimo speak English?" she asked curiously.

"Not that I know of," Ted answered. "But, since Madame Chiang will tell you she speaks for her husband, and indeed for all of China, it won't be a problem."

Nathan snorted. Genie, for her part, was intrigued that the Generalissimo allowed his wife such freedom. Such power. It was not a privilege normally granted to wives in a public setting—at least not in her experience.

Madame Chiang's smile was warm as they approached. "Welcome!" she greeted them in English. "You must be Miss Baker and Mr. Sterling. Thank you for returning our dear Lieutenant Younan to us. China is forever in your debt."

Only the faintest of accents colored Madame's soft drawl.

Nathan bowed slightly. "It was our pleasure."

"I hear you are returning to the United States," Madame Chiang said, her dark, intelligent gaze flitting between Genie and Nathan.

"We are," Nathan said, leaving Genie no room to respond. "We leave tomorrow."

*Tomorrow?* Genie struggled not to stare at Nathan while Madame wished them a safe journey. Had he planned on telling her their travel plans before they actually left Kunming?

Madame Chiang turned to her. "And best wishes to you on your upcoming marriage. May you enjoy many happy years together."

Genie almost choked on the ghastly thought. "Thank you," she managed.

"One last thing." Madame leaned forward, her smile fading. "When you get to the United States, please remind your countrymen of China's long friendship with them. Encourage them to reach deep in their pockets and send support to China, both monetary and military. After all, we share a common enemy as well as a common dream."

"Of course, but I'm not sure what I can do . . ."

"You can do much." Madame Chiang's expression became almost fierce. "Have you not a voice? Talk to your friends, to all the wives and mothers in your circle. Spread the word that China needs their help. It is too important to leave something so crucial in the hands of men alone."

Genie stared at Madame Chiang, the notion of women having any sort of impact on matters of state seeming as improbable as men giving birth.

"I can't believe this," Nathan said with a derisive laugh. "After decades of your government demonizing foreigners, calling for a purge of all non-Chinese peoples from your borders, you dare ask us to help you?"

Genie stiffened at his blatant rudeness, sure that he was going to get them thrown out. While she, too, had been spat upon and called a "white devil," she certainly didn't hold Madame accountable for it.

Ted looked horrified, too.

After a moment of frosty silence, Madame inclined her head ever so slightly. "You may do as you choose, of course. I hope you will enjoy dinner."

Recognizing a dismissal when she heard one, Genie began backing up. "Yes, thank—"

Nathan's grip on her elbow tightened, holding her in place. "Wait."

Switching to Mandarin, he turned to face Generalissimo Chiang. "The peril facing the Middle Kingdom is of its own devising. If your government would devote as much attention to driving out the Japanese as it does to fighting the Communists, you would not need to ask assistance from your Western friends."

The Generalissimo's hitherto pleasant expression vanished, and Genie's breath seized. They would be arrested for sure now. Of all the ways Nathan could demonstrate his improved mastery of the language, this absolutely wasn't it.

"Your youth makes you rash," the Generalissimo said tersely. "However, as you are our guest tonight, I will forgive your rudeness. Once. As to your mistaken belief that I should allow the Communist threat to go unchecked, you should consider the words of your own President Lincoln, a very wise man. He said a house divided against itself cannot stand, and I completely agree. These Communists you wish me to ignore are dividing the Chinese people, while Stalin rubs his greedy hands, eager to make the Middle Kingdom his own. Such a calamity I cannot and will not allow."

Nathan opened his mouth as if to argue, but he was interrupted by an American-looking officer materializing beside them. Genie almost collapsed with relief.

"Excuse me." An older man dressed in a uniform similar to Ted's except complete with insignia smiled genially at the group. She guessed he must be a high-ranking officer, not only because he stood with the unconscious ease of a man used to being in charge, but because Ted had abruptly straightened.

"I'm sorry to interrupt," the man said in English, bowing slightly to the older couple. "Madame Chiang, could you please let the Generalissimo know that dinner is about to be served?"

Madame smiled at the man, the tension of the previous moment vanishing. "Of course, General. Thank you."

"General," Ted said as soon as the Chiangs had drifted off toward the dining room, "may I present Miss Baker and Mr. Sterling. Miss Baker, Nathan, General Chennault."

General Chennault nodded. "It's a pleasure to meet you. And thank you for returning Ted to us. Though it's a pity he couldn't have brought his plane back with him."

A dull flush crept up Ted's cheeks. "I did the best I could, sir."

"I know you did, son." The general clapped him on the shoulder, all smiles. "But it still leaves us short a plane, which is why I'm sending you to Cairo tomorrow, to ferry another one back."

"Yes, sir. And I won't let you down."

"Never thought you would. And now, if you would be good enough to show Miss Baker and Mr. Sterling to their seats, I'll finish spreading the word." Chennault bowed slightly to Genie. "It was a pleasure meeting you."

"Likewise." She waited until the general had continued on his way before turning to Ted. "Cairo? Why, that's half a world away! How can he possibly expect you to fly that far?"

He smiled in amusement. "Not in one straight shot. I'll have to stop and refuel along the way. Same as you will on your flight to Calcutta tomorrow."

Her brain stuttered to a stop. "Flight?"

"Sure. Didn't Sterling tell you? Chennault got you tickets on a CNAC flight—that would be China's national airline—and he had to boot a couple of dignitaries to do it, too." Ted laughed even as her stomach twisted in pure terror.

"I can't . . ." She drew a deep breath and tried again. "I can't go up in a plane. They crash!"

"Don't be ridiculous," Nathan said coolly. "The flight leaves at sunup, and you will be on it. No excuses."

"Can't we go by boat?" she said, her panic growing. "I'm feeling so much better, I could readily handle another week of travel down to the coast. And I promise to take care of myself on the journey this time and not get sick again."

"I'm glad to hear it, though I have to wonder about your sincerity, considering how you're dressed tonight." Nathan gestured at her dress. "Someone with a lick of sense would have worn far more fabric to keep away the chill. Instead you chose to look like a harlot."

She flinched, stung by the unfairness of his attack, even as she was appalled to find her eyes filling with tears.

Ted slid between her and Nathan, forcing the slighter man to step back. "What the hell is your problem, Sterling? First you insult the Chiangs, and now Miss Baker. And the fellows you've bunked with these past few days are none too happy with you, either."

Nathan's face flushed. "Should I stay silent when men who should know better stagger home drunk boasting of the women they bought, while letters from their sweethearts back home lie open on their bunk? And what of diplomats who extoll us all to make sacrifices for 'the good of all' while they line their own pockets and see more to their own comfort than that of others?"

"And what of narrow-minded religious blowhards who pretend to speak the truth of the Lord and yet forget He reserved that right of judgment for himself?" With a disgusted sound, Ted turned his back on Nathan to face Genie. His dark eyes gentled. "For what it's worth, I think you look nice tonight."

Gratitude squeezed her chest. "Thank you."

Ted escorted them in silence to the dining room. He introduced them to the two Kunming businessmen and their wives who would be sharing their table, and then he left to find a seat with the pilots. The men and their wives graciously welcomed them, their faces lighting with relief when Genie responded in the local dialect.

The Chinese guests nodded gravely when she mentioned she was on her way out of the country. The men agreed that her father was right and said they had considered leaving themselves because the opportunities for advancement were surely more abundant overseas, away from the war. The women expressed their condolences, for they had heard the food was awful, and the countryside not nearly as beautiful.

None of the comments cheered Genie. Already crushed in heart and spirit as well as supremely irritated with Nathan, she dejectedly twirled her chopsticks in the delicately sauced noodles. If the Lord had any mercy, one of the gathered company would offer to take her back home, an offer she would have accepted in a heartbeat.

After dinner was finished, and the applause following the lengthy speeches given by General Chennault and Madame Chiang had faded into lethargic postmeal conversation, Nathan excused them both. He didn't talk on the way back to AVG Hostel Number One, where she was staying. Nor did she. It wasn't until she got back to her room that the tension of the evening finally slid from her shoulders. The respite was brief, though. Tomorrow she would be leaving China, perhaps for a very long time. And leaving on an airplane, no less.

She sank onto her narrow bed and stared unseeingly out the window. If only the planets had aligned differently, maybe Ted would never have been shot down. Then her father would never have rescued him, and she might still be in her village. Her little family would still be intact, her friend ready for their next walk up the mountain to feed Wu Fang.

She drifted over to the window and looked out through the snow toward the peaks, toward the east, toward home. The swirling snow winked in the light and then blurred as tears filled her eyes. *Baba* . . .

*The Lord gave, and the Lord hath taken away.* She could almost hear her father's beloved voice, and yet the comfort was thin. She knew he was right. If this was truly the Lord's will, then so be it. She had no choice but to submit, and yet . . . she didn't want to.

*Ah, Yu Jie.* The snow seemed to reverse directions, and a memory of Zhenzhu rose before her. *A boat can't always sail with the wind. Sometimes the boatman has to steer into it to find safety.*

Genie's fingers curled into a fist, her heart twisting in indecision, the two halves of her soul never having seemed so disparate as they did tonight.

"I'll go, *Baba,*" she whispered into the icy darkness beyond the glass, "because it is what you want. But I'm coming back. I promise."

# Chapter 11

Genie wiped her palms on her long skirts, looking anywhere but at the large twin-engine airplane with the blue-and-white logo and initials of the China National Aviation Corporation emblazoned on its aluminum exterior. Nervous perspiration dampened her skin, chilling her as the wind whipped across the airfield. Wondering where Ted was this morning, she turned her attention to the fighters, painted green and tan and with fierce, toothy snarls on their noses, sitting off in the distance. She couldn't imagine the kind of courage it took to fly one, let alone fly it toward enemy territory.

Nathan stood next to her, huffing into his clasped hands to warm them, his collar turned up against the cold. Despite his obvious impatience, he hadn't yet said a word about her reluctance to climb the metal stairs into the plane. Maybe he sensed her fear. Or perhaps he was nervous as well. It was one thing to be on the ground and watch a plane soar overhead. It was quite another to get in one, entrusting one's life to the contraption's ability to defy gravity.

"Miss, you need to board if you're going." The young American smiled encouragingly at her as he stamped his feet to stay warm, his hands shoved deep in his flight suit's pockets.

"All right." She curved her lips into what she hoped was a smile.

"And don't hesitate to ask the pilots if you can't figure out the seat belt. It's likely to be a rough ride, and there's no stewardess on board today. No coffee service for the same reason. But the view on top should be nice."

"Wonderful," she said, aware she didn't sound very enthused.

Nathan stooped to pick up their two recently purchased suitcases and started toward the metal airstair positioned at the rear of the plane. With every cell of her body crying out in objection, she followed him. Her knees shook so badly on her way up the steps she was afraid she would fall.

It was pleasantly warm inside the plane, almost hot, with a peculiar stale smell to the air. While Nathan stowed their suitcases with the others on a metal rack, she scanned the interior of the cabin. Of the twenty-one seats, all upholstered in green and cream, only two were unoccupied, a silent reminder of the two military officers who had been bumped from the flight to make space for her and Nathan. The seats were arranged in seven rows, with a narrow aisle between seats one and two. Through the square, curtained windows she could see the airport and the mountains beyond.

"Which seat do you want?" Nathan asked, gesturing toward the two empty ones that were conveniently next to each other. She wondered if that had been arranged in advance as well.

"I don't care."

Being by the window would give her a better view, one that Ted had rhapsodized about not too long ago, on the trail. But it might also mean seeing her death seconds before it happened, because planes did crash. Or at least have very hard landings, like Ted's plane, and that hadn't sounded like much fun, either.

"Actually, not the window one," she said.

"Fine. Follow me."

A murmur of conversations in both Chinese and English filled the cabin as she walked up the narrow aisle. While two or three of the passengers were in uniform, the rest were well-dressed civilians, both white and Chinese. Her attention caught on one particular family. White like her, the mother looked to be close to tears as she clutched a fretful baby in her arms. Her young son played happily with the window shade while the father stared off into nowhere, his face haggard and pale. She wondered if they, too, were being forced to flee because of the war.

Nathan took his seat, and Genie sat beside him. Barely a second later, the door in the back thudded shut, making her jump. A uniformed pilot—a handsome Chinese man with a scar through one eyebrow—strode past her and down the aisle on his way to the front. He disappeared through the opening in the front of the cabin.

She leaned over in time to see someone—she couldn't tell if it was the pilot or not due to the man being backlit—pulling down a folding seat in the narrow hallway, cutting off her view of the forward part. Then the engines sputtered and then roared to life, and she forgot about the pilots.

Her fingers dug into the armrests as the growl escalated into a deafening roar and the plane began to roll forward. Nathan leaned forward to peer out the window, temporarily blocking the view. At first it didn't feel much different from her ride in the truck, with the same bumps and decelerations. Then the plane turned, and turned again, and the engines began to snarl in earnest. Genie was pressed back into her seat by the sudden acceleration, and her heart stuttered.

For what seemed like an eternity, the plane bounced and swayed. Genie closed her eyes to hold back sudden, desperate tears. *Please, Lord, let me live. I want to see* Baba *again. And Zhenzhu. Please* . . . She was going to die. She just knew it. They all were—everyone on the plane.

The plane shuddered, and she bit her lip hard enough to taste blood. Then the ride abruptly smoothed out. She held her breath, waiting for death. Seconds passed with the engines' growl unchanged, and then it dawned on her. The plane was airborne. She was flying.

A strange sensation fizzed through her veins. She slanted a look at Nathan to see if he felt it, too. His face was pressed to the window, his attention rapt. Curiosity overrode the remnants of her fear. She leaned closer to look over his shoulder. The city slid out from beneath the wing, the cars and buildings diminishing to the size of toys, then even smaller. Wisps of white briefly obscured the view, and then a solid wall of pale gray slid around the aircraft, erasing the world.

Flying through the clouds didn't feel so different from being surrounded by fog in the early morning. Beginning to relax, she tentatively looked around the cabin. A few of the passengers were still pale, but most either chatted with their seatmates or read newspapers. Even the little boy had settled down to pester his mother with questions. Genie smiled to herself, a little humbled by his lack of fear.

Nathan leaned his head back against the seat and closed his eyes.

Light flickered outside the window, and then sunlight flooded the cabin. She leaned across Nathan to see the clouds stretch out below them like dazzling white snow, freshly fallen in a thick blanket. It looked thick enough to walk on, and she imagined herself walking across the clouds toward the rocky peaks jutting up like a miniature range. She almost expected to see the iridescent dragons of folklore flying around the distant ones. Or perhaps a celestial tiger, its orange-and-black coat sparkling in the sun, padding on silent paws from one side of the Middle Kingdom to the other.

Suddenly the seat dropped out from under her. It reappeared mere seconds later, the impact hard enough to click her teeth. She grabbed Nathan's arm just as another violent shudder racked the plane, her pulse kicking into high gear.

"What's happening?"

He sighed and pried her fingers off his arm, not even bothering to open his eyes. "Didn't you hear the ticket agent? Honestly, Eugenia. It's a good thing you have me along. He warned us the ride might get rough."

The plane lurched sickeningly to the side, and she closed her eyes against the rush of nausea. Silently reciting every psalm she could remember, she clung to the armrests like a lifeline while the plane shimmied and fell through the air. She tried not to think of the mountains she had seen sticking up through the clouds, or how far the plane had risen above the earth. After another hard jolt, she remembered the ticket agent mentioning seat belts. With fumbling fingers, she found the metal ends and figured out how to connect them.

Around her, all the conversations began to quiet down bit by bit. The baby started to cry, its piercing wails rivaling the pulsing snarl of the engines in strength. Genie gritted her teeth against the sound of the terrified child and hung on as the plane lurched through the air like a drunken farmer. She closed her eyes, hoping that would help. It didn't.

A slight cough and then a soft retching sound came from her right. Heart sinking with dismay, she opened an eye. Nathan was leaning forward, a fist pressed to his lips. His skin was dotted with perspiration. He shifted in his seat. Guessing his intent, she jumped up in time to let him shimmy past. Her own stomach clenched as she heard another passenger vomit.

Desperate for distraction, she slid her gaze out the window as she sat down again. A huge snow-covered peak drifted past, this time close enough to touch. Horrified, she immediately sank back into her seat and closed her eyes, feeling uncomfortably close to panic. Out of psalms to recite, she switched to prayer.

"If you clutch the armrest any harder, you'll dent it," someone said in a familiar, amused-sounding drawl.

"Ted!" Her eyes flew open to find him smiling down at her, his hands braced on opposite seats to keep his footing.

"How are you doing?"

"All right," she lied. "Nathan is having a hard time of it, though."

"He's not alone." Ted gave her a once-over, and then squatted in the aisle beside her. "Would it help if I explained the science behind flying? You're looking a tad nervous there, sport."

"I—I don't know." No sooner had the words left her mouth than she suddenly became weightless, only to slam down in her seat a second later. She squeaked in terror.

"Easy." His hand covered hers in what was meant to be a comforting gesture. Instead it sent her pulse into a frenzy as heat from his hand coursed along her nerves. Still, she couldn't for the life of her pull away.

"Have you been on board the whole time?" she asked, immediately realizing it was a silly question but needing to refocus her thoughts on anything other than where their skin touched.

"You didn't see me up front? I thought you did when I pulled down the jump seat."

"That was you?" she asked in surprise, and then wanted to kick herself. Of course it was; he had just said so. Apparently being this close to him caused brain failure.

"It was. But as I was saying, no matter what it might feel like, the plane isn't going to drop out of the sky." Amusement laced his voice.

"How do you know?"

"Physics." This time he actually had the gall to smirk.

The plane shimmied, and she clutched the armrests again, her irritation vanishing.

"What if the engines fall off?" The moment the words left her lips she wanted to call them back, afraid she had jinxed the plane.

Ted eyed her death grip and sobered slightly. "That's very unlikely to happen. And even if we did lose power, the plane simply becomes a glider, which is no harder to land than a powered aircraft."

Terror held her silent.

"Look, you've been in a boat before, yes? It's the same principle." He held out one hand level to the floor and then angled his other hand until it butted up underneath. "This is the plane, and this is the wind, or more accurately the relative movement of the air with respect to the plane. But never mind that. Long story short, the relative wind rushing under our wings holds us up, just like water sliding under a boat.

"And like water, this relative wind can have waves that lift the plane up and down. Some days the waves are smooth and you'll hardly notice them, and other times—like today—the waves are a lot rougher. And so is the ride."

As if to punctuate his words, the cabin shuddered violently. Her heart skipped a beat, and even Ted had to brace himself on the seat ahead of him.

"You sure we won't crash?" she asked, truly wanting to believe him.

"Positive. Well, mostly. Mountain waves *can* be a bit dicey. It's not so much the engines we worry about falling off as the wings."

Her stomach cramped. "You're not helping."

"Sorry." But the sparkle in his eyes said otherwise. And the fact that he could joke about such a thing somehow, perversely, made her feel a little better.

"Here." He stood suddenly. "I know something that might help, if you're up for it."

She hesitated. Nathan had yet to reappear, and as curious as she was about whatever Ted had in mind, she should probably check on her escort. Her father would expect it. Reluctantly, she turned around in her seat and searched the faces behind her.

"Sterling's huddled in the back where you can't see him, waiting to use the lavatory," Ted said as if guessing her thoughts. "Do you need me to go ask his permission to come up front?"

Something in his tone pricked her pride.

"No need. I'll do whatever I want."

One of his eyebrows slid up. His gaze turned assessing. "Is that so?"

"Yes." Her heart skittered at her temerity.

A small smile touched his lips as he glanced down the aisle again. "Well, all right, then. It feels like it's smoothed out a bit, so follow me."

On the short journey to the cockpit, Genie realized Ted was right—the air had smoothed out. The baby had even fallen into an exhausted slumber in her mother's arms. Curious looks followed her into the narrow space between the cabin and where the pilots sat. Luggage and mail sacks strained against the cages lining both sides, except for one section on the left where half a dozen radios in black boxes were mounted. Cable and wires snaked along the ceiling. Then Ted squeezed behind one of the pilots, and she could see out the front.

A dizzying array of black-faced dials faced her. Large and small, with white-painted numbers and pointers, they were mounted on a broad black panel beneath the windshield. The pilot on the left reached out to adjust one of the five levers mounted on a silver housing between the seats. It was all rather overwhelming. She couldn't even imagine trying to learn what all those levers and gauges did.

Ted tapped both pilots on the shoulder to catch their attention. "Gentlemen," he said loud enough to be heard through the men's headsets. "This is Miss Baker. Genie, this is Captain Joe Chin."

The pilot on the left was the one she had seen earlier, the one with the scar. He nodded while keeping his eyes out the front. "Welcome," he said in unaccented English, surprising her. Even Madame Chiang's English hadn't been as good.

"And this is First Officer George Willits," Ted said, gesturing to the pilot on the right. Genie had barely registered the American name and blond hair when the pilot turned and smiled broadly over his shoulder. Blue eyes looked at her over the top of his sunglasses.

"Glad to have you aboard, Miss Baker," he said with a wink. His drawl was even thicker than Ted's.

"Thank you."

Ted waved his hand at all the electronics. "So this is the cockpit and the panel. But don't get hung up on all that. The real attraction is the view."

At his prompting, she finally looked out the front window. Her breath caught.

The thick blanket of clouds had dissipated sometime in the past half hour, exposing a broad sweep of green and brown that faded into a dusky slate blue at the horizon. The rocky peaks still loomed off to either side, but their snow-covered heights were rapidly being replaced by foothills covered with ever-thickening vegetation. The colors were muted from the height but still stunning as the earth raced toward them, only to disappear silently beneath the nose.

Entranced, she crept closer, being careful not to touch anything.

"What do you think?" the American pilot asked.

She looked up at the deep blue of the heavens and followed the color down to where it became a milky white on the horizon. Endless. Enticing. A place where anything could exist. The ground continued to slide beneath the plane, a mere afterthought with no consciousness of their passing.

"It's . . . incredible. I feel so powerful, so free. Like a bird soaring over the earth."

The Chinese pilot began to laugh. Joe was his name, if she remembered correctly. "Now you've done it, Younan."

"Did I say something wrong?" Cheeks burning, she glanced back at Ted, afraid she had ruined everything with her silly comment.

"No, no. Not at all," he said, not looking a bit upset. In fact, he was smiling. "What you said is what every pilot has felt or thought at some point. It's what draws us into the air and makes us do what we do."

"Younan's right," Joe said, his attention back on the gauges. "Though it's probably only fair to warn you—once you're bitten by the flying bug, the only cure is to learn how to fly." He glanced at the blond pilot, George. "How we doin' on fuel?"

Genie shook her head, the possibility alone making her weak-kneed. "Oh no. I couldn't."

"Why not?" George asked while checking the gauges and jotting down numbers on a clipboard. "It's not like women can't fly. Surely you've heard of Amelia Earhart."

She hadn't, actually, but her pride wouldn't let her say so. "I mean that I have no call to learn such a skill, not unless I could find a way to serve the Good Lord by flying. It would be wasteful."

George turned in his seat again. "Far be it from me to argue with the man upstairs, but I think you're denying yourself one of the greatest pleasures put on this God-given earth."

Joe shot him an amused look.

"What? I said one of the greatest pleasures, not *the* greatest pleasure. And it looks like we have forty-five minutes of fuel, so we should make Lashio, no problem."

"Speaking of Lashio, how close are we?" Ted asked.

Chin made another adjustment to one of the levers. "We're about fifty miles out, so if Miss Baker wants to see anything else, now's the time."

"Maybe I should go back," she said, not wanting to overstay her welcome. And Nathan might be missing her by now.

Ted gestured toward the window on her right. "Not till you look out there. You likely had too many clouds before to really appreciate the view."

"There were a lot of clouds." She edged toward the window, the siren call of his suggestion too strong to resist.

The view of the ground was better from the side, and she soon spotted a waterfall, the bright water cascading down a rocky cliff. Ted leaned down beside her, his face startlingly close to hers as he peered out. She could smell his breath, clean and minty from the gum he was chewing.

"It never gets old." His tone was reverential, as if he were gazing on some holy relic.

With an effort she refocused her attention on the view.

"We're about to start descending," George called from behind her. "Which means we're liable to hit a few bumps. Perhaps Miss Baker would like to take her seat?"

"Oh yes. Thank you." She stole one last look out the front at the awe-inspiring panorama while Ted shifted back out of her way.

Nathan was waiting for her, back in his seat. He nodded toward the front. "I see Younan found you."

"He wanted to show me the view from the front, to make me feel better about flying."

"I bet." Nathan closed his eyes, his complexion still pale. "And how providential he should be on the same flight as we are."

She studied him for a moment, not missing the sarcasm in his voice, and wondered if she had missed something. Could it be he was jealous? He had made it clear he didn't love her, and she had made it clear she wouldn't marry him. Or at least she thought she had. Yet he bristled every time Ted was near, as if he were defending his territory.

The engines were throttled back to a steady purr, and a subtle shift in her seat told her the plane had started to descend. Leaving the problem of Nathan aside, she watched the deep green of the jungle get closer and closer. Soon roads appeared and then individual buildings. Sooner than she wanted, the ground was only feet away. A series of fences flashed by the window, and then a firm thump shook the plane. The plane continued to rattle its way down the runway, slowing as it went.

"Please tell me we're in Calcutta," Nathan said hoarsely.

"Lashio." She frowned as the plane taxied toward a crowd of people gathered in the ramp area. She wondered if perhaps there was a dignitary on board with them, or somebody famous.

The plane eased to a stop, and the engines shut down. The passengers began talking in relieved and buoyant tones. The blond pilot, George, exited the cockpit and strode down the aisle. He winked at her as he passed. She bit her lip, hoping Nathan had missed it. He was in a bad enough mood without his thinking she'd been flirting with the CNAC pilots, too.

Fresh air, redolent with humidity and the musky vegetative smell of jungle, rushed through the fetid cabin as the back door was opened. Shouts came from outside, and the plane rocked slightly as the airstair was lowered. Restless, she stared out at the hangars and the jungle beyond while brown-skinned workers replenished the fuel in the wing tanks. It was hard to comprehend she was already in another country, and come nightfall she would be in yet another.

A white couple boarded, thin lipped and eyes haunted. More refugees fleeing the war, she decided as they spoke softly to each other in French, the lady's eyes red as if from crying. Her heart went out to them as they took the two empty seats. Then to Genie's surprise, three more people boarded. While they moved toward the front of the plane, George let two more on.

"The ticket agent warned me about this," Nathan said sotto voce, his eyes still closed.

"About what?"

"That they might have to overboard the airplane. The general consensus is that the British will lose Burma any day now, so the airline has agreed to try to get out as many people as they can. For a price, of course."

An ear-splitting scream came from outside the plane. Everyone in the cabin fell silent. A second passed, and then an almost inhuman wail echoed off the buildings.

Chin shouted something from the cockpit, his words not quite making it back into the cabin. Passengers on the side closest to the hangars pointed to something, and Genie tried to angle her head to see around them. With so many people standing in the aisle, she didn't dare leave her seat for fear of losing it.

"Excuse me. Let me through." Ted worked his way down the aisle, his expression tight. He passed her without making eye contact and then was out the back, clattering down the airstair.

"Hey!" The anger in his voice was distinguishable even at a distance. "What do you think you're doin'?"

A man responded, but his words were lost beneath another wail. This one ended in a gut-twisting shriek that made the hairs on Genie's neck stand on end.

"Jesus," George muttered from the back.

Nathan half rose in his seat, and Genie could feel his agitation. But then how could anyone hear those awful sounds and not react?

"What's going on?" he called back.

George swore softly again, all geniality gone. He turned his attention to the rapt passengers. "Folks, it looks like we've got a reluctant traveler. Is there anyone willing to give up their seat? Because we can't have an unconscious gal in the aisle."

A dozen people began talking at once, but Genie didn't hear a single offer of a seat. She tugged on Nathan's sleeve.

"Tell him she can have my seat. I'll just ask Ted if I can sit up with him and the pilots."

Nathan ignored her, his attention focused on the door.

A commotion on the airstair had Genie craning around in her seat. The back of Ted's shoulders appeared in the door, and George shifted back against the luggage rack. Next through came a young woman hanging limply in Ted's arms, her legs supported by someone just out of sight. Then Genie got a better look. The woman was dressed in the long skirts and drab colors of a missionary.

"Nathan—" Genie said, her heart in her throat.

"I know," he hissed angrily. Then he raised his voice. "Bring her here. She can have my seat."

# Chapter 12

Nathan climbed over the top of her as Ted and another man eased down the aisle with a moaning woman in their arms. Genie scooted over to the window seat so it would be easier for the men to deposit the girl, for it was clear now that the poor thing was no older than Genie, and perhaps a little younger. Ted's jaw was clenched as he and the other man propped her into the seat, though from effort or anger she couldn't tell. The girl had gone limp and unresponsive.

He met Genie's eyes. "If she gives you any trouble, call for me."

"There's no need," the other man said calmly, his voice accented in a way that made Genie think English wasn't his first language. "She is my responsibility. I'll watch over her."

Ted shot the man a hard look. "What if the morphine wears off before we land?"

"I was assured it wouldn't. If it does, the doctor has given me another syringe to use."

The rear door slammed shut, and George edged his way forward past all the people sitting in the aisle. "That's it. We can't squeeze on another soul and expect to get this bird off the ground. Younan, move it."

Ted looked as if he wanted to say something more to her but then gave way to the other pilot.

Genie took a deep breath and glanced at the pale, still girl next to her. Her narrow chest rose and fell in shallow, fast breaths; her thin face was streaked with tears. Genie's chest squeezed with sympathy.

"Don't judge us too harshly," her escort said softly. "She has been through so much, she had become unreasonable."

She glanced up doubtfully at the man. Solidly built and not much older than she, his reddish hair stuck out from under a black flat-brimmed hat, and his round face was framed by a ragged beard. Shadowed gray eyes met her scrutiny steadily and without affront. His plain white shirt was stained from sweat and traveling, a condition only partially covered by his loose black vest buttoned above equally black trousers. Yet he appeared not a bit self-conscious over how he stood out from the other more conventionally dressed passengers. Instead he exuded a calm steadiness that reassured her.

Her father had the same kind of presence.

Questions burned on her tongue, but she lost the chance to ask them when the engines fired to life once again. The girl next to her stiffened and moaned. Her escort took her hand and began to sing in a low, pleasant baritone. The girl calmed.

Not wanting to intrude, Genie looked out the window. The airplane took much longer to lift off than she remembered coming out of Kunming. From her window, she watched the jungle rush by faster and faster, the plane swaying while it jolted over the ground, as if debating whether to leap into the air. Genie held her breath and prayed: she would be good, obedient, grateful, anything if she could survive the next couple of minutes.

The ride smoothed abruptly, and slowly—very slowly—the ground receded. Her fear dissipated in a rush of excitement. Ten feet. Twenty. Trees rushed so closely beneath the wings, she could almost imagine herself reaching out the window and touching the branches.

Slowly the hills once more became small green ripples in the earth, and the occupants of the cabin seemed to exhale as one. Apparently she hadn't been the only one to notice their less-than-spry ascent.

She glanced at the girl's escort and found him staring sightlessly at their clasped hands, his mind clearly elsewhere. A troubled elsewhere, if his bowed shoulders were any indication.

"Are you missionaries?" she asked, hoping to turn his thoughts to a more pleasant vein.

He glanced up at her. "Were. Our mission was destroyed by the Japanese."

"Oh." An awkward silence stretched as Genie struggled to think of what next to say. Happily, he made the decision for her.

"I am Brother Marcus Krauss, most recently from Thailand."

"Eugenia Baker, from Kweichow Province, China," Genie said readily, happy to be back on safer conversational ground. "And Thailand? Where is that?"

"You probably know the country as Siam. The government only recently changed the name to reflect its independence, which is somewhat ironic now that the government has kowtowed to the Japanese." The sudden edge in his voice left no doubt who he blamed for the loss of his mission.

"Are you and your wife hoping to start over somewhere else?"

His eyebrows flashed up. "Oh, this isn't my wife. This is my sister, Lavinia."

"I beg your pardon," Genie said, embarrassed and a little confused. The two looked nothing alike. Where he was square and sturdily built, Lavinia was reed-thin, almost to the point of being frail. Her hair was dark, almost black, beneath her white cap, her skin translucent without a single freckle that so marked her brother's countenance.

"No need to apologize," he said gently. "We are strangers to you, so how would you know? And to answer your question, no. At least not right away. I need to take Lavinia back to the States first, to stay with our parents for a while. She is . . . not doing well. Her husband was killed—murdered, actually—in front of her, along with several others of our group."

"How awful!"

"Yes." His gaze dropped to the fragile hand in his grasp. He was silent a moment, and then he gave a shaky exhale. When he looked up again, his eyes were clear, resolute. "So where are you and your husband headed?"

"To the United States as well. And Nathan isn't my husband. My father sent him along as my escort. Like you, my father is a missionary, but for the Blessed Souls Society. He's been serving in China for over twenty-five years. Nathan was sent to help him eight years ago."

"And you served as well?" he asked with what appeared to be genuine interest.

"I suppose. In my own way." Her cheeks heated under his steady regard. "I was helping my father translate the Old Testament into Yue Chinese."

"A worthy cause, to be sure. Will you continue once you reach the States?" he asked curiously.

"I—I guess I never thought about it. I've been so focused on the journey to my aunt Hazel's house in California."

"Ah, the West Coast. Beautiful country, though it can't compare to western Pennsylvania, where my family lives."

She hesitated. "Forgive me, but does everyone in Pennsylvania have an accent similar to yours?"

"In my town, yes. But then most of us grew up speaking German and only used English at school. Though perhaps not so much anymore, now that Germany has declared war on the US."

"So you grew up in two cultures like I did." She hesitated. "Do you ever feel conflicted, as if you don't know which country you belong to?"

"I am a man of God, so everywhere is my country. No"—a muscle worked in his cheek as he gently brushed a strand of Lavinia's hair out of her slack face—"divided loyalties trouble me not. My struggle is remembering we are all the Lord's children and worthy of forgiveness, even those who would slaughter civilians without provocation."

"May the Lord have mercy on their souls." The phrase, which she had heard her father say a hundred times or more, seemed woefully inadequate given the situation, but she had no idea what else to say. She couldn't even begin to imagine the horrors he and his sister had lived through.

He gave a short nod, his eyes not quite meeting hers. "Just so."

Deciding she had probed enough, she leaned her head back and tried to sleep the rest of the flight. Luckily, the air was much smoother on this side of the mountains. In what seemed no time at all, she awoke to Ted's voice informing everyone it was time to buckle up for landing.

Genie glanced at the girl beside her, but she was still out cold. Even the thump on landing didn't seem to disturb her. If not for the slight rise and fall of her chest, she could have been dead.

Genie shivered at the thought of all the girl had been through.

This time when George threw open the door after landing, a different flood of scents filled the cabin, a concrete reminder that she was in yet another country. Her third in less than twelve hours. Her mind could scarcely comprehend it. As the aisle emptied of passengers, Brother Marcus assured her he would be back for Lavinia and then left with the others. Afraid Lavinia would awaken, leaving Genie to handle the situation, she hardly dared breathe while the other passengers filed past—some openly curious, others politely looking away.

After the cabin had emptied, Ted appeared in the cockpit doorway, a bag slung over his shoulder. His brows gathered into a single dark line as he approached. "Did he abandon her?"

"No." Genie bristled, feeling a strange need to defend the missionary. "Brother Marcus—who is Lavinia's real brother, by the way—said he would be back once everyone got off."

"And that would be now." His gaze flicked to the back of the plane. "Sterling, you up for helping carry this poor girl off?"

With a guilty start, Genie realized she hadn't thought of Nathan once on the flight from Lashio. She peeked over the top of her seat to see him wipe his face with a handkerchief. He was still unnaturally pale, but he looked better than he had.

"If you can hold up a minute," George called up the airstair in a lazy drawl. "I see a wheelchair coming this way."

"All righty, then." Ted relaxed against one of the seats. "I meant to ask earlier, but where are you two staying? I thought we might share a taxi. Save some dough."

Nathan pocketed his handkerchief. "I don't know yet."

"I see." Ted studied the other man for a moment. "You do know there's hardly a bed to be found in the whole city thanks to the war, let alone one suitable for Miss Baker."

"I'm not worried," Nathan said coolly, and Genie felt a subtle rise in tension between the two men. "If worse comes to worst, I'm sure we can spend the night in a church."

"What's the holdup?" Joe asked, coming up behind Ted, a brown leather satchel in his hand. "I've got places to go, people to see."

"We're waiting for a wheelchair and discussing hotel rooms. Miss Baker here doesn't have a place for the night."

Joe's scarred eyebrow crinkled as he frowned. "That's no good. Maybe she could try the Grand? I'd give her my room, but I need a good night's sleep. We're flying some execs home tomorrow, and if I'm dog-tired they might get the wrong impression."

"I've got it handled." Nathan waved them on. "Go ahead, please. We'll be fine."

The pilot didn't move. "I'm sure you will. But I can't leave the plane until all the passengers are off. Company policy. Even though we're on British soil, you can't be too careful about sabotage. Not with a war on."

Genie hurriedly stood. "Oh, I didn't know—"

"Sit down, Eugenia," Nathan said impatiently. "No one can go anywhere until Mrs. Schmidt is safely off."

Genie shot him a questioning look as she sat, wondering how he had learned the young widow's last name.

"Chair's here!" George called back.

Ted unslung his bag and tossed it onto a seat. "I'll pick her up and then, Sterling, if you'll catch her under the arms, I can take her legs."

Nathan hesitated, and Ted swore softly.

"You're not going to endanger your soul if you accidentally touch her breasts. Pretend she's a guy, or else switch places with me."

"Just get on with it, Younan," Nathan snapped.

Ted reached down and hauled the girl out of the seat, his shoulders straining to control her dead weight as he eased her into the aisle. Nathan slid his arms under her armpits.

"Got her," he said, his pale skin flushing slightly as he adjusted his hold.

Ted wrapped the girl's long skirts around her legs and then lifted her up. Slowly, awkwardly, they carried her toward the stairs. Chin grabbed Ted's bag and nodded toward the door.

"After you, Miss Baker."

An unexpected reluctance to leave the plane kept her in her seat. Even though the experience of flying had been frightening, especially right at the beginning, the truth was she had never felt more alive than when looking out the pilots' window and watching the landscape rush beneath her. Now that she was safely on the ground, the desire to relive it was nearly overwhelming.

Mr. Chin's scarred eyebrow arched in silent question at her delay. With a small sigh, aware that they both had places to go, she pushed the desire away and stood. Flying had been a wonderful, once-in-a-lifetime thrill, but she was a missionary's daughter, not a pilot.

By the time Genie exited the plane, Lavinia was already seated, slumped over in the wheelchair, with Brother Marcus holding the handles. Nathan stood beside Marcus, deep in conversation, leaving Ted to help her down the stairs.

"Here's what we're going to do," he said in a low voice as he escorted her over to Nathan. "I'm giving you my room for the night. If I have a roommate, I'll kick him out."

"No, don't—" she started.

"Hey, Sterling," he called over her head. "I think I've got a solution to your problem, at least temporarily. How 'bout we discuss it over dinner?"

Nathan hesitated. "I don't think eating would be a good idea yet. At least not for me."

Ted turned to her. "How 'bout you, Miss Baker? Are you hungry?"

Now it was her turn to hesitate, habit warring with desire. She should follow Nathan's lead and refuse, despite being ravenous. It was what Nathan expected of her. It was what her father would expect.

"I am," she said, shocking herself.

Ted's dark eyes warmed with approval, and the corners of his mouth curved into a smile, sparking a glow of satisfaction in her own chest.

"Be ready at seven," he said, giving her a wink. Then he strode over to the two missionary men. "Here's my idea . . ."

# Chapter 13

At twenty past seven, Genie skidded to a stop on the polished marble floors of the Grand Hotel lobby. Panting to catch her breath, she craned her neck and scanned the faces of all the men packed into the elegant but very busy room. Soldiers of all sorts and nationalities stood in groups talking, or dozed on the upholstered couches and chairs. Others read mail while leaning against one of the gilt-and-white columns. None were the right height or build or had the right shade of ink-black hair.

Her chest constricted. *Oh please, oh please, oh please, let Ted still be here.*

It was Nathan's fault she was late. One would think a man who was still in the throes of travel-induced nausea would have better things to do than lecture her on the pitfalls of female vanity and the inherent wickedness of men.

Relief made her knees weak as she saw Ted standing by the front doors, talking with a couple of fellows she didn't know. He was laughing at something someone had said, his posture relaxed and confident, a man sure of both himself and his place in the world. Something like envy stole through her veins, but it was soon lost beneath pure feminine admiration as she worked her way closer through the crowded lobby. The gold hue of the gaslights made his tanned skin glow like polished bronze, and his slicked-back hair was as black and glossy as a raven's wing. He glanced her way and then smiled, his teeth startlingly white in his handsome sharp-edged face.

Nathan's dire warnings rang in her ears. *Women are weak in the ways of the flesh . . . unfit for the male world . . .*

Her steps faltered. Was this fluttery feeling in her veins weakness? Or was it only excitement that for a moment, an hour or two, she might be in the company of someone other than Nathan? Someone she admired. Someone much more interesting who could tell her about the country to which she was traveling.

In any case, she doubted her virtue was in any danger tonight. Perhaps if she were more petite and feminine, like Li Ming, it might be; however, she had no illusions as to her own appearance. Too tall, too masculine, too red of hair, she was unlikely to spark desire in any man's breast, let alone someone as worldly as Ted.

Drawing a deep breath to bolster her courage, she started toward the front doors. Ted was a good person. He wouldn't ridicule her if she made any mistakes at the restaurant. And even if he turned out to be bad company, she still needed to eat. Nathan had volunteered to sit with Lavinia, who had yet to awaken from her narcotic dreams, while Brother Marcus scoured the city for another hotel room.

"Sorry I'm late." She flashed Ted a quick smile as she stopped in front of him.

"No apology necessary, now that you're here and I don't have to eat alone," he said with a wink, and her heart raced a little faster.

He introduced her to his companions, their names forgotten the second after she heard them, and then whisked her outside to a waiting cab.

"Where are we going?" she asked as Ted opened the back-seat door for her.

"I thought we'd celebrate your first meal in a foreign country by going to one of my favorite clubs in town—unless Sterling needs you back right away."

"He didn't set a time, actually," she said quickly, ignoring the stab of conscience. The imprecision of Nathan's parting command to be "quick about it" might be interpreted a number of different ways. If she chose to define *quick* as a couple of hours, surely that was her prerogative.

As she climbed into the cab, she could feel Ted's speculative gaze but chose to ignore it.

While she waited for Ted to finish giving directions to the cab-driver, she smoothed the blue fabric of her dress down over her knees, glad that Natasha had insisted on her taking it. Ted jumped in and closed the door. All of a sudden, she was very aware of how small the cab's interior was and how close Ted's thigh was to her own.

She smoothed her dress again.

"I hope I look all right," she said to break the silence after the cab pulled away from the hotel.

"Like a thousand bucks. Which is a compliment, by the way," he added at her questioning look. "When you first showed up, I was worried Carlton and Spitz were going to try to invite themselves along."

Not sure how to respond to that, she didn't, though she guessed Carlton and Spitz must have been the two soldiers at the door. She smoothed her skirt again.

He shifted toward the far door, opening up more space between them. "You know, I was kind of surprised Sterling didn't put the kibosh on your coming tonight."

"Kibosh?" She squeezed her hands together in her lap, hoping he had moved farther away out of concern for her comfort and not because she was somehow repellent.

"A stop." His lips curved in the semidarkness of the cab's interior. "You never read Dickens?"

"Who?" She hoped the shadows would hide her blush of embarrassment.

"Guess not." Then he continued, "I think you'll like the 300 Club. Before the war, it was a private club. Women had to be escorted by a member, and nonmembers were admitted only by invitation. Now pilots and military officers are also allowed as unofficial members—officers because they are helping defend the city, and pilots because the proprietor likes them, being one himself."

"Sounds grand."

"It is. More important, I like the food. And most nights they have dancing."

"I don't think I've ever danced," she said, thinking the club sounded fantastic. "I mean other than when I was a baby."

"We can definitely fix that tonight, if you're up for it."

She searched his face to see if he was serious. He was, and her breath caught. Excitement doubled her heartbeat. Afraid of seeming too eager, she tore her gaze away. Outside the open window, the city flew by.

"Calcutta is beautiful, if you can look past the beggars and the kids rotting with leprosy," he observed from behind her. "And the smell. I swear it's worse than Kunming."

Frowning at that last bit, she leaned toward the window and sniffed. Not surprisingly, the acrid stench of sewers and animal dung weighed heavy in the air, but it was a smell she associated with any big city—a natural outcome of too many people and animals living in too little space. The air was also thick with an oily mix of smoke and smog, tasting almost metallic on her tongue—the smell of progress.

Yet there was also an unfamiliar cloying undernote of spice and incense lingering in the night air. To her the combination didn't seem all that offensive, but perhaps American cities smelled different?

Before she could ask, the cab slowed and turned onto a private driveway. A pale stone edifice rose in front of her, capturing her imagination. Lush gardens, studded with exotic flowers like shy jewels, surrounded the porticoed entrance. The cab stopped, and Ted opened the door. The heady scent of night-blooming flowers rushed in, and somewhere the delicate splashings of a fountain echoed off the courtyard's limestone walls.

Like a princess from a fairy tale, she got out of the cab and entered unfamiliar territory. She stooped to pick up a faded blossom off the immaculately swept tiles while Ted paid the cab fare. She rolled the silky pink flower between her fingers, marveling at its existence.

Twenty-four hours before, her world had been one of frost and barren ground. Tonight, through the whim of fate, she was enveloped in gentle summerlike heat, with the heady fragrance of exotic flowers and rich, fertile soil. It was almost too unreal to believe.

Ted came up beside her and held out his arm. "Ready?"

She hesitated, suddenly unsure whether she should touch him, which made no sense at all. It wasn't like he was a stranger. She had spent three days on the trail with him—slept with her head on his shoulder, for heaven's sake—and had even knocked him to the ground. Yet tonight everything felt different, more . . . real.

"Never mind." His jaw tightened as he stepped back.

"No." Instinctively, she reached for his arm and slipped hers through, her decision made in a heartbeat. "Now I'm ready."

His slow smile erased all thoughts from her brain. In a daze she let him lead her to the entrance, where a turbaned dark-skinned man stopped them and then waved them through after Ted pointed to the gold wings on his shirt front.

"So what do you think?" he asked as they passed a polished mahogany sideboard with a sparkling crystal vase filled with scarlet flowers.

"I feel underdressed," she whispered. From down the hallway came the sound of laughter and male voices as well as the unfamiliar strains of Western-style music—the kind she'd only ever heard over the radio when she had lived in Hankow.

"You're not," he murmured over the growing buzz of conversation. "I'd tell you again how nice you look, but I wouldn't want it to go to your head, you being engaged to another and all."

He gave her a teasing wink, yet his words sparked a ripple of unease. She disliked lying in general, but most particularly to someone she admired and liked. Perhaps it was wrong of her, but tonight she wanted to forget about Nathan and his matrimonial plans. For one night, she wanted to forget about the war and the danger to her family and friends. To be, for a moment, a carefree girl out with a handsome man, one who made her feel attractive, desirable . . . lovable.

"No, you're right," she said, pushing those dangerous thoughts away. "We can't forget about Nathan."

Before he could respond, someone hailed them.

"Younan! Miss Baker!" A man's voice cut through the sea of conversation and music. "Over here!"

Genie turned and saw a slightly disheveled George Willits, the blond CNAC pilot, waving at them from the corner. She followed Ted through the blue haze of cigarette smoke, past white linen–draped tables that practically staggered under the weight of perspiring drinks and empty bottles of beer. Everywhere there were men. Men in uniforms or linen suits. Men drinking at the bar or smoking at tables. Men laughing, arguing, staring . . . at her.

She moved a little closer to Ted, suddenly aware of how few females were present. Here and there, she spotted women in uniform. Over by the bar she saw a handful of girls in brightly colored dresses. She also saw how closely the young men hovered over them.

"You made it," George said with a wide grin as she and Ted got closer. After winking conspiratorially at her, he gestured with his beer bottle to the man seated at the table with him. "Joe here was just talking about you, wondering if you were coming tonight."

"Well, I did." She smiled tentatively at Joe. "Hello, Mr. Chin."

The Chinese pilot stood politely, his scar hardly noticeable in the soft light of the chandeliers. "Good evening, Miss Baker. And please, call me Joe."

George kicked out a chair with his foot. "Have a seat, you two. And, Younan, now that you're here, settle an argument for us. What's the word on Burma? How much longer will we be able to use Lashio for refueling?"

"Off the record?" Ted said as he scooted the chair out farther for her and then waited for her to take a seat. Once she was settled, he and Joe sat down. "Maybe a month at the most. We're taking too many losses to hold the base much longer, especially with no new planes coming through. Why?"

George leaned forward. "Because without Lashio, we're going to have to start flying the Hump, and I don't have to tell you how much fun that's going to be. Damn the Brits, anyway, for pulling out."

"It's not like they have a choice," Ted retorted as he tried to flag down a waiter.

"Wait, are you saying Britain is pulling out of Burma?" Her stomach twisted. Even with her limited knowledge of world politics, she knew that the fall of Burma would leave yet another undefended border for China.

Ted rubbed her back reassuringly, releasing a flood of heat in her body. "It hasn't fallen yet, Genie. And your village is a long way from the Burmese border. Don't worry."

She bit her lip, simultaneously wanting to lean into and away from his touch.

He lifted her chin until she met his gaze. "Your father will be fine."

She wanted to trust the earnestness in his dark eyes. She truly did, but her fears wouldn't let her.

"Of course," George said, breaking the moment, "if the Chinese troops would stop looting their own supplies long enough to mount an offense, we might not be in this fix. I swear, half the stuff we deliver disappears onto the black market seconds after it's unloaded."

"That's not fair!" Genie exclaimed, turning to face him. "Our soldiers would never steal from their own army. Not when the survival of China is at stake."

George raised a blond eyebrow. "*Our* soldiers? You Chinese or American? I mean, I understand Chin's confusion, being a Chinaman born in Baltimore and all."

"Actually, I suffer no confusion whatsoever," Joe said calmly. "You're the one who can't decide."

George drained his beer bottle and set it on the table. "You know what? You're right. Can I get you something to drink at the bar, Miss Baker? The waitstaff is unbearably slow tonight, and I'm in need of another beer."

"That's very kind of you," she said, racking her brain for something that would make her sound sophisticated and mature, like the other women here tonight. "Do they have punch?"

George staggered to his feet. "If they don't, I'll tell the bartender to go get some. Younan? Chin?"

Ted slid her a considering look. "Gin and tonic for me, and change Genie's order to a club soda with a twist of lime."

"Did I order something wrong?" she asked Ted with a frown while Chin said another beer would be fine.

"No, but I happen to know the bartender here likes to spike the punch, and I'm guessing you still abstain from liquor?"

Her cheeks heated under his steady regard. "Would you think less of me if I said yes?"

"Not at all," he said. "In a place like this, I would say it's wise."

"Oh. Thank you for looking out for me, then."

He tilted his head in acknowledgment and then turned his gaze to the room. Genie fidgeted as an awkward silence fell over the table. She wished she could think of something clever to say, something that would interest these men, who had seen and done so much more than she had.

Joe cleared his throat. "The band is good tonight. Just right for dancing."

"Do you think so?" she asked, eager to keep the conversation going. "I was telling Ted earlier that I've never danced."

"That's right." Ted abruptly scooted his chair back, startling her. "And I promised you a dance lesson, Miss Baker."

"Shouldn't we wait for our drinks first?" she asked, still perplexed by his sudden shift in mood.

"It's not like they're gonna go anywhere without us." He cocked an eyebrow. "Or are you afraid to dance with me?"

He held out his hand to her.

"What about Joe?" She stared at his hand, her heart racing with excitement and nerves.

She wasn't completely ignorant of dance positions. To be done properly, a woman would have to allow a man to stand very close to her. To touch her. Not inappropriately, of course, but still . . .

"I'll be fine," Joe said with a slight smile. "You kids run along, and I'll watch your drinks."

"If you're sure . . . ," she said, but Ted was already tugging her out of her chair. Giving in to the inevitable, she followed him to the small dance floor, where several other couples already danced.

The infectious rhythm was so different from the music she had grown up with, the tunes a little discordant even. But none of that mattered once Ted turned her in his arms. His tan shirt with its gold wings over the pocket and the perfectly tied knot of his brown tie was all she could see. She frowned slightly as a pleasant, almost spicy fragrance teased her nose, reminding her of forests and crushed mint.

She glanced up, and her suspicions were confirmed by his smoothly shaved jaw. "You changed clothes."

His lips twitched. "So did you."

Yes, but he had likely bathed, something she hadn't had time for with the fuss over the still-unconscious Lavinia and Nathan's lecture.

"First off, you gotta relax," he teased as he set her left hand on his shoulder and took her right. "Dancing is supposed to be fun."

"I know." She inwardly winced at how shrewish she sounded. With an effort, she forced herself not to think about baths and the weight of unwanted responsibilities. Better to focus on Ted's shoulders, which were so wonderfully solid and strong under her palm, and on the flexing of his muscles under her fingertips. It was like holding on to sunwarmed granite. Her skin was nearly scorched by the heat radiating through the smooth tan fabric.

"So dancing is easy," he continued, oblivious to the turn her thoughts had taken. "All you have to do is follow my lead. Meaning, if I move this way"—he stepped to the right, taking her with him—"you follow. And if I move this way . . ."

He stepped to the left.

"I follow?" she guessed as he tugged on her hand, urging her to move with him.

"Just so." His smile deepened, revealing a faint dimple on one side.

Her breath caught, and she managed to completely miss her next cue to move. She hurried to mimic his movement, only to be left behind again when he switched directions.

Mentally kicking herself, she made herself focus on the dance. Finally, her feet caught on to what they were supposed to do, and she made it through the rest of the song without a mistake.

Pleased with herself, she grinned up at him. "This is easier than I thought."

"Told you." His dark eyes sparkled with humor and approval.

Suddenly self-conscious, she glanced at the couple next to them. The serviceman twirled his dance partner in and out of his arms. The girl laughed, her face flushed and happy.

"Are we going to dance like that?" she asked.

He chuckled. "Not tonight. You gotta walk before you can run."

To her delight, he didn't release her when the song ended. The next song was faster, requiring more concentration on her part. A silence fell between them that should have been awkward, but it wasn't. His movements remained smooth and controlled, his muscles relaxed under her fingers. She had the sense that he was enjoying himself, so she stopped worrying and sank into the moment.

Ted hummed softly to himself as he added a turn to her repertoire of dance steps, not even wincing when she stepped on his foot.

"Sorry!"

"I'm fine. Don't worry about it. You're learning." He went back to humming.

"You know this tune?"

"'Begin the Beguine.' Fred Astaire danced to it in *Broadway Melody of 1940*. Wonderful flick. You even look a little like Eleanor Powell, except for the color of your hair."

"Who?"

"That's right, you wouldn't know. I bet you didn't get too many movies in your town."

"No." She paused for a second to get back on beat and then continued. "Though when we lived in Hankow, my father took me to see several. Mostly Chinese ones directed by a friend of his, but once we went to see one starring Shirley Temple."

"No offense, but I'm having trouble picturing your father at the movies."

"Why? He quite enjoyed them, actually. Particularly if they demonstrated good morals. One of his favorites was—oh, how should I translate it—*Spring Dream in Peking*. I think that's close. Anyway, it was about a man who falls in love with an evil woman, who encourages him to seek success through trickery and corruption. Of course it all falls apart, leaving him with nothing but a memory, a 'spring dream.'"

"Not exactly light fare for a young child. How old were you at the time?"

"Ten, I think. It was the last movie I saw before we moved to the mountains."

"That had to be quite the adjustment. Did you miss the city?"

"No." Her answer was easy and immediate. "I had everything I loved with me, so there was nothing to miss."

He was quiet a moment, and she sensed he was turning something over in his mind. "You're an interesting girl, Miss Baker. Not what I expected."

"My father used to tell me I was one of a kind," she said with an embarrassed laugh. Then unexpected despair swamped her, and she couldn't breathe. "What if I never see him again?"

Her damp cheek was suddenly pressed against smooth fabric, Ted's arms tight around her.

"It's all right. You'll see him again. If not in this world, then in the next."

"I thought you didn't believe in heaven," she said around a sniff. His heartbeat was steady under her ear.

"Some things stick, even after you grow up."

She pushed back in his arms and searched his dark eyes, her heart full. "Because you want to see your mother again. Like I want to see mine."

"Yeah." He held her gaze for a long moment, and she felt as though she could fall into the mahogany depths, never to resurface. "We should probably go back to the table. Our drinks have arrived."

She leaped back, mortified by how she had been staring at him. *It's embarrassing how you throw yourself at him.* Nathan's words sank like a dagger into her chest.

"It looks like Joe ordered us some food, too." Ted gestured for her to lead the way. "Good man!"

She started for the table when she caught sight of George by the bar. He was chatting with a dark-haired woman in a green dress that left little to the imagination. Unexpectedly, his hand slid down the woman's back to rest familiarly on her buttocks.

Actually, he was doing more than resting his hand on the silk-clad cheek; he was actively massaging it, the emerald fabric bunching under his fingers.

Genie tripped.

"Hang on. You all right?" Ted asked, steadying her.

"Yes . . . I . . . does George know that woman?"

Ted turned to follow her gaze. After what sounded like a muffled expletive, he immediately redirected her movements, cutting off her view. "Forget you saw that."

"But he was . . ." A curious tension curled deep in her body as she sought the words to describe the scene, her mind's eye caught by the sensual ripple of silk as it caught between his fingers, the displacement of the woman's soft flesh beneath the fabric. Heat climbed up her neck, leaving her flushed, shaky.

"Doing nothing you needed to see. I guess they've lowered their standards since the last time I was through."

"What do you mean?"

"Never mind. They'll be leaving soon enough."

Joe stood politely as she reached the table. "You kids have fun?"

"When did they start letting birds in?" Ted asked angrily before she could say a word.

Joe looked around the club. His eyebrows rose when his gaze reached the bar area. "Well, well . . . so that's why George sent a waiter back with the drinks."

"Warn me if he starts to bring her in this direction," Ted growled as he pulled out her chair. She sat, still at a loss as to what was going on.

"No worries about that," Joe said, resuming his own seat. "They're heading toward the door."

"What . . . ," she began, and then the pieces began to fit: Ted's discomfort, George's hand so low, the tight dress, "birds" . . . *birds of paradise*, her father had once called them. "That woman was selling herself? She was a prostitute?"

She knew about prostitution, of course. The world's oldest profession was mentioned several times in the Bible, and missionaries everywhere worked to stop the trade. She just hadn't seen a fallen woman in the flesh before. Nor ever thought she'd know, no matter how tenuously, a customer of one.

Ted sat beside her, his dark eyes apologetic. "I'm sorry, Miss Baker. They tend to show up anywhere there are soldiers, tonight being no different. It used to be they had to work their trade outside the club, but I guess times have changed."

Joe only shrugged and stubbed out his cigarette in the metal ashtray.

Her gaze flicked to the bar again. Joe was right. George was gone. Both he and the girl, actually. Her stomach clenched, but not with disgust as she had expected. Her emotions weren't nearly that uncomplicated. To her shame, beneath her discomfort also lurked a certain fascination.

Picking up her fork, she couldn't stop herself from wondering what would happen next. Where would the two conduct their business? In a room with a bed? An alley? Would they both disrobe? Or only the girl?

Would she, the girl, like it?

At that thought, she forgot to swallow and breathe separately, and choked. She hurriedly reached for her club soda as Ted smacked her on the back.

"Are you all right?" he asked.

She managed a smile over her glass. "Fine."

The rest of the meal passed in relative quiet. Ted concentrated on eating like a man who hadn't seen food in days. Joe smoked more than he ate, seemingly lost in his own thoughts. Her own appetite subdued by worry and nerves, she picked at the unfamiliar and spicy food on her plate. Her attention kept drifting toward the dance floor and the laughing couples.

If only Ted would ask her to dance again . . . or, of course, she could suggest it herself . . .

But she didn't.

At last, Ted settled up the bill, and the evening was over.

Chin stood and bowed politely as they started to take their leave. "It was a pleasure dining with you, Miss Baker. Perhaps we'll meet again."

"Perhaps when I return to China," she said, smiling at him.

He returned her smile, but it was touched with a sadness she didn't want to see.

She *would* return to China, and soon. The war couldn't go on forever.

Ted hailed another cab, and soon they were on their way back to the hotel. Part of her rebelled, not wanting to let go of the evening quite yet. She had loved dancing with him, enjoyed listening to him discuss politics, and she held his admission that he wanted to see his mother again close to her heart. There was so much she wanted to thank him for, so much she wanted to say into the warm velvety darkness of the cab.

"Was that woman really selling herself?" The words were out before she realized what she was asking, and then she wanted to sink through the seat. That was *not* what she had intended to say.

Ted sighed. "Genie, you need to forget you saw any of that. Sterling will skin me alive if he finds out."

"Was she?" She might as well find out, now that she had asked.

"Yes. And before you ask, no, I have never been with one, so any other questions you have on the subject will have to wait for someone else."

"Oh." His admission eased the knot in her stomach. "Why not?"

"Because I can't get past that they're somebody's sister or daughter. Maybe even mother."

Ted opened his door and swung his legs out of the car. With a start she realized they were already at the hotel, and the evening was well and truly over. She slid out his side while Ted paid the driver. Then the cab was gone, leaving her and Ted alone on the sidewalk in front of the hotel.

"Well, here you are, Miss Baker," he said, his easy smile back in place. "Back at your hotel, safe and sound."

A curious panic gripped her as she realized this might be the last time she saw him.

"I enjoyed the evening tremendously. I'd like to go on being friends. Can I write to you?"

He was already shaking his head before she had even finished her question. "I'm not sure that would be a good idea, Genie."

"Why not?" She searched his face in the dim streetlight. "Friends write to friends all the time. And we're friends, aren't we?"

"And what would your fiancé say about you writing other men?"

"He's not my fiancé," she protested, but she could tell from his expression he didn't believe her.

He took a step back. "Genie, look—you're a swell kid, and I enjoyed getting to know you."

"But you're not interested . . ." Her voice trailed off, her emotions too raw to voice. Abruptly, she turned her gaze to the darkened buildings down the block, afraid she might cry if she looked at him.

"I didn't say that," he said a touch sharply.

"Then why can't I write you? Am I so repellent?" she cried, and then pressed a fist to her lips to seal in her despair. She would *not* embarrass herself any further.

"Oh hell." He pulled her into his arms and held her tightly. She reveled in the feel of his body against her cheek, the strength of his arms, and the beat of his heart, steady and strong beneath her ear.

"Genie, sweetheart, it's been a hard couple of weeks for you. But once you get to the States and you're safe with your aunt, you'll forget how you feel right now. I'll be just some pilot you knew, some guy who taught you to dance."

"That's not true."

He tipped her chin up. "It *is* true. You have your whole life ahead of you, with much better men waiting to make your acquaintance. If not Sterling, then someone else. Someone you'll have more in common with—"

"How can you say that?" Angry tears blurred her vision as she pushed back out of his arms. "We've both lost our mothers; we've both been forced to leave the lands of our birth. We have lots in common. Or am I just too ug—"

"Genie, stop." He caught her, his fingers flexing into her shoulders as she tried to turn away. She resisted as he pulled her toward him, her mortification beyond what anybody should handle as he forced her to look at him. And then his lips were on hers. Her breath caught. She hadn't expected that. A queer numbness, almost like a hum, not at all unpleasant, spread through her blood. The warmth of it sang all the way down to her toes, and she clutched his shirt to keep herself from tilting along with her world.

Her first kiss . . .

Too soon his mouth left hers, taking a part of her heart with it. She struggled to breathe normally as he brushed a strand of her hair out of her face. She shivered under his touch.

"Take care of yourself, Eugenia Baker." His voice was soft, tender. "And stay out of trouble. I don't want to read about you in the papers."

"You too." *Stay alive,* she wanted to add. *Please.*

Stepping back, he gave her a brief salute with his first two fingers and smiled. "Roger that."

Then he turned and walked off down the darkened street. After a heartbeat or two, he began to whistle, and her heart followed the sound. When he was gone, she turned and entered the hotel.

"It's about time you came back."

She jumped and whirled to face Nathan. "What are you doing here?"

"Not making a spectacle of myself, for one." There was no mistaking the frost in his eyes. "I can only be thankful Brother Marcus didn't see you."

She turned toward the lobby, hoping to hide the flush stealing up her neck. "I would hardly call a kiss goodbye a spectacle."

"I disagree. And it shows a weakness of character that, frankly, I find concerning."

She drew a deep breath to rein in her temper. "It was a kiss, Nathan."

"With someone who is neither family nor fiancé."

She threw up her hands in exasperation. "And have you never kissed someone who wasn't family?"

"No. I haven't." An answer that didn't surprise her in the least. He gestured across the lobby. "I'll accompany you to your room."

"That's hardly necessary."

"Perhaps not, but I insist. And I've decided you're right," he said as they began to walk. "We are not well suited to each other. I'll not trouble you with talk of marriage again."

# Chapter 14

"Eugenia." Someone shook her shoulder, interrupting her dance with Ted. She pushed the disruption away. Whatever they wanted could wait until later. Right now she was exactly where she wanted to be . . . in the gardens outside the club . . . with hidden birds chirping in the foliage. She slipped back into Ted's arms, and he smiled lazily at her.

Her skin tingled with anticipation as his dark eyes glinted with wicked intention. He was going to kiss her.

"Genie!"

The voice was louder, more insistent. She frowned with annoyance as she recognized the intruder. What did Nathan want with her now? Couldn't he see she was having one of the best dreams of—

Her eyes snapped open. Sunlight flooded her brain, and she winced. Slowly the details of an unfamiliar room swam into view. No, not unfamiliar. She was in a hotel room, in Calcutta, sharing the room with . . . She jerked upright, all remnants of sleep sliding away.

Her gaze swept the room. Nathan was standing beside her bed, dressed for the day. Brother Marcus stood just inside the door, and . . . *Oh Lord.*

She snatched the sheet up to her neck, even as the bearded missionary flushed and tried to look anywhere but at her.

"Genie, where is Lavinia?" Nathan's tone, as frigid as a snow-fed mountain stream, yanked her attention back to him.

Her heart thudded painfully as another peek around the room told her what she had already guessed. Lavinia was gone.

"I'm sorry, I don't know. She was here last night."

"I'm fully aware of that. I was the one, after all, who walked you back to your room after dinner. Remember?" His thinly veiled sarcasm did nothing to lessen her panic.

How could she have missed the girl leaving? She blinked away the sudden burn of tears. Yes, she had been tired, but Brother Marcus had entrusted her with the safety of his sister. She had failed him. Honor demanded that she try to remedy the situation.

She leaned forward, reaching for her blouse lying folded at the end of the bed. "I'll go look for her. If you'll give me a moment to dress—"

"There's no need, Miss Baker." Marcus focused his gaze on the opposite wall. "She won't get far without money or passport. But thank you."

"Perhaps she was hungry and went to the hotel's restaurant," she said, not quite seeing what passports had to do with anything. Her brain sorted through all the possibilities. "Or maybe she's in the communal shower area. We should check the lobby, too."

Nathan and Marcus shared a look. That's when she realized they were keeping something from her. Something important.

"We can check those areas if it will make you feel better," Marcus said, his gaze returning to the wall. "However, knowing she cannot succeed without the right documents, really there is nothing to do but wait until she realizes it as well."

"She's trying to find a way back." The statement felt right the moment she said it. Then another worse thought occurred to her, and her stomach twisted. "You didn't sedate her yesterday merely because she was afraid of flying. There was something else."

Marcus held out his hands in a silent plea for understanding. "We had to leave, and she was being unreasonable. To stay was no longer safe for any of us. So many of our friends had already lost their lives to the war. I couldn't allow her to die, too."

Of course not. Genie's father had said much the same thing when he had ordered her out of China. The difference was she had listened and ultimately obeyed the edict, no matter how much it had hurt. Lavinia had apparently been of a different mind and had fought back. And the result? Both of them were now in India against their will, caught between the immutable forces of men and war.

Or maybe not. Lavinia was at least still fighting for what she wanted. Disconcerted by the thought, she dropped her gaze to the bedspread.

"The consulate will be open until three," Nathan observed to Brother Marcus. "Between the two of us, we can check the airport and harbor. Eugenia can wait here in case she comes back."

"No," Marcus said sharply. "The risk is too great. I won't be responsible for either of you being arrested."

Arrested? Startled, Genie looked up.

Nathan waved his hand dismissively. "I care less about that than what we discussed last night."

"And that will be only as the Lord ordains." Marcus turned to leave, and then paused. "However, if she's still missing when you get back from the consulate, then you can help me look."

"What's this about being arrested?" she asked after Marcus had left.

Nathan shot her an irritated look, and it occurred to her that he, unlike Brother Marcus, seemed to have no problem seeing her half-undressed. In fact, her near nakedness seemed to have no effect on him whatsoever.

"Turns out we're in India illegally because we don't have visas, a fact that should have prevented us from buying airline tickets in the first place."

"No one asked us for them yesterday."

"Probably because we deplaned with the flight crew, and the customs agent missed us. Brother Marcus alerted me to the matter last night when we were discussing train tickets. I meant to tell you, but the little performance you and Lieutenant Younan put on at the door distracted me."

She ignored his dig, a glimmer of hope lifting her spirits. "You mean if the police catch us without the right paperwork, they might send us back to China? I have to say, I wouldn't mind such an outcome."

"Genie, be reasonable. Suppose we're returned to Kunming, what then? Do you think your father will welcome you back with open arms? The country is in imminent danger of being overrun by the Japanese. Or did you forget there is a war going on?"

"How could I forget?" she snapped back even as her chest constricted sharply with the reminder. Indeed, she would count herself lucky if she could forget, even for a blessed second, that grave danger stalked not only her father and Zhenzhu and her village, but also the two CNAC pilots she had met yesterday who were likely already on their way back to Lashio. And Ted was probably on his way to Cairo to pick up another warplane.

"Well, you managed to forget your responsibility for Mrs. Schmidt," Nathan said as he headed for the door. "Hurry and get dressed. I'll be waiting in the lobby."

Silent recriminations filled the room as the door banged shut behind him. She glanced dejectedly at the dented pillow beside her. How had she missed the widow leaving? Granted, Genie had been exhausted from the long day of travel, but she wasn't usually a heavy sleeper.

Guilt and self-blame swamped her. To keep from being pulled under, she focused on an image of the widow safely returned, whole and hearty. Holding on to that fragile thread of hope, she got out of bed and quickly dressed. As she coiled her long braid on the back of her head, she expanded her prayers to include the safety of every person she knew. Then, mouth full of hairpins, she silently added another prayer, while pinning her hair into place, that she would see them all again. A final prayer that such a gift would be granted sooner rather than later was added as she checked her appearance in the mirror. Satisfied that Nathan could find nothing to object to, and with her Holy Trinity of concerns addressed, she took a deep steadying breath and left the room.

The early-morning humidity already had her perspiring by the time she reached the lobby. Nathan stood near the front desk. The lobby wasn't nearly as crowded as it had been the night before; still, almost every chair was taken, some by sleeping soldiers, their legs stretched out, their uniforms rumpled as if they'd been there all night. Guilt nicked her.

Yes, she was a woman, and it would have been unseemly for her to sleep in the lobby. And yes, Lavinia had been in a vulnerable state, so it made sense that Ted had wanted them to have his room. Yet these men sleeping out here, these men who were risking their lives to push back the demon called war that threatened them all, surely they were more deserving of a soft bed than she was.

"Good, you're here." Nathan gave her outfit an approving glance before setting off for the front doors.

That he didn't even bother to see if she followed him sparked a slow burn of resentment. An instant comparison to Ted's courteous behavior the night before was no less damning. Thank goodness Nathan had decided he no longer wanted to marry her.

Dazzling sunlight blinded her the second she stepped outside. The acrid stench of garbage, exhaust, and unwashed bodies stung her nose, and she fought the urge to hold her breath. While the chaos and smell of the city had been present the night before, that seemed a pale shadow compared to what assaulted her now.

Nathan took her elbow and pulled her, still half-blind, onto the sidewalk. She struggled to keep her feet as he guided her through the throng of humanity. No longer separated from the populace by the windows of a taxi, she was struck by the diversity. Here were native men in their loose-fitting white garments; there, thin dark-eyed women were draped in long jewel-like sashes. Western-garbed businessmen—British and Indian—hurried to their appointments. And seemingly everywhere were military personnel in their various uniforms and caps.

What she didn't see was anyone who might be Lavinia. The few Caucasian women who were out and about wore knee-length dresses or skirts, with small hats perched on their heads and purses that matched their short-heeled shoes. It astonished her that Nathan and Marcus weren't more concerned over the frail girl's disappearance. To be out here alone, with no passport and no visa to save her from prison, was a terrifying prospect. If Li Ming had been the one to go missing, Genie would have been scouring the crowded sidewalks, searching everywhere, frantic with worry.

"How far to the consulate?" she asked, an idea taking form. She practically had to shout the question to be heard over the growl of grinding truck gears as they slowed to avoid both animals and people spilling off the curbs.

"The man at the desk said it was about a mile." Nathan wiped the perspiration from his face with a handkerchief.

"Shouldn't we report Lavinia's disappearance to them? She's an American citizen, after all. At least I think Brother Marcus said they were both from the States."

He pulled her to a stop to let a streetcar pass. She gazed at the humming cable overhead and was thrown back in time. For a moment, memories of what felt like an impossibly long-ago childhood in Peking drove thoughts of visas and missing widows from her head. Then the train disappeared down the block, and her worries returned with a vengeance.

"Sister Lavinia's disappearance is none of our business," Nathan said as he took her by the elbow and guided her forward. "Should Brother Marcus feel the need to file a report, he knows where to go. He was with me when I asked directions."

She bit the inside of her cheek to keep from arguing, knowing it would be pointless. With growing anxiety she searched both sides of the street for a glimpse of a slight woman in a long skirt. It was harder than she would have guessed. Everything about Calcutta seemed to have been designed to overwhelm the senses. Beggars with open sores sat along the walls, while well-dressed businessmen hurried blindly by. Modern trucks and cars fought for space on the streets, zooming around horse-drawn carts and rickshaws. Dogs fought in the gutters for garbage, often with bone-thin children in rags. Above them, the skyline was a jarring mix of Greek and Roman temple facades and fanciful, multi-tiered buildings with open balconies plastered with colorful advertisements. The lettering was all swirls and curlicues, the meanings rendered slightly ominous by her inability to decipher them.

*Oh, Lavinia, where are you?* Did the widow feel as lost and disoriented by all the chaos as Genie did?

"You would think Calcutta would be more civilized after two hundred years of British influence," Nathan said as he steered her past a native wearing nothing but a loincloth and white paint. The man smiled at her, exposing toothless gums.

"Maybe it doesn't wish to be civilized." She eyed a policeman nonchalantly diverting traffic around a large cow lying in the middle of the street.

"Let's hope the rest of India isn't as bad." Nathan tightened his grip on her elbow in preparation to cross the street. They dashed between cars, earning several honks and shouted curses, and then up the steps of an unpretentious-looking building. The only thing that suggested this might be their destination was the Stars and Stripes flying out front.

Inside, the air was relatively cooler, a fact for which she was exceedingly grateful as perspiration snaked between her breasts. A single electric fan in the corner of the uncarpeted, sparsely furnished reception area labored to create a breeze. Plucking her damp blouse off her skin, she drifted over to a large bulletin board covered with official-looking notices.

At first glance, they seemed innocuous enough, typed simply on official letterhead. It wasn't until she read them that a curious light-headedness stole over her. There, between the notices of immigration requirements and ways to stay safe, was the US declaration of war on Japan dated December 8, 1941, and a second declaration, this time against Germany and Italy, dated December 11. Her sense of unreality deepened as she read the words, "To bring the conflict to a successful termination, all the resources of the country are hereby pledged."

All the resources. She knew from the war in China that meant not just money or equipment or raw materials, but also the people, men in particular. Young men like the ones she'd met in Kunming. Like Ted. She closed her eyes and forced herself to breathe.

Nathan rang a bell for service, and Genie turned just as a clerk appeared from the back. Perhaps not surprisingly, the fellow was in shirt sleeves, his coat lost to the heat and humidity, and his dark tie was loosened slightly. Friendly blue eyes peered at them from behind wire-rimmed glasses, his thinning brown hair slicked back off his forehead.

"Well, hello. Americans looking to leave the country and in need of assistance?"

"How did you know?" Genie asked in surprise, and then her pulse leaped. "Did someone come in earlier with the same problem? A young woman, perhaps?"

"Eugenia, please." Nathan shot her a quelling look before turning to the clerk. "You're correct on both accounts. Any chance you can help us?"

The clerk gave Genie an odd look as he bent to open one of the file drawers. "You're the first people to come in today, but inquiries have been steady. Almost everyone is in a hurry to leave the country after the new travel advisory."

"I heard there's a US troop ship headed to New York later this week," Nathan said. "One that is taking civilians aboard."

Genie tried not to stare at him. This was all news to her.

"Ah. I'm afraid that sold out within weeks of being announced." The clerk pulled out a small stack of papers. "But I do have brochures for several ships headed to Great Britain in the next couple of months."

Nathan shook his head. "I'm afraid I told Miss Baker's father I would return her to her family in the US, so Britain is not an option. Is there any way to see if a ticket becomes available, perhaps due to illness or changed circumstances?"

"You could take your chances and show up on the day of departure. But all your documents would have to be in order."

"Which brings me to our second problem: Miss Baker here is in dire need of a passport and any necessary visas to make her stay here in India legal."

As Nathan explained the situation, the clerk stopped smiling. Several times he interrupted to have Genie verify the information. Then he told them to wait and disappeared into the back offices. Fifteen long minutes ticked by, during which she was sure the Indian police were going to burst through the door any second and cart her away.

Then the clerk reappeared. He led them down a narrow hallway lined with file cabinets and then showed them into an office. An older man in his midforties stood as they entered. Silver streaked his temples, and his face was deeply lined by the sun and responsibility.

Two electric fans buzzed softly as they cooled the room, a clear sign of rank.

"Welcome. I'm Robert Buell, US Consul for Calcutta." Mr. Buell gave them a brief smile and gestured toward two leather-upholstered chairs across the desk from him. His manner, while gracious, also held an edge of impatience, as if his mind were on something else. "How can I help you?"

While Nathan explained their situation for a second time, Genie eyed the large framed maps of India and the world hanging between the windows. Like her father, she adored maps. China was easy to pick out. Less easy was her province. She squinted, trying to read the tiny print on the world map, curious whether the country next to Burma said "Siam" or "Thailand." Did Sister Lavinia really believe she could travel across two countries on her own?

"Are you and Miss Baker planning to get married before leaving the country?" the consul asked. Genie's attention immediately recentered on the men's conversation.

"Oh, we're not engaged," Nathan answered smoothly as the consul made some notes on a piece of paper in front of him. "Merely traveling together."

She blinked. Was Nathan aware of how scandalous his response made their relationship sound?

The consul's eyebrows rose slightly as he glanced up at her. "Miss Baker?"

"Mr. Sterling is escorting me—at my father's request—to my aunt's house in California," she clarified, and then asked, in case she'd missed it, "Is it true there's a ship leaving for New York soon?"

"There is." The consul sat back and considered her for a moment. "And as you can imagine, with the Japanese approaching, every available berth sold out in a matter of weeks. However—and I'm not sure I should even mention it—I was talking to an American businessman earlier this week who wasn't going to be able to use his ticket. And to be clear, he only had the one."

"Which means one of us would have to stay behind, assuming the gentleman hasn't already given it away." She glanced uncertainly at Nathan, the prospect of perhaps having a chance to return home to China skittering along her nerves.

"One is not a problem," Nathan said without hesitation. He held up a finger to shush her. "Miss Baker will take it, assuming it's still available. Meanwhile, what about our travel papers?"

"Since the gentleman was counting on me to resell it, the ticket is available. I'll have my assistant handle the transaction. The travel visas you can probably get today, depending on the workload of our British counterparts. Issuing a new passport, of course, takes more time." Mr. Buell paused and drummed his fingers on his desk as he considered. "However, under the circumstances, and with no name changes, it might be possible to procure before the ship sails. Though everything is taking longer with the war."

Nathan nodded. "Understood."

The consul's gaze fell on her again, and she fought the urge to squirm.

"Understand that I'm not officially recommending this," the consul said at last. "But go to the Calcutta police and tell them your wallet was stolen, along with all your papers. I'll have Jack prepare an official letter vouching for your identities and intentions. They'll likely balk, but if you're insistent enough, they'll reissue you the visas you need. If they prove wholly recalcitrant, have them call my assistant."

She stiffened, aghast at the suggestion. "But that would be a lie."

Nathan's fingers dug into her arm, silencing her. "And where will we pick up Miss Baker's passport?"

"I'll arrange to have it at our consular office in Bombay, so you can pick it up on the way to the dock. I'll certainly try to expedite things on my end. However, if plans go awry, my counterpart in Bombay may have an idea of what to do." The consul stood. "Be sure to see my assistant on your way out so he can get all the necessary information as well as your ticket."

Nathan rose as well and shook hands with the man. "We will, and thank you."

The consul's gaze rested on her again. "By the way, in case you didn't hear in China, India has become a bit unsettled. There's been a push in recent months for Indian independence, which has resulted in a few civic disturbances around the country. At the moment, the situation is peaceful enough, but tension is growing. So be careful. Should you be caught up in a demonstration, the locals might not necessarily know or care that you're not British."

"Are you saying we're in danger?" Anxiety threaded through her. "Because we have a friend who's—"

"Thanks for the warning." Nathan seized her elbow again, his fingers biting in hard enough to make her eyes tear up. "But we've traveled extensively through rural China for almost a decade, so being regarded as 'foreign devils' is hardly new. We'll be fine."

The consul smiled slightly. "Then I wish you safe travel to Bombay."

On the way back to the clerk's desk, Genie's thoughts whirled. She had never considered the possibility that they were all just trading one dangerous situation for another. Poor Sister Lavinia! Nor could she see how one ticket was going to help, unless Nathan intended to send her on alone. Only, he wouldn't. Would he? He'd made a promise to her father.

"Nathan—" she began on the way out of the consulate, after all the documents had been filled out and photographs taken.

"Whatever your questions, they will have to wait. I'm not discussing anything until I've talked to Brother Marcus." He all but bolted down the steps, the hastily sketched map to the police station in his hands.

She was forced to hurry after him. The consul's precious letter confirming her identity—the only thing standing between her and a Calcutta prison—was in Nathan's coat pocket. "What does Brother Marcus have to do with—"

Nathan grabbed her arm and hauled her around to face him. "Eugenia, your father put me in charge of this trip. Not you. So when

I say we'll discuss this later, that's exactly what's going to happen. Understand? And not another word about Sister Lavinia."

Her arm ached from the layer of bruises forming under his grip. Tears of frustration burned in her throat at the sheer depth of her powerlessness. A hundred passersby eyed her, yet she knew none would help should she try to protest. It wasn't fair.

It wasn't *right*.

"Do you understand?" Nathan repeated.

"Yes," she managed finally. Then her anger boiled over and she yanked her arm free. "But I don't agree."

# Chapter 15

By the time Nathan and Genie returned to the hotel, it was nearly five in the evening. She trailed him into the relative cool of the lobby, exhausted, hungry, and thoroughly disgusted not only with Nathan but with herself. Despite her abhorrence of lies, her precarious situation had forced her to remain silent while Nathan lied to the police and then to the British consulate. Nor had she been able to withstand Nathan's wintry demeanor following her outburst. Her need for his assistance ended up trumping her determination to ask if another American girl had been by, and she felt awful about it. Not one of her finer days.

Still, the truth was, as much as she longed to be free of Nathan and his petty tyranny, traveling halfway around the world by herself would require more worldly experience than she currently possessed. And being trapped in India with a revolution brewing within while an enemy threatened from without? The possibility made her blood run cold.

Pausing to let her eyes adjust to the interior dimness, she listened to the lobby buzzing with activity as usual. Nathan waved at someone, and then she spotted Brother Marcus sitting not far away. A slender dark-haired girl was perched on the couch beside him. Genie's spirits lifted immediately.

"Brother Marcus, Lavinia," Nathan said, heading toward them. "You're back."

"Brother Nathan. Miss Baker. I hope your day was successful?" The young red-haired missionary stood, a wide smile untangling itself from his beard.

"It was." Nathan clasped the man's hand. "And it appears yours was as well."

"Indeed. Lavinia . . ." Marcus turned to the silent girl next to him, and his smile faded a bit. "These are our new friends I was telling you about."

Sister Lavinia glanced up, and Genie's breath caught at the savage anger blazing in her intensely blue eyes. Then the girl blinked, and the emotion disappeared as if it had never existed. "Forgive me if I fail to say I'm pleased to meet you, because I'm not."

"Lavinia," Marcus said sharply.

"Oh." Her eyelids fluttered briefly. "Am I to lie now? Pretend that they weren't among any number of passengers who could have stopped my abduction? Stopped you from dragging me away from the body of the person I loved best, leaving it unburied for the dogs to devour?"

Genie inhaled sharply. Desecration of a corpse was bad enough in any culture, but Zhenzhu would say there was no worse fate than to lie forgotten and unhonored after death. It was why Wu Fang had cut across the Nationalist line to retrieve his beloved wife's burial marker, losing his arm in the process.

"Desist, Lavinia." Marcus's voice was low, hard. "You know there was no time. Nor were you the only one who suffered."

"Yet I was the only one dragged onto the plane," Lavinia shot back.

Brother Marcus's face flushed dangerously. "Have you forgotten John's letter?"

Lavinia paled and dropped her gaze to the carpet. Seeming to shrink in on herself, she went utterly still.

The transformation was unsettling. Such forced obedience also touched some hidden nerve inside Genie.

Nathan cleared his throat. "We were able to secure one more ticket for the ship to New York."

"So we are up to three." Marcus exhaled and massaged the back of his neck. "'Tis not ideal, but perhaps we will think of something over dinner. At the least, we need to discuss our travel plans to Bombay."

"Of course. Let me check for messages, and then we can depart." Nathan placed his hand on the small of Genie's back, making her start. "Will you watch Eugenia for me? I've dragged her all over town today, and she's likely tired."

She stared at him. Now he was worried about her? Not when she had told him all afternoon she would like to sit or at least get a bite to eat? He gave her a small smile and left for the front desk. Calling on her last reserves, she schooled her face into a polite, vacant expression. Maybe it was her mood, but the opulence surrounding her, the richly polished wood, the marble- and gold-accented pillars, seemed a slap in the face to the poverty she had seen in the streets today.

With her irritation only increasing, she let her mind return to the problem of the three tickets. The inescapable fact was either she or Nathan was going to end up left behind, stranded in India without friend, or family, or money. It likely wouldn't be her, since Nathan had promised her father she would get to the States. And likely not Lavinia, if Marcus's behavior in Lashio was any indication.

So that left Nathan behind and gave Genie a new escort, which might not be all bad as long as she willingly got on the boat. *But what if Lavinia refuses, and Marcus resorts to sedation again? Will you once again idly stand by and let him?* Genie's conscience squirmed uncomfortably. Though in her defense, she hadn't known the particulars of Lavinia's reluctance.

Nathan touched her elbow. "Eugenia, we're leaving now."

Genie hesitated, the thought of Lavinia being physically forced to do something against her will not sitting right with her. Hadn't her father raised her to be a champion for the downtrodden?

"Wait," she said, coming to a decision. Her heart thumped unsteadily as three pairs of eyes turned to her, but she stayed the course. "Lavinia and I need to return to our room first."

Lavinia's eyebrows lifted fractionally.

Nathan openly stared. "Why?"

"Ah . . . feminine reasons." She had trouble holding his gaze. "And I don't want to go alone. There are too many men in the hotel. I—I don't like the way they look at me."

"Fine. I'll escort—"

"No! I mean . . ." She paused as she racked her brain for a rational objection. "Lavinia might have something I, ah . . . need."

Her cheeks heated with the lie, her second one in as many minutes. She held her breath, sure he would see through the fabrication.

Instead, it was he who looked away. "All right. But be quick about it."

She turned to Lavinia, but the girl was already on her feet. Together they silently crossed the lobby, Genie debating the best way to start what was likely to be a delicate conversation. Once they were out of sight of the men, she slowed her steps. She glanced down the hallway and saw they were alone. Good.

"Mrs. Schmidt," she began in a hushed voice.

The young widow gave a slight shudder. "Call me Lavinia, please."

Genie hesitated, a little surprised. "All right. I gather from your disappearance this morning that you don't want to go to the United States."

"You have gathered correctly, though you can see how well my wishes have been honored thus far." Anger and something else—pain?—flashed in the girl's blue eyes.

"I'm sorry for what happened in Lashio," Genie said quietly, guilt pricking her. "I thought you were afraid of flying."

"And now?" Lavinia snapped. "Now that you know the truth, do you hold my brother blameless?"

"No. And again, I'm sorry." Genie held the girl's cold stare, trying to convey her emotions silently. *We are the same. We are women, trapped between the walls of men and war.*

Lavinia looked away, her eyes suspiciously bright.

"You heard we've only three tickets," Genie said, pressing ahead. "That means one of us gets left behind. If you want it to be you, I'll do what I can to make sure that happens. That no one forces you to leave against your will again."

Lavinia glanced toward the lobby. "Perhaps we should continue to the room."

Once they were safely inside, Lavinia plopped down onto the mattress. She turned an assessing gaze on Genie. "I'm assuming you really don't need any supplies?"

"No. I wanted a chance to talk privately. Nathan would kill me if he thought I was condoning feminine rebellion."

"As would Marcus." Lavinia studied her for another second. "We can talk, but first—why are you trying to help me?"

The question confused her. "Why wouldn't I? It's clear you are unhappy; should I not try to help?"

"So it's not because you're trying to be rid of me because of my curse?" Lavinia asked flatly.

"Curse?"

"I thought perhaps my brother had mentioned it. Perhaps told your fiancé."

"Oh, Nathan isn't my fiancé."

"Husband, then?"

Genie gave a strangled laugh. "Heaven forbid. I would no more marry Nathan than I would your brother."

Lavinia tilted her head and studied Genie. "My brother isn't a bad person. Some even say he's passably handsome."

"He drugged you to get you out of Burma!"

Lavinia shrugged slightly. "You didn't seem to care before; what's it to you now?"

"Look, do you want to stay in India or not?" Genie asked, a little exasperated with the widow's seeming inability to stay on topic even though they were pressed for time.

Lavinia's gaze slid out the window. "No. Have you seen the women on the street? Starving and forgotten, holding children half-rotted with leprosy . . ."

"Perhaps if you returned to Burma?"

"With what money?" Lavinia said bitterly. "I checked the ticket prices at the harbor and at the rail station. Or at least I tried, since many of the ticket sellers wouldn't even talk to me because I'm a woman. And to whom would I return? To the rest of our group, who think the Good Lord abandoned them because of me?"

Genie hesitated. The curse again. Her father would tell her such notions were foolish, and yet Zhenzhu wholly believed in them, often tucking protective talismans in nooks around the house to ward them off, but never where Genie's father would find them.

*Stay away from the girl,* she could almost hear Zhenzhu whisper in her ear. *Lest you become infected by misfortune as well . . .*

Li Ming would likely agree, having been raised on the same fairy tales as Genie, tales rife with demons and enchantments.

But her father would tell her that charity trumped all, and she was, if nothing else, her father's daughter.

"Curse or no," she said, suppressing a twinge of unease, "if you're saying you want to travel to the States, I will support you. If you don't, I will do my best to see that you stay. But I should think you'd want to go, since your brother said he was taking you home to your parents. Isn't that worth leaving the war behind for a bit?"

"Not if your father swore he'd kill you the next time he saw you."

Genie blinked, sure she hadn't heard that right. "Pardon?"

Lavinia's gaze fell to her hands, and she drew a deep breath. "I appreciate your concern, but I'm starting to think he's right. My death would solve so much . . ."

"Lavinia! Don't even joke about such a thing," Genie said, truly aghast.

Lavinia glanced up, her blue eyes wells of pain. "Who's joking? I no longer have anything left to live for . . ."

"It only seems that way now because you're grieving the loss of your husband and your friends," Genie said firmly, remembering the tales of how distraught her father had been when her mother died. "You mustn't give up."

"I am not grieving John's—" Lavinia's expression became shuttered, all emotion vanishing from her eyes as she stood. "We should rejoin the men. And to answer your question, what I want is immaterial. Marcus is set on my return, and only an act of God would change that."

Lavinia's words turned out to be prescient as Nathan argued for more than two hours over dinner that Marcus should sell him one of his tickets. Brother Marcus didn't agree, adamant that his sister return and equally assertive that he should accompany her. Nathan, not to be outdone, had brought up his promise to Genie's father. His *personal guarantee* of her safe arrival at her aunt's house in California. The only shared ground between them was that both women would be aboard the ship no matter what.

Lavinia stopped pushing the curried lamb around her plate long enough to shoot Genie an I-told-you-so look.

The spiced tea Genie had been savoring became like sand on her tongue. There was no way to avoid a showdown between the brother and sister now. If Ted had still been in town, she would have been sorely tempted to run away herself. Having stood up for her once, he wouldn't have turned her away this time. Or Lavinia, either. Because of course she would bring the widow with her.

As the four of them finished dinner in taut silence, memories of the night before haunted her. It was impossible to imagine two more different evenings. Ted and the CNAC pilots had actively engaged her in conversation. Had asked her opinion. Had made her feel included, even when the topic was something she knew nothing about.

She had even laughed, something she couldn't imagine doing tonight.

"Be sure to lock your door," Marcus advised once they were back at the hotel. "We found men sleeping in your hallway this morning."

"Perhaps they were tired," Lavinia said breezily as she hooked her arm through Genie's, momentarily startling her. In her experience, only family members or people of long acquaintance ever casually touched one another.

Marcus pointedly turned to Genie. "The train leaves very early in the morning. Either I or Brother Nathan will come for you around five a.m. Can you please be dressed and ready to go?"

Genie hesitated. "Are all four of us going?"

"Yes, of course. When I was out looking for Lavinia this morning, I purchased enough tickets for us all. Though things look worrisome now, I still have hope that, once we reach Bombay, the Good Lord will see fit to provide one more berth for Brother Nathan. So don't worry, Sister Eugenia. Have faith."

When he smiled, his eyes crinkled at the corners, and Genie realized Lavinia had been right: that if she had met him under different circumstances, she might have considered him attractive, kind even.

The realization gave her pause. How difficult it was to know someone's true nature on appearance alone.

Lavinia tugged on Genie's arm, propelling her toward the hall. "Five will be fine."

Marcus scowled at his sister. "No more running away."

"How can I, when you hold my passport?" Lavinia asked bitterly.

Once they were back in the room, the door safely locked, Lavinia's spirits seemed to lift. While they got ready for bed, she asked about Genie's travels, and about the flight from Lashio in particular.

"Were there any open seats on the airplane?" Lavinia asked, taking a seat on her makeshift couch-bed. Genie had offered to share the bed this time, or even switch places with the girl. Lavinia had only laughed, saying she would probably end up on the floor anyway, since she was no longer used to soft mattresses.

Genie pulled her nightgown over her head. The worn linen settled over her skin like an old friend. "Not a one. People were seated in the aisle."

"That's the way it was in Thailand, too. Too many people and not enough airplanes." She plucked at the bedspread, her expression turning sad. "Did Marcus tell you that's how we lost so many of us?"

Genie hesitated. "He said the Japanese overran the mission."

"We were supposed to leave a week earlier. Marcus had been worried for months because Phibun, the prime minister, had been steadily bargaining away the country's freedom, trying to prevent a Japanese occupation." She paused. "Thailand means 'Land of the Free.' Did you know that? It seems rather ironic now.

"Anyway, Marcus heard rumors that there were going to be flights out of Bangkok ahead of the Japanese invasion. So we journeyed the twenty miles south to the royal air base, even though John was desperately sick. But there weren't enough airplanes, or rather airplanes that weren't already commandeered by the military. We were told to come back. That was December 6. Two days later Bangkok fell, and we were trapped."

She stopped and bit her lip as a tear slid down her cheek. She dashed it away, almost angrily.

"You returned to the mission?" Genie asked gently, even though she knew the answer.

Lavinia nodded and opened her mouth as if to speak. Instead, a choked sob escaped, and she crumpled into a ball. As if a dam had been breached, tears slid down her face unceasing as she rocked in silent misery, her fist pressed to her mouth to smother any sound.

Genie's chest ached as she sank down beside the young widow. It was clear from the depth of her grief that Lavinia must have truly loved her husband, despite her earlier protestation. As for the rest of her tale, Genie couldn't even imagine living through so much horror, especially since Lavinia couldn't be much older than Genie herself was. If anything, she might even be a bit younger.

On impulse she hugged her, hoping to convey comfort.

A shudder ran through the thin girl's body, and she pushed herself back. "Don't touch me. I"—she scooted a little farther away, her breathing ragged—"I'm fine. I didn't sleep well last night."

Genie wasn't surprised, considering all Lavinia had been through recently. "I'm sorry I upset you. I shouldn't have—"

"It's all right." Lavinia smiled as if to reassure Genie, but it was too fleeting to work. "Go to sleep. Lord knows that's what I'm going to do as soon as you turn out that light."

Afraid anything she might say would only make the situation worse, Genie silently turned out the light and then crawled into bed.

Ted was twirling her, and she knew she was back at the 300 Club, though all she could see was his handsome dark eyes smiling into her own. The troubles of the day melted off her as she leaned back in his arms, her long skirts wrapping themselves around her legs, making it hard to dance. She was laughing in exasperation, trying to shake her legs free, when a little monkey raced across the floor, startling her.

Then the music dissolved into a discordant jangle as white-coated waiters chased after it. In growing unease, she watched as the tiny creature jumped onto one of the crystal chandeliers. The glass beads tinkled sharply as the lights began to rock dangerously while the frightened animal jumped from one to another and then another. The rocking became wilder and wilder, the base of the chandelier starting to tear loose from the ceiling. She turned and reached in a blind panic for Ted just as it crashed on top of him. In a heart-stopping instant, everything went black, vanishing completely except for a loud steady pounding.

She listened in terror, wondering what new calamity was about to strike.

It took a few seconds, but then she realized it was her heartbeat thudding in her ears, and she was awake. A little shiver ran along her skin. Edgy and aching for Ted's presence, she turned over on the mattress and stared out into the dark.

A silvery glow around the edge of the shade beckoned her.

Since she was awake anyway, she eased out of bed, careful not to make any sounds that might wake Lavinia. Crossing the room, she pulled back the edge of the shade. The buildings and streets outside her window were awash with moonlight. She wondered where Ted was sleeping tonight, if he were somewhere nearby. If only she could go back in time to those nights on the trail, when he had slept not ten feet from her, she would know what he looked like, relaxed and asleep in the moonlight. Or maybe not so asleep . . . Her lips curved as she remembered their kiss.

"Genie." Lavinia's whisper made her jump guiltily.

Spinning around, she saw Lavinia's shadowy figure sitting up on the couch. "I'm sorry. Did I wake you?"

"No." Lavinia seemed to shiver slightly, and then she freed herself of the blankets and padded softly across the ornate carpet to stand beside Genie at the window. She looked out at the dark buildings across the street. "I was already awake. And wondering if you cared who accompanies us to America, Marcus or Mr. Sterling?"

"Not really."

"I think . . . I think I would prefer your Mr. Sterling—that is, if you truly have no plans of your own to marry him."

"I don't," Genie assured her quickly.

"Good, because I think Marcus might agree to stay behind if Mr. Sterling and I were to become engaged."

Genie blinked. "Engaged? You've only known him a few hours. And you've been widowed less than a month; you can't know what your heart is feeling yet."

"My heart has nothing to say in the matter; I'm only interested in survival. At dinner he mentioned he wanted to start his own mission in Africa, as soon as he found a wife who would help him. Do you think he could be persuaded I am that person?"

She stared at the young widow for a moment, wondering if the girl was out of her mind. "You can't be serious."

"I know you don't like him, but if he married me"—Lavinia rubbed her arms as if chilled—"I would be out from under Marcus's thumb."

"Lavinia, no. You'd only be jumping from the pan into the fire."

Eyes washed silver in the moonlight turned to Genie, their intensity almost frightening. "As long as he doesn't beat me, I'm willing to risk it. Because I can't go home, Genie, and there's only one way Marcus will let me board the ship without him: if I'm under the oversight of a soon-to-be husband."

Genie shook her head. "No, there's got to be—"

"There isn't." Lavinia's slender fingers grabbed Genie's arm with surprising strength. "I cannot pass backward through time to return to my love, so if I'm to live, my only way forward is to marry Nathan. I'm not asking you to understand, only for you to help me. Please."

Genie hesitated. Would she be doing harm by agreeing to help? Lavinia seemed so sure this was what she wanted, and Nathan wasn't a bad man. He had never lifted a hand against her, no matter how vexed, and it wasn't as if Lavinia didn't understand what being a missionary wife would entail. Would it be so different from the arranged marriages back home, in China, where the bride and groom sometimes didn't even meet until the ceremony?

*If it's what she wants* . . . Genie could almost hear Li Ming's gentle, practical voice in her ear. Could almost see her dearest friend shrug her delicate shoulders as if to say, "Why not?" *Has she not known enough sorrow in her short life?*

Genie exhaled her doubts and threw caution to the wind. "Tell me what you want, and I'll do my best."

# Chapter 16

*"Panta rei,"* Nathan told Genie four emotionally draining days later. "The only constant is change," he continued, needlessly translating her father's favorite quotation from Heraclitus as they left the Bombay consulate. "And besides, I thought you liked Mrs. Schmidt."

"I do," she said as she watched her brand-new passport get tucked into his coat pocket. It still irked her that the clerk in the office had handed it to Nathan without the slightest hesitation, even though she had been standing right there. "But are you sure you want to marry her?"

"Absolutely. She's attractive, young, God-fearing, and has a pleasant personality." The last bit was no doubt a jab at her. "I'm sure she'll be a marvelous mother to our children."

Genie tried not to dwell on the nauseating thought as she followed him down the sidewalk. How her friend had managed to spend the entire train trip gazing up at Nathan in utter rapture, while Nathan went on and on about how her life could be improved through careful reading of the Bible and by following his instructions, was beyond Genie. She would have strangled Nathan in the first twelve hours.

It had gotten to the point where Genie was forced to leave the compartment on a regular basis to save her sanity. Even more telling, by the end of the trip, Brother Marcus had taken to joining her on her walks through the train.

If it hadn't been for her talks with Lavinia at night, when the widow seemed to shed Nathan like a skin and the world seemed to right itself, Genie would have given up all hope on their friendship. Instead, their late-night musings had given her tantalizing glimpses into Lavinia's past, deepening Genie's affection for the widow.

They had compared childhoods, which were more similar than not. Both had come from conservative religious families and had been raised in farming communities, though Genie had never actually worked as a farmer. Both had been schooled by their fathers, though Lavinia had benefited from having a mother who was willing to teach her how to cook. Zhenzhu had jealously guarded her kitchen, telling Genie she should devote her energies elsewhere.

Lavinia had told Genie about her best friend, Anna Christina, growing up, and how they would climb trees together. Genie, in turn, had told Lavinia about Li Ming and her amazing gifts with weaving and embroidery. Lavinia had turned wistful at that, saying it was one of her trials in life to love beautiful fabric but to have absolutely no talent when it came to creating it or using it. Her wedding dress had been a borrowed one from one of her sisters . . .

"Are you sure she's even ready to remarry?" she asked Nathan as they headed toward the harbor. Genie frowned slightly as it occurred to her that Lavinia's reminiscing had stopped at her marriage. "She's only been a widow since December. I doubt she's had time to grieve."

"Brother Marcus and I actually talked about that. He's of the opinion—and after the last four days, I feel compelled to concur—that remarriage is exactly what she needs. That her recent spate of disobedience was likely tied to her being mooring-less, adrift without male guidance."

She almost snorted. If anything, Lavinia had been rebelling against male interference. On the other hand, his conclusion seemed to be exactly the one Lavinia had wanted him to draw: that she would be-have—or at least behave better—under Nathan's watch.

Brother Marcus waved to them from his place in line on the jetty. Lavinia was nowhere to be seen.

"We're all set," Nathan told Marcus as they joined him in line. "You have the tickets?"

"And your luggage as well," Marcus said, handing Nathan an envelope. "As soon as the purser has checked all your documents, you'll have to get a health screening from the ship's surgeon." Marcus pointed to another line farther down the dock. "And then once he clears you, you'll be free to board. Sister Lavinia is already aboard and waiting for you."

Genie looked up at the enormous gray ship and wondered if her new friend was somewhere up there peering down at them. The ship took up the entire length of the dock and soared nearly eight stories into the air. The sheer distance between the lowermost deck and the water made her dizzy. *Less a ship than a floating mountain.* The harbor waves washed up and splashed restlessly against the hull, rocking the smaller boats motoring by, but not the ship.

She squinted into the noonday sun, at the ring of decks that proclaimed the vessel's prewar heritage as a cruise ship. Sticklike appendages jutted off the uppermost decks.

"Are those guns?" she asked as a chill ran down her back.

"Of course," Nathan said, an impatient edge to his voice. "There *is* a war going on, Eugenia. Do you really think the captain is going to sail a military vessel through enemy-infested waters without some manner of defending himself?"

"I guess . . . I guess I didn't think about it."

"Obviously."

The line inched forward, and Genie couldn't decide if she wanted it to go faster or slower. As tired as she was of standing, she was in no hurry to get on board, either. As long as she stayed on shore, she could cling to the very faint hope that everything would fall through, and she could go home to China.

Brother Marcus cleared his throat. "The boat isn't scheduled to depart until four. Would the two of you care to join me in town until then? Once all your paperwork is approved, of course."

"Perhaps I will," Nathan said as they advanced toward the purser. In preparation, he pulled her passport along with his own from his pocket. "Genie will go aboard as soon as she clears the health screening."

"Actually, I'd like to go shopping." Her fingers itched to yank her passport out of his hand. "I'd love to pick up a newspaper, to see if there's any news of home. And I haven't had a chance to buy a single souvenir so far."

"And how are you going to afford all those purchases?" he asked coldly.

"With my father's money, of course. I'm sure there's enough to spare for a few gifts. They don't have to be expensive. I'm sure Zhenzhu and Li Ming would be thrilled with anything from Indi—"

Nathan cut her off. "And once you buy said gifts, then what? You do know it's unlikely the parcels will get delivered. Not with the war on."

"Maybe not right away, but my father travels to Kweilin at least once a year. That's where he goes to pick up letters from my aunt."

"The last one being three years ago."

Her heart skipped a beat and then two. "But the letters in his desk—"

"Are all old. For all your father knows, your aunt might not be alive. It was one of his concerns about this trip."

The cacophony of the wharf faded as she searched Nathan's face for some sign he was lying. He wasn't. Her stomach twisted painfully. "Why didn't he tell me?"

Nathan shrugged. "He didn't want you to worry. And if we had continued our engagement, it would've been immaterial. I would've taken care of you, no matter what."

"But now I'm on my own?" Disbelief and a kind of horror stole her breath.

"Don't be ridiculous. I'd hardly abandon a woman to the streets. I only brought it up so you would understand the situation and be prepared."

"Prepared to wait out the war without friend or family, you mean."

She looked across the broad jetty toward the exotic buildings of Bombay. The sight no longer entranced her as it had several hours earlier. Now it only reminded her of how terrifyingly far she was from home.

"Perhaps Sister Eugenia could come into town with me?" Brother Marcus asked calmly, reminding them both of his presence. "Sometimes even the closest of traveling companions can benefit from time apart."

"Would you mind?" Nathan said, surprising her. She expected him to refuse strictly out of spite. "I could finish my errands more quickly unencumbered."

"It would be my pleasure. You have taken a load off my shoulders. I would be remiss not to return the favor."

"Thank you, and all will be fine. *She* will be fine; don't worry," Nathan replied rather cryptically.

Marcus hesitated and then nodded.

At last the purser, fully dressed in a white US Navy uniform, checked her and Nathan's tickets, passports, and luggage. Finding it all acceptable, he entered them onto the passenger manifest and then pointed them toward the line to see the ship's physician. After a quick physical inspection and being asked about exposure to any communicable diseases, they were handed a green card to present to the officer on deck. They were also given strict orders to be aboard no later than three thirty. Latecomers would be left behind. No exceptions.

"Don't make me regret my decision," Nathan said coldly as they walked across the crowded pier to rejoin Brother Marcus. "I'm depending on you to behave."

"I'm not a child, Nathan," she snapped.

"Good. Keep that in mind."

With an effort, she schooled her expression into one of resigned compliance, an effort she had to redouble when Nathan handed Marcus money along with her passport. The desire to snatch both away from him and then tell Nathan off burned hot within her. Only fear of what her father might think should word of such bad behavior get back to him restrained her. It wasn't until Nathan disappeared into the crowd that she allowed herself to breathe again.

"Thank you for offering to shop with me," Genie said, finally turning to face Marcus. "Are you sure you don't want to go to the States with us instead of Nathan?"

He smiled ruefully. "What I want does not matter. Our lives are all in the Lord's hands, and I now suspect it His wish that I continue His work here in India."

"But don't you wish you could go home?"

"My home," he said slowly, his gaze sliding out over the jetty, "is wherever I am. That way it can never be taken from me. It is a good way to live." He glanced back at her, his eyes shadowed with pain. "A path you might wish to pursue."

"Because the Japanese might overrun my village like they did your mission?" She drew a deep breath to dispel the sudden wave of anxiety that accompanied that thought. *Lord, keep them all safe.* She exhaled and refocused on the conversation at hand. "Lavinia never speaks of it, but she has these terrible nightmares . . ."

"My sister is plagued by many demons," he said with a weary sigh. "Which is why I wanted to thank you for your kindness to her. Her life hasn't been easy, even before the massacre."

"She told me she's cursed."

He winced. "Don't put too much stock in what she says. She is grieving the loss of her husband, and a good friend. And, I'm ashamed to say, there were those in our group who blamed her for our misfortune. It hurt her greatly."

"Why in the world would they think that?" she asked, truly horrified by such cruelty, especially when Lavinia would have been freshly widowed at that point.

"It doesn't matter," Marcus said firmly. "Lavinia is free of them now, and she knows what she needs to do to be restored to grace. All will be well."

"So she was guilty?" she asked hesitantly, not quite sure how to take his pronouncement. Lavinia had seemed so tenderhearted and compassionate on the train trip, willing to drop whatever she was doing if Genie needed to talk about her fears for her family or of the looming ocean voyage.

"Not for the attack. For that, the Japanese bear full responsibility." Then he sighed once more and looked down. "Though I will say trouble follows my little sister like a hungry dog, and always has. It was something my parents hoped to change by sending her to Thailand."

"It doesn't sound like it worked."

"No." He removed his flat-brimmed hat and dragged his fingers through his hair. "But I didn't mean to burden you with family troubles. I only meant to thank you for helping make the journey easier on all of us."

A smile slowly found its way back onto his tired face, and he gestured toward the city streets teeming with life. "Shall we?"

# Chapter 17

"Eugenia, have you seen Lavinia?" Nathan's head popped around the edge of the sheet Genie was pinning to the clothesline, nearly giving her a heart attack. He clutched the brim of his straw fedora as a gust of sea breeze threatened to steal it.

"Did you try the cabin?" She pulled another sheet out of the laundry basket and hung it next to the first one. After twelve days at sea, she couldn't wait to sleep on clean linens again. While it didn't bother her to do her cabin's laundry, she had heard the shocked dismay of the more upscale passengers when they had learned the navy expected them to do their own.

"Of course I did." His voice held a touch of annoyance, but when wasn't he annoyed with her these days? "I also visited the women's Bible study, and she wasn't there, either. Do you think she's ill?"

In a stroke of luck, a gust of wind billowed the freshly hung sheet, briefly obscuring him from view, because at that very moment a movement on deck directly above them caught her attention. It was Lavinia herself, long skirts whipping in the wind, stopping two sailors to talk. Or rather, more likely, to bum a cigarette.

Genie sighed, irritated with both Nathan and her friend for putting her in the middle of their relationship. "You were just with her at breakfast. Did she look ill to you?" she asked, pushing the basket to the right, forcing Nathan to pivot toward the rail, further obscuring his view.

"No, which is why this is so concerning," he said, clutching his hat again. "We were going to meet at eleven, and she never showed. We wanted to tell you our good news together."

"Which is?" She shook out a pillowcase even as she kept one eye on Lavinia, who was now laughing with the sailors. *Come on, Lavinia. Get your cigarettes and move already.*

"Mrs. Schmidt has agreed to be my wife!" Nathan said proudly.

Her hands stilled. It wasn't as if she hadn't expected him to propose to her friend. From the moment the ship had cast off, he had hovered over Lavinia like an overprotective mother hen, which was likely why her friend would periodically disappear on him. A girl had to breathe, after all. Especially if she was going to be shackled to the likes of Nathan for the rest of her life.

"Congratulations?" she finally managed.

"I was expecting a bit more excitement," he said drily.

"It seems a bit hasty, is all." She shook out a pillowcase, hoping to distract Nathan's attention. The sheets had settled down, leaving Lavinia exposed again. "You've only known her three weeks. That's not much time to really know someone."

Like that she'd taken up smoking to calm her nerves.

"Actually, that's another reason I wanted to talk to you. We'll be docking in Cape Town in two days' time, and I think it best if only Lavinia and I went ashore. We haven't had much time alone together since the train trip, and I had planned to surprise her with an outing."

She stared at him, the pillowcase in her hands forgotten. Surely she hadn't heard correctly. "Are you saying I'm to stay aboard?"

"I won't be able to chaperone you while I'm with Lavinia, and your father would have my head if I let you go ashore alone. If there's anything you'd like me to pick up for you, like soap or toothpaste, give me a list, and I'll see that it gets purchased."

"Are you sure that wouldn't be too much to ask? Because Lord knows I wouldn't want to intrude on your time with your fiancée," she said, a slow fury building in her blood.

"There's no need to be rude, Eugenia. I'm trying to find a mutually agreeable solution here."

"Of course." Sarcasm seeped into her voice. "Never mind that I'd be stuck on this boat, missing my one and only chance to ever set foot on African soil."

He rolled his eyes. "Don't be so melodramatic. I'm only asking for one day, Eugenia. One day without you tagging along so my fiancée and I can become better acquainted."

She clenched her hands behind her back, fighting the impulse to push him overboard. Her fingernails dug into her palms, the pain bringing tears to her eyes as she fought to be meek and polite, as she had been taught.

"Did it ever occur to you that maybe your fiancée might want less time with you, and that's why you can't always find her when you want to?" She blurted the words out before she could stop them.

There was a beat of silence as her betrayal of Lavinia's confidence hung in the air. Desperately she wanted to call the words back. Her friend would never trust her again.

"Unbelievable," Nathan said with a half laugh. "You kiss another man in front of me, and now you have the temerity to be jealous?"

"Jealous?" She almost choked on the word, all her anger rushing back. "You can't be serious. You are positively the last person I would ever waste my affections on."

"That's right. You'd rather play Jezebel to some pilot—someone who has undoubtedly already forgotten your existence—shaming your father and making a mockery of his ministry."

She winced inwardly at hearing her own doubts voiced aloud, but she would be damned before she would let Nathan gloat. "We were talking about my going into Cape Town, not any imaginary transgressions with Lieutenant Younan."

"And I'm telling you why your bad behavior in Calcutta is exactly why you're not going ashore. I cannot depend on you to behave as a properly brought-up Christian woman."

"That's not fair!"

"I don't care about fair. I care about obedience. Your father put me in charge of you, and I will not be remiss."

"You . . ." She struggled to think past the conflagration of rage incinerating her brain. "You're awful. Vile. Despicable."

"And keeper of your passport. Let's not forget that, should you be inclined to try to go without me. Lavinia has already learned her lesson on that subject. Perhaps it's time you learned it, too."

"Gah, how I hate you!" She spun away before he could see the tears escape her eyes. The wet streaks were cold on her skin despite the bright sun. She couldn't breathe. Couldn't draw even the tiniest inhalation.

"While I regret your sentiment," he said coldly, "I will nevertheless do what I feel is in your best interests. Am I being clear?"

Holding her breath in an attempt to maintain control despite the anger buffeting her, she nodded once.

"Excellent." Smug victory colored his voice, making her want to scream. "And if you see Lavinia, tell her I'm looking for her. And don't spoil my surprise."

She made herself hold absolutely still as he walked away, her fingers gripping each other so tightly her knuckles ached. Once he was gone, her breath escaped in a furious whoosh.

Shaking and nauseated, she abandoned the laundry basket and went to the rail. Far off in the distance, a charcoal line smudged the horizon, barely visible to the naked eye. Africa: the Dark Continent—vast, mysterious, untamed. How nice it would have been to say she had once set foot on its fabled shores. Now it was only one more point marking her distance from home.

Despair gripped her heart as the ocean crested and crashed against the ship in unceasing waves. As beautiful as she had come to find the endless water, she would trade the view in an instant to be back in her mountains among the tall fragrant cedars, back with the people who loved her and would always love her. Back to a time before the war had stolen everything.

She closed her eyes and let go of the present. The sea spray became icy drizzle from low-hanging clouds. The crash of waves became nothing more than the thrashing of leaves before a gathering storm. Behind her, the village and its fields blanketed the narrow valley. If she turned, she would see her father's home there at the edge. Li Ming's laughter, like the tinkling of tiny metal bells, floated on the wind, and Genie shivered, having forgotten her cloak in the study.

Smoke from the morning's cooking fires filled her head, tangy and sharp . . .

"Is he gone?" Lavinia asked from beside her.

Genie jumped, the scene dissipating like mist, the acrid smoke of a cigarette filling her lungs. Her cheeks were wet. Embarrassed, she wiped them before glancing at her friend, who had so many more reasons to cry than she did.

"For the moment. Did you know he means to leave me aboard when we reach Cape Town?"

"I did." Lavinia's startlingly blue eyes studied her intently, and Genie wondered what she saw there. Despair? Defeat? Lord knew the undertow of both was pulling her under at the moment.

Her friend opened her mouth as if to say something but then seemed to change her mind. She lifted the cigarette to her mouth, her gaze darting out to sea. When she exhaled, she let the smoke stream to the side, away from Genie. "What else happened?"

"I told him you were avoiding him," she admitted. "But he didn't believe me."

Lavinia laughed, but it sounded tired. "I'm not surprised."

Genie studied her friend anew. Wisps of dark hair, having pulled free from her long braid by the wind, curled around the young widow's face. The skin beneath her eyes was shadowed, bruised looking. Nathan was right about Lavinia needing rest, but not because she was working too hard. Genie was one of the few people who knew Lavinia rarely slept at night because of bad dreams. Now she wondered if perhaps those nightmares had as much to do with Lavinia's future as her past.

"You don't have to marry him, you know."

Lavinia made a noncommittal sound as she kept her gaze on the horizon. Her cigarette dangled from her slender fingers as if forgotten. Finally, she spoke. "Do you believe in curses?"

"No, not really."

"I do. So does my family. It's why they forced me to marry John and then shipped me halfway around the world. Only misfortune followed along in my steamer trunk, and it ended up killing everyone I loved."

A chill ran through Genie. "No curse was responsible for the Japanese attack. So don't even begin to think that. The war killed your husband. Not you."

"Are you sure?" Lavinia turned, her blue eyes as brittle as broken shards of glass. "Because, the Lord as my witness, I hated John. Hated him with every fiber of my immortal soul."

"You can't mean that!" Genie protested, shocked by her friend's blasphemy.

"Why? It's true." Lavinia's fingers trembled as she lifted the cigarette to her mouth. "He took my father's advice and, after we were married, tried to exorcise my curse through strict discipline. I wasn't allowed to talk to anyone unless he was present, wasn't allowed to speak at all unless spoken to, and I was locked in a closet if he had to go somewhere without me. But it was all for my own good, you see. So no one intervened, even when he tried to beat the curse out of me."

Genie stared at her friend, shocked into wordlessness. No wonder Lavinia had never before spoken of her marriage.

Flicking an ash over the side, Lavinia bit her lip and blinked, as if to stop tears. "After one particularly bad night, I tried to take my own life. Marcus finally spoke to him then, and things got a little better. At least until . . ."

The rest of the sentence went unspoken as Lavinia hurriedly took another draw off the cigarette, but Genie heard the words anyway. *Until the Japanese attacked.*

"Anyway," the widow said after blowing another stream of smoke to the side. "The Good Lord has seen fit to give me a second chance with Nathan, and I don't intend to squander it. Nothing can be as bad as what I've already lived through."

"I see." Genie rubbed her arms, not quite sure what to think of Lavinia's story. It seemed so far-fetched, and yet . . .

Lavinia slid her an enigmatic glance. "I never properly thanked you for your help with Nathan. I feel bad that I've done nothing for you in return."

"Don't. I really didn't do anything."

"You kept Marcus busy on the train, which made all the difference. Tell me how I can return the favor, and I'll do my best."

*Help me go home* was her first thought, which she squelched immediately because it was currently beyond anyone's ability to grant. Her second one, *be my friend,* was even more pathetic, and one Lavinia wasn't likely to understand. How could Genie explain that, despite all the time they had spent together and the confidences they had shared about their lives before the war and their worry over their future in the States, she still had the inexplicable sense that Lavinia was holding back? Perhaps the subtle distance was out of grief, or maybe Lavinia found her somehow lacking—Genie didn't know—but it left her feeling lonelier than ever.

"I wish I could experience Cape Town firsthand," she said finally. "But I think I ruined any chance of that by insulting Nathan."

Lavinia tamped out her cigarette on the railing. "Perhaps, but leave Nathan to me. We still have a couple of days; things could change." Then she laughed, and the shadows lifted momentarily from her eyes. "Did I tell you I've devised a little test for my besotted fiancé? I'm going to cut my hair every night, a half inch or so, and see how long it takes him to notice."

"You might go bald first."

"Maybe, though I doubt it. He's always saying he sees me for who I really am, and I'd like to believe him. Some days I feel almost . . . invisible."

Genie understood the feeling. After so many times of being shoved aside, of having her opinions overlooked, it was hard not to feel that way. "Maybe you should cut my hair, too, and see if he notices."

Lavinia's eyebrows lifted. "You would risk it? He's likely not going to be pleased."

"He already thinks I'm incorrigible. Besides, think how much more modern I'll look with short hair."

Lavinia laughed. "Fine. Let's do it."

# Chapter 18

Seagulls showed up the next morning, though the ship didn't seem to be any closer to the African coast. At lunch, despite the sign exhorting passengers to not feed the birds, Lavinia kept tearing off pieces of her sandwich and tossing them to the hungry scavengers. Nathan pretended not to notice, which only made Genie's irritation with him sharper. She had no doubts that if she fed the birds, he would throw the proverbial book at her.

Appetite gone, she looked out on the sparkling ocean and enjoyed the cool breeze as she waited for the other two to finish. With very little to do, having finished the laundry yesterday, she was in no hurry to leave, especially on such a nice day. A happy consequence of the voyage being sold out was that the mess hall was too small to accommodate all the passengers, so tall benches had been set up on the promenade for the more able-bodied passengers, such as the three of them, to take their meals outside whenever weather permitted, which was most of the time. On days like today, with the deck above providing a kind of awning to shade her from the hot sun, she couldn't imagine wanting to eat anywhere else.

A sailor ran past them, startling her from her reverie. Equally startled, Lavinia's gull squawked and bolted out from under the bench in a frenzy of flapping wings. Nathan shot her a disapproving look and

then went back to conversing with one of his new missionary friends, an American whose family had been serving in southern India.

Genie glanced at Lavinia.

*Did you see that?* She mouthed the words.

Lavinia nodded, equally silent as she eyed the seagull, which was circling back for more food. It was shooed away by two more crewmen—officers, by the look of their khaki uniforms—strolling aft. One held a stopwatch, the other a stack of clipboards. Their pace was leisurely but purposeful.

Genie bit her lip, her lunch all of a sudden not sitting quite right in her stomach. The passengers had been warned that there would be emergency drills. The hard truth was that the ship might encounter a German U-boat at any moment, especially once they rounded the cape, and it would only take one well-aimed torpedo to sink them. Everyone needed to be ready.

Not ten minutes later, the general alarm bell rang out. The children at the next bench shrieked and covered their ears. Genie tensed as a short eerie silence settled over the deck and everyone waited for the next series of bells. Her heart fell as the expected alarm sounded: six short rings and then a long one. The signal to abandon ship. Almost as one, the diners collected their families and began heading for the stairs.

She scrunched her napkin in her hand, waiting for Nathan to move. Her urge to follow the others had her shifting restlessly from one foot to the other as Nathan returned to eating, his friend having joined the rest.

Lavinia shot her a look, the warning clear in her bright blue eyes.

*Wait. Wait.* She breathed in and out. Once. Twice. As much as she wanted to obey the alarm, she didn't dare move until Nathan suggested it. Her chances of making it ashore depended on her obedience to his will, no matter what.

Nathan finally set his glass down, having finished the last of his tea. "You two clear the trays while I retrieve the passports from the cabin. I will rejoin you at the lifeboat station."

Genie didn't hesitate in snatching up both his tray and her own. Lavinia joined her on the way to the refuse station, where they handed their trays to the kitchen help. The young man smiled reassuringly at her, and she reminded herself that this was only a drill. There was no real danger.

Together, she and Lavinia hurried toward the stairwell, joining the tide of passengers. Out on the lower deck, an officer was shouting instructions through a bullhorn: *Single-file lines! No suitcases! Children with parents! No talking!* Working their way through the throngs of people already lined up, Genie and Lavinia arrived at their assigned meeting point, where a sailor checked their names off on his clipboard.

Taking her place in line, Genie looked up at the lifeboat being winched down from above. "Do you think we'll actually have to get in the boats?"

"I certainly hope so. Think of the adventure," Lavinia said almost longingly as she edged closer to the railing. As she leaned and peered over, the wind whipped her long skirts around her legs, as if trying to trip her.

"Terror, more like. And I'm warning you—if you fall in, you're on your own," Genie said, her pulse spiking as Lavinia leaned even farther out. "I don't know how to swim."

Lavinia straightened, her eyebrows lifted in genuine surprise as she glanced back. "You don't?"

"No. There were only rivers where I grew up, and not ones you wanted to swim in."

"We lived next to a lake and swam all the time. My brothers taught me."

"Lucky you."

"You know, there's a swimming pool on the lido deck," a man said from behind her.

Genie turned around, only to be greeted by a conspiratorial wink. She felt her cheeks heat with embarrassment, as the man was far more attractive than she had expected, with broad shoulders, sun-streaked brown hair, and lively hazel eyes. His deep tan spoke of someone who spent a lot of time outside. She guessed he might be in his thirties.

"Likely you could find someone to teach you," he continued with surprising seriousness. "It's not as if there's a whole lot else to do on board."

"And who are you?" Lavinia asked coolly as she linked her arm through Genie's.

"Oh, sorry. Dick Pelton." He grinned and held out his hand to Lavinia. "Photographer for the US government and documentary film specialist. Before the war, I also worked in Hollywood—not that I'm bragging."

"And we're missionaries," Lavinia said, ignoring his hand. "So there's no need to brag. We're not interested."

"Lavinia!" Genie exclaimed, shocked by her friend's rudeness. She turned to Mr. Pelton. "I'm Eugenia Baker."

"Nice to meet you." His fingers were pleasantly warm as they shook hands.

"And this is my friend Mrs. Schmidt." Genie gestured toward Lavinia, who gave a visible shudder at the name, but how else was she supposed to introduce the widow? "She was recently in Burma until her husband was killed by the Japanese."

"My condolences, Mrs. Schmidt," Mr. Pelton said. "I was on your flight from Burma. That had to be very difficult."

"Please call me Lavinia. Hearing my married name is too painful at the moment."

"Of course."

Genie stared at Mr. Pelton. "Did you say you were on the flight from Lashio?"

"I was. And on the train from Calcutta."

She narrowed her gaze. "How is it I never saw you?"

"I don't know, but I remember seeing you—not many people in India have red hair." He turned to Lavinia and frowned slightly. "And speaking of red hair, what happened to the fellow who boarded the plane with you? I'm assuming now that he wasn't your husband."

"He wasn't," Lavinia agreed.

Nathan joined them and said, "Here, put this on." He handed Genie a life jacket.

Not needing to be told twice, she slipped it over her head and began fastening the straps while Nathan helped Lavinia put hers on.

"Let me," Mr. Pelton said, taking one of the straps from her hand and untwisting it. "It's easier to fix this now, before it gets wet."

"Wet?" A jolt of panic, like an electric shock, numbed her fingers. "We're not actually going into the water, are we?"

"One tries not to, but waves do splash up once in a while." One corner of his mouth lifted as he expertly threaded the buckle. Without asking, he tightened down her other straps, and as each one grew snugger, she became more and more aware of how close his fingers were to her breasts.

"You put life jackets on other people often?" she asked in an effort to distract herself.

"Not often. However, as a boy growing up on the coast of California, I think I spent more time on the water than off. At least until I discovered girls." He winked.

Her cheeks heated, and she hurriedly looked around for Nathan, hoping he hadn't seen.

He hadn't. He was standing close to Lavinia, gently brushing strands of windblown hair from her face, his expression open and unguarded. Boyish.

Something panged in her chest, but it wasn't jealousy. Not exactly. Just a pained awareness that she had never inspired such a look from him.

"Looks like we might not get wet after all." Mr. Pelton nodded down the deck, and she followed his gaze. The captain, identifiable by the gold bars flashing on his shoulder boards, was speaking with the officer holding the stopwatch. He gestured to the boat swinging briskly in the wind, and the officer nodded. A piped whistle split the air, and then a second later the all-clear sounded.

"Oh, thank heaven," she breathed as the boat was slowly winched back up. The sailor with the bullhorn began shouting dispersion instructions. Passengers were to hand their life jackets to crew members or stack them along the wall.

"Dickie! There you are." A slender, very blonde woman with a deep-blue scarf holding back her hair appeared out of the crowd. Her tortoiseshell sunglasses hid her eyes but not the striking angles of her face. Genie was positive she had seen the woman before but couldn't remember when or where.

"How ever did you end up over here?" the woman scolded as she breezed past Genie without a second glance, her dramatically red lips already in a pout. "All the interesting people are on the other side. Tell the captain there's been a mistake so you can line up with us next time."

"Why should I? Look at all these people I haven't met yet." He gestured at the departing passengers.

"Oh, you tease." She linked her arm with his. "Come, join me at the bar. All this running around has made me thirsty. Bess and Larry will be there, too, I'm sure."

"In a moment." He smiled at Genie. "It was a pleasure finally meeting you, Miss Baker. And Lavinia. Please give her my best."

"Of course, but . . ." She stopped, realizing that Lavinia and Nathan were no longer nearby. In fact, they were nowhere to be seen. She turned back to Mr. Pelton, but he was already drifting off, arm in arm with his lady friend. On a ship overloaded with people, she was alone.

"Excuse me, miss." A young sailor, one who looked barely old enough to shave, gave her a brief tired smile. His arms were full of cast-off life jackets. "Do you need help?"

She hesitated, still feeling a little sorry for herself. Then, realizing how pathetic that was, she pulled herself together. Alone didn't mean helpless. Her fingers began unfastening the buckles. "No, thank you. I can do it."

# Chapter 19

Excitement hummed in Genie's veins as she leaned over the railing and studied the pier far below her. Ever since the ship had steamed into Cape Town late last night, she'd been on razor's edge, one moment sure her good behavior of the past few days would sway Nathan's thinking, the next terrified that it hadn't been enough. Nothing had been said one way or the other over breakfast, so maybe, just maybe . . .

She inhaled, filling her lungs with the air of Africa. *Africa!* Behind the heavy odors of oil and fish from the dock, past the smells of salt and engine exhaust, she fancied she could detect the rich scents of jungle and savannah, the spicy musk of unfamiliar flora and fauna.

Below her, evidence of the war was everywhere. Soldiers with rifles slung over their shoulders strolled along the dock while white-capped sailors tossed crates from flatbed trucks to the ground. The small open-aired cars growling up and down the harbor front were all painted in drab camouflage paint. Not far back from that, long rows of canvas tents formed an entire town of their own.

Then she lifted her gaze to the large flat-topped mountain soaring up, green and mysterious, from the center of town, and she felt her breath catch. She bounced on the balls of her feet, too agitated to stand still. The need to feel solid ground under her and to be surrounded by something other than water was fast becoming a compulsion.

Impatient, she glanced over her shoulder for Nathan and Lavinia. A deep, thrilling chorus of powerful engines pulled her attention to the horizon. A quartet of fighter planes tore through the sky, the bones in her chest vibrating as they zoomed over the ship and then out over the ocean, holding a tight formation as they banked to the left, back toward the city. Her heart galloped unsteadily as the snarl of their engines, which had just seconds ago filled all the empty places on deck, faded until the shouts and thumps of crates being unloaded once more could be heard.

"Genie!" Lavinia's voice, so close, made Genie jump. "We're here."

Spinning around, she started to smile, her eagerness back. Then she caught the strained smile on Lavinia's narrow face. Genie's heart stuttered, the teasing words she had been about to utter dying on her lips.

"I'm sorry we took so long." Her friend's gaze drifted past Genie's shoulder. "Nathan wanted to verify there would be a meal service for passengers remaining aboard. Which there is, so that's good."

Disbelief rapidly coalesced into fury. She whirled on Nathan, who had, of course, let Lavinia break the bad news to her. The coward.

"I'm not going ashore?" she asked slowly, to be sure there was no mistake.

Nathan made an exasperated sound. "Really, Eugenia. We've already discussed this."

"Yes, but I thought . . ."

"Thought what? That your continued selfishness would be somehow overlooked because of your recent spate of good behavior? Hardly." His features hardened as he tucked Lavinia's arm into his own. "Your father would be mortified if he could hear you now, putting your happiness ahead of others. You should be ashamed of yourself."

"Ashamed, why?" she asked incredulously. "Because I want to experience Africa for myself? I should think that's exactly the kind of thing my father would want for me. He never, ever—not even once—indicated that the furthering of one's knowledge was anything but noble and good. So who are you, my appointed escort, to deny me this experience? If anything, you should be ashamed of yourself. My father trusted you to do right by me, not pursue your own selfish desires!"

Lavinia shook her head imperceptibly, her eyes hard with warning as Nathan first paled and then flushed. Genie cringed inwardly. She had really done it this time.

"If you had ever truly cared about your father's desires"—Nathan's tone was sharp enough to cut steel—"*you*, instead of Mrs. Schmidt, would be my fiancée. I can only thank the Lord that your imprudence saved me from such a fate."

Her breath caught at the injustice of his remarks. She was still searching for the right retort as Nathan tugged Lavinia toward the gangway, taking her freedom with him. There had to be something she could say. Lavinia, for her part, kept glancing over her shoulder, her expression intent, but Genie couldn't respond. Her feet were rooted to the deck.

Her friend leaned in and said something to Nathan. Then she was running back to Genie. She threw her arms around Genie's shoulders and hugged her tight. Genie stiffened at the unexpected show of affection.

"I tried to change his mind, but don't despair," Lavinia whispered in a rush before releasing her. "I put it in Nathan's pillowcase. Top bunk, second row from the left. Don't get caught."

And then her friend was gone, rushing back to Nathan's side. Genie blinked in confusion. *Don't get caught.* Don't get caught doing what—?

Like a summer sunrise, understanding blossomed. The urge to run after her friend and hug her rolled in as fast as her depression was swept away. If she had Lavinia's message right, she might yet walk on African soil.

With renewed hope, she hurried inside to Nathan's stateroom. Her gaze swept the passageway as she nervously lifted her hand to knock on the door. While it was one thing to be caught searching one's own cabin, it was quite another to be found going through someone else's, particularly one assigned to the opposite sex.

All was quiet, which didn't surprise her. Most of the ship was probably already ashore. Still, her knees shook as she rapped on the metal door. When no one answered, she knocked a little louder. She willed her breathing to slow while she waited to see if anyone would respond. *You have every right to be here. Calm down.* Rationally, she knew no one would fault her for retrieving her passport, if that was indeed what Lavinia had been talking about. The passport was hers, after all.

Silence crouched beyond the door, perhaps benign, perhaps not. Praying that it would be the former and that her legs wouldn't give out, she turned the handle. The door was unlocked. Silent as a shadow, she slipped into the cabin and scanned for sleeping occupants. Like the cabin she shared with Lavinia, everything of luxury and comfort had been stripped from the room except a small sink and a mirror. Four rows of steel-framed bunk beds, each with three cots, had been squeezed into the small space, leaving barely two feet between rows. As a result, all the baggage was stowed either on or beneath the beds, which would make her task easier.

Reassured that she was alone, she headed for the second row of bunks.

"Breaking and entering a new skill they teach missionaries these days?" a man said from the doorway.

She spun around, her heart jumping nearly out of her chest. "Mr. Pelton, hello."

"Hello, yourself." He propped his shoulder against the doorjamb and lifted an eyebrow. "Is there something I can help you find? Your escort, perhaps?"

"Oh, Nathan is already ashore." She furtively wiped her damp palms on her skirt and tried to guess his mood. Dressed in a dark-green cable-knit vest and pressed brown tweed pants, his gold-streaked hair neatly slicked back and his hat dangling from long, slender fingers, he was the very picture of casual elegance. And privilege. And likely not the kind of man to view petty theft kindly.

"I know this looks bad, but I promise, I'm not doing anything sinister. I'm looking for my passport so I can go ashore. Because I forgot to tell Nathan to buy me postage stamps to mail these." She pulled the letters she had written over the last few weeks from her skirt pocket, thankful she had them with her. "They're for my father and aunt."

"I see." He studied her, his hazel eyes almost green in the filtered light. "You know, I'm headed into town this morning. I could post them for you."

"No! I mean, thank you, but I wouldn't want to impose. Besides, I'm looking forward to the adventure."

"Of course." He continued studying her, making no move to leave the doorway. "Is there any particular reason your passport is here and not in your cabin?"

A lie would be the fastest way to gain his support, but she couldn't make herself utter the words. Exhaling in defeat, she slumped against the bunk post. "Nathan didn't want me going ashore today. He wanted to spend all his time with Lavinia—the widow you met. They're engaged. So he hid my passport."

"Best wishes to them both, but I'm not clear why that required your being left behind. Is there another reason he doesn't want you leaving the ship, like you're traveling under a false name? A criminal fleeing justice?"

"No!" she said, horrified he could think such a thing of her.

His expression eased into a smile. "Relax. I was only teasing. Go ahead and search for your passport. Then I'll help you find that post office."

"I wouldn't want to impose . . ."

"No imposition at all. My companions were planning to spend the day shopping, which I'd just as soon avoid, so this works out perfectly. I can be your knight in shining armor and have a good reason to miss out on a day of utter boredom." He winked at her.

A sudden nervousness fluttered in her stomach, and she turned back to the bunks. Mr. Pelton was far too sophisticated to be flirting with her, so she didn't know how to take his comments. She counted off the bunks again, and the passport was right where Lavinia said it would be. Stress rolled off her shoulders like rain off oilcloth. Silently thanking the quick-witted widow for somehow arranging to have the passport left behind, she tucked it into her pocket next to the letters. Then she fluffed the pillow and returned it to its original place. Nathan was bound to find out, but the longer she could put off that unhappy occurrence, the better.

"Got it?"

"Yes." She turned to him and smiled, unable to hide her relief.

"You know," Mr. Pelton said, stroking his jaw thoughtfully, "limiting yourself to a quick trip to the post office seems hardly worth all this cloak-and-dagger effort. How about I show you around Cape Town properly? I know some wonderful little restaurants, having been here before. We could have lunch."

"Surely you have better things to do. Won't your friends miss you?"

"Not really. Their tastes run toward fashion and glamour, two things that don't interest me much. Likely a byproduct of my having spent too much time in Hollywood." One corner of his mouth quirked up beguilingly. "Come on. It'll be fun. You know you're itching to see the world."

She bit her lip. Having Mr. Pelton escort her to the post office was one thing. Staying ashore, having lunch with a man she didn't know very well, and spending extended time in his company without a chaperone? That was quite another thing altogether. Yet the temptation of seeing more of Cape Town pulled at her.

"No, I'd better not," she said, ruthlessly stomping on her disappointment. To refuse his offer was the right thing to do, no matter how much she hated it.

"Are you sure?" he asked with what sounded like genuine disappointment. "I was hoping to take you downtown to this local soda fountain I know of where the milkshakes are absolutely crackerjack."

"I'm sorry . . . soda what? Cracker what?" It was as if he had suddenly switched languages on her.

"Soda fountains. You know, where you can get sodas and drinks? And crackerjack, as in excellent, like having caramel popcorn in a box . . ." An arrested look entered his eyes. "When did you say was the last time you were in the States?"

She gave an embarrassed laugh. "Never. I've only ever lived in China. I was born there."

"No kidding?" He considered her another long moment, one brown eyebrow cocked. "Your English is so good, I never would've guessed. Tell me, have you ever had a burger or a milkshake? Ever watched a baseball game? Had apple pie?"

"No." She shifted uneasily. "At least I think not. Is it bad that I don't know what half those words mean?"

"Not necessarily, though it'll make for one heck of a culture shock when you get to California. And it's all the more reason you should come with me into town. I can point out the similarities, giving you a leg up on all things Americana, starting with a bottle of Coca-Cola."

Relief flooded her as she remembered the fizzy, caramelly brown beverage. "Wait, I've tried that. One of the nurses in Kunming gave it to me. It was actually rather good."

"Well, that's a start." He straightened and gestured down the passageway. "Shall we go? It sounds like I've got my work cut out for me."

She hesitated again. If Nathan saw her, she would be in deep trouble. Still, from what she had seen on deck, Cape Town was a big city. If she kept a sharp eye out, she should be able to avoid him.

"All right, I'll go. But only if we can stop and get a newspaper along the way so I can check for news of home, and if you promise to have me back right after lunch."

"Deal." He stepped back into the passageway and let her lead the way.

Up on deck, they were hailed by a group of fashionably dressed people. One was the imperious blonde from the lifeboat drill. The woman lifted her gloved hand in a half-hearted greeting as Genie and Mr. Pelton approached, her expression hidden beneath her wide, flat-brimmed hat and tortoiseshell sunglasses. As they got closer, her wildly red lips compressed into a flat line.

"Whatever took you so long, Dickie?" she asked, not bothering to spare Genie so much as a glance. "Half the day is gone, I swear."

"Patience, Kitty dear. The shops have barely opened." Mr. Pelton greeted the other two people, a petite brunette with a pretty smile and a sunburned blond man. The man had his arm draped possessively over the brunette's shoulder. She leaned happily into him, a diamond the size of a pea on her left hand.

Mr. Pelton turned back to her. "Genie, I'd like you to meet Kitty, Bess, and Larry. Reprobates, all, but I call 'em friends. Gang, I'd like you to meet Miss Genie Baker, recently of China."

"Are you going with us?" Bess, the brunette, asked brightly. The genuineness of her enthusiasm was in sharp contrast to Kitty's glower. "It should be ever so much fun. I, for one, can't wait to get off this boat!"

Mr. Pelton shook his head. "No, my dear. Genie and I are off to find a post office, a newspaper, and then maybe a museum or two."

Kitty wrinkled her nose. "A museum? How awful. All those dusty exhibits and stuffy rooms. You might as well lock yourself in a stateroom and read a history book."

"Oh, it's not as bad as all that," he said wryly. "You should try it sometime. You might find it edifying."

Kitty stuck her tongue out in reply, and Genie stifled a gasp. To her surprise, Mr. Pelton only laughed, not seeming the least bit put out. Genie couldn't even imagine how Nathan would have responded to such disrespect.

The conversation turned to a list of must-visit stores and restaurants as the group started down the gangway. Kitty strode ahead as Bess and Larry sauntered arm in arm, seemingly happy to chat with Genie and Dick. The four of them weren't even halfway down when Kitty reached the pier. She called out to two passing soldiers, who stopped and waited for her. She said something and the soldiers laughed, and then she made a great show of straightening the taller one's collar, leaning in very close. Her smile became wide and dazzling as her hands dropped to his chest and lingered. Then she looked up the gangway at Mr. Pelton, her smile all teeth.

Nervously, Genie glanced at the man beside her. It was clear the blonde was trying to bait him, yet there was no rancor in his expression. In fact quite the opposite. She would swear he was on the verge of laughter.

"You're not upset with her?"

"With Kitty? Not a bit." His voice was as relaxed as his posture. "Kitty can't help being . . . well, Kitty, any more than I can help being me. And right now, she's peeved because I won't come to heel like a well-trained lapdog."

His smile deepened as he watched Kitty spin away from the soldiers in a huff.

The bemused longing on the soldiers' faces after she left was almost comical. But it also gave Genie pause. First Nathan's tenderness with Lavinia, and now Kitty's effect on the soldiers. How was it those two women knew how to turn men into besotted slaves, whereas she hadn't a clue?

"Penny for your thoughts?"

Shoving aside her self-doubts, she managed a smile. "I'd save your money, Mr. Pelton. They're not even worth that much."

He winced. "Dick, please. 'Mr. Pelton' makes me feel positively ancient."

"You mean you're not?" she teased. To her surprise, he didn't smile at her joke. Instead shadows entered his eyes.

"Sometimes I wonder," he said quietly. "Sometimes a soul can see too much." Then he gave a rueful laugh. "But listen to me, spoiling a perfect day with a beautiful girl. A day already being cut short by said girl's heartlessness."

"I'm hardly being heartless. Honestly, you've already got me agreeing to more than I initially planned."

"True." He gave her a lopsided grin. "But that doesn't mean I can't try for more."

# Chapter 20

"So speaking of more," Dick said three hours later as they finished their lunch. "How about one more hour before we find you that newspaper and head back? There's another truly modern miracle you've yet to see: the department store."

"Oh, I don't think—"

"That you can pass up such a chance? You're right. You can't." Dick leaned his chair back and gave her a cheeky smile. "Besides, you're just getting started on your lessons in everyday Americana."

"To be honest, I don't know how much more I can absorb. Which is not to say I'm not grateful, because I am. Truly." She swirled a french fry in a dab of ketchup, both new foods to her and rapidly becoming her favorites. "It's so strange. A month ago, I thought I knew everything about the world. Everything I needed to, at least. But now I'm starting to think I'll never know enough."

"Traveling can do that to a person."

She sighed and drew a sharper pattern in the tomato condiment. "Do you think the war will go on much longer?"

"Well, considering the wrong side is winning at the moment, a speedy resolution might not be in anyone's best interest."

"Ted said we're losing ground in the Orient, that England is pulling out." She stabbed the french fry into her plate until it crumpled as she fought back sudden tears. *Lord, please let Ted be alive and safe.*

"Ted being . . . ?"

Wiping her fingers on a napkin, she drew a deep, steadying breath. "A friend of mine. He's a pilot with the AVG. You might have seen him. He was on the flight out of Burma, too."

"He was?" he asked, suddenly more alert.

"I'm surprised you didn't notice him. He came back and talked to me several times. He was on his way to Cairo to ferry a plane back to make up for the one he crashed not far from my village. Only he'll tell you it wasn't a crash but a forced landing." The memory of how emphatic he had been on that point made her smile. "He's actually the reason I'm here in Cape Town. My father was looking for a way to get me to safety, and then the Good Lord dropped a Flying Tiger in his lap. Almost literally."

"Does your tiger have a last name?"

"Yoo-nen." She sounded it out. "It's Turkish. His family moved to the United States when he was young."

"And now he's fighting to defend his adopted country." Dick stroked his jaw thoughtfully. "That has real possibilities. An American immigrant saving an American missionary from a war-torn country. There's an interesting symmetry there."

"What are you talking about?"

He shot her a quick, reassuring smile. "Nothing. Just thinking out loud. Any idea if Ted is short for anything, like Edward or Theodore?"

"No, I'm sorry."

He waved away her apology. "Nothing to be sorry about. Ready to continue your education?"

Once again, she tried to demur, and once again, she found herself giving in. In truth, the department store, which had more clothes and goods displayed than she had seen in her entire life, was worth seeing, as were the moving stairs Dick called escalators. He also used the time to continue her lessons on American slang. She couldn't wait to go over it all with Lavinia, though perhaps it wouldn't be as useful for a missionary wife.

The weather was so beautiful when they left the department store, Dick had no difficulty convincing her to take one more side trip, this time to a city park. After almost two weeks aboard a ship, she loved being surrounded by the rich, earthy aroma of trees and plants.

"Hard to believe we're in the midst of a world war when surrounded by such tranquility, isn't it?" he mused as they strolled past flowering shrubs and manicured lawns. He tipped his hat back to catch more of the sun on his face. "A man could get used to it."

"It's so odd. In my village, we never would've known there was a war going on if not for Wu Fang's radio. Everything was so very peaceful."

"I know what you mean. I was in Borneo, scouting locations for a film, when Pearl Harbor was attacked. I had just rolled into the hotel after a day of gorgeous scenery, when the freighter boys—Dutch freighters—asked if I had heard the news: America had joined the war! I didn't believe it at first, and then I did, and my heart sank."

"Why?"

He was quiet a moment as he pulled a nut out of the bag they had bought and tossed it toward a pair of inquisitive squirrels. "When you were in China, did you by any chance see any of the cities that got bombed?"

"Only Kunming. My father stopped letting me travel with him when I was ten."

He turned to study her. "How old are you now?"

"Twenty-two."

"You're very honest," he said with a small smile. "Most women I know wouldn't answer so readily."

Her cheeks heated. "Lying, even by omission, is still a sin. At least in my book."

Something flickered in his eyes, and he turned back to the squirrels, fishing out another nut. "In answer to your question, I'd seen too much carnage in Europe already. Photographed it for newspapers. Filmed it for newsreels. Lived it firsthand. I wouldn't wish it on my worst enemy, let alone a fellow American."

"Wait, I thought you worked in Hollywood."

"I do, but I also like to travel, hence the news work." He gestured toward an official-looking cream-and-white stone building at the end of the avenue. "Want to try the museum?"

She noted the lengthening shadows and shook her head. "It's getting late. I really should be getting back."

"All right." He tossed the empty bag aside. "Let's go."

"No argument this time?" she asked, a little shocked.

"Nope. I figure we've been out long enough for a first date."

"First date?"

"I'm teasing, Red." He cocked his head as if at a sudden thought. "You don't happen to have a photograph of you and your pilot friend, do you?"

"I only wish. Though there was a photographer at the dinner in Kunming, where the Chiangs thanked Nathan and me for saving Ted's life, which was ridiculous, since he was never in any real danger."

"Wait. By the Chiangs, do you by any chance mean General Chiang Kai-shek and his wife?"

"Yes, why?"

He shook his head in wonder. "Unbelievable. This just keeps getting better and better. Do me a favor, will you? When you get back to the ship, write it all down for me. I know several newspaper editors who would give their right . . . er, arms to run this kind of feel-good story."

"Oh, I don't think—"

"Don't get shy on me. The American public is starved for good news right now, and it doesn't get much better than this! One of our boys, a Flying Tiger no less, risking his life to save one of our own. It's an editor's dream. And think how proud Ted's friends and family will be to hear of his heroics. And his girl, too! She'll be flying on cloud nine, the envy of all the other gals."

"Of course. His girl." Why had she never considered that fact before? Of course Ted had a girl back home. He was too handsome and nice and at ease around women not to. And it would explain why he was so good at kissing. And why he hadn't wanted her to write him.

Her chest started to hurt. She had been so stupid.

"So is it a deal?" Dick asked. "I could write the copy and have you proof it. We can work on it tonight, and then I'll wire it off before we leave port tomorrow."

"Um . . . all right," she said, the ache around her heart turning into outright pain as she pictured Ted's girl. She would be beautiful and poised, with shorter dresses and curled hair, like Kitty or Bess. Someone who wasn't her.

Dick peered at her in concern. "Are you okay?"

"Fine," she said, almost choking on the lie. And here Dick thought she was so honest. What a laugh. She'd been lying to herself since the very first moment she had laid eyes on Ted and hadn't realized it until now. All those fantasies she had built around him because he was her first kiss, her first infatuation, her first everything. But she wasn't his first. He had a whole other life, reducing her to nothing but an asterisk. A footnote. Perhaps not even that.

*No wonder he pushed me away.*

"Genie, we don't have to do the story if—"

"No, it's fine. You're right, I should think of Ted and how proud his family would be. And his girl."

"Are you sure?"

She summoned a smile despite the bleeding hole where her dreams used to be. Dick had been nothing but kind to her all day. Letting him publish the story seemed inadequate payment for all she had seen and experienced today. If she was in pain now, she had no one to blame but herself. "I'm sure."

"Well, well!" An unfamiliar man's voice echoed down the path. "Look who we meet outside the museum. Is it too late to run away?"

"Larry!" Dick grinned at the man who was strolling up the sidewalk with Kitty and Bess on his arms. "No need to bolt. We're actually on our way back to the ship, so Cape Town's museums are safe from you three for another day."

"Excellent. Mind if we join you? It's past time for my afternoon cocktail, and I'd just as soon drink on board as try to navigate that gangway later."

"I also think he's out of money," Bess whispered, and Genie could believe it, judging by the slew of bags hanging from his wife's arm.

"Oh, come now," Dick said with a laugh. "He still has a shirt on his back. He's gotta be good for a few more guilders."

"What are you saying?" Larry said in mock horror. "I thought we were friends, Pelton!"

Dick shrugged. "You know I can't stand to see a damsel in distress, and Bess here looks so sad." He chucked her affectionately under the chin. "Surely one more bangle won't break the bank."

Larry frowned. "No, but it might sink the ship. You have no idea all the packages that are already stowed aboard. I doubt there's a pair of shoes left untried in all of Cape Town."

"You poor man," Dick said with feeling, even as Bess smiled sweetly.

Kitty rolled her eyes. "Are we through here?"

"We are," he said, slinging his arm around Kitty's narrow shoulders and pulling her close. He bestowed a quick kiss on her cheek, earning a grimace from the woman, but she didn't pull away. "Say, do any of you happen to have a camera along? I'd like to snap off one or two pictures before the light gets any worse, and in return I'll pay for processing the whole thing."

"I might," Bess said, stopping to rummage through her bags. "Larry, did we finish the roll down on Sea Point?"

"No idea, but the crank still turned, so I bet Dick could squeeze another couple on there."

Bess pulled a smallish black-and-silver box out of one of the bags with a flourish and held it up. "Ta-da. One camera, as requested."

Dick took it from her. "Holy smokes. A Leica, no less. Excellent."

Genie stared as he turned it over in his hands. "That's a camera? It's so small."

"Small, perhaps, but with some of the finest optics in the world. It's also manufactured in Germany and currently unavailable in the US. Wherever did you get this, Bess?"

Bess shrugged. "Howie gave it to me for Christmas."

"Good man. I wonder if he got it through some backdoor diplomatic channel." Dick began checking various dials on the camera and peered through a part of it. "I heard Leica sent a lot of their employees out of the country ahead of the border closing in '39, most of them Jews. I wonder if one of them sought asylum through his office."

"I wouldn't know. Howie never talked shop when he was home."

"No, I suppose not. Say, do you have any more film? Just in case."

"Aboard the ship."

"I may need it later. Come over here, Genie, and let me see if I can use the park as a background."

"Wait, you're going to take a picture of me?"

He peered over the top of the camera at her, his dark eyebrows arched in bemusement. "That was kind of the point of my borrowing Bess's camera."

"Oh no. Don't." She backed away, horribly aware of how unfashionable she looked next to Kitty and Bess.

"Genie, a story like this needs a photo to do it justice. And you'll look just fine. Trust me. Taking people's photos is what I do for a living."

"But my dress . . ."

"Is exactly what the public would expect a missionary girl to wear."
He took her hand and pulled her around to face the sun. "Kitty, Bess,
do you want in the photo, too? It wouldn't hurt to add a famous socialite and wife of a diplomat to the portrait of our intrepid heroine."

Kitty studied the polish on her fingernails. "I'll pass."

Larry gave Bess a little push. "Go on. Here's your chance to get
your picture in the papers."

"But I don't have any connection to the story," Bess said with a
frown as she came up beside Genie.

"I'll say you're keeping her company on the voyage home." Dick
raised the camera to his face.

"Wait, what about Larry?" Genie asked. "Shouldn't he join us?"

Kitty burst into laughter. "Oh, please do, Larry. And make sure to
have your arm around Mrs. Whitcomb for good measure."

"That's not funny, Kitty," Larry said coolly.

"But the irony is so delicious. A sweet, innocent missionary girl
and . . . well, us." Kitty's blue eyes glittered as she swept her hand to
include the other three Americans.

"Stow it, Kitty," Dick said, his voice taking on an angry edge. To
Genie's surprise, Kitty bit her lip and turned slightly away, as if hurt.

"Maybe taking a photograph isn't a good idea," Genie said cau-
tiously, still not quite sure what had just happened.

"Nonsense," Dick said, back to his normal cheerful self. "I know
you want to get back, but all I need is one measly photograph. One
snap, and it'll be over before you know it." He raised the camera to his
face again. "Smile, girls!"

Bess slid her arm around Genie's waist and gave her an encourag-
ing squeeze as the shutter clicked.

"Excellent." Dick wound a little lever on the top and then raised
the camera again. "And one more for good measure."

Another click, another wind of the lever. Genie's cheeks ached
from holding her smile.

"And that feels like the end of the roll," Dick said with a satisfied smile, looping the camera strap around his neck. "Can you kids get Genie back to the ship for me? I want to get this roll developed today, or by tomorrow morning at the very latest."

"Sure," Larry said as Bess came back to link her arm through his. "Cutting it kind of close, though, aren't you? We're scheduled to sail at noon tomorrow."

"Got it covered." Dick caught Genie around the shoulders and pulled her close enough for her to smell the not-unpleasant musk of his sweat beneath his cologne. Then he released her. "And don't worry; I haven't forgotten that you want a paper. I'll pick one up and give it to you when we meet later to go over that copy."

# Chapter 21

Starving for breakfast and nearly out of time before the galley closed, Genie clattered down the outer deck stairs as fast as she dared. She had stayed up way too late poring over the newspaper—the one Dick had brought her in exchange for the hopelessly boring story she had written on her meeting Ted and the Chiangs—and had completely overslept. Not that she had gotten much rest for all that, for the news reports from Burma had been troubling, with Japanese and Chinese forces massing on either end of the country, preparing for all-out battle.

One short article had mentioned an air fight for control of the skies over Burma and that the Allied side had been victorious despite being horribly outnumbered, but there was no description of the casualty rate or who had taken part, except for a mention of the planes: Hurricanes and Tomahawks. She didn't know a lot about airplanes, but she could've sworn the Tomahawk was the kind of plane the AVG flew.

Her stomach growled as she spun on the landing, heading toward the next set of steps. She almost ran over the top of someone in the process. Two people, in fact, who were coming the other way. To her surprise, one of them was Lavinia.

She grabbed the railing to catch her balance. "Oh heavens! Sorry, Lavinia."

She turned to Lavinia's companion and blinked in surprise. It was Kitty, with a cigarette in hand and a silent dare in the arch of her perfectly drawn eyebrows. Genie's hand reflexively tightened on the stairs' handrail.

"Kitty?" Genie glanced between the two women, her stomach sinking at the slow realization that Lavinia and Kitty were not in the same place by unhappy accident. They had been walking together.

Oh no, no, no. It was bad enough that she had to tolerate the blonde's presence when she was with Dick. She really didn't want to share Lavinia, too.

*Be nice, Genie. We are all the Lord's children.*

"Genie." Lavinia looked startled. Then she smiled brightly. "Have you met Miss Van Nuys?"

"I have, but only in passing." She stuck out a hand and pasted on a smile for Lavinia's sake. "I'm Eugenia Baker, but call me Genie."

Kitty exhaled a stream of smoke to the side and flicked an ash from her cigarette onto the deck. "Miss Baker, how nice to see you again."

*So that's how it's going to be,* Genie thought, letting her hand drop to her side. *And to think I'm risking starvation for this* . . . "I didn't have a chance to thank you for your help yesterday. So thank you."

Kitty eyed her coolly. "It seemed the least I could do, since you're helping Dickie."

Lavinia's brow puckered as she looked from Kitty to Genie and back. "What are you two talking about?"

"I didn't get a chance to tell you last night, but it turns out I needed to have my ticket in addition to my passport to get back on board. Which wasn't your fault," Genie added quickly when her friend paled. "I didn't think of it, either. I mean, how were we to know? In any case, they weren't letting anyone on without a ticket, so my only option was to have someone run aboard and look for Nathan—you can imagine how keen I was on that idea."

"Or else be vouched for by someone who had a ticket. Someone who could sway the soldiers' minds." A slight smile curved Kitty's red lips as she flicked another ash. "Namely me."

"Yes." Genie's smile faded. The whole episode had left a horrid taste. Watching Kitty blur the young men's minds with lust for a second time had been depressing enough. When she found out later that what they had done wasn't just against the rules but had been outright illegal and that the soldiers would be court-martialed if anyone found out, she had nearly thrown up.

"How lucky for you, Genie," Lavinia said, eyes wide in honest concern. Then she turned to Kitty, her expression softening. "And thank you for helping her. I had totally forgotten about the ticket."

Something flickered behind the blonde's cool facade. "I did it for Dickie, but you're welcome. And honestly, I didn't remember, either."

"Wait, you both were in on getting me ashore?" To her surprise, a feeling very like jealousy pricked Genie.

"I asked her for advice after Nathan turned out to be more stubborn than expected," Lavinia said, the concern coming back into her eyes. "But she won't tell anyone, if that's what you're worried about."

Genie shot a look at Kitty, who merely raised an eyebrow, daring her to question Lavinia's claim. With an effort, she tamped down on her irritation. "I guess I didn't realize you two were friends."

"We met not long after the ship left port. She was the one who suggested I might cut my hair to be more fashionable." Lavinia's face brightened as she continued, "Did you know she designs clothes to be sold in her father's department stores? That's why she was in India—to find inspiration for next year's swimming suits. Which is how we got to the subject of women knowing how to swim and, in particular, how you never learned. Can you believe it? She offered to loan us a couple of suits so I could teach you!"

An utterly different emotion gripped Genie. "Wait, I never said I wanted to learn."

Lavinia started to frown. "Don't you want to? Think of all the fun we could have. Whenever we're bored, we could go to the pool instead of attending another Bible study or hymn sing."

"I'd rather take up cards."

"Genie, I'm serious." Her friend's chin took on a familiar stubborn tilt. "It's dangerous to be on a boat if you don't know how to swim. You're going to learn, and that's final."

"Learn what?" Nathan asked suddenly from behind Genie, making her jump.

"To play deck tennis," Lavinia said without missing a beat. "Miss Van Nuys was just inviting us to play in a friendly tournament. Oh! I'm sorry. Have you two met? Nathan, this is Miss Van Nuys—"

"Call me Kitty," she said, holding out a gloved hand.

Nathan hesitated and then shook it. "Kitty."

"Nathan is my fiancé," Lavinia continued.

"You're a lucky man," Kitty purred in a husky voice.

Nathan cleared his throat and released her hand. "Er . . . thank you. I agree."

"Well, I must be off. I'll see you all later." Kitty's cool gaze rested on Lavinia for the barest of seconds before she turned away.

"Eugenia," Nathan said after Kitty had left, "I've been looking all over for you. I wanted to apologize. You were right; your father would have wanted you to experience Cape Town. There's not much time left before we leave port, but if you'd like to go down to the dock and at least have a look around, I'd be happy to accompany you."

Disbelief and anger left her momentarily speechless. "My, how . . . generous of you."

"Not at all," he said, completely missing her sarcasm, which didn't surprise her. His ego was a fortress, unassailable. "Besides, it'll give us a chance to talk. I feel like our relationship has become strained over the course of the trip, unnecessarily so, and I think it's high time we worked on repairing it. We have less than a month before we reach the States and I deliver you to your aunt, a transition that will go much more smoothly if we're on friendlier terms. Don't you agree?"

She briefly closed her eyes as she struggled for composure. A good person, perhaps a better person than she, would accept the olive branch he was extending, no matter how delayed or stunted or pathetic. Nor could she refuse to go after making such a fuss yesterday. Not without arousing suspicion.

And much more important, her father would demand she accept it. "Fine. When would you like to go?"

"Now, if you'd like. Lavinia, darling, would you like to come with us?"

"No, thank you. Now that we have plenty of water again, I'd like to wash my hair." Her friend edged backward, and Genie narrowed her eyes as Lavinia's gaze flicked in the direction of Kitty's departure. Or maybe not. It could all be in her imagination. "I'll see you two later."

"Lavinia said you had some letters you wanted to mail?" Nathan asked, pulling her attention back to the matter at hand.

"I already sent them with someone else." Which was close to the truth, if not true exactly.

"Oh. Good." He seemed at a loss as to what else to say. Gesturing for her to lead the way, he waited until she moved before falling beside her. A strained silence fell between them as they descended the stairs to the deck with the gangway.

Finally, she couldn't stand it any longer. "It looks like you and Lavinia are getting along," she said as a kind of peace offering.

His shoulders relaxed as he smiled. "Oh, Genie. I never thought I could be so happy. She's like a miracle, a gift from heaven. We see eye to eye on so many things."

Genie rather doubted that. More likely her friend was only telling Nathan whatever he wanted to hear. And while it wasn't her place to criticize her friend's strategy, it did leave her uneasy. In her mind, marriages should be built on honesty. "So when's the happy day?"

"Not for a while yet. I want to ask her father's permission first, when we go to visit him."

Alarm shot through her, and she almost missed the next step. "Does she know this?"

"Yes and no. We've discussed the matter, but I haven't told her my final decision. Truth be told, she was being rather unreasonable about the whole thing." He glanced at her. "Has she said anything about it to you?"

"Only that she has no desire to return home."

"Yes, well, I think that's patently ridiculous. Family is one of the Lord's sacred institutions. Whatever her misgivings, we will overcome them."

"You might want to tell her," she said carefully. *Especially since avoiding her father was the only reason she agreed to marry you.*

"If the need arises. Otherwise, it is my decision to make, and I would ask that you not upset her unnecessarily."

She stopped at the top of the gangway. "You're asking me to lie?"

He stopped as well. "No, I'm asking you to not bring it up."

"And are there things you tell her not to bring up with me?" she asked, her temper sparking. "Decisions about my future that you feel I'm better off not knowing?"

"Of course not. I think we've always been perfectly frank with each other."

"But you won't extend that same courtesy to your future wife?"

He hesitated. "My relationship with Lavinia is different."

"For which I'm eternally grateful. I would hate being lied to, especially by someone who professed to love me."

Anger flashed in his eyes. "You're awfully quick to judge, considering."

"Considering what?"

"Do you really think your father told you everything? Hardly."

"What don't I know, Nathan? You've told me about my aunt and about his wanting us married. What else is there?"

"Nothing." He took a deep breath as if reining in his temper and gestured toward the gangway. "Shall we?"

So much for improving their relationship. She hesitated, debating whether to press him on what her father hadn't told her. Then she decided he wouldn't tell her anyway, so she stalked onto the swaying platform, her gaze firmly on the soldiers at the end and not on the foaming water below. They were checking documents of people waiting to get on the ship. A whole long line of people carrying suitcases. More people fleeing the war. Where they were going to stay on the already crowded ship, she had no idea.

As she got closer, she recognized the soldiers as the ones she had talked to last night. For an instant she was overjoyed to see them, because it meant they hadn't been court-martialed. Then the other shoe dropped, and her heart stuttered. They were likely going to recognize her, too. And say something. Which meant Nathan would find out she hadn't stayed on the ship yesterday.

She immediately reversed direction. It wasn't that she was afraid of his reaction to the news, but of her own. Her self-control was too frayed to deal with another one of his temper tantrums.

Nathan caught her. "Where are you going?"

"I've changed my mind. A few minutes walking on the pier isn't worth my missing breakfast."

He refused to let her go. "This is your one and only chance. If you head back now, I'm not asking again."

She shook off his hand. "Don't worry."

"And you have to tell Lavinia that this was your fault, not mine. I won't have her angry at me because of your intemperance."

She stilled, suddenly putting two and two together. "This wasn't your idea, was it? This whole 'take Genie ashore and repair our relationship' thing. That was Lavinia's suggestion, wasn't it? Only you're getting around to it a day late, and now you're trying to appease her."

"There is no appeasement necessary," he said stiffly. Then he added, "All the same, you will tell her?"

Deliberately, coldly, she turned away from him without answering and ran up the gangway. Even though her appetite had fled, she headed toward the galley. Whirling around the stairway corner, she almost ran smack into Dick.

"Hello, again," he said, catching her by the arms to steady her. "I was hoping to see you at breakfast, but you weren't there. Are you all right?"

"Fine. In fact, that's where I'm headed now. I got a late start is all."

"Then I'd best not keep you. You've got ten minutes." He edged past her, turning the whole time to keep talking. "And I've got to hurry if I want to wire the story before the ship sails. By the way, the photo turned out spectacularly, in case you wondered."

"Wait, did you need me to look at—"

"No time. I'll show you the final copy when I get back. I will see you, won't I?"

"Why wouldn't you? It's not like I'll be anywhere but on the ship."

"Good, because there's something else I want to show you, something I think you're going to like."

"Like what?" she asked a little warily, hoping she hadn't given him the wrong impression yesterday.

"Don't worry," he teased. "What I want to show you are magazines. Lots and lots of them. You said you wanted to learn more about American culture, and here's your chance. A whole stack of *Life* magazines, chock full of ads and photographs, all for your enjoyment. And some newspapers, too, in case yesterday's wasn't enough."

She threw aside any thoughts of impropriety. The chance to learn more about the war that was threatening her home and everyone she loved overrode everything else. "I would like that. Thank you."

He winked at her. "Thought so. Now if you see Kitty, tell her I'll be back shortly."

Ah, yes, Kitty. Genie would have preferred not to talk to the woman at all, but she would for Dick's sake. "All right."

Dick frowned, reversed directions, and came back to her. "What's wrong?"

"Nothing." She rubbed her arms, chilled by a sudden breeze. "I don't think Kitty likes me much. Though she seems to like Lavinia just fine. She's even loaning us swimsuits so Lavinia can teach me to swim. Not that I want to learn."

"Everyone should learn, but now might not be the best time. The pool is pretty cold. It might be better to wait another week or so, until we're closer to the equator. The nights won't cool off the water quite so much." He paused. "And you said something about Kitty and Mrs. Schmidt?"

"Apparently they're best of friends now." She tried to keep the jealousy out of her voice, but she kept seeing the open admiration in her friend's face. "I didn't even know they knew each other."

"How odd. Kitty usually doesn't associate with . . . unless? No. Though being a missionary doesn't necessarily preclude . . . But still, it would be unusual." He seemed to have forgotten she was still standing there.

"What are you talking about?"

Surprise flickered in his hazel eyes as he registered her question, and she realized she'd been right. He had forgotten her.

"Never mind." She turned away, her spirits plummeting. "I'd better get up to the galley. If I see Kitty, I'll let her know."

He stopped her with a gentle touch on her arm. "Genie, what's wrong?"

"Nothing. Truly. I'm just not myself today."

He gave her shoulder a gentle squeeze. "Go get some breakfast, and we'll talk more when I get back, all right? I've got to run now, but no more moping about. You hear? Think about the pile of magazines just waiting for you."

"All right," she said, managing a small smile.

"I'll see you soon." After one last reassuring shoulder squeeze, he was gone.

# Chapter 22

"Today is the day!" Lavinia exclaimed as she entered the cabin. "You've managed to put me off for three weeks, but not this time! The weather is perfect, and Nathan's busy until noon."

A scrap of floral fabric plopped on top of the glossy photo spread of New York City. Genie pushed it to the side and kept studying the pictures, trying to glean as much information about American culture as she could. They would be docking in less than a week, and she didn't feel at all prepared.

The fabric reappeared, this time separating itself into two separate scraps. "Come on. Time's a-wastin'."

With a slow dawning of horror, Genie looked up from the magazine. "Tell me that's not a swimsuit."

"It is, and Miss Van Nuys apologizes, but that's the only one she thinks will fit you, because you're so long-waisted."

"I won't even pretend to know what that means, especially since it doesn't matter. I'm not learning to swim."

"Then just come in the pool with me."

"No."

Her friend's blue eyes took on a determined glint. "Either put that swimsuit on, or I tell Nathan you've been spending several hours a day in Mr. Pelton's cabin, alone with the man. Unchaperoned."

"You wouldn't. For heaven's sake, most of the time he isn't even there. And even when he is, we aren't doing anything. We're just friends."

"Do you really think Nathan will believe that?"

Genie growled in frustration because, no, Nathan wouldn't. He would believe the absolute worst of her, and he'd make sure everyone else did, too. "Fine. I'll do it."

Two minutes later, she almost reversed her position on the matter. The swimsuit Kitty had chosen for her bared not only her arms and legs but also her midriff. Granted only two inches of it, but she might as well be walking about in her underwear. "Kitty hates me."

"She does not." Lavinia finished tying the belt on her terry-cloth robe. "If she did, she wouldn't have loaned you a suit at all."

"But look at me. I can't go out like this. I think I'd rather drown."

"Genie . . ." Lavinia touched her arm, her fingers cool, her blue eyes beseeching. "I know you're afraid. But we can't let our fears stop us. I know, because every day I make myself get out of bed and face the world, no matter how bleak or frightened I feel. And while I do it partly for Nathan, mostly it's for you. Because you stood beside me when even my own brother would have turned away. Your friendship gave me hope."

"And yours has cheered me greatly, but that doesn't mean I'll swim for you." And if that made her a coward, so be it. Then she added, out of fairness, "And your brother does love you."

Lavinia waved the correction away. "Nevertheless, if anything happens to the ship, and you were to drown, I would never forgive myself. So, for me, will you please be brave and at least try?"

Genie hesitated, terror warring with friendship. "Fine. I'll try."

Her friend beamed. "Thank you. There's a robe there on the bunk, and I've got towels."

Already regretting her decision, Genie slowly followed her friend out into the passageway and then out onto the stairs leading to the lido deck. She had hoped to put off this day indefinitely. Following Dick's advice, she had first tried to convince Lavinia to wait until they reached the equator before trying to teach her to swim. That she might do better if the water was warmer. Lavinia had flatly disagreed and had roused Genie early the day after they had left Cape Town . . . only to find the pool closed on account of the weather. Genie had never been so thankful.

The rough seas and rain had continued for another week, and then she was able to plead off one more week due to her cycle. These last few days, she had tried to avoid the issue by just plain hiding from her friend—not the most respectable of activities, but she had been desperate. Unfortunately, Lavinia was particularly tenacious.

Despite it being so early in the day—not even 10:00 a.m.—there were entirely too many people lounging around the pool for Genie's comfort. She drew a deep breath and glanced up into the cloudless azure sky. Lavinia was right; it was a beautiful day. And also one that was likely to cause a different sort of problem for her, besides the whole drowning problem.

Against her better judgment, she would be exposing parts of her body that had never seen a glint of sunlight, and if her face and arms were any indication, those parts would soon be bright red. Unlike the lithe golden creatures stretched out on towels around her, she didn't tan. She burned and then freckled.

Pale was her preferred state. Pale was something she was actually good at. Pale was a valued quality in China, where women went to great lengths to stay out of the sun. So why was she about to risk losing all that now?

"Ready?" Lavinia said, sounding entirely too cheerful.

Genie eyed the ship's glimmering swimming pool as if it were a banded krait: beautiful and deadly and ready to strike if one got too close.

"Don't look so terrified," Lavinia scolded softly. "When has water ever hurt you?"

"When I was eight, our last summer in Hankow, a ferryboat capsized on the Yangtze River. My father and I were nearby when we heard the shouts. My father helped haul as many people as he could out of the water, but many didn't make it." She shuddered, remembering the pale and sightless eyes of the drowned who had also been pulled out.

"That's dreadful! But perhaps many of those people died because they didn't know how to swim. They might still be alive today, if only someone had taught them."

"Or one could just avoid boats."

Lavinia rolled her eyes. "What are we on, Genie?"

"I try not to think about it."

"And what about yesterday, when someone thought they had spotted a submarine trailing us, and the whole crew went to battle stations? What if it hadn't been a false alarm? Miss Van Nuys says we're entering some of the most dangerous waters in the Atlantic, because we're nearing the States."

"Miss Van Nuys could be wrong."

That earned her a sharp look, but honestly, she was tired of hearing Miss Van Nuys this and Miss Van Nuys that. It was bad enough that her friend kept disappearing with Kitty for hours on end, leaving Genie bored and lonely. It also meant she had the unpleasant task of placating an irritated Nathan when he stopped her, looking for his fiancée. Having to listen to her friend go on and on about every little thing the blonde said each day positively set her teeth on edge.

"Oh look! There she is," Lavinia said, the warmth in her voice leaving no doubt as to who *she* was. "And your friend Mr. Pelton, too."

Genie's lungs froze as she spotted Dick's sun-streaked hair and familiar build on the other side of the pool. She swallowed a sudden surge of panic. Baring herself to strangers she had more or less come to terms with, but she hadn't considered his being here. For some reason that made the whole situation much, much worse.

Sure, she and Dick had been spending a lot of time together, but she didn't let herself think anything of it. He was interesting because he had seen so much of the world. And he was easy to talk to as well as being easy on the eyes. But he was also older, more worldly, and something of a flirt. So while his interest in her was flattering, she had learned her lesson with Ted: just because a man was nice to her didn't mean he wanted her affections in return. And if her pulse leaped a tiny bit every time Dick smiled, every time he touched her, she knew better than to take it seriously.

She pressed her hand to her chest to ease a sudden tightness. "Did you tell him I was coming?"

"No." Lavinia frowned irritably at her. "Why would I?"

She sneaked another glance across the pool. Dick stood with his back to her, talking to Larry and Bess, who both sat in chairs, swimsuits on, ready to sunbathe. He laughed and something twisted inside her. "I don't think I can do this."

"Nonsense. We've put this off long enough." Lavinia grabbed her arm and dragged her resolutely toward the pool. "I won't have your death on my head, not when we can do something to prevent it."

"What about Nathan—does he know how to swim?"

"Don't change the subject. We're talking about you, not Nathan." She stopped by some abandoned deck chairs and draped two towels across them. "Ready?"

"No."

Lavinia sighed. "It won't be that bad. Promise. And don't forget: I'm going to be just as exposed as you. But then so is every other woman out here this morning, and they haven't been struck down by the Lord for indecency."

"At least you got the one-piece suit," Genie groused as her fingers fumbled with the knot on the belt. A decidedly light-headed sensation ~~~~ ~ ~~~ ~~~ She couldn't believe she was actually doing this.

ng a pretty suit in a blue-
breath. *In for a penny, in*
rection, she did the same.
her bare skin as she turned

ie's arm. "We're going to
n, and put our feet in the

not risking Nathan's wrath
finitely going all the way in

—"

tty said, interrupting Genie
d like a model for *Harper's*
ite outfit that showed off the
a spurt of envy.
nost purring as she gave them
can see how they fit in the
back." Then she said, ~~~~ ttle small on you, Miss Baker. But you, Nia, you look positively divine."

Nia? Genie glanced at her friend, only to find Kitty adjusting Lavinia's swimsuit. As Genie watched in uneasy fascination, Kitty slid her fingers under the fabric straps and then slowly smoothed them back over Lavinia's shoulders. Lavinia flushed and looked away as if embarrassed. For an uncomfortable second, Genie wondered if she should intervene, though on what grounds she wasn't quite sure.

Kitty gave Lavinia's suit one last tug before stepping away. "Go try them out in the pool. See what you think."

As if released from a spell, Lavinia sprang into motion and grabbed Genie's hand. "Come on. No backing out now."

"Wait . . ." The wind teased her bare skin, making her shiver despite the hot sun.

"Feet in the water, Genie," Lavinia ordered.

*It's no different from taking a bath. Stop stalling.* Obediently, she sat down on the concrete edge of the pool and then, after another moment of hesitation, slipped her feet calf-deep into the pool. The icy bite of the water made her gasp.

"It may feel cold now, but you'll get used to it quick enough," Dick said from close beside her, making her start. She hadn't noticed him come up. "Hi, Lavinia," he said over her head. "Teaching our girl to swim at last?"

"If she'll let me."

"Of course she will." Dick clapped Genie on the back. "Our girl here isn't a coward."

She slid him a look even as her skin sizzled from his touch. "How do you know?"

His expression turned serious. "Would you feel better if I joined you? It'll only take me a moment to get changed."

"No!" She winced as her voice echoed around the deck, drawing looks from the sunbathers. Still, the prospect of trying not to drown with a half-naked Dick in the pool beside her, distracting her, perhaps moving close enough to touch . . . She took a deep breath to quiet the flutterings in her stomach. "I'll do better on my own."

"You sure? I'm a good teacher." He winked at her as he stood.

"Excuse me," Lavinia said loudly, "but I can teach Genie just fine by myself, and I'd like to get started, since we don't have a lot of time."

He hesitated, his brow furrowing slightly. Then it smoothed. "Of course. Good luck."

Genie watched him walk away, around the edge of the pool, back toward Larry and Bess. Then she rounded on Lavinia. "That was rude."

"Was not. It's not like we need him. Anyway, you were correct—he'd just distract you." Lavinia pushed herself up and off the edge of the pool. She sank beneath the water and then resurfaced in a rush of water. She laughed, a bright, joyous sound as she paddled in the water, magically keeping her head above the surface. "Oh, how I've missed this. Come on in, Genie. It's not so bad once you're in."

"How—how are you doing that?"

"It's easy. And look . . ." She stopped moving, and her head dipped slightly. "It's only four feet deep, so you'll be able to touch the bottom whenever you want."

"Oh." Feeling foolish, she slid forward and dropped into the pool, not giving herself a chance to think. Her breath promptly left her as cold engulfed her, the water rushing up her nose and into her ears. Panicking, she thrashed against the suffocating pressure until her toes scraped painfully against concrete. Instinctively her feet pushed against the solidity of it, and her face cleared the surface. She gasped at the air desperately.

"Genie, stop trying to drown yourself and just stand!" Lavinia's exasperated voice cut through the haze of terror.

*Focus. You're not going to die. Believe.* Pulling herself together, she straightened her spine and concentrated on the feel of the pool bottom under her toes and the warm air on her face. She sucked in one breath, two. Her heart rate began to slow as the water pulled and pushed on her in gentle sways, warming by degrees.

"See? Nothing to it," Lavinia said cheerfully.

Genie experimented with a few tentative steps. It was a curious sensation, moving through the water. The water both resisted and supported, making her feel slightly buoyant.

"You ready to try floating?" Lavinia asked. "It's really easy."

Genie swished her arms experimentally under the surface. It took more muscle than she had expected, and much of her nervousness returned. "No, thanks."

Lavinia sighed and beckoned her with her hand. "You can't learn to swim if you don't know how to float. So come here."

She hesitated and then gave herself over to Lavinia's instruction. Soon she had learned to lean back in the water and to arch her back just so to keep her face out of the water. Or mostly out of it. She had almost caught the knack of it when two teenage boys dove into the pool and began swimming laps.

Every time they swam by, waves would splash over her face, and she would panic and slip below the surface. After several minutes of torture, where she swore half the pool water had ended up in her lungs, she began to lose patience with both the boys and herself. She *would* master this if it took all day, or week, or even the rest of the voyage.

"Do you want to take a break?" Lavinia asked after Genie resurfaced for what felt like the hundredth time. "We can always try again later."

Genie coughed and wiped the water from her eyes. "I'm not giving up until I can swim from one end of the pool to the other, like those fellows."

Lavinia gave her a dubious look. "All right, but let's keep it simple for now. Like with the dog paddle. It's easy and keeps your face out of the water."

"My face would be happy about that."

Lavinia laughed softly. "Fine. But be forewarned: it's tiring and slow."

And so the next lesson began. The boys, apparently wanting a break from trying to kill her, hauled themselves out of the water. Their skin, brown as nuts, sparkled with water. Perching on the edge of the pool, they proceeded to watch her and Lavinia with great interest.

She did her best to duplicate Lavinia's movements, but her ungainly paddling was nothing like what the boys had been doing. Worse, despite Lavinia's assurances, her face still slipped below the water, or at least her nose and mouth did. She was about to call it a day when a resounding boom thundered overhead. Startled, she promptly sank. She immediately reached for the bottom with her foot.

It wasn't there.

Panic flooded her veins as she flailed, trying to pull herself up to the surface. Her lungs burned with the need to breathe, but there was only water. It pressed in on all sides, heavy and immovable. Another muffled whump, and then an arm, muscular and warm, whipped around her waist. Seconds later her head was above water. She gasped in sweet lungfuls of air.

"I've got her." The deep bass reverberated in her bones as the man and her bobbed in the pool. The man began swimming, towing her toward the edge. Sounds returned in sharp detail: the small, percussive slaps of water, the excited exclamations of a woman nearby, the rasp of her own breath.

The edge of the pool appeared, and she lunged for it, the man releasing her just as she latched on.

Bess knelt down in front of her, her pretty brown eyes wide. "Are you all right, Genie? I'm so glad Larry noticed you were in trouble."

Genie wiped the water from her eyes and recognized her rescuer as Bess's husband. She didn't know if she was happy or disappointed it wasn't Dick. "Thank you."

"Not a problem," Larry said. He pushed himself up and out of the pool, water sluicing off his body. "But I think you're done for the day."

Lavinia swam up just as Larry was reaching down and hauling Genie out of the water. "What happened?"

Genie shivered as a breeze cooled her wet skin. "I went under and couldn't find my footing."

"That's because you were in the deep end," Larry said, accepting a towel from Bess.

"Deep end?" she echoed hollowly.

Lavinia had the grace to look apologetic. "It only goes down to six feet. I didn't think it would be a problem. Another couple of seconds and you would've found the bottom on your own."

"What is going on here? Eugenia, is that you?" Nathan's shocked voice echoed across the lido deck.

Genie stiffened. For a brief second she considered plunging back into the water to escape him, but it was too late. Her appointed watchdog was already on his way over, his face white with anger. If only she could reach her robe, but it sat at the far end of the pool, along with her towel.

A soft splash came from where Lavinia had been holding on to the edge of the pool. Genie looked, but her friend had disappeared beneath the surface and was now a shadowy figure slipping silently away.

Genie bit her cheek in frustration. Once again, Lavinia was leaving her to face a furious Nathan alone. *So much for standing beside me in my time of need.* Next time she saw the widow, they were going to have a frank discussion about what it meant to be friends.

# Chapter 23

Genie winced as Nathan dragged her down the passageway, his fingers digging painfully into her upper arm. He flung open her cabin door and shoved her through.

"Stay here," he snarled, his face flushed and furious. "And change out of that . . . abomination. You and I are overdue for a discussion about the company you've been keeping, but after I find Lavinia. You haven't seen her, have you?"

Genie glared at him, tempted to tell him his fiancée was likely hiding in the cabin behind her. Instead, she rubbed her upper arm where his fingers had dug in—the ache telling her a bruise was already forming—and decided she wanted to deal with Lavinia first. "No," she said, stretching the truth only a little. "She's disappeared on me, too."

With a growl, he left and slammed the door after him.

"I'm so sorry," Lavinia said in a small voice. "He was supposed to be busy until lunchtime."

Genie whirled around. The widow stood between the bunks, fully dressed, her wet hair pulled back into a thick braid. One might never know she had been swimming not ten minutes before. Fury scalded Genie's veins as she stalked toward her duplicitous friend. Lavinia's eyes widened with uncertainty.

*You should be worried, traitor.*

Lavinia backed up a step. "He's never cut short his morning Bible study sessions before."

"How would you know?" Genie said shortly. "You're always with Kitty, leaving me to cover for you."

"Not always." Lavinia paused. "Does Nathan know I was with Kitty?"

Genie threw up her hands in exasperation. "Why would he care? My point is you are always abandoning me—like just now at the pool—and I'm sick of it."

"Does Nathan know?" Lavinia asked again, her voice rising in agitation.

"Forget Nathan, Lavinia. I'm talking about us, our friendship. Friends don't abandon friends in times of need."

Lavinia sank on to one of the lower bunks, her fingers digging into the bedding. "I'm sorry. I was distracted by the gun firing and didn't see you go under. Then Nathan showed up. I—I couldn't face him."

*So that's what that boom was, the deck gun.* It should have occurred to her sooner, since the crews had been having firing practice all week. Still . . .

"Did you really believe we could go swimming without him finding out?" Genie asked, all her irritation returning. "With all those people watching us?"

"It was a risk, but I was willing to take it, because I care about you. Because I don't want you to die." Lavinia's voice quavered as she said the last bit, and her thin face crumpled.

In a heartbeat, Genie's anger vanished. She knelt and hugged her friend as the girl began to cry. Sometimes it was so easy, here on the boat, to forget all the awful things the Lavinia had lived through, all the losses she had suffered in Burma and earlier.

"I'm not going to die. At least not anytime soon," she amended, not wanting to tempt fate with an untruth.

"Y-you don't understand," Lavinia sobbed. "You and Nathan are my only friends. If anything happens to either of you, or should Nathan decide not to marry me . . ."

"You'll be fine," Genie said, exasperation taking over again. "I know you don't want to go home, but surely your parents will let you stay with them a bit while you decide what to do. Or else one of your sisters or brothers? What about Marcus?"

"Marcus has washed his hands of me. He would never say so aloud, but I know he blames me for John's death and for the others', too. And it's not that I don't want to go home; I can't. My father has promised to kill me if do."

Genie privately doubted that. Even though Lavinia had claimed as much in the past, no father, at least in Genie's experience, would ever wish to harm his own child. Fathers might be distant, or busy, but she could never doubt that they loved their offspring. "Does Nathan know of your concerns?"

Lavinia shuddered delicately as she pulled away. "He knows I have no wish to go home."

Genie bit her lip, torn between wanting to warn her friend and the need to keep her word with Nathan. She went for a middle ground.

"I wonder if he knows the depth of your worries," she said carefully as she stood up. The swimsuit had become cold and clammy, reminding her she needed to get changed before Nathan returned. "I've noticed you are far more open with me than you are with him."

Her friend picked at the worn quilt covering the cot. "It's because I need him. I need this marriage. The Lord has given me another chance, and I'm not going to spoil it. As soon as we're married, everything will be fine." Her hand fisted the faded material.

"Lavinia, do you even love Nathan?"

"Love doesn't matter. Being able to eat, having a roof over one's head—those things matter."

"Yes, but you don't have to be married to have those things. We both know women can work to support themselves. The US can't be any different than China or Thailand in that respect."

"Work, sure. But I'd still need someplace to go home to at night, someone who's willing to support me until I can support myself." Lavinia jumped to her feet and began to pace the narrow aisle between the cots.

"So ask someone to help you. If not your family, what about friends, or families of the missionaries you worked with? Or even the Church itself? Good grief, Lavinia. What have we been doing all these years if not helping women in this exact situation? Are there no missions in America?"

Lavinia picked up Genie's discarded robe and began folding it.

Genie stopped dressing long enough to narrow her gaze at her friend. "Or is it that you're too proud to ask for charity?"

"No, not too proud," she said, staring at the robe in her arms. "Too different. No one will want me. Not for long."

Genie wanted to shake her. "If this is about that stupid curse, forget about it. We've been practically living in each other's pockets for the last month, and I've yet to see any sign of it."

Lavinia's eyes flashed. "Because I've not let you see it."

"Then maybe you should, because until you do, I refuse to believe it even exists. In fact, what kind of friendship do we have if you feel like you have to keep things hidden from me? If you keep lying to Nathan, what kind of marriage do you hope to have? You say you can't survive without us, but how important can we really be if you won't extend us the common courtesy of at least being honest once in a while?"

"You don't know what you're asking."

"I'm asking you to trust us with the truth. Or at least me, if no one else. And before you tell me I won't understand because I've nothing to lose, know that I'm just as alone as you are. My aunt, whom I've never met, let alone ever corresponded with, could be dead for all I know. And Nathan is not about to let me live with you two while I try to locate my mother's family. So if anyone is likely to end up on the street, it's me."

"Never." Lavinia looked stricken. "I would never allow that to happen to you."

Genie scoffed as she tucked her blouse into her skirt. "So you say now, because Nathan isn't here to gainsay you, but I know better. You would never stand up to him if he said no." She snatched the two halves of the damp swimsuit off the bunk. "I'm going to go return this."

"That's not true." Lavinia reached out and caught Genie's arm. "Who got you your passport so you could go into Cape Town?"

"By going behind his back and stealing it!"

"And putting my relationship with him at risk in the process. I haven't forgotten how you stood up for me in Calcutta and then helped me on the train. You think I'm exaggerating, I know, but truly you saved my life."

Genie shook her off. "Well, I'm done saving you if this is the thanks I get. From now on, if Nathan asks where you are, I'm going to tell him."

Lavinia stiffened. "You think you're any better at standing up for yourself? Tell me—who was prepared to stay aboard the ship that day in Cape Town because Nathan told her to? And what about today? Did you get to the end of the pool like you wanted? Like you swore you would before you quit for the day? Or did you once again give in because Nathan told you no?"

"I was done swimming, anyway. Nearly drowning can have that effect on people."

"You inhaled a little water. So what? You could have tried again. You were doing fine before they fired the deck gun. Or are you the type of girl who gives up after a little setback?"

"That is *not* fair. I didn't want to go swimming in the first place."

"And yet there you were," Lavinia said silkily.

Anger ripped through her as Lavinia's accusation hit its mark. "You know what I think? I think you should ask Nathan about his plans for when you two get to America. Then come talk to me about who stands up to whom."

Genie jerked the door open and then slammed it shut behind her, not waiting for a reply. Lavinia had some nerve, accusing her of having no backbone. Yes, she was on a ship bound for the US against her will, but she had come far since then. She was being the tree Li Ming had asked her to become. She was making her voice heard.

After all, had she not stood up to Nathan, refusing to marry him even though he and her father had both wished it? Had she not gone into Cape Town with Dick, even though Nathan had expressly forbidden it? Had she not sought out information on American culture without Nathan's approval, thus better preparing herself for her future?

*Yet whose voice was really being heard?* her mind whispered. *How many times did you tell Nathan you wouldn't marry him, but it never mattered, not until he had made up his own mind? And what about Cape Town? Would you have even gone if Lavinia hadn't helped you? Would you have thought to learn about the States if Dick hadn't suggested it?*

*And what about your oath today to make it across the pool?*

Genie thumped her fist on the wall in anguished frustration. "Stop it. Stop it!"

"Stop what?"

She gasped and whirled around. "Dick!"

He smiled faintly and ran his gaze up and down her. "Other than being mad at the wall, are you okay? After Bess's description of what happened at the pool, I was afraid I'd find you in pieces. In fact, I was just on my way to your cabin to see if you needed rescuing."

"No." She drew in a deep, shaky breath, trying for a calm she didn't feel. It was bad enough he had caught her acting like someone bound for the asylum. "Well, I might need rescuing from myself, but not from Nathan."

He stepped closer and gently brushed her jaw with the back of his knuckles. The tenderness in his touch made her want to cry. Her fight with Lavinia had left her so bruised.

He dropped his hand. "I'm glad you're okay. And I'm sorry I got you into trouble. When your escort asked me where you were, I didn't realize swimming was verboten."

She laughed weakly and wiped her eyes. "I don't think it was the swimming, per se, as much as the swimsuits."

His perfect eyebrows rose. "Really? You weren't dressed any differently than the other gals. You looked adorable and thoroughly American."

She gave another small laugh, but this time with a much lighter heart. "How did you know that's exactly what I needed to hear to feel better?"

"It's my special curse," he said with a wink.

*Curse.* Her lightened mood vanished as she thought of Lavinia. The need to make things right with her friend squeezed her chest. "I'll talk to you later."

He reached out as she turned to go and stopped her. "Genie, what's wrong? What did I say?"

She eyed the closed cabin door nervously. "It's not you. I yelled at Lavinia a moment ago and said some awful things. But she was right, and I need to apologize."

"As should I for ratting you gals out. How about we apologize together?"

She hesitated, not at all sure that what she wanted to tell Lavinia was anything she wanted Dick to hear. "I'd rather talk to her alone."

"Well, you'd better do it quick," he said, his gaze narrowing at something over her shoulder. "Because her fiancé appears to be coming this way."

"Oh heavens!" With a start, she grabbed Dick's arm and pulled him quickly down the passageway with her. Nathan was the absolute last person she wanted to talk to. Nervousness ate away at her as she and Dick strode down the narrow hall, sure she would hear Nathan calling after her any second now. Blue-painted light bulbs marked the distance . . . one, two, three.

At first she had thought blue lights pretty, until she found out they were only one of the many precautions the crew had taken to prevent enemy submarines from spotting them; the blue hue was apparently almost invisible at night. Their presence now only compounded her sense of danger.

"It was cowardly of me to leave Lavinia to face Nathan alone," she admitted as they neared a corner and freedom. "Though he never yells at her like he does me."

"I wouldn't beat yourself up too much about it. From what I've seen, Mrs. Schmidt handles her fiancé just fine. Practically has him eating out of her hand most of the time."

"Still, I feel like I should be there for her. On the other hand, if he started in on me again, I'm afraid I wouldn't be able to hold my tongue, which would only make things worse."

"I doubt you would say anything that wasn't justified."

His steps slowed once they were around the corner and out of sight. She let go of his arm, embarrassed she had held on to him as long as she had. Worse, she had a sudden urge to lean against his chest, to walk into his arms with the hope he would hold her tight, driving away all her doubts . . .

*Gah, Genie! Stop. He's not interested in you that way.*

Dick gestured to the damp swimsuit hanging forgotten in her hand. "Since you want to avoid Sterling, how about we go swimming for a bit? Let things settle down between the lovebirds before we apologize, and then we can all have lunch together."

Torn between worry for Lavinia and dread of having to deal with Nathan, Genie glanced back the way they had come. "I'd have to change first."

"There's a changing room by the pool you can use." A teasing smile curved his lips. "Come on. I was devastated to find I'd missed out on seeing you actually swim."

"Thrashing about, more like." Deciding discretion was the better part of valor, she turned toward the exit. "Where were you, anyway?"

"Getting my own suit. You were doing so well, I thought I'd join you."

She eyed his tan pants and white shirt. It was the same outfit he'd had on earlier.

"I left it with Larry and Bess," he said, answering her unspoken question. "I hadn't changed yet." He held out his arm. "Give me another chance to see poetry in motion?"

"More like a train wreck," she said with a grimace as she took his elbow. His arm felt wonderfully solid and steadying under her fingers, a sensation that comforted her perhaps a bit more than it should, given Lavinia's accusations just minutes ago. Nevertheless, she didn't let go. "Let's get changed. I wanted another chance to get across that pool anyway."

# Chapter 24

"I'm sorry we didn't get you swimming again. Kitty can get worked up about the damnedest things," Dick said as he pulled out a chair for her in the ship's bar. Besides the sailor in his light- and dark-blue enlisted man's uniform listlessly wiping down glasses from the night before, they were the only ones inside. Maybe it was her mood, but the remnants of the boat's luxury status—the wood paneling and mirrored shelves—gave the room a strange, haunted air. Like so much else in the world, the ship's grandeur had been reduced to a tattered shadow of itself by the war.

"Like I said before, I don't think Kitty likes me very much," she admitted, taking a seat by the window, which had been cracked to catch the ocean breeze. "And it was her swimsuit, so she had every right to ask for it back."

Dick took the seat across from her. "Ask, yes. Rip out of your hands, no." He laughed. "I think our Kitty might be a bit jealous of you."

She scowled at him, not at all amused by his friend's rudeness moments ago. "I don't see why. She's the glamorous one."

"Jealousy is rarely rational. Though if I had to guess at a reason, I'd say she's miffed because the two people she's currently most interested in are both more interested in you."

"Who, Lavinia?"

"And me." He gave her a wry half smile that sent her heart skittering nervously. Surely he didn't mean "interested in" her as anything more than a friend. She wasn't nearly sophisticated enough to interest him that way. And yet . . .

Seemingly unaware of the sudden turmoil he had touched off inside her, he pulled a cigarette case from his trouser pocket and sat back. "But enough about Miss Kitty. I want to make sure you're all right after your misadventures this morning."

She took a deep breath. "I'm fine. Or will be if I can keep avoiding Nathan."

Dick snorted as he shook out a cigarette. "Talk about people not liking someone. I don't think he's said word one to me this whole trip."

"He just doesn't know you."

"Or more accurately thinks I'm a bad influence," he said with a laugh as he struck a match.

"I don't see why. You're always a perfect gentleman."

"You're sweet to think so." He lit his cigarette and then waved his hand to douse the match. "But he might have a point. After all, I introduced you to Bess and Larry."

"Why should that bother him? They both seem very nice. And I like how Larry dotes on his wife. All husbands should be so attentive."

"That's the problem. Larry isn't her husband." His lips quirked as she stared at him. "I thought you realized after Kitty spilled the beans back in Cape Town."

"But . . ." She thought back to that day in the park, to Kitty's comment about the photo and Larry's angry reaction. And then she recalled how Larry's hand had rested on Bess's bare thigh at the pool this morning, while Bess leaned her head on his tanned shoulder, her wedding ring glinting in the sunlight.

"Where is her husband?" she asked, feeling a little ill.

"India, working. He's attached to one of the consulates and couldn't get away." He perched his cigarette on the edge of the ashtray and gave her an amused look. "Still think they're nice?"

"I . . ." She couldn't find the right words to express the tumult in her head. "Does Bess not love her husband?"

"You'd have to ask her to be certain, but I assume she does. I also know she's angry with Howie for sending her home alone. Likely she's afraid and perhaps a little bored. Who knows why people cheat. I'm guessing the reasons are as individual as the people themselves."

"And Larry?"

"An opportunistic hound dog. Still, you can't fault his taste in women."

"Actually I can." Genie rubbed her temples. "I don't know what to think. Bess has always been very nice to me. Nice to everyone, as far as I can tell. But what she's doing is wrong. Adultery is a sin. I want to blame Larry, because I don't like him as much, but she's the one who's bound to another."

"Morals are the very devil, are they not?" He laughed and picked up his cigarette again. "Still, good for you for trying to figure it all out. And good thing you know so little about me, or I doubt we'd still be friends."

"Are you really that awful?"

He exhaled a stream of smoke and then, not meeting her eyes, he tapped an ash into the small tray. When he finally lifted his gaze to hers, she was struck by the myriad colors of his irises: brown, gold, green, even a little blue. "So what were you thinking of doing once you got to the States? Any plans?"

"Well, I'm going to my aunt's house."

"And then what? Go to church picnics, knit socks for soldiers, pray for the war to be over?"

"Is there anything wrong with that?" she asked, a little stung.

"Not at all, if you're inclined along those lines. It just seems to me that for someone like you it might be a little . . . well, stifling."

"For someone like me?" she asked slowly.

"Someone with an affinity for adventure."

She shook her head. "You're wrong about that."

He raised an eyebrow. "Really? Then who went into Cape Town with a virtual stranger? Went swimming today despite having zero experience? Even flew in an airplane with no visible qualms?"

"That last one isn't entirely true. I had my doubts at first, but then Ted explained everything to me, and I felt much better."

Something dark flickered in his eyes before he looked away. "Tough business, being a pilot these days. They don't last very long."

"What do you mean?"

"Of course those AVG boys are some of the best," he went on without answering her question, which only increased her unease. "All the same, a gal like you would be smart not to lose her heart to one."

"Probably so," she agreed, her anxiety building. "But what did you mean, they don't last very long?"

"War is dangerous business, Genie. And a pilot isn't only fighting enemy pilots but the airplane itself. I have a buddy who's a test pilot for Vultee Aircraft, a fellow with over a thousand hours of flight time—he learned to fly in the Great War—and he says they're sending boys up with less than thirty hours in these planes. Planes unlike what they were trained in. Planes that are faster, trickier, and flat-out harder to fly."

She suddenly found it hard to breathe. "Ted never mentioned any trouble, other than his plane running out of fuel. But he says he thinks a bullet nicked the fuel line."

"Or maybe he had a bad gauge. Or maybe a leaky fuel line that had nothing to do with a bullet. Truth is, the best pilot in the world can be brought down by a bad plane."

"Does America produce bad planes?" The idea seemed to border on sacrilege and ran counter to everything she had read in the newspapers, where the US was the greatest, the best, and would win the war in no time.

"Compared to Germany? We're a decade behind in design and production. The government is leaning on the industry to catch up, and they are—well, they would be if they could get enough workers. The armed forces are vacuuming up all the able-bodied men just when the industry needs them most. Which is what made me wonder what you were going to do while you waited out the war. Because you could work, if you wanted."

"Work?" The suggestion caught her off guard. She knew women worked, of course, but usually only if they had to, not because it was their choice.

"Where does your aunt live?"

"Bakersfield, California."

"You're kidding," he said, brightening. "That's just a hop, skip, and a jump from LA, my hometown. It's beautiful country, though a bit different from what you're used to. What we call mountains are nothing like the ones in China."

China. A sudden longing to see her mountains again seized her. She had been gone almost six weeks. Her father, Zhenzhu, Li Ming . . . Lord, how she missed them. And worried about them.

She glanced out the window at the sunbathers lying around the pool, drowsy in the hot sunshine, unconcerned that there were people busy fighting the enemy right now, fighting for their lives. People like Ted, who was likely back in Kunming, flying his new plane over those mountains, hunting for the Japanese, risking his life to defend her family while she sailed away.

"What time is it in China?" she asked suddenly, tearing her gaze from the deep, brilliant blue of the water just beyond the railing, the glare off the small waves so bright, it was making her eyes water. Or at least that was what she told herself.

"Let's see—we're not quite halfway around the globe from there, so . . . maybe a ten-hour difference. Nine o'clock at night? Why?"

Nine o'clock. The airbase in Kunming would be shut down for the night, all the pilots safely on the ground. She closed her eyes and prayed that Ted was among them, joking about his day, getting ready to "sack out." She couldn't even begin to pray for her father's safety; the fear cut too close to her heart. *Lord, watch over them; watch over them all.*

"Hey." Dick's hand settled over hers on the table. He gave her fingers a gentle squeeze. "Don't cry. I can't abide damsels in distress."

Opening her eyes, she wiped her cheeks with her free hand. "I'm sorry, and I'm not so much in distress as tired and wishing I could go home. Everything was so much simpler there."

"And what would Miss Eugenia Baker be doing if she was home right now?" His teasing lilt tugged at her spirits, and she tried to smile.

"Nothing that would interest you, I'm sure."

He squeezed her hand again. "Try me."

"Well, right now I'd be getting ready for bed because it's late, and candles are precious."

"Then what if it were daylight?"

She turned her gaze out the window again and let her thoughts stretch out. "I was working on translating the Old Testament into Yue Chinese before I left. So I'd be in my father's study, working while Zhenzhu cooked. Or maybe I'd be out in the fields . . ."

The mountains rose up around her, the air so clean and fresh. Earthy. In her mind's eye she gazed up at the jagged peaks, her heart reaching out and over them . . .

She stiffened. *No, that's not right.* If she were home again, she wouldn't want to leave. She would be glad to return to the simple life, where she knew her role, where everyone did. Where the line between right and wrong was understood. Where she knew exactly what each day would bring . . . and what it wouldn't.

"Genie, what's wrong?" Dick asked sharply.

Her gaze slid to his. The concern she saw there steadied her, even as the problem became clearer. "What if I can't go back?"

He frowned slightly. "Are you worried your village won't be there?"

"Of course, but more than that . . ." She bit her lip, wondering whether she dared say what was truly worrying her, if it would change his opinion of her. She took the plunge. "What if I return, only to find I don't belong there anymore? That I've somehow changed too much?"

"Ah." Understanding lit his eyes. "Did no one warn you about the ravages of time? That innocence lost can never be regained?"

"The only constant is change," she whispered, hearing her father's words for the first time for what they really were: a warning. *Panta rei.*

"You're not alone. Every sailor on this ship, every young fellow being shipped overseas, every one of your pilot friends . . . anyone who's ever left home changes. Their perspectives broaden with their experiences. Or they should. I have, unfortunately, met people who ended up even more narrow-minded than when they started. But I chalk that up to fear."

Fear . . . that was exactly the emotion gripping her. "What do I do?"

"Hi, kiddos. Ready for lunch?" Bess asked cheerfully as she stopped by their table. "I'm famished, and whatever they're cooking today smells divine."

Dick glanced questioningly at Genie. "Shall we?"

She hesitated as Larry came up and possessively wrapped his arm around Bess's waist. The revelation of the other couple's less-than-respectable relationship still unsettled her.

If only she could go back in time to when she had been oblivious. "Thanks, but I think I'll wait for Lavinia and Nathan."

Dick eyed her curiously for a moment and then relaxed back in his chair. "I'll wait with Miss Baker. You two run along, and we'll see you shortly."

"You didn't have to do that," Genie said after the pair had left. "I know they're your friends."

"Acquaintances, more like. And besides . . . you're much more interesting."

She laughed without humor. "I find that very unlikely."

His gaze dropped to her lips, and his eyes darkened. Her breath caught at the change. Alarm, awareness, heat all rushed through her veins. Then he blinked, and the intensity was gone. "You sell yourself short, Miss Baker. And, given the time, perhaps we should return to your cabin to see if Lavinia is ready for her apology and lunch?"

"Oh, of course." Horrified that she had so totally forgotten about her friend, she shot to her feet. "I wonder that she hasn't come to find me already. We always eat together."

"Miss Baker? Miss Eugenia Baker?" A uniformed naval officer crossed the bar to her, his tanned face grim. He wasn't the captain, but there was enough insignia on his shoulders to mark his high rank.

"Yes." She glanced at Dick nervously, but his attention was fully focused on the officer.

"I'm Lieutenant Andersen, and I'm afraid I have some bad news."

Her knees gave way, and she thumped down in her previously discarded chair. Her ears buzzed dreadfully, her greatest fear about to be realized. "My father?" *How could they have found out? How could a message find us here, in the middle of the ocean . . .*

The officer frowned slightly. "No, your travel companion."

And then, just like that, she could breathe again. Then her heart cramped painfully. "Lavinia?"

"I'm here about Mr. Sterling," he corrected, a touch impatiently. This time he had her full attention. "I'm very sorry to have to tell you this . . ."

A chill of premonition dredged its way through her soul. *No, no, no.* She raised her hand to stop him.

"There was an accident. Not more than an hour ago, Mr. Sterling fell down the number three stairs and landed badly. Very badly. In fact, Mr. Sterling is dead. I'm sorry."

Genie's vision grayed, and then she saw nothing more.

# Chapter 25

"Genie . . ."

Vaguely, she registered an icy glass being placed in her hands.

"Come on, drink."

She did and then immediately choked as a harsh liquid burned its way down her throat. The fog of unreality that had gripped her vaporized in an instant. She gasped for breath, the bar swimming back into view. As the fire in her throat died to a raspy, manageable burn, her consciousness fully returned. Abruptly she became aware of Dick crouched beside her chair, his hand on her back.

"Are you all right?" he asked gently.

She felt the weight of a dozen stares, the silence in the bar almost deafening. Embarrassment became unreasoning anger. What were they waiting for? For her to scream? Throw herself on the ground and wail? Cry?

Not that she could do any of those things with her lungs feeling as if they were caught in a vise. Every inhalation hurt, as if she were no longer breathing air, but water. Maybe she had drowned after all, and this was some kind of horrible after-death dream.

She glanced up at the officer, who seemed real enough. His expression reflected the discomfort one would expect in such a situation. She licked her dry lips. "Are you sure it was Nathan?"

"Yes, miss."

Her world collapsed again. Even though she hadn't felt anything but antipathy for the man for months now, that didn't mean she wanted him to die. He had been her one constant on the trip. The one person she knew wouldn't fail her. Her one last link to home.

*Home.* "I must get word to my father," she said, a strange restlessness driving her to her feet. "He needs to know."

"Later," Dick said, pushing her back into the chair.

The officer shook his head. "I'm sorry, miss, but we can't risk communicating with shore right now. It'll have to wait until we make port."

"But that's . . ." She struggled to do the math in her head, her brain still fuzzy with shock. "A week away."

"At least," the officer agreed solemnly.

She shivered. Her father would be devastated. Nathan had been like a son to him and would have become family in truth if she and Nathan had married. And yet that possibility had died long before today. Died because she had refused to marry without love, and Nathan had chosen to love . . .

"Lavinia," she gasped as her mind cleared more. "Does she know? We have to tell her."

Her friend would be destroyed by the terrible news. *"You and Nathan are all I have . . ."* She turned in her chair and grabbed Dick's arm, her fear for Lavinia overriding her own. "We have to find her before she finds out from someone else."

The officer cleared his throat. "If you mean Mrs. Schmidt, she already knows. She was there when it happened."

"She was . . ." Her brain whirled in a thousand different directions, but what kept rising to the forefront were her parting, angry words to her friend. *Ask Nathan . . .* It defied reason, but could Lavinia have . . . ?

No. She couldn't even finish such an awful thought. Even if Lavinia and Nathan had argued over her going home, it would have been just that: an argument. And how had the officer put it? It was an accident.

People could and did fall down stairs, especially on ships. That Lavinia had been present was nothing more than an unfortunate coincidence. If anything, the widow was bound to think the accident was somehow tied up with her curse. Of all the awful things that could happen . . .

She turned to Dick. "I need to talk to Lavinia. Immediately."

"She's with the captain at the moment," the officer said, shifting uneasily, as if he wished he were somewhere else. "He's filling out all the paperwork for the investigation."

"Investigation?" She stiffened in protest. "Surely he doesn't think she has anything to do with it."

"It's SOP, standard operating procedure, for the navy, miss. Any death aboard ship needs to be dutifully investigated and documented." He paused. "He'll likely want to talk to you, too, since you were traveling together. There's also the problem of what to do with his personal effects."

She blinked. Of course, his things . . . something had to be done with them. She hadn't even thought of that. It wasn't like Nathan needed his clothes or his papers or his personal kit anymore. He was through with earthly conventions. Unfortunately, she was not the best person for the job. Despite all they had been through recently, she knew appallingly little about his personal life.

"I'm afraid I have no idea who should get them," she admitted reluctantly. The tragedy in that simple statement brought tears to her eyes. Poor Nathan. Surely somewhere, someone loved him. A mother or father or sister . . .

And yet if she were to die now, would she be in the same position? Was anyone left in her village to mourn her, and would anyone know to contact them if so?

The thought chilled her.

"The captain will also want to know if there's anything the navy can do for you," the officer went on, pulling her back into the present.

"Anyone we can contact on your behalf? He isn't keen on putting two women ashore with no male to help out."

She massaged the sudden pain in her temples. Oh Lord, she hadn't thought of that, either. Nathan, no doubt, had had their entire journey planned out, but unless he had told those plans to Lavinia—which seemed unlikely, the more she thought about it—they had died with him. Unless . . .

"Can the captain see me now?" she asked.

Ten minutes later she was seated outside the captain's office, waiting for him to finish with Lavinia. Genie was alone, which suited her just fine. Dick had wanted to accompany her, but she refused. She needed time to herself.

The door latch clicked, and Lavinia came out, accompanied by a somber Kitty. For once Genie wasn't stung by seeing them together, though it struck her as odd that Lavinia hadn't asked for her instead. Still, her heart wasn't so small as to begrudge the widow whatever comfort she needed. Not at a time like this.

"Genie," Lavinia cried upon seeing her. Her tear-ravaged face crumpled as she flung herself into Genie's arms. The girl's sobs tore at her heart, and soon they were both crying.

"Miss, the captain will see you now."

Genie glanced up for Kitty, but she was gone. Typical. All her goodwill toward the woman dissipated. She tightened her hold on her friend, not at all happy that she was going to have to temporarily abandon Lavinia again. "I've got to go in."

Lavinia's fingers dug into Genie's arms. "Don't leave me."

"I won't. I just need to see the captain." She drew a deep breath as she untangled herself from the girl's grip. Anger drove back her tears. Anger at Nathan for not being more careful. Anger at the war for forcing them into this situation to begin with. *None of this should be happening.* And yet it was.

"We'll be fine," she continued, pushing her friend back slightly to make eye contact. "Wait for me, all right? I'll be right out."

Lavinia nodded and blotted her face on her sleeve.

Genie hurried through her interview as quickly as she could. In truth, she had little to add. No, she didn't know if he had any family in the States. No, she didn't know if he had made any travel arrangements for her and Lavinia once they reached New York. No, she didn't know the address of the mission headquarters, or the name of anyone else who might need to know of Nathan's death. But she might be able to find out, if she could go through Nathan's things . . .

The captain rejected the idea, but then, when she pointed out that she needed to retrieve her passport and other travel papers from Nathan's personal belongings anyway, he grudgingly relented. But only if she agreed to take on the duty of bundling up all Nathan's belongings and shipping them somewhere—anywhere, he didn't care—just so he didn't have to deal with the problem. Yes? Good.

He gave her until supper to get it done, or else he would have one of his men see to it.

Relieved and a little puzzled he hadn't given the task to Lavinia, who was Nathan's fiancée, after all, Genie hurried out to tell Lavinia the news. Only her friend wasn't there.

Fear prickled up Genie's neck. Lavinia, even on the best of days, could be impulsive—frighteningly so—and today was not a good day. Her friend's entire world had imploded not an hour ago. And there was Lavinia's belief that she was cursed.

Retrieving her passport would have to wait.

With growing panic, Genie spent the next hour searching every deck, checking every stairwell, and triple-checking their shared cabin. Lavinia was nowhere to be found. Finally, in desperation, she sought out Kitty, who was lingering over lunch with Dick. The woman's cat eyes flashed with dislike as Genie approached.

Dick, on the other hand, looked relieved. "There you are! I was just wondering if we should organize a search party. Lunch is almost over."

"I'm looking for Lavinia. Have you seen her?"

"I wouldn't bother looking. If Nia wants to be found, she'll let you know," Kitty said, her lips curving ever so slightly.

It took all Genie had not to slap the mocking smile off the blonde's face. "Maybe Lavinia's well-being is nothing but a joke to you, but I know her better, and I'm worried."

"You only *think* you know her," Kitty shot back.

"Girls, please." Dick held his hands up. "A catfight will not help. Do you or do you not know where Lavinia is, Kitty?"

When she didn't answer right away, Dick pinned her with a hard look. Kitty shifted slightly in her chair and sighed. "Fine. She said she needed to get something from her fiancé's cabin."

"Why didn't you just tell me?" Genie snapped. The hurt that Lavinia had confided in Kitty but not her congealed with her fear, creating a hard knot in her stomach. Why hadn't Lavinia waited for her? They could've gone together. After all, Lavinia knew Nathan had Genie's passport as well.

Lord, she was so, so tired. The tumultuous events of the morning crashed down on her like a rockslide.

Dick was instantly beside her, his hand under her elbow. "Easy, there. Do you want me to come with you to find Lavinia?"

As much as she wanted to sag against him and let his kindness override the horrors of the morning, she shook her head. She was too emotionally drained. "I need to do this alone."

He let her go, and soon she wished she hadn't been so hasty. Her knees were shaking by the time she reached Nathan's cabin. As she lifted her hand to knock, she wondered whether she was going to have to sit down in the passageway for a moment. No one answered, which didn't mean anything. If Lavinia was inside, likely she wouldn't want to give her presence away.

Trying the latch, she found it unlocked. Inhaling for courage, she eased the door open. She swept her gaze around the interior. The last thing she wanted was to catch one of Nathan's cabinmates in a state of dishabille. Her attention caught on an upper bunk.

"Lavinia?" she gasped in shock.

From her perch near the ceiling, Lavinia regarded Genie with a peculiar expression, as if she didn't quite recognize her. In truth, Genie almost didn't recognize her friend. Lavinia's long hair had been hacked off with neither precision nor skill, leaving jagged ends sticking out in all directions like a black halo. Combined with the vacant, other-worldly blue of her eyes, the effect was disturbing. Terrifying, actually.

"Lavinia, what's going on?"

Lavinia tentatively touched her scalp, and a bubble of laughter escaped her, sending a chill down Genie's spine. "You mean this? I decided that since he never once noticed, after all these weeks, I might as well finish the job."

"I see. Do you still have the scissors?" Genie asked carefully. There was no blood indicating her friend had harmed herself, at least not yet. She wanted to keep it that way.

"I threw them over there." Lavinia waved her hand across the room. "I didn't need them anymore."

"I see," she said again, this time with relief. Without taking her eyes off Lavinia, she eased the door closed and locked it. The last thing she wanted was someone else walking in and witnessing her friend's odd behavior.

"Did you want me to cut your hair, too? I didn't think to ask."

"No. I like it this length. Actually, I'm here to pack Nathan's things."

"Really? I thought you were here to retrieve this." Lavinia held up Genie's passport. It took everything Genie had not to leap for it.

"That, too. Can I have it, please?" She extended one hand and held her breath.

Lavinia cocked her head, her unblinking gaze never leaving Genie's face. She whipped the passport behind her back.

"No," she said with a slight shake of her head. Her eyes became glossy with unshed tears. "You'll just leave me. Like Nathan."

"I won't leave you." Her heart broke for her friend. "And Nathan didn't mean to. It was an accident."

One tear wound its way down her cheek. "Maybe I should follow him."

"No!" Then Genie continued more calmly. "Don't. We'll stick together, and things will be all right."

"Your aunt won't want me."

"It doesn't matter what my aunt wants," Genie said firmly. "You're my friend, and I won't leave you in the lurch. If need be, we'll find jobs and a place where we can room together. Dick was just talking about how easy it is to find work in the US now there's a war on. We'll stick together and be just fine."

Lavinia shook her head again. "You don't mean that."

"I do. When we get to the States, you'll come with me to California. I won't leave you behind." Genie put her heart into the beseeching gaze she sent her friend, praying Lavinia would see and understand that she had meant every word.

After a long, tense moment, Lavinia slid down from the bunk, her eyes haunted. "I won't grieve him. I didn't for John, and I won't for Nathan, either."

Genie bit her lip, noting the slight tremble in the girl's shoulders and her ruined hair. Whether her friend knew it or not, she already was grieving. "All right."

On a shuddering exhale, Lavinia handed Genie her passport. "I'm going to lie down."

Genie let her friend edge past her. "Did you find whatever it was you were looking for?"

Lavinia paused at the door and then opened it. "I did."

"Are you going to go see Kitty?" Genie hadn't meant to ask the question, but some small, jealous part of her wanted to know. Had to know.

Lavinia's fingers turned white as they gripped the door. "No," she said, not turning around. "I'm done with Kitty. I'm done with all of it."

# Chapter 26

Nathan was buried at sea the next day, a Monday. Lavinia chose to stay in bed, claiming a headache from the overnight change in the weather. As Genie shivered in her winter sweater, under leaden skies, waiting for the naval chaplain to finish reading the funereal scripture, she wasn't sure she could blame her friend. The ship's crew stood at silent attention, their faces by turn somber or reflective. Nathan's burial was an unwelcome reminder that death stalked them all.

The chaplain's voice died off, and the canvas-bound shroud slid off the stern of the ship and into the ocean. The dark waters churned and thrashed as the sea consumed the unasked-for offering.

Genie looked away, unable to watch as the white bundle faded beneath the surface. A sorrow deeper than she had expected pierced her. Nathan had always been one of the constants in her life. He had been the rasp on which her identity had been honed, the unshakable pillar that marked the path down which she had traveled. Of all the people who now surrounded her, none of them had been with her in China. None of them had been in her home. None of them had known her father.

A cold rain began to spatter as the sailors filtered away, their duty done. Finally, there was no one left to stand with her. She was well and truly alone.

The rain started to fall harder, dampening her skin despite her wool dress and sweater. Wrapped in a fog of unreality, Genie hardly felt the chill as she drifted back to her cabin. Her friendship with Lavinia had yet to be repaired after the swimming disaster. It weighed on her, even though truly there had been no time with all the paperwork and preparations for the funeral—things that had fallen on Genie, since Lavinia had pretended to be asleep and had refused to see anyone, including a very angry Kitty.

It also weighed on her that she had less than a week to figure out how to get them from New York to California on her own. Nothing in Nathan's personal effects had indicated that anyone would be waiting for her when the ship docked. In fact, there was no evidence he had even tried contacting her aunt.

"I'm back." Genie closed the cabin door behind her. Lavinia didn't reply. She lay huddled under the covers, a motionless lump, exactly where Genie had left her.

Sighing inwardly, Genie shrugged off her sodden sweater and hung it to dry. "The chaplain did a nice job."

Lavinia made no indication that she had heard.

Genie reached out and gave her friend's shoulder a gentle squeeze. "You alive in there?"

"Unfortunately, yes," Lavinia said coldly.

Genie took a deep breath and then let it out. *Patience, Genie.* Grief could do strange things to a person. It wasn't Lavinia's fault that her world had been turned upside down yet again. To be honest, she wasn't doing so well herself, with all her worries about the future.

Suppressing a shiver, Genie plucked the wet wool from her skin as she crossed over to her trunk to get a dry outfit. "You ready to get up and get something to eat?"

"What's the point?"

"Surviving." She shrugged out of her wet things. "Whether we like it or not, life goes on."

"For people like you, maybe."

Genie's fingers paused on a button. "What do you mean, 'people like me'?"

Lavinia rolled away and pulled the covers up.

"Oh, no you don't." Genie hurriedly tucked her blouse into her skirt as she rounded the bunk bed. "Your curse didn't have anything to do with Nathan's accident."

"I watched him die, Genie." Tears welled in Lavinia's already swollen eyes. "I tried to help him, but he was . . ." A choked sob tore itself from her throat. "Why does everyone who loves me die?"

"Not everyone," Genie said in exasperation. "Marcus loves you, as do I, and we're still around. As is Kitt—"

Lavinia sat bolt upright, her tear-stained face hard. "No! Don't even say her name. I hate her."

"Whatever for?" Genie asked, surprised and a little alarmed by her friend's sudden vehemence.

"Because this is all her fault. All of it. I wish we had never met."

"Kitty had nothing to do with Nathan's failing to pay attention to the stairs," Genie said, her exasperation returning. "The fault is his and his alone."

Lavinia didn't answer. Instead, she fell back on the cot and buried her face in the pillow.

Genie perched on the edge of the bunk and stroked her friend's back. "I know it feels too soon, but we have to make plans for the future. First, are you coming with me to California to live with my aunt? You know I want you to. Both because you're my friend and because I need your help getting there. I can't do it alone."

"Yes, you could," came Lavinia's muffled reply.

"Then how about I don't *want* to."

Lavinia rolled to face her. "Why? You haven't needed anyone up until now."

"That's not true. Nathan handled everything."

"Yet you complained about it at every turn, and now you're free."

"Yes, but I never wanted to be *this* free." She took Lavinia's hand when her friend would have rolled away again. "And I certainly don't want to be free of you."

"Why? You would be better off if you were."

Genie could have screamed in frustration. "Lavinia, that's it. No more secrets. What is this curse I should be so afraid of? Tell me."

"How do I explain something that has no explanation? How do I describe the anguish of wanting something so desperately, only to have that one thing elude you, over and over? No, worse, to have it ripped away irreparably by death or disaster?"

"You're not making any sense."

Lavinia sat up and took Genie's hand. "If you could have one thing from life, just one, what would it be?"

Genie's chest constricted at once. "A chance to go home."

"And then what? Live with your father the rest of your life?"

"Why not? He needs my help to complete his dream of translating the Bible."

"*His* dream, Genie. Listen to yourself. What about your dream? When you were home, did you long for nothing?"

Had she? An uncomfortable restlessness pricked her as ghosts seemed to stir at the edges of her memory. Ghosts of childish dreams of real adventures, of being brave and banishing demons, and then returning as a heroine. As someone important. Someone worthy of respect.

She gave her head an angry shake, scattering the ghosts. "We were talking about curses, not dreams. Stop trying to change the subject."

Lavinia withdrew her hand and sat back. "I'm not. For me, they are one and the same. I have only ever wanted to love and be loved in return." Her face crumpled. "I was so close this time, but now Nathan is dead, and I am alone again."

Forgetting her own problems, Genie reached for her friend as Lavinia began to cry in earnest. "Hush. Accidents happen. Wars happen. None of that was your fault. Nathan may be gone, but you still have me. We'll go to California together to live with my aunt. And when you feel better, you'll find love again. You'll see."

*When you were home, did you long for nothing?*

Lavinia's words haunted Genie long after her friend had calmed down and fallen into an uneasy slumber. Like Lavinia, she supposed she, too, would like to love and be loved. Her heart did still ache a little when she thought of Ted, but she hadn't fallen apart after he'd pushed her away. And as much as she secretly hoped Dick liked her, securing his affections wasn't exactly her dream. Though she wouldn't mind if she did. Dick was . . . exciting. Always in motion, always thinking. She liked that about him.

Nor had she lied when she said her goal was still to go home after the war. She loved her father and Zhenzhu and desperately wanted to see them again. Yet living there for the rest of her life, hemmed in by the mountains, isolated by race and culture, alone with her translations . . . she wouldn't call that her dream, either. If she was honest with herself, a part of her had always been envious of her father's adventures. Traveling the breadth of India and then visiting Cape Town had only whetted that appetite.

Was that her dream, then? To see the world? Except, when Nathan had offered her a chance to see Africa as his wife, she had been singularly unmoved.

*If you could have one thing from life . . . what would it be?*

The question was deceptively simple, yet Genie found over the next few days, as she labored over creating a travel itinerary that would get her and Lavinia to California, that she had no easy answer for it.

Too many conflicting emotions would rise up within her, giving her a headache.

More often than not, she would shove the question aside. Unless a miracle happened, the war was likely to drag on for at least another six months, if not a year. Perhaps longer. She had gleaned that much from candid conversations with the captain. And even if said miracle did happen, she had Lavinia to consider. Until her friend recovered her footing after this latest blow, Genie had resolved to stay with her. No one should be alone when grieving so many deaths in so short a period. So there was no point in trying to determine what she wanted. All that mattered in the foreseeable future was already set.

The final few days aboard ship disappeared entirely too fast, like snowflakes landing on a mountain stream. It was only at Dick's gentle prodding that she made herself leave Lavinia's side long enough to go on deck for their arrival in New York Harbor.

Hovering between terror over her upcoming journey across the United States and worry about leaving Lavinia alone in the cabin—her friend having retreated into an almost catatonic state of grief—Genie watched the shoreline silently slide by. It was her first glimpse of her new home, her new country. Some might argue her real country.

To be fair, New York City was majestic in the early-morning sunlight, as grand as the cities of Bombay and Cape Town and yet in a class entirely its own. Off to one side, Lady Liberty loomed on her island of exile, welcoming Genie to the golden gleaming shores. Yet a deep loneliness stole over her. This was her parents' land, not hers. There was no pull on her heart, no reaching out to her soul.

"Miss Baker." Lieutenant Andersen, the same officer who had told her of Nathan's passing, joined her at the rail.

Her stomach twisted. "More bad news?"

"Yes and no." He took a deep breath. "The communications officer on shore was able to send your cable to your father. So you can rest easy on that count. However, I'm sorry to report he was unable to reach your aunt at the address you provided, and further checking with the telephone operator resulted in no leads. Apparently she and your uncle moved out of town a year ago, with no forwarding address."

"Uncle?" This was news to her, and the shock of it temporarily overrode the fact that her aunt was missing. Did her father know Aunt Hazel had married?

"Is there anyone else we might try on your behalf?"

His question brought her new situation into sharp focus, abruptly replacing her surprise with sheer panic. She pressed her hand to her chest, trying to calm her suddenly pounding heart. "No, no one."

"I'm sorry, miss."

"Wait." She grabbed his arm when he started to turn away. "Did you by any chance get my aunt's married name?"

"Sharkey, miss. Mrs. Arthur Sharkey."

"Thank you." Genie released his arm, even as her thoughts whirled. "And tell the captain not to worry; I'll be all right. And Mrs. Schmidt, too."

The officer nodded and then left. Genie hardly noticed for the chaos in her head. Her entire plan had hinged on Aunt Hazel helping her with both practical and financial matters. Not only did Genie have no idea how to handle the purchase of train tickets and lodging, but apparently what little money Nathan had left her was becoming less valuable with each passing day due to a recent spike in inflation—a word she barely understood even after the captain explained it several times.

*How did I end up like this?*

The answer was easy: the war.

She glanced again at the New York skyline and the busy harbor front. Perhaps she and Lavinia should skip the trip to California and stay here and look for work. After being on the move for almost two months straight, she had little desire to keep traveling. Particularly when there would be no one to greet them. Perhaps it would be better to save what little she had left and find her and Lavinia a room to let while she tried to locate her aunt.

But what if she couldn't find her? What she knew about finding a job was rivaled in its meagerness only by what she knew of finding a place to stay.

"What a heavy sigh," Dick said, joining her at the rail. "I take it the view doesn't move you?"

"It's not that. My aunt is MIA," she said, using some of her newly learned slang. She rubbed her aching temples. "Lieutenant Andersen just stopped by to inform me. Honestly, I can't think how anything else in this journey could possibly go wrong."

"The ship could sink before we weigh anchor. But let's not think about that."

"No. Let's not." She laughed softly, her mood lifting a bit. "How is it you always know what to say to make me feel better?"

"It's a gift." He smiled at her, but a haunted sadness in his hazel eyes remained. One that had been there too much of late. As if sensing her concern, he looked away at the passing buildings. "So what will you do?"

"I don't know. I can't help but feel this is somehow my fault." Her gaze fell to the rail, where her knuckles were white from gripping the metal so tightly, as tight as the guilt gripping her chest. "I keep thinking that if I hadn't been so short with him, if I hadn't wished myself free—"

"That he wouldn't have died?" Dick asked sharply. "Don't flatter yourself. The universe doesn't work that way. Sterling fell down those stairs all on his own. It had absolutely nothing to do with you. You weren't even there."

But Lavinia had been, and despite Genie's direct question, her friend hadn't actually said what her "curse" was. All Genie knew was that it had something to do with love and it supposedly killed people. Perhaps her friend had a murderous temper? Genie discarded the idea as ridiculous almost as soon as it surfaced. Yes, Lavinia could be impulsive, but Genie hadn't seen any signs of intemperate violence.

"I'm sorry all this has fallen on your shoulders," Dick said, interrupting her thoughts. "But I have an idea, if you'd like to hear it."

She gave herself a mental shake. "Of course."

"I've got an apartment in LA where you and Lavinia can stay while you look for your aunt. LA isn't far from where you said your aunt last lived. And it's not like I'll be using the apartment anytime soon," he added when she started to protest. "Uncle Sam has already booked my services for the next six weeks. Plenty of time for you to get back on your feet."

"Where will you be?"

"DC and then . . . places I probably shouldn't mention."

"Because of the war?"

"Yes," he said. "Anyway, the apartment's not large, but there's a bed and a fold-out couch and a private bath. The neighborhood isn't bad, either. And thanks to the government, the rent's already paid through the end of August, so you wouldn't have to worry about that right away. What do you think?"

She drew her first free breath in what felt like ages as a whole layer of stress dropped away like snow off a branch. "I don't know what to say. That's very generous of you."

"Not at all. It's the least I could do for a friend in need."

"Is that what we are, friends?" She glanced up at him, aware of the wistfulness that had crept into her voice.

"Ah, Genie . . ." A small smile quirked his lips as he raised his hand and brushed an errant strand of hair from her face. She leaned into his touch, the warmth of his fingertips on her skin releasing something inside of her, making her feel less frightened and alone.

His smile deepened as he tucked her hair behind her ear and continued in a low husky voice that made her shiver, "In a perfect world, we would be much more than friends."

She glanced up, and her breath caught at the sincerity in his hazel eyes, now more green than gold. Her pulse skittered as his fingers gently slid to the nape of her neck. Her thoughts scattered in utter disarray; she wasn't sure whether she should pull away or lean in. The tobacco and spice of his aftershave wrapped around her senses as he bent closer, making her heart pound harder.

"You are such a treasure." His breath feathered over the sensitized skin of her ear, and her entire being shivered this time. The urge to run got infinitely stronger, but so did the one to stay. "A wondrous creature I could spend the rest of my life getting to know."

"Oh, I'm not—" she began, trying to impose reason, but the battle was lost the instant his lips touched hers. Any misgivings were drowned by shock and then bliss as he deepened the kiss. Then she stopped thinking at all.

Her arms slid up and around his neck. In response, he pulled her tighter against him until there was no space between them anymore. Part of her knew that her behavior was improper, but it felt so wonderful to let go and, for a moment, forget. To feel so desired, adored . . . wanted . . . all the things she secretly craved. She couldn't have walked away if she had tried.

Dick finally broke the kiss and drew back. Dazed, she stared up at him. Both of them were breathing hard. The experience had been so different from when Ted had kissed her, she didn't know what to think. She didn't remember feeling quite this off-balance before, almost terrified. Like she had done something wrong.

"I'll make the call as soon as we make port." He cupped her face with his hand. She had never seen his eyes so green. "Don't worry. I'll take care of everything and then come see you as soon as my assignment is up."

She forced her brain to think. "Wait. I can't just move in . . . I've got Lavinia with me, and we're almost out of money."

"Already thought about that. Remember when I said I had a friend who worked for Vultee? I'm sure I could land you both positions there, if you don't mind being around airplanes all day."

A laugh of amazement escaped her as excitement fizzed through her veins. "I would love it. And I'm pretty sure Lavinia won't mind, if it means we get to eat."

He seized her hand and then dropped it to touch her face again. His expression was tender. "Thank you for letting me do this for you. I've been so worried since Sterling passed away."

"It's I who should be thanking you!" she said, shaking her head, still not quite able to believe the change in circumstances. "I have no idea what I've done to deserve such kindness."

A sudden shadow passed over his face as he slid his fingers over her jaw, his touch feather-light. "With you, it's easy to be kind. You make me want to be a better man, better than is likely possible."

Her chest constricted, caught between the need to comfort him and confusion that he should be in need of it. But then he smiled as if nothing were wrong and squeezed her shoulder. "We're going to be docking soon. Why don't you check on Lavinia and make sure she's all packed? Once we're all ashore, I'll make sure to find you two, and then we can all head to the train station together."

"That would be lovely." Then she added, now that he was no longer touching her and she could think again, "But I don't want to inconvenience you. I'm sure I can figure out the train schedules myself. LA should be an easy enough destination."

"You mentioned you were short on money?"

"If Lavinia and I economize, we should be fine." At least she hoped so, because the alternative of borrowing money from Dick, too, was more than she could bear.

His lips quirked into a lopsided smile as he gazed down at her. "Not that I doubt your abilities, but I would feel better if I went with you. Just to be sure you were all right."

Wonder filled her that such a man as Dick had come to care about her. He had seen so much, been so many places, known so many women. It was beyond flattering, and a little terrifying.

She swallowed the nervous lump in her throat. "I should go check on Lavinia. And tell her about the change in plans."

Not waiting for a response, she hurried away, praying she wouldn't trip. Her legs were shaking badly as her body tried to absorb all that had happened in the last half hour. She uttered another prayer as she reached the cabin the door that the news about her aunt and the arrangement with Dick wouldn't drive her friend further into the dark world that had gripped her.

"Lavinia, I'm . . ."

She trailed off as she saw a very pale Lavinia sitting up on her bunk, with an immaculately attired Kitty standing not far away, near the porthole. Kitty's eyes flashed with open hostility as she glanced at Genie. The air in the cabin was electric with tension.

Keeping her eye on the pair, Genie closed the door behind her. "Hello, Kitty. Did I interrupt something?"

Kitty straightened her gloves with a sharp tug on each wrist. "Not at all. I was just leaving."

*I bet,* Genie thought as she walked deeper into the cabin. The spots of color blooming high on her friend's cheeks sparked a feeling of dread within her. "Are you all right, Lavinia?"

"Oh yes. Miss Van Nuys just offered to buy us tickets to California," Lavinia said tightly. "Isn't that nice?"

"*Offered* might not be the right word," Kitty snapped.

Lavinia turned to Genie, her eyes unnaturally bright. "Of course I accepted, because I so want to fly in an airplane again. Don't you? And this time I intend to be awake the whole time, so I can enjoy it."

Genie's heart beat unevenly. Did she want to fly again? It had been her secret dream since landing in Calcutta. *But the expense . . .*

Reluctantly, she turned to Kitty. "That's very generous of you, but we can't accept. There's no way I'll be able to repay you."

"Oh, we don't have to, do we, Kitty?" Lavinia said with a cold laugh, and a chill slid up Genie's spine. This was a side of her friend she hadn't seen before. One that was frankly a little frightening.

Kitty's red lips compressed into a hard, thin line, and the tension in the air ratcheted up another notch. Her kid-gloved hands tightened into fists and then opened, only to fist again. "No. Mrs. Schmidt and I have agreed the tickets are to be a gift." She glanced at Genie. "She said you're going to California?"

"Yes, Los Angeles," she said slowly, still not sure she should accept. Something about the deal felt off. "It turns out we'll be staying at Dick's apartment for a few weeks. The address I had for my aunt is outdated, and it might take some time to find her."

Kitty laughed darkly. "And how like Dick to swoop to the rescue of a pretty girl!"

"If you mean how like him to be kind in general, then yes, it was," Genie said, her patience with the woman wearing thin.

"You didn't accept, did you?" Lavinia asked, drawing Genie's attention back from the infuriating blonde. To her surprise, her friend looked stricken, her face drawn and pale.

"He won't be there," Genie reassured her friend quickly. "He'll be away on assignment for at least six weeks, so there's nothing improper about it."

"And so the plot thickens," Kitty said with a mocking smile.

Lavinia narrowed her eyes at Kitty. "Genie, did I ever mention that Miss Van Nuys was there when Nathan fell?"

The smile dropped from Kitty's perfectly drawn lips. Her expression hardened. "Don't push, Nia."

To Genie's surprise, Lavinia paled again. Real concern for her friend had her stopping Kitty as the blonde brushed past her. "Wait, what's going on between you two? Why are you even here? It's been over a week since Nathan died, a week where you couldn't be bothered once to check on Lavinia."

"We all have reasons for what we do, Miss Baker," Kitty said coolly. "Reasons we may or may not share, but they are still there. It would be wise of you to remember that."

"Is that a threat?"

"More like a warning that if you sleep with vipers, you will get bitten."

Lavinia shot to her feet. "How dare you—"

Kitty turned to Lavinia, her expression diamond-hard. "I wasn't talking about you, Nia, dear. We have an agreement, remember?"

Lavinia collapsed back onto the cot as the door slammed shut behind Kitty.

Genie's stomach twisted as a plague of doubts clawed at her. She had accepted Dick's offer because having a place to stay would make things so much easier for her and Lavinia. But what if it was a mistake? What if it *was* improper, and she would be branding her and Lavinia as loose women before they even had a chance to settle in to their new city?

Lord above, she wasn't ready for this. The future yawned in front of her like a set trap. One false step and she might never make it home. It didn't help that Genie now had new worries about Lavinia, too. The last few minutes had renewed her suspicions that Nathan's death hadn't been accidental. Yet the depth of Lavinia's grief was real and argued against any involvement on her side. Maybe Kitty, whom Genie hadn't even known was there when Nathan fell? Yet how could she be sure Lavinia hadn't been lying about that? She knew her friend wasn't above shading the truth when it suited her.

So many secrets and half truths—it was all enough to make Genie want to give up and retreat to her bed, as Lavinia had.

*"You're not going to be one of those girls, are you?"* Mrs. Greenlee's words reached out unbidden from Genie's memory, the disgust as

clear as the day Genie had first heard them in the Kunming hospital. *"Someone who refuses to get on with the business of living simply because there's a war . . ."*

The business of living—that's what this was, and Natasha was right: she needed to get on with it, experience or no.

# Chapter 27

Dick seemed surprised by Kitty's generosity but gave no indication that Genie shouldn't take the woman up on her offer. "It might solve a lot of problems, actually," he said as they waited in line to claim their luggage off the dock. "I hear train seats are hard to get these days, thanks to Uncle Sam using the rails to move his troops around. I hadn't even thought of flying."

"Don't you think I should at least ask why she's buying us tickets? The tickets out of China were so expensive!"

Dick shook his head. "I'd say best to let sleeping dogs lie on this one. Lavinia and Kitty are both adults. If they're satisfied with the agreement, why question it? A day and a half of flying sure beats more than a week by rail."

"That it does." She glanced behind her to where she had left Lavinia sitting on a bench, waiting for Genie to return with their bags. Satisfied that her friend was safe and not going anywhere, she turned back to Dick and smiled. "And I admit I'm excited by the prospect of flying again."

"I bet you are." He returned her smile with one of his own, and her heart added an extra beat.

"Ah, here are our two lovebirds." Kitty glided up beside them in a scarlet traveling outfit. The jacket was richly embroidered with black thread and shiny black beads, and a small matching hat with a black lace veil perched at an angle on her smooth blonde hair. In a word, she looked expensive, though that wasn't what set Genie's teeth on edge. It was the dismissive glance Kitty flicked over Genie's best and recently hemmed to midcalf skirt and practical but perfectly presentable wool sweater. "We really must do something about your wardrobe, though."

Genie inhaled deeply for patience. "Why? There's nothing wrong with the way I'm dressed."

"No, you wouldn't think so," Kitty said as she waved to the porter carrying her bags, and then pointed to where he should wait for her. "But I'm afraid I must insist on it, as well as a professional haircut for Lavinia. She looks a positive fright at the moment."

"Oh, come on, Kitty . . . ," Dick began with a disbelieving laugh.

Kitty raised a gloved hand to silence him. "No, Dick, darling. If they are to fly as guests of my father, they simply must look the part. It'll be hard enough to get tickets as it is."

"Then maybe you shouldn't bother," Genie said, even though everything inside her rebelled at the idea of being cooped up in a train for another week.

Kitty arched one perfectly drawn eyebrow. "You don't get a say in the matter. And because I'm saving you a bundle in travel costs, you should have no problem affording a new outfit and a trip to the salon. I'll make an appointment for you both as soon as I reach my apartment."

"Surely we won't have time," Genie said, her stomach turning at the possibility of having to take on these new expenses. "Don't we need to get to the airfield?"

"Oh no. I doubt I'll be able to get you tickets before Friday."

"But that's five days from now!" Her unease turned into horror. "What on earth are we to do until then?"

"Ask Mrs. Schmidt. I'm sure she'll have some idea." Kitty reached into her purse and pulled out a small card.

"Kitty, you're not being reasonable," Dick said with a bemused frown.

"Don't interfere, Dickie. This is between me and Mrs. Schmidt. I wouldn't cross her if I were you." She turned back to Genie and handed her the card. "This has my phone number on it. Call when you are situated, and my assistant will give you directions to the salon. I'll also have some clothes picked out for you both. Oh, and don't worry: I'll give you a special discount on them."

Unless the "discount" meant free, the clothes would still be more than they could afford. Genie wanted to scream. Or cry. Or perhaps both. Why, oh why did Nathan have to die and leave her in this fix?

Genie shook her head. "I think we'll skip the flight and travel by train as originally planned."

"Then you'll be traveling alone, Miss Baker. I gave my word to Mrs. Schmidt I would fly her to California. And unlike some, when I give my word, I always keep it." Kitty turned to Dick, and her icy demeanor thawed considerably. "Don't be a stranger, Dickie. DC isn't as far as all that. Whenever you have some free time, be sure to come up. You'll always be welcome."

"I'll keep that in mind," Dick said, giving her a quick kiss on the cheek. As Kitty strode down the dock toward a row of cars waiting for passengers, the porter and all her bags following after her, his look became speculative. "Do you happen to know what happened between Kitty and Mrs. Schmidt?"

"No idea, but if I had to guess, I would say it had something to do with Nathan. Lavinia let it slip that Kitty was there when he fell."

His eyebrows rose. "Really?"

An awful thought resurfaced. "You don't suppose Kitty, well, pushed him, do you?"

He was already shaking his head. "No. Kitty may seem cold as ice, but she's no killer. The other day I saw her dress down a sailor for using a seagull as target practice. She was nigh on hysterical, she was so upset."

"Then I'm back to having no idea." She drew a deep breath, trying to steady her nerves after this latest change to her plans. "Since it looks like we're flying after all, you wouldn't want to help me find an inexpensive place to stay, would you?"

"I wish I could. Unfortunately, duty calls. The train station I could've managed, since I'm headed there myself." He hesitated. "Are your finances really as bad as all that?"

"Worse. But I'll figure it out." Meaning she couldn't stomach being any further in debt to him. And then there was her self-respect to contend with. Nathan hadn't seemed concerned about their lack of funds, which meant she couldn't be, either. Not unless she wanted to admit that women were indeed inferior when it came to solving problems.

She could almost feel Nathan smirking at her from the far side of the veil.

Determination boiled up inside her. She would not fail at this.

A poster stuck to the side of the taxi stand caught her eye. It showed a stormy sea battering a stone lighthouse, only instead of a beacon at the top, there was a large red cross. She didn't even need to read the large block letters telling her to "Join the American Red Cross." She instantly recognized the symbol from when she lived in Peking and was well aware of all the good work the Red Cross Society had done there. It was like a sign from heaven.

All she had to do was find a local office and explain that she and Lavinia were war refugees and in need of assistance, and everything would be fine. The Lord had provided, just as her father had always promised her.

With renewed spirits, she claimed Lavinia's and her luggage. Dick helped them hail a taxicab and load the bags into the trunk. While the driver asked a police officer for directions to the nearest Red Cross office, Dick helped Lavinia into the back seat. Then he turned to Genie. "You sure you'll be all right?"

"Absolutely." And she meant it, too.

He tenderly touched her cheek, his eyes almost overbright with emotion as he gazed down at her. "I can't wait until we can be together again."

Her breath snagged in her chest, her heart too full of wonder and gratitude to speak. For some unknown reason he had chosen her, and she thanked her lucky stars he had. She would never have been this optimistic about her future without him, not after losing Nathan and having the additional burden of a grieving Lavinia. And certainly not after learning her aunt had disappeared.

He leaned forward and kissed the corner of her mouth. A wonderful warmth curled through her despite the chilly breeze of the water. Compared to their last kiss, it was unbearably chaste, but likely much more appropriate to the surroundings.

He gave her a heartbreakingly sad, sweet smile. "Au revoir, Miss Baker."

In a daze, she let him help her into the taxi and then shut the door. As the taxi driver began to drive away, she waved out the window. To her disappointment, he was too busy loading his own luggage into the next taxi to see her.

"Genie, did you see this?" Lavinia said in a tight voice.

Reluctantly, Genie turned and glanced at her friend.

Lavinia held up a newspaper, her eyes wide, her face paper-white. "Someone left this. It's from today."

Frowning, Genie took it from her and scanned the *Brooklyn Daily Eagle* headlines. And then she saw it: "Chinese Fight Jap Drive to Split Burma: Hand-to-Hand Battles Rage in Toungoo Streets—Situation 'Critical.'"

A million shades of fear seized her as she skimmed the rest of the article: fear for Li Ming's fiancé, for Ted, for the CNAC pilots, for all the civilians . . . and especially for her father and Zhenzhu, as this last border between China and the Japanese invasion was about to be breached.

"Oh no," she breathed.

# Chapter 28

A mild breeze caressed Genie's skin as she paused at the top of the airstair. She blinked against the bright spring sunshine, the tang of oil from the airport mingling with the more agricultural scent of damp earth filling her nostrils. Palm trees waved softly by the terminal building, as though bidding welcome. But it wasn't until a quick scan of the area around the plane revealed no police officers hanging around, ready to arrest her, that some of her stomach-churning fear of the last week began to ease.

For reasons Genie could only guess at, Kitty had failed to mention, when she had handed over the tickets, that civilian travel in the United States had all but ceased after Pearl Harbor. Any seats on the few remaining commercial flights were for the exclusive use of military personnel or civilians traveling on war business—not thrill-seeking missionary girls.

Lavinia had picked up on it right away and had concocted a story where she and Genie were traveling for Kitty's clothing company, which was designing a new uniform for field nurses. Genie, less comfortable with lying, would nod and privately wonder how Kitty's father had been able to get the tickets. Though perhaps things weren't any different in the States than they were in China, where everything was for sale, given the right price.

On the way down the airstair, with no unusual flurry of activity starting up, she relaxed a little more. She glanced up at the snow-dusted hills that formed a solid wall to the east. While substantial enough to be considered mountains, they lacked the jagged poetry of the ones back home. *Home.* Her stomach twisted again, this time with sorrow and worry for her father and Zhenzhu.

The newspapers she had picked up in New York and Saint Louis had reported next to nothing on the fighting in Burma or China. She wished she had a way to know if her father was safe. If only he had agreed to come with her, she could have asked him what he had thought of this vast country, the country of his birth. He had rarely spoken of it, and she had never thought to ask. Now that she had spent the last two days viewing the States from the air, she was filled with questions. Had he been to Saint Louis, where she had overnighted between flights, and seen the mighty Mississippi River? Or the Grand Canyon, which the stewardess had pointed out as it passed in the distance off the wingtip?

What would he think of her decision to come to LA? She could well imagine what he would say about her kissing Dick—and Ted before that—but she was a woman full grown. Her virtue was still intact despite kissing two men. And she knew from the earthy talk of the village women that, unlike what the missionary wives had told her, one didn't get pregnant from kissing a man.

As long as Dick was gone on assignment, she could see nothing improper about her and Lavinia staying in his apartment. It would be only temporary, in any event. As soon as she started working at Vultee, saved up a little money, learned her way around the city, and understood how renting an apartment in the States even worked, she and Lavinia would move into a new place. Easy as pie. All she had to do was figure out how to hire a taxi to take them to Dick's place, and they would be set.

Her stomach shifted uneasily again. To distract herself, she straightened the cuffs of her new fawn gloves and then looked out at the large swaths of camouflage nets strung across the airfield. From the ground, it was easy to see the branches and pieces of fabric stuck in the netting and to see that many of the "buildings" crammed between the runways were merely sheets of plywood. From the air, though, the whole thing had taken on a completely different look. The airport had ceased to exist, becoming instead what appeared to be a suburban neighborhood. She had actually had a moment of panic as the plane centered itself to land on what looked like a city street. Then they had descended lower, exposing the artifice.

"Maybe asking for airplane tickets wasn't such a good idea," Lavinia said weakly, interrupting Genie's survey.

Genie glanced at her friend's pale sweaty face and felt a moment of compassion. "I suppose now's not the time to tell you that I loved every second."

Because she had.

Something about being unchained from the ground and being able to see for miles in every direction had filled her with joy. Even the turbulence over the mountains of Colorado, uncomfortable and a little frightening as it had been, hadn't dampened her enthusiasm. She found herself wanting to know more about why it had been rough there, and how the pilots had found their way over them when there were no roads to follow.

Genie took her friend's arm. "But just think—you made it! *We* made it. And you never have to fly again if you don't want to."

Lavinia expelled a shaky breath. "Which I don't. But you're right. We did make it. New city, new us."

"Exactly," Genie agreed. She stole a glance over her shoulder at the airplane, wishing she could climb back on. Someday, when the war was over and civilians could fly again, she was definitely going to buy a ticket and go up. It didn't matter where. China had an airline, so why not? She even knew two of the pilots.

She and Lavinia claimed their suitcases and then followed the other passengers through the beautiful stucco and red-tiled terminal building into the late-day sun. Military trucks rumbled by on the street out front. She searched the few cars parked in front for a taxi. Already planning ahead for the next step, she didn't immediately hear her name being called.

"Miss Baker. Mrs. Schmidt. Over here!" A petite blonde waved from down the sidewalk. The girl's red lips were stretched in a wide smile that showed off pearly white teeth. She hurried over as fast as her pencil-slim skirt would let her. Her pert velvet hat—pinned off center to accentuate her rolled hair—bobbed with each enthusiastic step.

"Sorry we're late," the girl exclaimed, her gray eyes bright with excitement beneath her perfectly plucked eyebrows. She bounced to a stop in front of them, fairly vibrating with high spirits. "How was the flight? I bet it was phenomenal. The weather couldn't be better. It makes me wish my lesson was today instead of tomorrow. Ready to go?"

"I'm sorry. Who are you?" Lavinia asked coldly. "And the flight was awful."

"Oh, I am so sorry! I'm Charity. Charity Newcombe." The girl stuck out her hand, Lavinia's rudeness having no perceivable effect on her sunny mood. "Mr. Pelton asked my uncle to meet you at the airport, to make sure you got to the apartment okay, and I thought you might be more comfortable if I tagged along. Not that my uncle is scary or anything. He's just so old! He doesn't know the first thing about how we young people live today."

"Genie Baker. And your uncle is . . . ," Genie prompted as she shook Charity's hand. The girl had a surprisingly strong grip.

"Fred Short, lead stunt pilot for Century Studios," Charity said proudly. "He also tests planes for the company where I work. And I hope where you two will be working, too! Uncle Fred has already set up interviews for you tomorrow morning, so we've got a lot to do before then."

"Tomorrow?" Genie repeated, her panic returning as Charity shook hands with a much less enthusiastic Lavinia.

"Uh-huh. But you don't have to start work right away. I'm sure Skip would let you take a couple of days to settle in." She pointed to a shiny, dark-blue sedan. "That's my uncle's car over there. Isn't it a beauty? Much nicer than riding the bus, which you'll get to do plenty of, since that's the easiest way to get around."

As they got closer, a short heavy-set man climbed out of the driver's side and waved at them. He looked nothing like she expected a test pilot to look. For one thing, he was much older—the hair under his hat was decidedly more salt than pepper—and he also had on a suit and tie. All the pilots she knew either wore uniforms or flight overalls.

"Now about tomorrow," Charity continued. "Skip—that's my boss—had only a couple of job openings on such short notice. There's one in the office pool—where I work—and two more on the shop floor if you two would rather work together."

Genie hesitated, completely lost as to why Vultee had a pool, or what one was expected to do on the floor of a shop. "I'll have to think about it."

"That's fine." Charity bounced on ahead to open the car's rear door.

"Afternoon, ladies." Fred Short held out his hands to take their suitcases. "Have a nice flight? I have to admit I was surprised when Dick said to meet you at the airport. Not many people get to fly these days, which is a real shame."

"I guess we got lucky," Genie said quickly before Lavinia could say something incriminating. "And thank you for picking us up, Mr. Short. I'm Genie Baker, and this is Lavinia Schmidt."

"Nice to meet you both," he said with an easy smile.

"Charity says we also have you to thank for getting us interviews for tomorrow."

"Yes, ma'am. I owed Dick a favor for getting me hired as a stunt pilot back in the thirties. Maybe he felt sorry for an old gimp like me."

"Or maybe he recognized a great pilot when he saw one." Charity gave her uncle a playful punch in the arm. Genie's eyes widened in shock, but Mr. Short seemed unperturbed.

"In any case," her uncle went on, "it was a lucky break. More lucrative than crop-dusting, and a heck of a lot more fun. Told him if he ever needed something in return to let me know. Didn't expect it would be so easy as picking up a pair of pretty girls from the airport," he said with a wink.

"Don't let him fool you," Charity said as her uncle limped around to the back of the sedan with the suitcases. "Uncle Frank is something of a legend in the Valley. He's so good, Vultee has him test out all their new designs."

"Not all of them." He opened the trunk and set the suitcases inside. "Only the ones they think might crash."

"Which scares my grandmother to no end," Charity whispered to them as her uncle made his way back to the driver's side. "Just last month he had to put a plane down in an orchard because the engine seized up. He's lucky to be alive."

Mr. Short paused on his way into the driver's seat and narrowed his eyes at his niece. "Luck has nothing to do with it, missy. It's skill and practice, and don't you forget it."

"Yes, sir." Charity rolled her eyes as she opened the door for Lavinia. While Genie waited her turn, she was reminded of something Ted had said about flying and luck. Except he had said it was better to be lucky than good. Zhenzhu would have agreed. Luck was everything in China. Still, Genie liked the idea of overcoming bad luck with skill. It was much more optimistic.

Mr. Short started the engine and pulled out into traffic. He glanced in the rearview mirror and caught Genie's eye.

"That was a right nice photo of you in the newspaper a couple of weeks back. Is it true you met General Chiang?" he asked.

"I was in the papers?" she asked, startled.

"Forget the general," Charity butted in, stars in her eyes. "I want to know about the Flying Tigers. Were they dreamy? No, forget that . . . of course they were."

"I only met a few," she said, belatedly recalling the photo Dick had taken of her in Cape Town and the attendant article. How long ago that day seemed. And the dinner with the Chiangs? Ancient history. "And the Generalissimo and his wife were very nice. Very polite."

"The Flying Tigers are my heroes," Charity said. "They and Amelia Earhart. I wonder if they'll ever find her."

"You don't think they will?" Genie asked carefully, still not sure who this Amelia person was and not wanting to admit as much. Not when she so desperately wanted to make a good first impression on Charity and her uncle.

Charity leaned forward, her blue eyes intense. "I hope so, but I think the Japs got her. I think she was flying over them, taking photographs for the government, and got shot down."

"Or more likely," her uncle said in a drawl so very much like Ted's it made her heart hurt a little, "she got lost, ran out of fuel, and crashed into the ocean. You ever been flying out of sight of land, Miss Charity? It ain't easy."

"How could I?" Charity sat back with a huff. "Florence has forbidden me from flying more than two nautical miles from the coast. At least until I get my license."

"Well, good for Flo."

"Wait, you're a pilot, too?" Genie tried to wrap her head around the idea. "They let women fly?"

"Well, of course, silly! You aren't one of those kooks who think Amelia is really a young man in drag, are you? And what about Louise Thaden or Blanche Noyes or Jackie Cochran, all winners of the Bendix

Trophy for air racing?" A smug smile twisted Charity's red lips. "Beat those men, fair and square."

"You should tell her about the flying program Vultee's got for its employees," Mr. Short said over his shoulder.

Charity's eyes widened. "Oh my gosh, yes! We definitely could use more lady pilots to show those men what's what. If you want, I can get you two pamphlets tomorrow when we go to the plant."

"Not for me," Lavinia said sourly. "If I never go up in another airplane, it will be too soon."

"The flight was a little rough today," Genie agreed soothingly, but her mind was otherwise occupied. The possibility of becoming a pilot had never occurred to her. Men were the ones who worked on and with machines. Men were the ones who drove cars, who commanded ships, who flew airplanes . . . and yet Charity said she was learning to fly.

"Well, there's no need to decide anything today," Mr. Short assured them. "Mrs. Schmidt looks like she's fading fast. Now Dick didn't get a chance to tell me a whole lot, on account of it being a bad connection. Will Mr. Schmidt be joining you ladies?"

"Mr. Schmidt is dead." The ice in Lavinia's tone should have rendered the conversation just as deceased, but Mr. Short seemed to have missed it.

His glance in the rearview mirror was sympathetic. "The war?"
Lavinia nodded stiffly.

"Well, that explains a lot. Dick can't resist playing hero for damsels in distress," Mr. Short said, his attention returning to the road.

Exhaustion swamped Genie as they drove. She tried to pay attention as Charity chattered on about the weather and the places they were passing, but her thoughts kept returning to the fact that she was finally here. She had made it to California in spite of all the trials and tragedies the war had thrown at her. She still needed to find her aunt to finish the journey, but the bulk of it was done.

Still, her relief was tinged with regret, and no little sorrow, for the one person who hadn't made it. His absence in the car became all the more conspicuous as Charity peppered them with questions and Lavinia never once mentioned her engagement, or even his name. It was as if Nathan had simply ceased to exist for her, his love erased. An unwanted body committed to the cold embrace of the ocean, with no grave to acknowledge his time spent upon the earth. No way for his loved ones, wherever they might be, to pay their respects.

It wasn't right. Common decency demanded that he at least have a memorial marker erected somewhere. Chinese tradition demanded it, too. Though she would deny any belief in ghosts if asked, she was enough a child of China to worry about Nathan's angry spirit—especially since they hadn't parted on the best of terms. Let the Lord keep his third of Nathan's soul, and the ocean her third.

Genie would have to talk to Lavinia about getting a gravestone made for him here in LA to safely anchor the last third. Just in case her father was wrong and Nathan wasn't entirely in heaven. Because the last thing she needed was to be haunted by a vengeful spirit. She had enough challenges already.

# Chapter 29

The next afternoon, Genie kicked off the slightly too small pumps Charity had loaned her for the interview and groaned with relief. As she leaned back on the couch in Dick's apartment, the deep glow of accomplishment that had simmered inside her the whole bus ride home from the plant blossomed, and she found herself grinning like a little child.

*I did it.* She was officially a secretary at Vultee Consolidated, due to start in two days' time. Later she could panic about not knowing how to type or take shorthand, but not now. Besides, Charity had assured her both skills would be easy enough to learn. For the moment Mr. Winston—or Skip, which was how all the office girls referred to him—had been happy enough that she could read and write in Chinese. Vultee didn't do a lot of business with China, but enough that the recent loss of their in-house translator to the draft had caused concern.

She rolled her head to the side, careful not to dislodge the pins holding her snood, and watched Lavinia put away the groceries.

"If you want to leave that for later, I'll do it," Genie offered half-heartedly.

"No, that's fine. You paid, so I'll put them away." Her friend paused with a bag of onions in her hand as she decided where she wanted to store them. "Do you find it odd that there is a complete lack of food in the cabinets?"

"Likely Dick didn't want anything to spoil in his absence. He does travel a lot."

Lavinia shot her a skeptical look. "Rice doesn't spoil. Neither does flour or salt."

"Maybe he doesn't like to cook?"

Lavinia opened a cabinet and put the onions inside. "Well, he obviously likes to drink. Too bad neither one of us does. There's enough alcohol in this apartment to float an entire navy."

Too exhausted to think of a snappy reply, Genie rolled her head back and closed her eyes. It was true that there were some things about Dick's apartment that weren't quite as she had expected. Nothing was hung on the walls. No photographs or knickknacks cluttered the small tabletops, which not only struck her as impersonal but also odd, given his profession and his travels. Then there was the record player in a beautifully carved wood cabinet stuffed with leather albums filled with records, but not a single book in the entire apartment. Not even a magazine or outdated newspaper, which struck her as even more curious than the lack of food, given his collection of printed news onboard ship.

"Scoot over."

Her eyes snapped open as she straightened. "I'm sorry. This is your bed, and here I am lounging all over it."

"I don't want to sleep, silly. I just want to sit down."

Genie moved to the far cushion. Lavinia collapsed onto the couch and sighed deeply.

"We did it," Lavinia said proudly, echoing Genie's earlier thoughts. "We are officially employed and capable of living on our own."

"You don't mind working by yourself on the factory line?" The question had bothered her all day, despite Lavinia's insistence that Genie pick which position she wanted to apply for.

"I'll hardly be alone." Her friend sounded amused, if a little tired. "And to be honest, I feel the same way about answering telephones as you do about handling a wrench. Besides, the pay is better on the line."

"I just feel like I'm abandoning you . . ."

"You're doing no such thing." Lavinia reached over and squeezed her hand. "I'm grateful to even be here. Without you, I'd either be on the streets of New York trying to sell myself or dead. So as far as I'm concerned, anything you say from here on out is fine with me."

"You would not be dead," Genie said sharply, unsettled and more than a little upset by her friend's casual mention of it. "I wish you would stop saying such things."

Lavinia released Genie's hand. "Nevertheless, I am in your debt."

"At least take the bed, and let me sleep on the couch."

Her friend sighed. "We already discussed this . . ."

"How about we share the bed?" she continued gamely. "There's plenty of room."

Lavinia sprang to her feet and went to the window. "The couch is fine. How many times do I have to tell you before you believe me?"

"When you convince me that sleeping on the couch isn't you punishing yourself for Nathan's death."

"I'm not. It's just . . . I haven't been sleeping well. So it's best that I stay out here, where I won't wake you." The bleak expression in Lavinia's eyes broke Genie's heart. Abruptly, her friend turned and walked into the bedroom. "Do you think Mr. Pelton would mind if I took one of his towels to the beach?"

"You're not coming with me to Chinatown?" she asked, still not feeling right about having the bed to herself, but it was also clear her friend was done discussing the matter.

Lavinia reappeared with a beach bag and towel in her arms. "Since I don't have the same fond memories of the Orient that you do, I'd rather not. And also unlike you, I find being near water soothing."

Genie eyed her dubiously. "Isn't it a little cold for swimming? It can't be much over sixty degrees out there."

"I'm not going in the water." Lavinia stuffed the towel into the bag. "For one, I don't have a swimsuit, though that's going to be one of the first things I buy when I save up enough money. And for another, it's only March, so the water is likely freezing."

Genie shivered in disgust. "Freezing or not, I can't imagine ever wanting to swim in the ocean. I'd much rather fly over it."

"I saw you brought home a pamphlet on flight lessons." Lavinia set the bag on the small metal dinette table and picked up the paper in question. "Are you really going to do it?"

"Absolutely. As soon as I figure out our money situation."

Her friend glanced at her. "Can I ask why? It's awfully expensive, and it's not like you'll be able to do anything with it."

"That's not true. You heard Charity yesterday. Women can fly in air races and across country—"

"But not as a job. Didn't you notice on our plant tour that there wasn't a single female pilot waiting to ferry a plane?"

"Maybe we just missed them," she said stubbornly.

"Maybe, but that still doesn't explain why you want to learn."

A plethora of emotions whirled up inside her, choking off her ability to speak. How to explain the rush she felt when the plane left the ground? And the awe she felt as it climbed into the sky, past cloud and peak? It was impossible, so she opted for something more concrete. "Remember how you said you almost made it out before the Japanese attack but didn't because there weren't enough pilots? Well, what if there had been one more? What if it had been someone like me?"

"Marcus wouldn't have flown with a female pilot," Lavinia said flatly. "And I said there weren't enough planes."

"Planes require pilots. And would he still have refused if he had known the consequences of staying behind?"

Lavinia's hand fisted around the pamphlet in silent distress, but Genie didn't back down. Her friend's tale of how people had been stranded and then slaughtered by the enemy because there hadn't been enough flights out had left an indelible mark on her soul.

Lavinia's gaze dropped to the papers on the table as she took a deep breath. "Likely not." Her fingers trembled as she replaced the pamphlet and began smoothing it out. Then she picked up the newspaper clipping Charity had given Genie. It was the article Dick had submitted right before they had left Cape Town. "This is a nice photo of you and Bess. I'm surprised Kitty wasn't in it. She was there, wasn't she?"

"She was," Genie said carefully, aware they were venturing into yet another minefield. "But I think she was afraid my poor sartorial choices might have ruined her reputation for fashion."

As she had hoped—no, prayed—Lavinia smiled. But it was tinged with sadness.

"Funny. I never worried about such things on the boat." Lavinia touched the photograph softly, as if to reach the person who was just out of sight. "How backward and gauche I must have appeared. And how ironic that she's not here to see how far I've come."

Genie didn't know how to respond. It was true that her friend looked utterly modern this afternoon, with her hacked-off hair now lying in artfully trimmed curls that gave her an avant-garde, almost doll-like appearance. The clothes she had borrowed from Charity's friend, since Charity herself was closer to Genie's height, showed off her trim figure. And the spark of hope that lit her blue eyes more often than not these past few days had driven the shadows from her pixie face.

And yet despite the outward improvement, Genie wondered how much her friend had healed on the inside. So much had happened since the beginning of the year, loss upon loss piling up, culminating in Nathan's death not fifteen days ago. Of course, if her own feelings were any guide, perhaps the latter calamity hadn't fully hit Lavinia yet.

Even though Genie knew Nathan was dead, had watched his body being swallowed by the sea, it still didn't feel quite real. It was as if her mind couldn't quite wrap itself around the fact. Part of her truly expected Nathan to reappear as if nothing had happened, ready to take charge of their lives again. It only followed that if she couldn't quite get over how surreal the whole thing felt, she couldn't even begin to imagine what her friend was feeling.

"Are you sure you don't want to leave the beach for another day?" she asked as Lavinia put all the papers into a neat pile again. "It'd be nice to have some company."

Lavinia looked up. "If you don't want to go by yourself, just say so."

"What?" she said, startled. "No. I was thinking of you. That maybe you didn't want to be alone."

Lavinia sighed. "Genie, it's all right. We've been shepherded all of our lives, never going anywhere by ourselves. Of course you don't want to go to Chinatown alone. It's something women like us were never allowed to do. Yet one of the things I most admired about Ki—Miss Van Nuys—was that she had traveled around the globe solo, and she had never given it a second thought. Such independence! No men telling her what to do. No women tagging along like nursemaids. I was so envious. Actually, I still am.

"The way I see it," Lavinia went on, giving Genie no chance to respond. "This would be a good test of us both. I'll go to the beach while you go to Chinatown. And we won't let our fear of being alone stop us. After all, other people go places alone all the time."

"I'm not afraid of being—" she began and then stopped, surprised by the small fluttering of anxiety in her stomach. Could Lavinia be right? In truth, she couldn't actually think of a time when she had gone someplace new without someone else going with her.

"But it's up to you," Lavinia said. "If you want me to come with you . . ."

"No." She took a deep breath, refusing to let such an inane fear stop her. "You're right. I should practice going places on my own."

"All right, then." Lavinia picked up her bag. "Let's have a look at the bus map and see what's running this afternoon."

They divvied up their money for bus fare and agreed on where to hide the apartment key in case they didn't get home at the same time. Then Lavinia left the apartment, the beach bag over her shoulder.

The wall clock ticked hollowly in the silence after her friend's departure. It was a little unnerving to find out how right Lavinia was and how little she liked being alone. Glancing at the clock, she saw she still had twenty minutes until her bus. Plenty of time to change her mind and put off her errands until tomorrow.

*Stop it, Genie. You're not a coward.*

Desperate for a distraction, she opened her bag and hunted around until she found what she was looking for. Sitting down, she unfolded the thin crinkly paper of the overseas V-mail, conspicuously marked with its bright red and blue borders, and picked up a pen. The apartment disappeared as she concentrated on the blank page. Where should she even start? So much had happened since she had last written him. A deep longing for one of his hugs welled within her. *Please, Lord, let him and Zhenzhu and everyone else be safe.*

As if in answer to her prayer, a sudden calm washed over her. She could almost feel her father beside her, steady and wise, waiting for her to speak. Tears filled her eyes as the ink flowed from the nib to the blank page: *Dearest Father. I hope you and Zhenzhu are well. I am in California, safe and sound, but I'm afraid the journey isn't over yet . . .*

# Chapter 30

Charity plopped down onto the office chair across from Genie and folded her hands expectantly. Genie ignored her and concentrated instead on the memo she was typing. It had taken nearly two weeks of practice to memorize the layout of the typewriter keys—the seemingly haphazard placement of the letters making no sense to her—but now, if she was on the ball like she was today, she could make the keys click as smoothly as a well-tuned engine. The rhythmic staccato, combined with the sounds from the other machines in the office, made a satisfying kind of music that she was loath to disturb.

"Ahem." Charity cleared her throat, and Genie missed a key.

Casting a sour glance at her friend, she backspaced to the beginning of the word. One mistake she could X out and retype. Two and she would have to start the form over. Silently she willed her friend to go away so she could focus.

Her friend didn't catch the hint. "So are you going to take lunch today or not?"

"Not." *XXXX.* Her finger pressed the key with savage intensity. "I'm working through so I can leave early without being docked. With two flight lessons this weekend to pay for, as well as a few other things, I need every dime of my paycheck this week."

One of the other things being Nathan's grave plaque, which she hoped to pick up after work. She had found a place in Chinatown that would make one for her even without a death certificate. Lord bless the Chinese for being such pragmatists. All it took was the right price and a little compromise on her part. Instead of the stone she had envisioned, which would have required a truck to transport, she had opted for the much smaller, lighter, less expensive option of a bronze plaque. She would have to attach it to something larger later, but that was the key word: later.

She started typing again more slowly. Leaving early would depend on her getting through her entire inbox, which left no time for mistakes.

"Two lessons? Holy cow, Genie. I swear you're at the airport more than the flight instructors." Charity leaned forward with a sly gleam in her eye. "Come clean; it's a fellow, isn't it? You met a pilot that you just can't get out of your head, and you want to impress him."

A sudden image of Ted's darkly handsome face made her fingers curl, and she almost hit the wrong key. Shoving aside the wayward thought, she advanced the form to the next box. "No, I just happen to like flying. Is that such a crime?"

"Well, no. But you didn't grow up around airplanes like I did, so it seems a little unusual. I mean, when was the first time you even saw a plane?"

"When I was sixteen." With no little relief, she finished the last line error-free. She carefully removed it from the typewriter and put it in her out-box. Then she picked up a blank form and began threading it into the platen. "My father took me to an aviation exposition in Shanghai that was in honor of Generalissimo Chiang's birthday."

"Really? I didn't know China had planes back then. You know what I wish? That I could go with you when you return to China. Just to visit. After all, I love Chinese food. And think of all the gifts I could find! My mother adores Blue Willow china. It would be fun, don't you think?"

Genie made a noncommittal sound. She had given up trying to educate the girls in the office pool that living in China wasn't like walking through LA's Chinatown. It wasn't just using chopsticks instead of forks, or all about the silk robes and hopelessly outdated court customs featured in Hollywood films. It was much more rich and complex, with ancient butting up against modern. They didn't want to hear about modern Peking, with its streetcars and electricity, or even Kunming with its modern hospital and Western-style university.

"Of course, we have to win the war first," Charity breezed on, thankfully looking like she was getting ready to stand up. Then she stopped. "That reminds me—did you see in the paper that Lee somebody-or-other is touring North America in her plane to raise funds for China? The article said she's a big-shot movie star in China."

Genie paused midturn of the carriage knob and glanced at her friend, suddenly all ears. "Lee Ya-Ching? Did it say if she's coming to LA?"

"I don't think it did. But wouldn't that be nifty! I bet she would love meeting you, another girl pilot, and one who could talk to her in Chinese. You two could even gossip about meeting Madame Chiang, because I bet she has, too."

An unexpected wave of homesickness slid between her ribs and straight into her heart. Without thought, she rubbed at the ache in her upper chest and then, realizing what she was doing, stopped. Hoping her friend hadn't noticed, she refocused on correctly aligning the paper in the typewriter.

How odd that walking through Chinatown only made her mildly nostalgic, whereas being reminded of that dinner with the Chiangs hit her so much harder. Maybe because she could so clearly picture Nathan that night, uptight and disapproving, and Ted in his uniform. It had been her first time in a Western-style dress . . .

She shook off the memory and prepared to type. "Let me know if you hear anything. In the meantime, if I don't get these forms typed,

I'm sunk. I have to leave early today, and I don't want Skip firing me for leaving things undone."

Charity waved Genie's fears away. "Bah, Skip would never fire you. Have you seen the way he looks at you? You could be all thumbs and still keep your job."

Genie's fingers twitched, and she only barely missed hitting a *j* instead of a *u*. She had indeed noticed the way her boss looked at her and had fervently hoped it was her imagination that he came out of his office every time she arrived for work, and that his gaze ran up and down her legs every time he passed her desk. But if Charity had noticed it, too . . .

"Baker, you've got a phone call," the department secretary called from the doorway, her voice as gravelly from cigarette smoke as Wu Fang's had been.

Surprised, she pushed her chair back, the casters squeaking as they moved across the linoleum floor. She couldn't imagine who might be calling her. Lavinia was working next door in the plant, and the gravestone maker didn't know where she worked.

She picked up the receiver on the department's communal telephone. "This is Eugenia Baker."

"Genie, it's Dick. Dick Pelton." His normally rich voice sounded thin and tinny through the phone. Still, it was the most welcome sound she had heard in weeks.

She turned her back on her friend's narrowed gaze and smiled, pleasure racing through her blood, warming her from the toes up. "Dick, where are you?"

"Believe it or not, I'm just down the road. In San Diego. What do you say I come up there and visit you, maybe take you out to dinner?"

Her heart leaped. "That would be lovely." Then she remembered. "Oh, but where will you stay? We've completely taken over your place."

He laughed, the familiar warmth and amusement melting the distance between them. "Don't worry. I'll stay with a friend. And I can't stay long, anyway. In fact, I was almost afraid to call for fear of getting your hopes up, only to have to cancel at the last minute."

"You wouldn't dare," she teased, hoping she sounded confident and mature.

"Not given a choice, but alas, my time is not my own. Nevertheless, I'm hoping I can steal away for at least a day, because I really want to see you."

"Ditto," she replied, afraid to say too much. From the sudden quiet in the room behind her, she was pretty sure the few remaining girls who had yet to leave were hanging off the edge of their chairs, trying to catch every word.

"Let's see, today is Friday, and weekends are a no-go for me. How about Tuesday? You free that day? I'll make sure to call first, before I leave, so you'll know I'm on my way."

"That would be perfect."

"And, Genie . . ." His voice became husky, deep. "Look pretty for me, will you? I've been dreaming of you for weeks, and I want to take you somewhere fancy."

The rush of nerves stole her ability to speak for a moment. Something more than dinner was at stake here; she could hear it in his voice, and it left her both dizzy and flushed. "S-sure."

After they both said goodbye, she hung up the receiver and turned to find Charity staring at her with moon-wide eyes.

"Well?" her friend asked as Genie made her way back to her chair, her legs as shaky as a newborn lamb's.

She released the breath she wasn't even aware she'd been holding. "Mr. Pelton wants to take me out for dinner."

"You mean Uncle Fred's friend?" Charity frowned slightly. "No disrespect intended, but isn't he a little . . . well, old for you?"

"Not really. He's only thirty, or maybe thirty-five at the most." Then happy disbelief made her laugh. "I can't believe he called."

Charity's eyebrows rose. "Are you sweet on him?"

"What? No," she said, ruthlessly jerking herself back to reality. "He's just a friend." *A friend who happens to be an extremely good kisser.* Warmth curled low in her belly as she remembered the details of that first kiss in New York.

"Oh, that's all right, then. For a moment, I thought . . . well, never mind. Since I've never met him, I thought he was my uncle's age."

Genie gave herself a mental shake. "He's not. And he's coming up next Tuesday, so maybe you'll get to meet him then. He also wants to take me somewhere nice, so I'll need your help to look my best."

"Look your best, eh?" A speculative gleam lit her friend's eyes.

"Baker. Newcombe." Skip's irritated voice made them both jump. He stood in the door of his office, arms crossed and scowling. Genie's skin prickled as his dark eyes locked on hers. She felt like a fly pinned to a specimen board. "Either get to work or clock out. I'm not paying you to gab."

"Yes, Mr. Winston," she and Charity both answered, though Genie suspected his comment was directed mostly at her.

Her supposition was borne out at the end of the day when he called her into his office to lecture her on how her wanting time off couldn't become a habit, and how he would expect her to work late in the future, if the need arose. Then, after reviewing her work, he kept his word and let her go.

It took longer than she expected to make her way to Chinatown and back. The buses were all packed to overflowing and running later than usual. As a result, she didn't get home to the apartment until after six. Her shoulders ached from carrying the nearly twenty-pound grave marker, but at least it was discreetly bound in paper and string, so no one had given her a second look on the bus. It took a moment of juggling to get her key out of her purse, but soon she had the building door open and was up the two flights of stairs to the apartment.

She opened the front door and peeked in. For reasons she couldn't fully explain even to herself, she hadn't mentioned today's errand to Lavinia. Her friend had been doing so well of late—losing some of her gauntness and having fewer nightmares, even making some new friends—that Genie was afraid to do anything to jinx it. Perhaps later, when she had saved up enough money to purchase a small grave plot, she would bring the subject up. That is, assuming she could sneak the package past her friend tonight.

The good news was that Lavinia wasn't in the kitchenette. The bad news was the pot of water on the stove starting to boil, which meant Lavinia had to be nearby.

Briefly, she entertained the idea of leaving the package in the hallway for a few hours, perhaps until bedtime, when she might be able to smuggle it in without Lavinia noticing. The problem with that, though, was the nosy neighbors, who were bound to notice it and then knock on the door to tell Genie and Lavinia that it was there.

She eased the door wider. Water was running in the bathroom, masking any sound she might make. Relieved, she tiptoed through the apartment and opened the front closet. The water pipes thumped as the faucet was abruptly shut off.

"Genie, is that you?" Lavinia called from the bathroom.

"It's me." She hurriedly shoved the package in the back of the closet and shut the door. "Sorry I'm late."

Lavinia came around the corner, toweling off her short dark hair. Her face was freshly scrubbed, too. And Genie wasn't sure in the early-evening light coming through the window, but her friend's eyes looked faintly puffy. "Did you hear Kitty is getting married? To a soldier, no less."

"Wow. That was fast," she said, a little shocked by the news. It hadn't even been a month since they had last seen the woman. "How did you find out?"

"Mr. Pelton. You just missed his call." Lavinia headed back to the bathroom with the towel.

Genie's pulse went through the roof with excitement at the mention of Dick. Then crashed with disappointment as her friend's words sank in. "Did you tell him to call back?"

"No," Lavinia called out from the bathroom, horrifying Genie with that single word.

"Whyever not?" she asked in disbelief.

"Because he said he wouldn't be able to." Lavinia reappeared, her hair now combed into some semblance of order. "Can you believe Kitty, though? She doesn't even like soldiers. She told me she hated everything to do with the war."

Genie followed her friend into the kitchen, suppressing her irritation with Lavinia's refusal to stay on topic. "Did Dick say anything else? Leave a message for me?"

Lavinia dumped spaghetti into the now-boiling pot. "Yeah. He said he's very sorry, but he'll need a rain check on your date next week."

"Oh." Genie's spirits ebbed. "Did he say why?"

"He's going to be out of the country." Lavinia set the timer and then turned to face her, a frown gathering on her delicate face. "When did you two start dating?"

"I don't know if you could say we're dating, exactly." A guilty heat spread up her neck, though, as she remembered the smoky purr in his voice when he asked her to wear something nice. She looked away from Lavinia's too perceptive gaze. "We're just friends."

"Well, for your sake, I hope you keep it that way."

Irritation surged within her. "What is it you don't like about him, Lavinia?"

"I never said I didn't like him."

"Don't lie to me," Genie snapped. "You haven't liked him from the moment you met him."

"Genie, I . . ." Lavinia made a frustrated sound. "Well, it's just you could do so much better than Mr. Pelton."

"In what way?"

"He's—" Lavinia shook her head as she headed back to the bedroom. "Never mind. Just don't do anything you'll regret, all right?"

"For the last time, we're friends," she said, following after her.

"That's fine." Lavinia opened one the bureau drawers and began digging through it. "Do we still have that card Kitty gave us in New York?"

"Why?" Genie asked, instantly on alert. "You're not planning on contacting her, are you? Because I'm not at all sure that would be a good idea."

"Why not?" Lavinia asked distractedly as she shut the drawer and opened a new one.

"Well, for one, she was pretty steamed at you the last time you saw her."

"She's making a mistake," Lavinia said without pausing her search. "And someone needs to tell her."

"It doesn't have to be you," Genie said a little desperately. "Lavinia, you're not contacting her."

Lavinia finally looked up, her brows drawn in confusion. "Why not?"

"Because I threw the card away ages ago." Which was the truth. It had been one of Genie's first acts once she had safely reached LA, as she had been so relieved to be done with the woman. "Let it go. If she had wanted to remain friends with you, she could've made an effort those five days we were in New York. But she didn't. She left all the arrangements to her personal assistant. Remember?"

Lavinia's gaze slid away, and her chin took on the stubborn set Genie knew all too well.

"And think of this," Genie continued, "think of how expensive those airline tickets had to have been. If you contact her, she might decide we need to reimburse her, which we simply don't have the money for."

"That won't happen," Lavinia said flatly. "She got off easy buying us those tickets."

Genie stared at her friend. "What do you mean?"

"Never mind." Lavinia exhaled and shut the drawer.

Renewed suspicion prickled like ice up Genie's spine. "Lavinia, did Kitty have something to do with Nathan's fall? You said she was there."

Lavinia glanced up, her blue eyes wide and oddly blank. "Did I? Then I was mistaken."

"Lavinia, what actually happened?" Genie asked sternly, no longer sure what to believe.

"I already told you: he fell." A note of desperation entered Lavinia's voice. "We were arguing over my going home, and in the heat of the discussion he didn't see how close he was to the stairs. I blame myself because I didn't catch him in time, but I didn't push him, Genie. Nor did Kitty. Nor did anyone. He fell."

"Then why are you angry at Kitty?"

"She was the one who put the idea of going to see my father into Nathan's head." Lavinia turned her gaze back to the bureau and stared sightlessly at it for a moment as Genie reeled under this new revelation. The deliberate malice of Kitty's action utterly confounded her.

"Why would she do that?" Genie finally asked. *And how could you care who she's marrying after that?*

"She hoped it would force me to call off the engagement. She'd taken a dislike to him and thought I could do better." Lavinia was silent a few seconds, and then she turned and gave Genie a tremulous smile. "But that's all in the past, now. New city, new us, right?"

Genie took a deep breath and let it out. "Sure."

For what other choice did she have, did either of them have, but to move forward?

The answer was none. *Panta rei.*

# Chapter 31

"Not bad!" Florence yelled from behind Genie, her voice barely audible over the engine clatter of the Piper J-3 Cub. Genie managed to twist her lips into a smile, grateful for the praise. Not that her instructor would see it, since she was sitting behind Genie in the narrow cockpit. "Not bad at all, kiddo."

Flo clapped her encouragingly on the shoulder, but Genie didn't dare relax her vigilance as the plane rolled down the runway. As the taxiway appeared on the right, she pushed on the rudder pedals to turn the plane. Her legs shook with fatigue and nerves, and her fingers were cramping from her death grip on the control stick. Maybe someday she would land without her pulse accelerating into the red arc, but she wasn't there yet.

"Taxi back to the flight line, will you?" Flo hollered from the back seat, and Genie's stomach fell to the soles of her new sturdy-soled shoes.

Today's lesson was supposed to be for an hour, but they had only been out thirty minutes. Despite her decent landing, she must have messed up badly enough somewhere else to need to be grounded, but where?

The engine loped along with her frantic thoughts. The takeoff had been good. So had her practice maneuvers over the hills. So why were they stopping early?

"Don't park!" Flo yelled again. "Just shut her down here."

Confused, Genie pulled the fuel mixture knob to the idle cutoff position. The engine sputtered and then died. The stark silence that followed echoed with her worries as she hopped out of the aircraft and waited for Flo to gather her things. Charity, who was also Flo's student, had never mentioned students failing before. Was she going to be the first? Her stomach twisted nervously.

Flo climbed out of the back seat and jumped to the ground. She turned to Genie and slid her aviation goggles up to the top of her head. "Remind me, how many hours you got now?"

"Eleven."

Flo glanced up at the cloudless sky and then over at the weakly stirring windsock. "Well . . . looks like the weather should hold for the next few minutes. What do you say you take her up on your own?"

"What?" Genie wiped her sweaty hands on her overalls to hide their sudden shaking as elation and terror flooded her. "Do you mean it?"

Flo laughed. "I wouldn't say it if I didn't mean it. So . . . what do you think? Ready to give it a go?"

Genie took several deep breaths and stared at the yellow Cub, feeling simultaneously excited and petrified. She was going to get to fly it solo. Now. All by herself. Just her and the plane. "You sure I can do this?"

"Absolutely. If the winds had cooperated last week, I would have soloed you then." Flo slapped her on the back hard enough to make her stagger. "You got this, China Girl. Just take your time and remember— if you don't like anything about the landing, anything at all, there's no shame in going around and trying it again."

"Do a go-around. Got it." Her feet refused to move.

"Come on. Don't tell me the gal who single-handedly rescued a Flying Tiger is afraid of a little challenge."

"I didn't rescue him," she said in exasperation, tired of having to correct everyone. "My father did."

"That's not what the paper said." Flo gave her a conspiratorial wink and then sauntered off toward the front of the airplane as if Genie flying solo were a foregone conclusion.

Genie wiped her hands on her pant legs again and silently cursed Dick for his wildly inaccurate article. Though being reminded of Ted did calm her a bit. What she was contemplating was something he did every day with ease, though he wouldn't be climbing into a little J-3 Cub but a much bigger, much more powerful Curtis Warhawk. Just thinking about flying such a beast made her pulse triple-time.

Forcing herself to breathe, she tried to imagine herself in Ted's shoes. How might he feel if he were asked to take her little Cub up? *It'd be a cakewalk.*

She glanced at Flo waiting expectantly by the propeller, ready to help pop the starter. She took a deep breath and let Ted's easy confidence flow through her veins.

*There's nothing to it.*

The world was in unusually sharp focus as she climbed back into the cockpit. She took the rear seat this time, where Flo usually sat, and let the familiar sensory details of the plane soak in: the musky, almost metallic odor of leather and oil, the acrid stench of hot insulation, the sharper tang of road oil blown in from the recently treated runway. The array of dials on the dash sat silent, still, waiting for the start of the engine. She ran her gaze over them, mentally reassuring herself that everything she needed to know was right here: tachometer, airspeed, compass, altitude, oil temperature, and oil pressure.

"Ready?" Flo called out, her hands on one blade of the wooden propeller.

Genie placed her feet on the rudder pedals, left and right, and breathed. Her right hand gripped the control stick. Her left was on the throttle lever, which was attached to the frame just beneath the window. She pressed down on the pedals with her heels to hold the brakes. "Ready."

Flo gave the propeller a hard turn and jumped back as the plane rocked slightly. Nothing. Seemingly unperturbed by the engine's lack of cooperation, she repeated the procedure. Again, nothing, and Genie started worrying. Maybe it was a sign she wasn't ready. Flo hand-propped the Cub one last time, and this time the starter caught. The engine fired to life, and Flo jogged away from the plane, out of the propeller's deadly reach, with her head ducked to avoid the grit from the prop-wash.

Still imagining she was Ted, Genie eased up on the brakes and added a little throttle. The plane lurched forward, and then she didn't need to imagine anymore. She was simply an aviator, taking her plane out. She could do this!

She taxied to the end of the runway, her head craning this way and that, looking for any traffic, human or mechanical. The ever-present possibility of unexpected engine failure had her scanning the gauges. Everything looked good. She stood on the brakes, wiped her hands, and then taxied onto the runway. She pushed the throttle all the way in, and the engine's pattering became deafening as it threw itself into its task of acceleration.

The Cub rattled and shimmied. Then the tail came up, and her feet added a little right rudder to hold the plane straight. Another second, another breath, and then everything smoothed out as the plane left the ground. Elation sparkled through her as the earth fell away.

She was doing it. She was flying all by herself.

At four hundred feet above the ground, she banked to the right, making the first ninety-degree turn of the airport traffic pattern she'd learned. Below her, the streets of Montebello stretched out in long lines. Spotting the tall building she used as a reference point for starting the downwind leg, she made the second turn. The familiar mountains that ringed the north and east edge of the LA basin were a deep blue in the hazy air, but she couldn't let herself be distracted by the view. Sooner than she liked, the third landmark of the pattern appeared dead ahead. She turned onto the base leg, the end of the runway off to her right.

A rush of things to check flooded her thoughts: airspeed, altitude, alignment, trim. The runway was just off the nose as she turned on final and began her slip to land. Her pulse thundered in her ears as she worked to keep the plane lined up correctly. The runway grew steadily larger and longer in her windscreen. The numbers whipped under the nose, and then she could no longer see the center stripes. On pins and needles, she waited for the jerk of the tires meeting the pavement, telling her she had landed. *Any second now . . .*

*Any second.*

The flight-school building rushed by, and her heart kicked as if hit by an electric jolt. The Cub was caught in ground effect, and was going to float all the way off the end of the runway if she didn't do something.

In a spurt of panic, she pushed the throttle open and the stick forward to start the go-around. The engine screamed in protest, and the plane shuddered as it tried to stall.

"Come on, come on, come on." She leaned forward, mentally willing the plane faster so it could shake free of the airstream hugging the runway and start climbing. Slowly, the Cub started to gain altitude, but not nearly fast enough. The telephone wires stretching across the road not two hundred yards from the end of the runway came into view. Adrenaline flooded her veins, drenching her in sweat.

*Why isn't it climbing faster?* She had full power, correct airspeed . . . the trim! It was still set for landing, not takeoff. Praying to the Good Lord above, she furiously cranked the trim handle nose up.

As if by magic, the Cub leaped up, and the wires passed harmlessly underneath, though much too close for comfort. She probably could have touched them if the windows had been open. She released a shuddering breath and forced herself to focus. She couldn't stay in the air forever. She had to land sooner or later, sooner being preferred.

"Come on, Genie. Concentrate." The sound of her voice centered her. "You can do this."

The first landmark appeared, and she turned. The second landmark appeared, and she started her downwind leg. This was her thirty seconds to think and prepare. She had come in too fast before, which was why she had floated instead of landed. *Control the airspeed by controlling the pitch. Control the altitude by adjusting power.*

Exhaling to steady her nerves, she turned base and then final. She was very conscious of the trim handle under her fingers as she adjusted it for landing. Once again the runway numbers disappeared under the nose. She used her peripheral vision to gauge her height off the ground and waited to make the flare. The plane caught a gust and danced to the side, but she didn't relent. She was in control. She would make the plane behave.

The Cub jerked slightly as the main wheels touched, and then she felt the smaller bounce as the tail wheel came down. Dizzy with relief, she held the plane to the centerline as it bumped and shimmied down the runway. The plane slowed, becoming docile and obedient once more. Trying not to rush, she guided the plane over to the flight line, taxied close to a reasonable tie-down for parking, and shut off the engine. Her ears rang in the relative silence, and every muscle in her body shook as she climbed out of the cockpit.

Pride filled her to near-bursting even as her shaking legs forced her to lean against the fuselage for balance. Holy angels in heaven, that was fun!

And terrifying.

And she couldn't wait to do it again. That is, if her flight instructor didn't ground her first.

Flo sauntered around the back of the airplane, her expression behind her sunglasses impossible to read. "Well, China Girl. How'd it go?"

"I came in too fast the first time and decided to go around."

"And?" her instructor drawled, her eyebrows lifting above her sunglasses.

"And I almost forgot to reset the trim," she admitted, since it was obvious Flo had seen the whole fiasco. A tense second passed with Flo saying nothing. Genie shifted uneasily. "Am I in trouble?"

Flo barked a laugh. "Lord, no. You got yourself into a hairy situation, and you didn't lose your head. What more can a flight instructor ask? I just wanted to let you sweat a bit so you won't let it happen again."

"No chance of that!"

Flo gestured toward the flight school. "Why don't we go in and talk about what we want to do tomorrow."

Genie followed her instructor in, elated and shivering as the cool April breeze dried her sweat. To her surprise, no one came over to greet them as they walked in. Pilots, being by and large a friendly bunch, almost always gathered around at the end of someone's flight, wanting to know all the details. At the moment, however, everyone was crowded around a card table, their voices raised in agitated discussion.

"I wonder what's going on," Genie murmured to Flo, who looked just as mystified as she was. As they got closer to the table, one of the instructors, an older balding man who flew with the more advanced students, turned and waved a newspaper in their faces.

"Did you gals see this?" he practically shouted. "Excuse my French, but hot damn!"

"Here, hold it still, Harry. My eyes aren't that good." Flo grabbed the man's wrist to steady it. Genie read the headlines, screamed in bold letters just below the masthead: "Tokyo Bombed!"

"What? When?" she asked, not quite able to believe the news.

A dozen voices piped up. "Early this morning. Doesn't say who's responsible, but it's gotta be us. No official word from Washington, though. Can you believe it?"

"Well, there's a piece of good news," Flo said, her voice shaking with emotion. "About damn time, too."

"Hey, Flo," one of the younger instructors called out. "You've got friends in the army air corp. Who do you think bombed ol' Tojo?"

"It's tough to say. A fully loaded bomber wouldn't be able to hold much fuel, which means they couldn't have come from here or even Hawaii. Maybe somewhere in China?"

"The AVG?" Genie asked excitedly. "Could they have been involved? They've got a base in Kunming."

"Hard to say. Whoever it was, though, I'd sure like to buy them a drink!" Flo said.

Resounding cheers met her suggestion. Then the discussion turned to picking possible refueling sites, a discussion boosted when someone brought out a map.

"Does this mean the war will be over soon?" Genie asked as she followed Flo over to the flight desk. Good news or no, there were still logbooks to be filled out.

"While that would be nice, I doubt it." Flo picked up a pen and began filling out that day's flight entry. "Did bombing Pearl Harbor make the US roll over and surrender?"

"No." Genie's hopes fell.

Flo, having finished the entry and signed her name, slid the logbook over to Genie. "It was a needed morale boost. I'll give you that. But I wouldn't buy that boat ticket home just yet. I have a feeling it'll be at least another six months to a year."

*Home.* A ripple of longing ran through her. She had been so caught up in the prospect of her father and Zhenzhu being out of danger soon, and all the AVG pilots like Ted being able to return to the States, she hadn't considered the impact of victory on herself. Yet with no war, there was no reason to stay in California. She could go home.

She waited for the rush of elation, but it didn't come. Instead, she thought of her job, her flying lessons, her raincheck with Dick. And what of Lavinia? She couldn't just leave and abandon her friend. Nor could she imagine Lavinia wanting to come with her to China.

"You all right?" Flo asked, and Genie looked up to see real concern in her flight instructor's eyes.

"Fine." She forced herself to smile. "Just tired after the flight. How about we look at the schedule to see when I can fly again?"

# Chapter 32

Genie plucked at her blouse, separating the thin fabric from her sweaty skin, while Lavinia checked the mailbox. The cockpit of the Cub would be an oven if she went flying today. Not that the July heat was all that oppressive. Certainly not like India. Yet the day was the warmest she had experienced since she had arrived in California three and a half months earlier.

"This is for you." Lavinia handed one of the two envelopes to Genie before relocking the small brass door.

Her hopes of it being a letter from her father faded as she read the return address: Society of Blessed Souls. "Are you sure there wasn't anything else in there?"

"Other than the telephone bill, no." Lavinia dug her keys out of her bag. "I'm surprised we haven't gotten a rent notice yet."

"Maybe Dick paid it before he left? You're the one who talked to him," Genie said, distracted by the envelope in her hand. She had sent numerous requests for information to the Society; she wondered which one they had finally gotten around to answering.

Her friend slid her an exasperated look as she unlocked the building door. "Genie, rent is rather important. We could wind up on the street if it doesn't get paid. Speaking of which, did you even look at that 'roommate wanted' list I gave you?"

"I did. They were all for a single person, and I'm not moving somewhere without you. And don't worry about the rent; I probably misheard Dick about how long he'd prepaid the rent. I had a lot on my mind at the time."

Considering the subject closed, Genie slid her finger under the envelope flap. Nervousness twisted her stomach as she pulled the letter out. The Society had employed both Nathan and her father. What if this wasn't a reply to her request for burial funds, but news of her father? Perhaps dire news? In her last communiqué with them, they had said they had heard nothing from her father in months, and to assume he was fine.

Her breath locked as she read the first few lines:

> *Dear Miss Baker,*
> *We're sorry for the delay, but our records still show*
> *Mr. Nathan Sterling as living in Kweichow, China . . .*

Exhaling with relief, she scanned the rest, picking out the words "request denied" and "death certificate." *Rats.* "Lavinia, do you, by any chance, happen to have Nathan's death certificate?"

"No. Why?"

"Without it, the Society refuses to believe me that he's passed on." She stuffed the letter back in the envelope and followed Lavinia up the stairs. The stairwell was filled with the savory-sweet smell of frying onions. Her stomach rumbled appreciatively.

"This wouldn't have anything to do with the bronze plaque in the front closet, would it?" Lavinia asked as she waited for Genie to catch up.

"You found it? I was going to tell you about it, but I was afraid you'd be upset."

"It's kind of hard to miss," her roommate said as they walked down the hallway. "And why would I be upset? If anything, I'm glad you did it. He was a good man."

Genie inwardly sighed in relief. "I was hoping to get it installed a while ago, but grave plots are more expensive than I thought. That's why I wrote the Society, hoping they might help out."

"Fat chance of that," Lavinia said coldly. "They didn't care about him when he was alive, so why should they now he's dead?"

"That's not true."

Lavinia stopped, her short dark hair practically lifting in anger. "Isn't it? To them he was just another soldier in the field, fighting the good fight, but ultimately as expendable as any boy in uniform. Same as me. Same as your father. Same as . . ." She shook her head, and her pin curls rippled. "Forget it. I'm done with that life. With all of it."

Genie bit her lip as Lavinia put her key in the lock. Even though her roommate's moods had been more stable of late, apparently Nathan's passing was still a sore spot.

Lavinia frowned, twisting the key one way and the other. "That's strange. Didn't we lock up this morning?"

"I thought so, but we were in a hurry."

Lavinia eased the door open. A black silhouette stood in the living room, his shape starkly outlined against the bright window. Genie jumped back and screamed.

The man stepped forward quickly, hands out, placating. "Whoa, it's me."

"Dick?" Genie could scarcely believe her eyes.

The light from the hallway illuminated the wary expression on his deeply tanned face. "I didn't mean to scare you."

"Well, what did you expect, showing up here without warning?" Lavinia snapped as she passed Genie and entered the apartment.

Dick frowned as he stepped back out of Lavinia's way. "I called and left a message with the Vultee switchboard operator. Didn't you get it?"

"No." Genie tossed her lunch box onto the kitchenette counter, a riot of conflicting emotions squeezing her heart. She wanted to throw herself into his arms, she was so relieved to see him, but nervousness—as well as Lavinia's presence and her obvious dislike of the man—held her back.

"I'm sorry." Hands in his pockets, he gave Genie a sad half smile. "Any chance you'll forgive me? I'd really like to take you out to dinner tonight. After this last assignment, I could use a little feminine company to remind me of all that's still good in the world."

Her hurt over not hearing from him even once during the last three months was no match for the shadows in his eyes. Wherever he had been, it was clear that fresh horrors had been laid upon old ones.

"Of course, but I'm not dressed—" she began, remembering his request from that day so long ago for her to look her best.

"No need to change," he said, his voice firm with sincerity. "You look lovely. Probably better than I deserve."

"Definitely better than you deserve," Lavinia said acidly from the couch.

"Lavinia!" Genie exclaimed, shocked, but Dick only laughed.

"I see Kitty was telling tales out of school again."

"Only to me," Lavinia said. Her expression remained stony.

"Would you like to come with us?" he asked, the amusement fading from his face. "Genie is in no danger from me, but if you'd feel better tagging along—"

"Of course I'm in no danger," Genie said, losing patience with her roommate. "And what in heaven's name is wrong with you, Lavinia? Do you know how much trouble we'd be in if it weren't for his help?"

Lavinia's gaze became troubled. "You don't *owe* him anything, Genie."

"That's where you're wrong," Genie said hotly. "We owe him everything at the moment."

"Genie, sweetheart," Dick said, interrupting her. "Why don't you freshen up while I talk to Nia and see if we can't come to some sort of agreement."

Lavinia paled at his use of Kitty's nickname for her, and Genie's loyalties began to slide the other way. She had no idea what was going on, but she wouldn't stand by while either one hurt the other. They were both her friends.

Lavinia glanced at her. "Go ahead. We actually do have things to discuss, and I won't be able to go to dinner with you two. Sheila and the girls are going to the cheap movies tonight, and I already told them I was coming along. I was going to ask if you wanted to go, but it sounds like you might have other plans."

"No, that's fine," Genie said honestly. Sheila wasn't one of Genie's favorite people, even though she worked the line with Lavinia and purportedly worked it with more swagger and attitude than most of the men. Maybe it was because no matter what Genie tried, Sheila still seemed to dislike her.

Dick smiled in reassurance. "Don't worry. We promise to keep it civilized."

Reluctantly Genie went into the bedroom and closed the door. Then she hurried into the bathroom and turned on the faucet. As quietly as possible, she flew back to the door and pressed her ear against it to listen. Muted murmurs were all she heard, thanks to the running water in the bathroom. She tried listening from a few different spots and then finally gave up. Disappointed, she returned the bathroom and turned off the water. A few quick repairs of her makeup and hair, and she was ready to go.

She opened the door to find that Dick was the only one there.

He smiled as he picked his hat up off the kitchen table. "Ready?"

"Where's Lavinia?"

"She said she had an errand to run, and to have fun." He opened the door into the hallway for her.

"What kind of errand?" she asked, narrowing her gaze.

"Does it matter?" He sighed in the face of her glare. "She's off to the post office. She had a letter for Kitty and asked if I had her most recent address."

"And you just gave it to her?" She wanted to shake him.

His eyebrows rose, clearly not understanding her irritation. "Why not? She has the right to write to whomever she chooses."

"Unless that person is utterly evil." With a growl, she grabbed her handbag off the chair. "The way Kitty sabotaged Lavinia's relationship with Nathan is unforgivable."

Dick sighed. "I wondered if you'd heard about that."

"I did. And now—no thanks to you—Lavinia is about to be back in touch with her." Heartsick for her friend all over again, Genie stormed into the hallway. Men could be such fools.

Dick followed her down the stairs. Once they were on the sidewalk, he guided her toward a shiny black sedan parked at the curb. As he opened the door for her, revealing the interior, her eyebrows rose despite her irritation. Butter-soft leather covered the seats, and polished wood with chrome accents made up the dashboard. Everything gleamed softly in the sunlight. Expensively.

While she didn't know a lot about automobiles, this one was definitely much nicer than the one Mr. Short had driven, and Charity had practically waxed rhapsodic over that one. Maybe cameramen made more money than stunt pilots?

She took her seat on the passenger side and then waited as he walked around the back of the car.

"So tell me what you've been doing with yourself," he said after sliding behind the wheel.

Deciding not to let memories of Kitty ruin her evening, Genie began to talk. While he drove across town, she told him about learning to type and her job at the plant. She told him about flying while they drove up into the hills. He asked the occasional question but otherwise didn't say much, which struck her as strange. He wasn't usually one to be so quiet.

Finally they reached the restaurant, an out-of-the-way spot with a breathtaking view of the valley and the ocean beyond. While Dick talked to the maître d', she wandered over to the edge of the veranda that ran along the side of the building.

"What a lovely place," she said as Dick came up beside her.

"And my date is even lovelier," he said, making her blush. He winked and took her hand, and all her nervousness returned. A white-aproned waiter appeared, breaking the spell, and together they followed the man to their table. Dick pulled a chair out for her, and the waiter handed them menus.

"This reminds me of the 300 Club in Calcutta," Genie said, admiring the rich paneling and fine china. "Well, except there are more women present, and fewer uniforms. And there's no live band or dancing. Or overhead fans . . ."

"So not very alike after all," Dick said with an amused expression as he picked up the wine list.

She laughed. "I guess not. But the feel is the same. Exclusive."

"Ah, but anybody can come here. The 300 Club is members and guests only."

"You've been there? You never told me."

"You never asked. Do you prefer red or white wine?"

She hesitated, not sure how to respond.

He glanced at her over the top of the card. "You still don't drink?"

"I've never had a good reason to, I guess. Whatever money I have left over at the end of the week is split between savings and flight lessons, not liquor."

"Your dates don't offer to buy?"

"Oh, I . . ." She glanced away as embarrassment heated her cheeks. "I don't date. I don't have time." Nor had anyone asked her, but she wasn't about to admit that.

"So I should be flattered, then?"

Her startled gaze lifted to his.

"That you've taken the time to have dinner with me, I mean." His hazel eyes were extraordinarily pretty in the low light. A slow smile curved his lips, and a very feminine kind of heat warmed her. "I can't tell you how glad I am no other fellow has caught your eye."

He reached out and took her hand again. Shivers of awareness raced up and down her arm. Once again, the waiter spoiled the moment by coming to take their order. Nervously, Genie snatched back her hand, barely hearing Dick as he ordered a bottle of the restaurant's best cabernet.

"If I never drink another bottle of warm beer, it'll be too soon," he said with real feeling after the waiter left. "That and homemade hooch. Boy, was that stuff awful. Could take the paint right off metal."

"I take it there were no bars wherever you were working?"

"There was precious little of anything except jungle and ocean," he said with a small laugh, except there was no humor in the sound, and shadows had crept back into his eyes. She wished she could drive them away permanently, but she didn't know how.

The waiter returned with the wine. While Dick examined the bottle, she tried to think of a topic to broach that wouldn't be war related. Unfortunately, she had used up most of her chitchat on the car ride to the restaurant.

"Did you hear Burma fell?" Dick asked before she could decide on a subject.

*So much for avoiding war-related subjects.* "I did. I read about it in the papers," she said, turning pensive as the waiter poured wine into a glass for her. "I wish they had written more about the situation in China, but I did see there was a string of recent U-boat attacks in the Caribbean. It made me think we were lucky on our voyage."

"In more ways than one," he said with a wink, making her heart beat a little unsteadily. Then he sobered. "I tried to find out what was happening in Kweichow, where you said you lived. You know, through back channels and fellow photographers. I'm afraid I couldn't find out anything more than what's being published."

"That's all right," she said, touched by his effort.

He lifted his glass, his expression becoming mock serious. "To reunions with old friends."

She started to pick up her water glass to return the toast but then changed her mind and set it back down. She lifted the wineglass. "To friends, old or not," she teased. She sniffed the deep-red liquid as he drank from his glass and was intrigued by the faint fruit smell. "Will I like this?"

"Maybe. Won't know unless you try it."

Taking a deep breath, she lifted her glass to him. "To trying new things."

He returned the toast, his green-gold gaze taking on a lazy heat. "To new things."

She took a sip. It was tangy and sweet and rich all at the same time. And faintly grapey. With her second sip, a pleasant warmth touched her tongue and then traveled down her throat as she swallowed.

"What do you think?" Amusement sparkled in his eyes.

"Am I supposed to feel any different?" she asked curiously, because nothing felt different. Certainly not different enough to justify the "demon drink" moniker.

"Not after two sips, certainly," he said with a laugh. Then his amusement faded as his gaze met hers. "I find alcohol relaxes me. Lets me forget what I've seen, if only for a while."

Her chest tightened, and she reached across the table for his hand. "I wish you didn't have to go back," she said, tears burning in her eyes. "Sometimes I really hate this war."

"Only sometimes?" he teased. His strong calloused fingers threaded through hers, becoming entwined.

Ellen Lindseth

"Can I tell you something? Something I haven't dared tell anyone else?" she asked, her stomach clenching with nervousness.

"I'd feel honored."

She bit her lip as a swirl of emotions built inside her. She let them go. "When I first heard that Tokyo was bombed, I was overjoyed because the war would be over and everyone would be safe . . ."

"But?"

"But then I realized how much I would lose by going home: my job, my apartment, my friends. My chance to get my pilot's license. And I found myself praying the war wouldn't be over *too* soon . . ." Guilt squeezed her throat. "What kind of horrible person would wish such a thing? Especially when every additional day means a day people's lives are endangered."

Instead of reassuring her, as she had hoped, he picked up his glass and swirled the contents, his face contemplative. "Say the war were to end tomorrow, would you have to go back immediately?" he asked finally.

"Well . . . yes. My father is expecting me."

"Is he?" He glanced up, his gaze sharp. "Because there's no guarantee that ending the war with Japan will end the civil war simmering in China. And I can't imagine a caring, loving father wanting his child to return to that kind of situation. Not if she's safe and happy somewhere else."

"But . . ." She wanted to argue but couldn't find the words. So much of what he said was true. Even before the Japanese invasion, her beloved China had been racked by political unrest. The war had solved nothing on that front. She had only to remember Wu Fang's contempt for the Kuomintang and the Generalissimo's anger at the Communists.

"And whether or not you wish for the war to be over won't change reality. One person's wishes don't hold that much power. What matters are actions, and in that regard you are entirely blameless, Genie. You're working in an aircraft plant, supporting the war effort, doing your best to bring this war to an end."

"You make it sound so glamorous, when all I'm doing is typing orders," she said, her throat still tight.

"Here, stop moping and drink up. After all, you're out with me." He winked at her. "What more could you want?"

She forced herself to smile as their dinners arrived. The conversation, as if by mutual consent, turned to lighter subjects. The more Dick drank, the more easily he talked, which thrilled her to no end, since he was a fantastic storyteller. For her own part, she found the more she drank, the better the wine tasted. And if Dick kept both their wineglasses full, she didn't have the heart to refuse him.

By the end of dinner, Dick was as relaxed as she had ever seen him, and she was feeling pretty good herself. The world had a kind of fuzzy glow that made the restaurant particularly delightful, the food excellent, and the company even better.

After Dick settled the bill, he came around the table to hold her chair.

"Ready to beat feet, my dear? And be careful standing up."

"Why?" she asked, mystified as she stood. The room tilted abruptly, and she gasped. "Oh my!"

His fingers closed around her elbow, keeping her from staggering. "It's okay; I've got you. Give it a moment."

Trying not to panic, she held very still and concentrated on the feel of his hand on her arm. Slowly the floor settled back into place, though her hearing still seemed slightly muffled.

"Let's get you to the car, and we'll go for a drive." His voice was warm on her ear, and she shivered. Everything about him called to her tonight. She wanted nothing more than to turn in his arms and lean against his solid chest, letting him fight off gravity and hold her up. "Nice and slow. You can do this."

His hand settled on her waist, setting off tingly, electric waves of awareness. Her skin became even more sensitive, the rub of her clothes become almost erotic. "Don't let me make a fool of myself."

"Never," he said firmly.

Trusting him, she concentrated on putting one foot in front of the other. It got easier as her legs started cooperating again. It actually wasn't so different from trying to walk across a deck in a high sea. Dick said goodnight to the maître d', and then they were outside in the fading twilight. In the semidarkness, she didn't see the khaki-uniformed man until they almost collided.

"Sorry, miss," the soldier said, pivoting to the side. "Didn't see you."

The familiar timbre and drawl of his voice halted her midstep. *It couldn't be.* Her eyes widened, and she spun around.

"Ted?" Her heart pounded in sudden joy. It was! There could be no mistaking the sharp slash of black eyebrows and the determined, angular jaw.

The soldier slowed and glanced at her with a slight frown. Her pulse became erratic as his familiar dark eyes met hers.

# Chapter 33

"Genie?" Ted's frown vanished, and a wide grin softened the edges of his chiseled, handsome face. "Well, if that don't beat all! It is you. I can hardly believe it. What the heck are you doing in LA?"

"I live here now," she said, her heart starting to function again.

"Do you now?" He gazed at her for another breath-stealing second and then turned to the well-dressed fellow with him. "You're not going to believe this, but this is Miss Baker, the missionary girl I was just telling you about."

The older man bowed slightly and smiled. "Miss Baker, it's a pleasure. I'm Stuart Jeffries, regional coordinator for war bond activities."

"Nice to meet you," she said politely. With his intelligent eyes, craggy face, and neatly trimmed mustache, he reminded her a little of General Chennault.

"Want to hear something crazy?" Ted said, turning back to Genie. "He thinks parading me around the country will get people to buy war bonds. Me, of all people."

"And why not?" Mr. Jeffries asked, sounding exasperated. "You're young, good-looking, and one of the famous Flying Tigers. Tell me, Miss Baker, would you buy a war bond from Lieutenant Younan?"

She ran her gaze appreciatively over Ted from the top of his dark, slicked-back hair to the tips of his polished brown shoes. "Absolutely."

"And there you have it," Mr. Jeffries said with a pleased look. "The young girls of America will eat you up."

Ted's cheeks pinkened beneath his tan. Genie's lips twitched as she bit back a smile at his obvious embarrassment. It served him right for being so ridiculously good-looking, and kind, and brave, and . . .

"Ready to go, sweetheart?" Dick touched her, startling her. She had somehow forgotten his presence.

Ted's gaze flicked to Dick's hand on her shoulder. His expression became politely blank as he held out his hand. "I don't think we've met. Lieutenant Ted Younan. Friend of Genie's."

"So I gathered," Dick said drily, letting go of Genie long enough to shake Ted's hand. "Dick Pelton, and I heard a lot about you on the trip home from India."

Ted raised an eyebrow. "All good, I hope. And where's that Sterling fellow? I'm surprised he isn't with you tonight."

"Oh, Ted," Genie said, slipping between the men. "There's so much you don't know—"

Ted's gaze flicked from her and to Dick. "Apparently."

"Nathan is dead." To her surprise, tears filled her eyes as she said the words. "He died on the way here. And then my aunt went missing."

"Oh, honey. You all right?" The genuine concern in his voice almost undid her.

"She's fine," Dick said coolly. His hand settled on her shoulder again, a silent reminder that she was out with him, not Ted.

Dashing the wetness from her cheeks, she forced herself to smile. "Dick was kind enough to find me a job and a place to stay, so yes, I'm fine. And you'll never guess what! I'm training to be a pilot."

"No kidding." Ted smiled, his attention all on her again. "That's terrific. Which airport are you flying out of?"

"Vail, over in Montebello."

"Sure, I know the field. Who's teaching you?"

"Genie . . ." Dick eased her back from Ted. "We've delayed the gentlemen long enough."

"Florence Palmatier," Genie said, resisting the movement. It felt so good to talk to Ted again. So much had happened since the night they had shared in Calcutta. "You should stop by sometime. I fly almost every weekend, if the weather's good. We could talk after my lesson."

Ted's gaze flicked toward Dick. "I don't know, Genie. I just got back to the States. For all I know, Uncle Sam could be shipping me out again."

"Before you leave, then? It's just been so long since I've talked to someone from home . . ." Her voice faltered as he held his hands up and backed away.

"I'll see, okay? No promises. It was nice seeing you, though."

Sudden understanding squeezed her chest. He didn't want to see her again, and why should he? He likely had a girl who would want all his free time spent with her.

Still, it hurt to be pushed away by the man who had given her her first kiss.

She pasted on a bright, fake smile, her good mood of a moment ago vanishing under the threat of tears. "Nice seeing you, too." She turned to Dick, her heart feeling as fragile as spun glass. "Ready?"

In silent support, Dick put his arm around her, and she leaned gratefully into his shoulder. Dimly she heard him say goodbye to the two men, and then they were walking to his car. She shivered as he opened the door for her in silence, the chill emotional rather than physical.

Memories of China, of her father's house, of Kunming, of the flight to Calcutta—all whirled about her like leaves before a wind, pulling her back in time, leaving her raw and exposed. It was as if seeing Ted had unlocked something inside her, and she was once more that scared and naive girl.

Dick got into the car, and she could feel the weight of his gaze. "So that was the AVG pilot. Have to say he's a bit different than I imagined."

She forced herself to shrug as if her heart weren't bruised and bleeding. "He's all right, I guess."

"You know, pilots aren't the most constant of people. Most of the ones I know have gals in every city."

She winced, thinking of the CNAC pilot in Calcutta and his prostitute friend. "I'm a pilot, and I'm not like that."

"No. You're something different altogether. Something special."

She blinked back tears as the rips in her heart mended a little. "Thank you."

"Aw, sweetheart. Come here." He reached over and pulled her across the leather seat to nestle close to him. "I shouldn't have given you so much wine. You just relax, and I'll get you home."

She rested her cheek against his chest and closed her eyes. "I'm sorry I'm not a better date."

He pressed a kiss to her hair. "You're fine—and the night's not over yet."

Exhausted from a long day at work and the effects of the wine, she closed her eyes and relaxed into him as he drove back to the apartment. At some point, she must have fallen asleep, because out of nowhere she felt lips on her temple. On her cheek. Slowly she came awake as Dick tilted her head up, his fingers warm under her chin. His lips touched hers in the softest of kisses, and she sighed. Then his mouth settled over hers with a gentle firmness, the pressure parting her lips, deepening the kiss.

The touch of his tongue on her jolted her into full awareness. Sudden panic had her pushing at him, but he didn't release her. If anything his mouth became more insistent. With an effort, she broke the kiss.

"Dick, stop!" Panting and disoriented, she looked out the car windows. Her heart pounded. "Where are we?"

"Your place." He slid his hands up her bare arms, releasing an electrical storm of sensations. "Or rather mine, technically. Why?"

She tried to get her brain to think, to focus, but it wouldn't. Everything felt strangely muddled and fuzzy. Part of her wanted to go back to kissing him. In fact, most of her did. Especially that secret, sexual part that lay low and deep inside her. Her pulse leaped.

Alarmed at the drift of her thoughts, she pushed back to gain a little space and worked on slowing her heart, her breathing. The car was silent, the engine shut off, the clock on the dash ticking softly. Outside the windshield were the familiar silhouettes of the buildings on her street, the lights shielded in accord with the coastal blackout.

"Is something wrong?" His voice was low and velvety soft.

She considered the question, her body shivering, already missing the seductive heat of his. "I—I don't know."

"Then, no," he said, the mesmerizing timbre of his voice dropping even lower. "Come here, Genie. Let me kiss you . . . please."

Her thoughts scattered like dandelion fluff as his hand cupped the back of her head. She closed her eyes as the familiar scent of his cologne filled her head, erasing her fears. His lips touched hers, and all her objections fell away. It was as if she had been lost for so long, and now she was found. He tightened his hold, and a flashfire of desire filled her veins.

Close was suddenly not close enough. She slid her hands under his coat and dug her fingers into the hard muscles of his back. He felt so good, so virile under her fingertips. A little purr of pleasure escaped her throat. She thought she heard him groan in response, but he kept on kissing her, over and over, deeper and deeper, until she couldn't think at all.

Her lips parted under his again as his hands, so provocatively hot through the cotton fabric of her skirt, found their way to her hips. One palm slid up to her waist, making her moan as desire lit up her blood. His fingers flexed, and her back arched without thought. Beneath her blouse her breasts ached, wanting his touch. Some small voice inside cried out a warning, but she didn't listen. Instead, she dissolved into the sensations of his lips gliding down her neck. She shifted restlessly, wanting something, something more . . .

His thumb grazed her nipple, and she gasped. Shock made her open her eyes. She stilled even as her heart drummed a fast tattoo, her rib cage barely holding it in. "Dick?"

His lips left her neck as he lifted his head. His expression was hard, almost savage in the shadows. Yet his touch was so, so gentle as he cupped her face. Almost reverently, he traced the line of her jaw with his thumb.

"Ask me up, Genie." His voice was like black magic. "Say the words. Let me come up and give you more. You know you want to."

Her breath caught with indecision. Aching and restless, she did want more. More kisses, more of his hands on her body, more of how he made her feel: like a woman, desirable and desired. But she wasn't naive. While there was a chance he would behave himself and not push to take her virginity, there was also the chance that he would push, and she wasn't at all sure she would say no. Not with the way her body wanted to arch against him, to feel his body press against hers, closer than close, like a magnet to steel.

*Good girls wait until marriage, Genie.* She struggled to focus on that one hard and fast rule. The one she had been taught since childhood. *Good Christian girls wait, no matter the temptation.* Except the missionary wives—nor her father, who never mentioned such matters around her—hadn't mentioned how tempting the fall would be. Here, cocooned in the dark, with the heat of Dick's body setting her nerve endings alight, the scent of him blending with his aftershave, she felt positively reckless and so, so alive. Her blood sang in her veins, rendering her powerful and powerless in the same instant.

*No, Genie. No.*

She swallowed as her body fought with her conscience. "I can't. It wouldn't be right."

"Are you sure?" His voice was impossibly deep as he pulled her back, his fingers tantalizingly warm on her arms. "Because everything about this feels exactly right to me."

When he kissed her this time, his kiss was harder, rawer. She couldn't help but respond affirmatively to his unspoken plea: *let me love you.* She squirmed against him, his need resonating within her, unleashing a strange wildness. She felt so beautiful, so wanted.

His hand slipped inside her blouse, the small shell buttons popping free. His fingers found her breast, and she arched her back with a gasp. He traced her nipple with his fingertips and then caught it between his thumb and forefinger and squeezed gently. Pleasure rippled through her, nearly making her pass out. She felt herself falling backward, his weight pushing her down onto the car seat, under him. It would be so easy to just give in . . .

Abruptly, her brain started working again. "Dick, wait! Stop!"

She stiffened when he didn't pause. Concern spiked through her as his mouth trailed hotly down her neck while he shoved her blouse aside, her breast fully exposed.

She tried to squirm away. "Dick . . ."

The sudden pounding on the window nearly gave her a heart attack. A woman, Lavinia, peered in wide-eyed through the driver-side window.

"What the . . . ?" Lavinia's muffled voice came through the window glass. "Genie? Are you okay?"

Dick swore softly under his breath as Lavinia began pounding again. Genie flinched, sure the glass would break.

"Pelton, darn you, you promised!" Lavinia was shouting now, sounding oddly close to tears.

Dick closed his eyes and leaned his forehead against Genie's. His breathing was fast, ragged. "I'm so sorry, Genie."

"It's all ri—" she began, reflexively wanting to comfort him.

Lavinia began rattling the door handle. "It's locked. Try the other side!" she yelled to someone Genie couldn't see. The passenger-side door opened a second later.

"Play time is over, lover boy," an unfamiliar female voice growled a second before strong hands grabbed Genie around the upper arms and began hauling her from the car.

Dick resisted for a moment and then let her go. "It's not what you think," he said, but it was clear he wasn't talking to her.

"Yes, it was!" Lavinia yelled back, nearly deafening Genie as she scrambled to her feet. "Can you tell me honestly you would have stopped if we hadn't happened upon you first? What is wrong with you?"

Inside the car, Dick ran his hands through his sun-streaked hair, his clothes still askew. Genie's chest hollowed with guilt and embarrassment. She had done that. Despite knowing better, she had clawed at him like an animal in her passion. Thank the Lord that Lavinia had shown up when she had; otherwise she would likely have abandoned her morals entirely.

He drew a deep breath and met Genie's gaze. "I'm sorry, sweetheart. Things got a little out of hand. Next time—"

"There will be no next time," Lavinia said hotly, her hand grabbing Genie's arm as the other person let go. "We had an agreement."

Dick's expression hardened. "Which I didn't break, so stop interfering where you're not wanted, or I might change my mind."

"Easy, cowboy." Sheila stepped out of the shadows, and Genie's spirits sank even further as she recognized Lavinia's friend. Now the whole plant would know of her shameless behavior. "Everyone's a little worked up at the moment. How 'bout you both let Genie decide who she wants to see and when?"

"Fine." Dick's voice was clipped. Then he slumped back on the car seat and ran his hand over his face. He looked truly miserable, and another wave of guilt threatened to swamp her. She had started it, after all. At the restaurant, when she had all but thrown herself into Dick's arms after seeing Ted. And all the kisses she had eagerly returned. All the caresses she had accepted and given.

"Dick . . ." Her voice broke. She wanted to tell him that it was okay, that she completely forgave him because it was partly her fault, too. But the words wouldn't form. Her legs, unsteady to begin with from the wine she had drunk, began to shake.

He met her gaze. "I'll call you later."

"No, she will call you, if she wants to," Lavinia snarled as she grabbed Genie's arm.

Then Sheila moved to block her view of him as Lavinia continued herding her toward the entrance of their building. The world blurred, and she realized belatedly that she was crying. No, make that sobbing. And worse, she didn't even know why.

# Chapter 34

"I picked up a second shift, so I'll be home late tonight," Lavinia said the next morning as she finished packing her lunch box. "So don't invite Dick up unless you think you can fight him off by yourself."

Genie felt like rolling her eyes, except the movement would likely hurt too much. She didn't know much about hangovers, but from the descriptions she had overheard at the office, she was pretty sure she had one now. Either that or her headache and upset stomach were from sobbing herself to sleep last night.

"You do remember this is his apartment, right? If he wants to come up, I can't exactly tell him no."

"You can tell him to wait until you either leave or have a chaperone." Lavinia paused in her packing long enough to give Genie a stern look. "I'm serious, Genie. He crossed a line last night, and he knows it. That he did it at all means he can't be trusted."

"So you keep saying, but you won't say what line was crossed, or what this agreement is between you two that he supposedly broke. Honestly, how can you expect me to just give him up if you won't give me a concrete reason?"

Her roommate locked the metal clasps on the box with a decided snap. "Can you honestly tell me you would've been fine with going all the way with him last night?"

"It wouldn't have gotten that far."

Lavinia slid her a disbelieving look. "Genie, he was in the process of undressing you in full view of anyone walking by."

Irritated and losing patience with both her friend and the snood she was trying to pin on, Genie tossed the tangled hairnet aside and picked up her brush. "The situation was as much my fault as his. If you're going to be angry, be angry with me, too."

Lavinia's jaw tightened fractionally. "No, Genie. He got you drunk and then did things he shouldn't have. Things he promised he wouldn't. So I have no forgiveness in me whatsoever where he's concerned."

"Well, that's too bad. Because I'm going to go on seeing him, assuming you haven't scared him away."

"If only we were both that lucky."

Genie rounded on her friend. "What is your problem with him? He's been nothing but good to the both of us since the day we met."

Lavinia's gaze dropped back to her lunch box. "I can't explain it."

"Can't or won't?"

She glanced up, her blue eyes intense as they met Genie's. "Can you just trust me on this? You know your friendship means the world to me. I would give my life for you, if I had to."

Genie huffed in frustration. "Wonderful. You would risk your life, but not the truth. Do you know how ridiculous that sounds?"

Lavinia slapped the table with both palms. "Darn it, Genie. You want truth? Fine. Try this one on for size: for all his charm, his generosity, has he ever, even once, said, 'I love you'?"

"Well, no. But I can tell—"

"That he has a reputation as a ladies' man?" Lavinia said sharply. "Because he does. And I would think you should at least think twice about having a man undress you who doesn't at least love you."

Genie stared at her friend, temples throbbing with anger. "Who said he was a ladies' man?"

"Does it matter?" Lavinia exhaled in frustration. "Genie, you're out of your league with Dick. Trust me on this. If you keep seeing him, you're going to get hurt."

"Trust you? Oh, that's rich, given all your secret agreements with people. First Kitty, and now Dick. Is there anyone else I should know about?"

Lavinia glanced at the wall clock. "Shoot, I've got to go, Genie. The bus will be here any minute."

"So catch our normal one," Genie said coldly, not missing that her friend hadn't answered her question. "Why are you going in early, anyway?"

"Because I said I would." Lavinia grabbed her box. "Remember about me being late tonight."

"We're not done discussing this," Genie said as her friend opened the door. "I'm getting fed up with all your prevarications."

Lavinia tossed a wave over her shoulder as she left. The door closed with a decided thump.

"Coward," Genie groused, but there was only the soft ticking of the clock to hear her. Since she still had a half hour before her bus came, she returned to the bathroom to give her snood another go. Standing in front of the sink, she rubbed her temples. Her earlier headache was back in spades, thanks to her argument with Lavinia. She also noticed in the mirror that one of the buttons on her blouse had gone missing, too.

"Lovely." She sighed and put her brush and snood down. Given the way her day was starting, maybe she should call in sick. Then she considered the effect on her pocketbook, which was already a little light thanks to the money she had squirreled away for future expenditures and the more immediate expense of flight lessons.

A quick search of the bedroom floor resulted in finding the lost button as well as several bobby pins and a dime. If she hurried, she could have it sewn back on and do her hair. All she needed was a needle and thread. She sat back on her heels and thought. It seemed to her Lavinia had been repairing a seam not too many days ago, and that she had pulled her sewing kit from one of her drawers in the tallboy by the window.

She hesitated and then went over to the piece of furniture in question and opened the fourth drawer, which, along with the next two drawers down, was Lavinia's domain. Her skin burned with nervous guilt as she gingerly sorted through her friend's things. Genie had never before violated her friend's privacy, and she hated that she was doing so now. Only this was an emergency, since she didn't have any other clean clothes, and she couldn't face Skip with a button missing.

Not finding the sewing kit in that drawer, she moved on to the next one, past the folded sweaters and extra socks. Feeling like a thief in her own apartment, she opened the last drawer and stopped short. It was like a memory box from a different world. Carefully she picked up the folded floral blouse, a vivid image of Lavinia in Calcutta coming to life. Here, too, was the skirt as well as a leather-bound Bible with water stains on the cover. There was also a small journal and a dog-eared black-and-white photograph of four somber-looking missionaries standing in front of a tropical landscape. Thailand, perhaps. She recognized Lavinia and Marcus right away, but not the gaunt man with his arm around Lavinia, nor the young woman standing to the side—near but not quite with the group.

Gently putting the photograph down, she shifted the clothes to the side, still hoping to find the kit. Instead, she found an envelope underneath everything. It was addressed in a spidery, weak hand to a Reverend Jacob Krauss in Pennsylvania. A chill ghosted up her spine as she stared at the unfamiliar handwriting. Marcus had threatened Lavinia with a letter that day in Calcutta, in the hotel lobby. Genie could still remember the instantaneous change in Lavinia's demeanor, from defiant to vacant. Was this that letter? It had to be, but where had

Lavinia gotten it from? Somehow Genie doubted Marcus would have just given it to his sister.

Nathan. That was who Marcus would have given it to, because who else would need it to keep Lavinia in line? Something dark and furious twisted inside of her. All those weeks aboard ship, had Nathan been holding it over Lavinia, the stick to reinforce the carrot? Love me or else? It made her sick just thinking about it, because of course he had. The Nathan she knew was insecure and petty enough to use any advantage he could find. It was enough to make her want to toss his grave plaque into the closest garbage bin.

It would also explain why Lavinia had gone straight to Nathan's cabin after his death. Not to grab Genie's passport, as she had first thought, but to find the one thing that would set Lavinia free of her brother's blackmail. And Nathan's.

Renewed questions surrounding his unexpected death pricked her. *I didn't push him, Genie. Nor did Kitty. Nor did anyone. He fell . . .*

She bit her lip as Lavinia's words echoed in her head. If ever her friend had told the truth, Genie would've sworn it was in that moment. And yet . . . She stared down at the envelope, the malevolent power of the thing almost pulsing in the still air. No one would ever know she had opened it, not if she was careful. Maybe if she read it, she would finally learn Lavinia's secrets. It wasn't like she would learn them any other way. And maybe, once she knew what haunted her friend, she could actually help her.

*No.* She shoved the envelope under the clothes and slammed the drawer shut. As much as she hated secrets, whatever was in that letter had caused Lavinia enough pain.

Returning to the bathroom, she dug through her toiletry bag and found a safety pin. The button and her curiosity would have to wait until Lavinia returned.

~

Forty minutes later the bus dropped her off outside the plant. While she waited at the traffic signal with the hundred or so other workers, her gaze drifted to the sky. Except for a few clouds off to the east, it was a beautiful morning. The wind was light, and the temperature cool. A perfect day for flying, if she hadn't had to work. However, if she didn't work, she wouldn't have the money to fly. So work it was.

The light turned green, and Genie forgot the sky. She let herself be caught up in the swell of humanity surging across the street, finding that little thrill she always felt as part of this massive effort—all these people, men and women, from all walks of life, united by a common cause—to stop the enemy in its tracks. It gave her hope that, despite the depressing news she read every day in the paper, the war would soon be over, and her father and Zhenzhu safe.

"Genie, over here!" Charity called out excitedly from near the entrance. Genie waved and began cutting her way through the tide of people between them. She quashed a twinge of envy on the way. Her friend looked stunning in yet another new outfit she had likely sewn. Genie felt the presence of the safety pin on her borrowed blouse all the more keenly. Maybe this weekend she should take up Charity's offer and let her friend teach her how to sew. She would have to put off a few flight lessons to buy the fabric, but she was getting so heartily sick of the few hand-me-downs the girls in the office pool had given her, it would be worth it.

"Hiya, Genie!" Charity eyes sparkled as she practically danced in her low-heeled pumps. "Guess what I found out last night?"

"That the blond pilot you met over the weekend has a thing for you?"

"No, silly! Though that would be lovely. Something much more exciting—the Flying Tigers are back in the States, at least some of them. And at least one is right here in LA!"

An image of Ted, handsome as ever in his uniform as he backed away, flashed in front of her eyes. She rubbed at the sudden ache beneath her breastbone. "Yeah, I know."

Charity frowned. "You know? How? Did you talk to Flo last night, too? And why aren't you more excited? I thought you liked the Tigers."

"I do, it's just . . ."

"Genie, Miss Baker." The familiar male voice came from behind her. Caught between joy and dread, she spun around to see Dick striding up the sidewalk. Her heart beat unevenly as she drank in the sight of him. He was impeccably dressed, as always, but it was also clear from the dark circles under his eyes that he had slept no better than she had last night.

All the doubts Lavinia had planted burned away. Dick had to be in love with her, even if he hadn't gotten around to saying as much. It was so obvious.

"I was hoping to catch you. I . . ." He stopped in front of her, his gaze touching lightly everywhere on her face, as if trying to memorize her. She noted the deep, unhappy grooves around his mouth and unconsciously reached up to smooth them away. Catching her hand, he glanced at Charity. "May I have a word with your friend? In private?"

Charity's eyebrows lifted. She looked questioningly at Genie. "Um . . . sure?"

"It's fine," Genie said, forcing herself to smile through her sudden nervousness. "This is Mr. Pelton, my landlord, of sorts."

Charity's eyes widened as she noted their clasped hands. She turned back to Dick with new appreciation in her eyes. "You're Uncle Fred's friend? I'm Charity Newcombe. It's so nice to meet you."

Dick hesitated and then released Genie to shake her hand. "Nice to meet you, too. But I'm sure you girls are in a hurry, and I don't want Genie to be late."

"Oh, right." Charity turned to Genie. "Do you want me to wait for you?"

"No, I'll be right there. Cover for me if I'm not."

"All right," Charity said, backing away, "but you know how Skip gets if we're late."

Genie shooed her friend away. "Five minutes and I'll be in."

She jumped as Dick's fingers closed around her elbow. It took everything she had not to turn and throw herself into his arms, but Charity was still watching. Still, she was desperate for Dick to hold her, to reassure her that the ugly things Lavinia had said weren't true.

"I had to see you, Genie," he said in her ear, sending chills up and down her spine. His voice was rough, raw. "Please tell me you aren't mad at me."

"Mad?" She gave a little laugh as she turned to face him, Lavinia's words echoing in her ears: *He crossed a line last night, and he knows it . . .* "Why would I be mad?"

Instead of answering, his gaze dropped to her lips. His eyes turned a mesmerizing green. "You have the most gorgeous mouth."

Surprised, she touched her lips. "Really? I was teased as a child. I was told it was too big, like a monkey's."

"Then they were wrong, because it's perfect. So kissable. If I could, I would spend all day kissing you."

A wave of heat suffused her blood, and her breath came a little faster as her body remembered a lot more than just kisses. "While I would like that, I'm pretty sure our bosses wouldn't. Because they'd want us to work. At some point."

"Likely." His lips quirked. Then to her dismay, he shifted back, increasing the distance between them. "Which is why I'm here. I came to tell you I won't be able to see you again for a while. I'm heading back out on assignment. But when I get back, I'd like to take you out again. If that's all right with you."

"Of course," she said, her heart sinking. "How long will you be gone?"

"They haven't told me. But don't worry about the rent. I'll take care of it before I go."

She shook her head. "Dick, Lavinia and I can't keep living off your kindness. It's not right, especially now we can afford to help out."

"I'm not going to charge you rent," he said flatly. Then he brushed her cheek tenderly with his knuckles. "Let me do this for you, Genie. Knowing you're there, safe, gives me peace when I'm out on assignment. Something to look forward to when I get home."

She shivered under his touch, her resolve scattering like dandelion seeds in the wind.

Lavinia just didn't understand. Dick *did* love her. His wanting to take care of her proved it. If Nathan had been in Dick's position, he would never have charged Lavinia rent. Or her, for that matter.

In China, women went to stay with their future in-laws all the time.

*Yes, but are you engaged to Dick?* a voice whispered in her head. *Has he ever said he loves you?*

She started to frown, her doubts starting to gather again. "Dick . . ."

"No time for arguments, sweetheart. I've got to go." He gave her a sad smile that momentarily squeezed her heart. Then to her dismay, he began backing away from her. "Take care of yourself."

*Don't you dare let him get away,* the voice prodded her, sounding a little panicked this time. And a lot like Zhenzhu's. *Make him say the words.*

The voice was right. "Dick, wait—"

But he was already disappearing into the workday rush of people.

"Are you planning on working today, Miss Baker?" Skip's voice made her jump.

She spun around, her pulse racing in alarm. "Mr. Winston, I didn't see you there."

"New boyfriend?" he asked coolly. "I thought you were too busy to date."

"I am. My flight test isn't for a couple of weeks yet. And Mr. Pelton isn't my boyfriend. He's my landlord."

"A rather friendly one, I would say." His gaze dipped to her breasts and then moved even lower. Her skin crawled as a slow smile curved his lips. "Maybe we should work on becoming better friends, Miss Baker."

"I would prefer to keep our relationship professional, Mr. Winston. If you don't mind." To her relief, her voice sounded much steadier than she felt. She probably could have skipped adding that last part, because it was obvious he did mind. His smile had faded into a frown, turning her knees into gelatin.

Her heart pounded in terror as the seconds ticked past. If he fired her, she was sunk. She needed this job, especially when she was so close to getting her license. On the other hand, she was getting sick and tired of men rolling over her objections. Dick may have just gotten away with it, but not Skip.

This time, she would stand up against the wind, even if it cost her.

The little voice inside her head cheered.

Skip tilted his head toward the plant. "You're late, Miss Baker. Let it happen again, and you're fired."

# Chapter 35

"Guess what today is," Charity said, sliding into the chair on the other side of Genie's desk.

"Friday, August 7." Genie wiped a bead of sweat from her forehead. The office was positively sweltering this afternoon thanks to the bright sunshine pouring in the windows. "At least that's what I've been typing all day."

Her friend smirked. "I didn't ask the date. I said guess the day."

"I don't know." She racked her brain. "The day I hope to get my license? I've got my final flight exam"—she checked the wall clock, and her stomach lurched from nerves and the heat—"in two hours."

Skin-prickling nausea had her grabbing the open Coca-Cola bottle near her typewriter and taking a hasty sip. Work . . . she needed to focus on work.

Charity's forehead wrinkled slightly. "Are you feeling all right?"

"I'm fine. It's just hotter than blazes in here."

Her friend sat back. "If you're worried about the flight test, don't be. Just because the flight examiner is an old fuddy-duddy and a stickler for details."

Another surge of nerves had Genie reaching for the Coke bottle. "You're not helping."

"Then try this: Today is your lucky day, because not only is that Flying Tiger still in town, but I did a little digging and found out he's been asking around about you."

"What?" The bottle almost slipped from her fingers. Hurriedly, she put it down. "Where did you hear that?"

"From Flo last night at the airfield, after my lesson." Her friend grimaced. "And for the record, getting my commercial license is a lot harder than I thought."

"Your instructor did warn you. And if you've known all day, why tell me now, right before my exam?"

Charity rolled her eyes. "Because I had to wait for Skip to leave. Don't even think I didn't see how he had you cornered in the mailroom earlier. Why do you think I sent Gloria in?"

"So she could witness my humiliation? I swear, if he gets any freer with his hands, I may have to slug him." Genie defiantly yanked the last memo from her typewriter, but her fingers shook as she prepared its envelope. "Between you and me, I feel like he's getting hungrier every day, and I'm what's on the menu. He already uses every excuse he can think of to get me alone. To be honest, I'm not sure how much longer I can take it."

"You'd leave me?" Charity looked stricken.

"I may not have a choice." She gathered up the envelopes from her afternoon's work and stood. "I just hope I pass my test today, because what I would really love is to find a job flying."

"You'll have to get your commercial license first," Charity reminded her. "And it isn't cheap."

Genie inhaled deeply and placed a hand on her unsettled stomach. "I know. But first things first. If I don't pass this test today, nothing else matters."

"You can always take the test again."

She could, but that would mean more money spent on lessons. More time spent dodging Skip's advances. More fear that maybe, just maybe, she wasn't smart enough or strong enough to turn her dream of flying into a reality.

And she wouldn't even think about trying to explain her failure to Ted, who had probably never failed at anything in his life . . . and also, inexplicably, had been asking about her.

Chiding herself for making mountains out of molehills, she turned toward the mailroom. As if her life weren't complicated enough. "I'm heading out as soon as I drop these off. So wish me luck."

"Good luck!"

The bus to Montebello dropped her off by the airport at a quarter to five. Heat radiated off the pavement, warning her of a bumpy flight to come. All that rising air would displace the cooler air above, creating all sorts of up and down drafts. *Wonderful.* Slinging her satchel that held all her flight gear over her shoulder, she worked on focusing her mind as she began the mile walk to the flight school. Now was not the time for self-doubt.

The flight examiner was an older fellow, grizzled and gruff. For over an hour they sat at a desk while he quizzed her on the mechanics of flight, basic airplane maintenance, weather predictors, map reading, aeronautical protocol, and anything else he could think of, each question getting harder and harder as the exam went on. It soon became clear that he was doing his best to fail her, but all those hours of studying paid off as she answered almost every question correctly.

The flight portion was little better. The dust haze over the valley made the glare so awful, her eyes positively ached from trying to spot any dark flecks that might be other airplanes on a collision course. With nervous optimism, she put the Cub through every maneuver on the handwritten list clipped to her knee board: crosswind takeoff, short field landing, turns around a point, stall recoveries, steep turns. Each success bolstered her courage.

And then it happened. Exhaustion from her long day at work and the more recent task of fighting the near-constant up- and downdrafts caught up with her, and she remembered a few seconds too late to check her altitude coming into the final stall recovery. Kicking herself as she saw how low she had gotten, she threw the throttle forward, but not fast enough.

"My airplane!" the flight examiner yelled from the back seat as the control stick moved in her hand. Instantly, she let go, obeying the command to cede the airplane.

Time seemed to stand still as she sat there stunned, her dreams disintegrating around her. She had failed. She was nothing. She was finished.

*No.* Something flared inside of her as all the frustrations of being a woman, of being told what to do, of being held back, erupted into a firestorm of anger. *This will not do.*

"*My* airplane!" she yelled over the roar of the engine as she took hold of the control stick and throttle.

Perhaps he was shocked that a student, let alone a female, would fight back. Or maybe he was only giving her enough rope to hang herself with. Whatever the reason, he didn't interfere as she maneuvered the Cub around to try the recovery again. With grim determination she set the stall up without losing altitude and executed the recovery correctly. Or at least she was pretty sure she had. Silence reigned in the back seat, which unnerved her to no end.

With all her tasks completed, she headed back toward Vail Field. Self-doubts ate away at her confidence. There was no way she was going to pass now. She hadn't asked for permission, she hadn't waited for instruction, nor was she, as a student pilot, qualified to just take control.

Feeling as if years were being stripped off her life for every minute that passed on the flight back, she couldn't hold back a sigh of relief as the runway came into view. Except she could see at a glance that she was coming in and too high and too fast. All extraneous thought ceased as she feverishly worked to correct the approach. Throttle, elevator, trim, rudder, aileron—her hands and feet worked the controls as she forced the plane to slow down without letting it stall or—heaven forbid—enter a spin on the turn to final. With the ground so close, there would be no time to prevent a crash.

Goosing the gas a bit on the turn, she gave her airspeed one last check and then centered the plane on the runway. The large painted numbers at the end grew larger in the windscreen as the plane floated down. Hot air from the surrounding roofs and streets pushed up on the Cub, bouncing it around. Gritting her teeth, she kept everything as steady as she could. The plane flirted with the runway, touching down and then ballooning back up. Her fingers tightened on the throttle, ready for the go-around. *Come on, darn you, land already.*

The plane dropped and bounced, and then the tires finally grabbed the pavement with a jerk. A wash of white-hot, adrenaline-fueled needles raked her skin, leaving her flushed and shaking as the Cub rattled and bumped down the runway. With an effort, she got her legs to cooperate long enough to steer the plane off onto the taxiway. A thousand shoulda-coulda-wouldas whirled in her brain as she pulled the plane into its tie-down spot and shut off the engine. A deafening silence filled the cockpit. On gelatin legs, she hopped out of the plane and pulled the cotton stuffing from her ears while she waited for the examiner to join her.

As she waited, a lone, crumpled paper scuttled across the tarmac, aimless and unwanted. Kind of like her dreams, now that she had torpedoed her chances of passing.

The flight instructor brushed past her without comment on his way to the flight-school building. Genie briefly closed her eyes, the temptation to run away overwhelming. Maybe she should skip going inside altogether and save herself the embarrassment of being told she had failed. Except that would be cowardly, and she wasn't a coward.

Drawing a deep breath, she squared her shoulders and forced herself to walk after him.

That was the problem with taking action: there were always consequences.

The screen door slapped shut behind her as she entered the office. The flight examiner was already seated behind the front desk. He ignored her as he wrote something on the form in front of him.

Without looking up, he held out his free hand. "Log book."

She pulled the stapled cardboard-covered book from her satchel and handed it to him. He opened it to the most recently filled out section and began writing.

"Sit," he said.

She pulled over a wooden chair and sat. Nervously, she wiped her sweaty hands on her twill trousers. Would he let her down hard or easy? *Please, don't let me cry.* A few other students came in and eyed her curiously. After what felt like an eternity, he laid the pen down and sat back. She braced herself for the worst.

"I'll be honest, Miss Baker," he said, his brown eyes intense behind his glasses. "There are a lot of people, male and female, who think women are inherently unqualified to pilot an aircraft. These same people can and will actively seek to have you fail. It's not unheard of for female pilots to be denied services by airport managers, or to have their planes sabotaged.

"That said, I've yet to encounter a piece of equipment that can tell the sex of its operator, so I try to keep an open mind. And I try to be fair, especially when a student's progress is of particular interest to another instructor I know and respect."

She nodded to show she was listening, even as she wondered if he was talking about Flo. Everyone liked her flight instructor.

The flight examiner drummed his fingers on the table, his gaze speculative. "If I pass you, any idea what you'll do with your license?"

Joy raced through her veins as his intent became clear. She had passed! Light-headed with relief, she felt like laughing and crying at the same time. "I'd like to find a job flying, sir. I can't think of a better situation."

"There isn't a whole lot of call for female pilots in California, though I hear they're looking for bush pilots up in the Alaskan territories. Or you could instruct. Air racing and performing are a no-go until the war is over."

"I wouldn't mind helping ferry aircraft around the country," she said, thinking of her company. "If we keep increasing production, and Uncle Sam keeps drafting our pilots, there's going to be a backlog soon."

"I like the way you think, miss," he said, sitting back. "But no commander in his right mind would let a little gal like you fly his planes. They're too powerful and hard to control."

"Yes, sir," she managed, though what she really wanted to do was protest.

Apparently approving of her restraint, he held out his hand and smiled for the first time. "Congratulations, Miss Baker. You are now officially a private pilot, with all the responsibilities and privileges the license grants you."

"Thank you." Her hand trembled with excitement as she shook his hand. No matter the restrictions on her future, she was a pilot. *A pilot!*

Flo whooped from the corner, and soon Genie was engulfed in a hug by her instructor. "This calls for a proper celebration. It's not every day the world gets another female pilot. I hereby declare that you and I are moving this party to Damon's."

"Where?" Genie asked as she pulled free to admire the brand-new endorsement of her logbook. It still didn't feel real. She couldn't wait to get her official license in the mail.

"Damon's Steak House in Glendale. Right by the Grand Central Airport." Flo slung her leather flight jacket over her arm. "I'm assuming you haven't had supper yet. No? Didn't think so. And neither have I, so let's go. I'll drive."

"I should probably call my roommate," she said, tucking the precious logbook into her satchel. Though in all likelihood, Lavinia wouldn't be home. It was Friday night, so she was probably out with the other line girls.

"I'm sorry," Flo said, looking suddenly abashed. "Was there someone else you'd rather celebrate with?"

"Not really." Her high spirits deflated a bit as she realized she really had no one else to call to share her good news with. Her father was beyond reach in China. Dick was out on assignment somewhere. Charity, who would understand her sense of accomplishment the most, was likely out on a date. It was a Friday night, after all.

Flo clapped her on the shoulder, shaking her out of her doldrums. "Then it'll just be us aviatrixes painting the town. We'll have fun, promise."

Genie gave her a grateful smile as she slung her satchel over her shoulder. Her instructor really was the best. "How fancy is Damon's? I've got the clothes I wore to work in my bag."

"Nah. You look fine as you are. Being so close to the airport, the waitstaff is used to pilots showing up in their flight suits. Even more so now the army opened up another flight school right down the street."

Genie's pulse skittered at the mention of the flight school, one thought replacing all the others: *Ted.* He was an army pilot, she was sure. And if Charity was right, and he was still in town . . .

"Give me a sec." Without waiting for Flo's answer, she spun on her heel and flew toward the bathroom to change.

# Chapter 36

Damon's was crowded by the time they got there, but the maître d' managed to find them a table. As Genie followed him past the other diners, the appreciative glances of the men made her glad she had changed.

Her only regret was that she was making Flo look rather dowdy by comparison, but her flight instructor didn't seem to mind. In fact, Flo seemed in her element here, stopping frequently to chat with one person or another. The men all seemed so at ease with her, laughing and slapping her on the back, asking if she wanted to sit with them. By the time she and Flo managed to reach their table and be seated, Genie realized that maybe her instructor had stayed in her twill pants and work shirt for a reason. Dressed as she was, Flo was less a female than a fellow pilot, whereas it was quite the opposite with Genie.

Genie smoothed her skirt as she sat down, wondering if she had made the wrong choice. If Ted did show up tonight, would she want him to see her as a pilot or as a woman?

The waiter handed them menus and then started to leave. Flo stopped him.

"Before you go, a bourbon on the rocks for me. And this brand-new private pilot over here will have . . ." Flo gave her a questioning look.

"Oh, I don't know." Genie bit her lip, unsure if she should order hot tea or something stronger. Unfortunately, her experience with stronger spirits was limited to what she had imbibed that one night over dinner with Dick.

The waiter shifted his feet impatiently.

She decided to go for it. "A glass of red wine?"

"What kind?" he asked brusquely. "And we only sell it by the bottle."

She stared at him, totally at a loss.

Flo tossed her a sympathetic look. "She'll have an old-fashioned, extra cherries." She leaned forward after the waiter left with their order. "If you don't like it, we'll get you something else. Don't worry."

"It's fine, I'm sure. If you couldn't tell, I don't drink very often. In fact, almost never."

"Nothing wrong with that." Flo sat back and stretched her legs out as she perused the menu. "What are you thinking of having?"

Genie scanned the choices and sighed. Everything in the States was so heavy and bland. Even the Chinese food in Chinatown didn't taste quite right. What she really wanted was one of Zhenzhu's home-cooked meals, but that would have to wait until war was over. "Honestly, I'm not that hungry."

"May I join you?" Ted's familiar drawl had her straightening her chair.

Flo looked up, and her expression brightened. "Of course."

"Ted!" Genie soaked in the sight of his lean face and naturally athletic grace as he pulled a chair over to the table. Everything inside her felt lighter, as if she could float right off her seat. "What are you doing here?"

He winked at her as he sat down. "A little bird told me you passed your flight exam. So I wanted to come say congratulations."

"Thanks. It was a huge relief."

"I bet."

"So you didn't have to fly tonight, after all," Flo said, signaling for the waiter to return.

"Nah. The lesson got scrubbed on account of a flat tire, which suited me just fine."

The waiter arrived, and Ted ordered a beer.

"Lesson?" Genie asked after the man left. She frowned slightly. "Are you an instructor now?"

He leaned back in his chair and stretched his long legs out in a position very similar to Flo's. "For the moment, until they can decide what to do with me. I think they're still holding out hope I'll consent to the war bond tour, but fat chance of that. I'd rather be stuck in the right seat for the duration of the war, teaching wet-behind-the-ears cadets how to fly, than be paraded around like some kind of fatted calf."

She cocked an eyebrow at him. "Would it really be so bad? I'd certainly buy a war bond from you."

A tired smile curved his lips as his beautiful dark eyes met hers. "So you've said before. But enough about me. It's you I want to hear more about."

Caught in the crosshairs of the familiar, tigerlike intensity of his gaze, she felt the fine hairs on her skin lift as if she were on the side of a mountain with a thunderstorm approaching. "What would you like to know?"

"If he's smart," Flo said with a laugh, "he'll ask if you're seeing anyone and then make his move."

Ted's cheeks pinkened, but his gaze remained steady. "As I was saying, I heard you're working at Vultee. That had to be quite a change for you. How do you like it there?"

"I like it far more than I thought I would," she said honestly. "I like getting a paycheck. And I like feeling like I'm making a difference in the war."

A fond smile stole across his handsome lips, making her heart catch. "I wouldn't expect anything less from you."

Her face now on fire, too, she hurriedly dropped her gaze to her menu.

To her relief, the topic of discussion switched to student pilots and the sad state of the army air corps. While Flo peppered Ted with questions about different aircraft and training techniques, Genie pretended to study the dinner choices.

She tried to pay attention to the conversation, as it all pertained to what she wanted to do in the future. Unfortunately, her brain had a different agenda. Instead she found herself focusing on the beguiling rhythm and cadence of his voice. It soothed her in a way she couldn't begin to articulate. He could be reading the dictionary for all she cared; she had been just as spellbound when she'd heard him for the first time, in her father's study.

"Have you heard anything from your father?" Ted asked.

Startled, she looked up. Her heart squeezed at the honest curiosity she saw in his eyes, but then he had met her father. Shared dinner with him. Traveled with him back to her village.

"No, not a word." Sorrow twisted through her. "I've written dozens of letters to him, but with the war, I've no idea if he's received a single one. I can only pray he and Zhenzhu are safe."

Wordlessly, he reached out and squeezed her hand. She tried to smile back, grateful that he didn't utter any platitudes. They would be lies in any case. Even though today's paper had touted a victory by the Chinese army, it had only been a small one. The Japanese were no closer to pulling out than they had been at the start of the war. And if the article on the front page of today's *Los Angeles Times* was true, India might agree to a deal with Japan in an act of independence from Britain. If it did, China would be lost.

Pushing away the horrifying thought, she focused on the here and now. After all, it wasn't every day she had the pleasure of Ted's company. She would be a fool to squander it.

She smiled at him. "Do you like instructing? The flight examiner suggested it as a job I might try if I wanted to fly for a living."

"Well"—he released her fingers and sat back—"there's always that one student who tries to kill you, like the cadet today who flipped the aircraft into an inverted spin."

"Overcorrected on his stall recovery, eh?" Flo said with a snort.

"Thank the Lord for altitude, that's all I've got to say," he said fervently, and Genie inwardly flinched, remembering her own earlier mistake with altitude. The waiter reappeared with a tray of drinks and then took the rest of their order. To her delight, Ted ordered dinner along with Flo. Still too nervous to eat much, Genie ordered only a bowl of soup.

"So you're serious about this flying business?" Ted asked, rolling his neck.

"I am. Though I think I'd rather be a ferry pilot than an instructor."

His eyebrows lifted slightly. "Really? Flying untested planes is dangerous work. You have to be prepared for anything."

"And an instructor doesn't?" She picked up her cocktail glass, hoping to hide her sudden nervousness. "Besides, I'd like to do something for my country. Something besides typing forms and volunteering to collect scrap metal. And getting airplanes to the boys who need them fits that bill."

"'Your country'?" His eyebrows slid up a bit higher. "Is the United States home now?"

She swirled the contents of her drink, the ice tinkling as she considered the question and the reason behind it. No doubt he was thinking back to when they had first met, when she'd considered herself Chinese through and through. "Yes and no. As my father would say, *Panta rei*. One has no choice but to accept change."

His beautiful dark eyes held her captive for a long moment. The empathy she saw there silently acknowledged all she didn't say. She felt some of her tension dissipate. As an unwilling immigrant to the States like herself, he had to understand the division in her soul.

"Ferrying might be fun," Flo said thoughtfully while Genie took a sip of her drink. "I hear they're letting gals do it over in Britain."

"That's because Britain's running out of pilots, male or female," Ted said drily. "Where do you think most of my students are heading?"

The possibility that Ted might be asked to join them made her blood run cold. She didn't like the idea of him being shipped so far away. He was the closest thing she had to family in the States, other than Lavinia and her still-missing aunt.

Which reminded her, now that she had a break before pursuing her commercial license, she could finally travel up to Bakersfield, where her aunt had last lived. Having already quizzed the neighbors by post, to no avail, she had decided it was time to try her luck in person. Maybe she would have better success.

Aware that the conversation had continued on without her, she tuned back in only to find her friends debating whether American engines were better than British ones. Having no opinion on the matter, she took another sip of her drink. The taste was a rather pleasant mix of sweet and sour, and as she drank, a welcome warmth began to suffuse her tired muscles.

Slowly, all the day's trials slid away. Skip was relegated to being nothing more than an annoyance. She had passed her flight exam, so she no longer had to obsess over her studies. She would still need to watch her pennies so as to build hours for her commercial license, but she could now take her time.

She tilted the glass up and finished the drink, marveling at how wonderful she felt. Perhaps if she sipped that last little bit . . .

Without pausing in his discussion, Ted reached over and gently guided her hand with the glass back to the table.

"Too much booze on an empty stomach is never a good idea," he said in response to her confused frown. "Trust me on this."

"Are you saying I can't take care of myself?" she asked, fighting a ridiculous urge to pout.

"No. I'm just looking out for you. Something tells me you don't have a lot of experience with the stuff."

She lifted her chin. "Why would you think that?"

He cocked his head, skepticism clear in his dark eyes. "Has the little missionary gal I met in China taken up drinking, then?"

Her bravado evaporated at the reminder of who she was, or at least had been. "No."

His laugh held no humor. "Didn't think so."

Dinner arrived, and Genie found she was much hungrier than she had imagined. Ted slid the bread basket to her without comment as he and Flo continued to swap flying stories. Amused by the one-upmanship, she sipped the water in her glass, her worries ebbing away again.

She wished the evening would never end. It had been a long time since she had felt this content—maybe not since she had left home six . . . no, seven months ago. And while she missed her father terribly, and Zhenzhu, and Li Ming, she was also aware that this kind of evening—sitting here with Ted and Flo, talking about what she loved, being listened to as if what she had to say was important—would never have happened if she hadn't left home. In China, she had been relegated to being a silent ornament at her father's dinner table, seen but not heard, like the other women, no matter how much she wished to speak.

It was such a queer feeling to both wish she were home and yet be glad that she wasn't.

Ted began to use his hands to illustrate a new fighter technique to a rapt Flo, and Genie fell back in time to that first night on the trail. Wu Fang and Nathan had hung on his every word then, too. The spicy, clean scent of his aftershave—the same one she had noticed when they had danced together at the 300 Club—tickled her senses. His hair was the same glossy black she remembered. Her fingers itched to glide through the short waves to see if the strands were as soft as they looked.

He glanced at her, his dark tiger gaze holding for a second as if he sensed the direction of her thoughts. A question lurked in the chocolaty depths: *What are you doing, Genie?*

What *was* she doing?

A stab of guilt made her tear her gaze from his. Dick was the one who had always been there for her, helping her after Nathan's death and her aunt's disappearance, finding her work, giving her a place to stay. He deserved better than to have her moon over another man in his absence. Yet that was just it—Dick was always absent. She had seen Ted as many times as she had seen Dick these last few months. And despite his passionate kisses, Dick was notoriously bad at staying in contact when on assignment. She could count on one hand the number of phone messages he had left, and not even a single letter or postcard.

She would never admit it to Lavinia, but recently she had started to wonder if her friend had been right about Dick not loving her. In which case, why shouldn't she admire the way Ted's khaki shirt stretched over his strong shoulders or the intriguing muscles of his forearms bared by his rolled-up sleeves, or be distracted by the subtle emotions playing across the angles of his exotic face or by how good he smelled?

Flo stretched her back and yawned. "Hey, you two—do you mind if we get the check and run? I've got a flight first thing in the morning."

"Not a problem," Ted said as he signaled for the waiter again. "I can drive Genie home. I'm off rotation tomorrow, so I'm in no real hurry."

Flo shook her head, even as Genie tensed with alarm. It was one thing to let her fantasies about Ted run wild in the relative safety of the restaurant. It was quite another to actually go anywhere alone with him. Not that she didn't trust him. She knew without a doubt he would behave as a gentleman. No, it was her own restraint she worried about. The old-fashioned had left her feeling decidedly fuzzy.

"I don't want to put Genie in an awkward spot," Flo said. "I'll take her."

"I don't mind," Genie heard herself say. "It'll give Ted and me more time to catch up."

Flo hesitated, but there was relief in her eyes. "If you're sure you're okay with it."

"Absolutely." Genie smiled as much to convince herself as her instructor. Ted made no comment either way as he settled the bill.

Before she knew it, the evening was over, and Genie found herself alone on the sidewalk with Ted. A whiff of his aftershave teased her again, and she fought the urge to lean closer to get a better smell.

"You all right?" he drawled softly.

The question shook her out of her thoughts and back into the present.

"Yes." She was glad the darkness would hide her furious blush.

Thankfully, he didn't say anything else as they set off down the sidewalk into the mild night. Ted had his hands in his pockets. She clutched the strap on her satchel like a lifeline to keep from touching him. Part of her still couldn't believe they were both here in LA, walking side by side beneath the stars.

"I went flying at night not too long ago," she said to break the silence. "The city lights were so lovely. Like a quilt of stars. I remembered how you said nothing beat the view from an airplane, and you were right."

"Did I say that?" He stopped by a dusty Ford pickup truck that wouldn't have looked out of place on one of the numerous farms in the area. "Well, I was wrong. There's one thing that does beat it."

"Like what?" she asked curiously.

He opened the passenger door and gazed down at her. "Seeing you again."

Heart fluttering, she let his comment slide and gestured at the truck. "Is this yours?"

"Airport's. I didn't have time to go home after my last lesson, so I borrowed it." He leaned in and grabbed a towel from behind the seat back and spread it over the cushions.

"Never know who was in here last," he said at her inquisitive glance. "And I don't want to be responsible for ruining your skirt. Which looks very nice, by the way."

"Thank you." His offhand compliment pleased her probably more than it should have.

He helped her in, and she straightened the light cotton fabric across her lap as he shut the door. Seconds later he jumped in on the driver's side and started the engine.

"Where to?"

She gave him her address and then admitted she had no idea how to get there.

"No problem." He shifted the truck into gear and pulled away from the curb. "I grew up here."

"I didn't know that."

"We moved here when I was thirteen, when my father was offered a position at Caltech. Have to say California winters beat the East Coast ones hands down. Don't know if I could ever move back."

The storefronts of Glendale slid by as they headed south out of town. "If the war were over, would your father return to Turkey?"

"Doubt it. His work is here. I'm here."

"If he did go, would you follow?"

"No." He gave her a sideways look. "Are you thinking of not going home after the war?"

"I don't know. I mean, I miss my father and Zhenzhu and my friends. And yet . . . my life there seems so far away. I'm not sure I would still fit in."

"I can see where it might be kind of hard to keep flying. Those mountains didn't leave much room for a decent runway."

"There is that," she said with a small laugh, but her mood slipped again. "I was thinking more that I've changed so much, my father might no longer recognize me."

"I sincerely doubt that. You don't look *that* much different."

"No, but I act differently. I'm more independent: I have my own income; I go where I want, when I want; I speak my mind."

"All good things, in my book."

"But that isn't at all how I was raised."

They had stopped at a traffic signal, the lights dimmed by hoods so as not to attract attention from the air and possible enemy bombers. On the corner a couple waited for the light to change as well, a sailor and his girl. While Genie watched, the sailor pulled his date in close and stole a kiss. Unexpected pain wound its way through her chest.

"Why did you reject me after we kissed in Calcutta?" she asked before she could stop herself, and then wanted to sink into the dusty seat cushion. A million apologies raced across her tongue, unspoken, as the light turned green.

He sighed as he put the truck into gear. "I didn't reject you, Genie. You were affianced to another, as you will recall."

"But I told you I wasn't. Is it because I'm ugly?" Her heart stopped the instant the words were out, horrified that she had actually asked that question aloud. She certainly hadn't meant to.

He shot her a disappointed look. "You should know better than that."

"Then why did you push me away and tell me not to write you?"

"You want me to be straight with you? Because the lifespan of a fighter pilot isn't all that great. It's why I don't date much. I don't want any gal getting too attached to me. I saw what my mother's death did to my dad, and I wouldn't wish that on anyone."

She glared at him. "Speaking as a gal, I would prefer making up my own mind on the subject."

He laughed. "I'm sure you would, Miss Speak-My-Mind Baker." Then his amusement faded and his fingers flexed on the steering wheel. "Genie, there's something I want . . . no, need to ask you. It's been nagging at me ever since I ran into you last month."

"Yes?" she prompted when he didn't continue right away.

He drew a deep breath. "I hope you won't be mad, but I asked around about that Pelton fellow . . . he's not pressuring you or anything, is he? I know it's none of my business, but I feel somewhat responsible. I mean, I'm the reason you're here in the States, and—well—I don't like the thought of someone taking advantage of you. If I had known that Sterling had died, or that your aunt wouldn't be here to greet you . . ."

"You would have done what, exactly?" she asked drily. "You were still in China."

"I don't know. It's just when I found out my little Genie Baker was running around with a married man, I felt I should at least ask if you were all right."

Her heart had no sooner warmed from the words "my little Genie Baker" when the second part of his sentence detonated.

"I'm doing what?" Surely she had heard him wrong.

He slid her a sideways glance. "Dick Pelton is married, Genie. You knew that, right?"

# Chapter 37

"No." She wanted to say more, but there was no air. Her fingers clutched the door handle.

"Genie, I'm—" He glanced at her, his jaw tight. "Damn, but I was afraid of this."

She swallowed hard, fighting to get her breath back. "I don't know who you heard that from, but Dick's not married. He couldn't be. For heaven's sake, I'm staying in his apartment. I think I would know if he had a wife."

"He's got a house up in Hollywood Hills. I asked Fred Short about it. Do you remember meeting him? Flew in the Great War and is now a stunt pilot for Warner Brothers?"

"Well, sure. That's Charity's uncle, but . . ."

"He's also a good friend of your Mr. Pelton. He wasn't wild about dropping you and your friend off at the apartment but figured as long as it was the two of you, it was likely on the up-and-up, so he kept his mouth shut."

"I don't believe it." A queer buzzing had begun in her ears. She shook her head to clear it.

"Fred has no reason to lie, Genie. But if you still doubt it, ask Pelton himself. Assuming he's man enough to tell you the truth."

"I can't. He's out of the country." She let go of the door and pressed her fingertips against her throbbing temples. "He has been for almost a month."

"Are you sure?" he asked, his eyebrows sliding up. "Because I saw a fellow in town not three days ago who looked a lot like him. He had a different, older woman on his arm, but I'd swear it was the same fellow."

"People look alike. It might have been someone else." But the doubts he had planted twisted through her stomach, leaving her light-headed and sweaty. "Why are you doing this? Why are you saying these things to me?"

His voice turned gentle. "Because you have a right to know. I'm sorry, Genie. Please don't cry."

Startled, she wiped the wetness from her cheeks. She hadn't even realized she was crying. Worse, if what Ted was saying was true, Dick didn't even deserve her tears. Everything between them had been built on lies: their friendship, her gratitude, her trust, their . . .

Her breath caught. *Oh Lord, forgive me.* If Ted's information was correct, then she had kissed another woman's husband. Happily, fervently kissed him. Had run her fingers through his hair her while he fondled her breast. Had even considered letting him do much, much more.

Her dinner surged up her throat, and she fumbled with the door latch. "Stop. Here."

Immediately he pulled the truck over to the curb, and she popped the door open. She was out of the cab before the truck had even stopped rolling. Shame and guilt vomited out of her onto the sidewalk. Every touch, every kiss remembered made her retch again. How could she have been so wrong about someone?

Ted crouched beside her, and her humiliation increased a thousandfold. She closed her eyes, trying to ignore both him and the stinking contents of her stomach on the concrete. *Please, Lord, let this all be a horrible, horrible dream.*

"You deserve better than to be some man's piece on the side. You know that, right?"

"Piece on the side"—what a brutal way to describe her shame. But then, this was Ted, who had never shied away from telling her the truth.

Tears welled up behind her closed eyelids even more furiously than before.

His hand cupped her elbow, and he began pulling her to her feet. "Come on. Let's get you home."

She resisted. "No. I can't go back to that apartment. Not now. Not ever."

"Genie, be reasonable. All your belongings are there. You can't just not go back. And if no one has said anything to you before, they're not likely to start now. So take a couple of days, have a plan in mind. You've got a roommate to help you."

He tugged again, and this time she stood without protest.

"Who else knows he's married? Flo? Charity?" her voice squeaked with distress. "How can I ever face them again?"

"Honey, I'm pretty sure if they had known, they would've said something. No one who knows you would ever believe you'd willingly go out with a married man."

She huffed in angry despair. "You believed it."

"Actually, no, I didn't. It was too out of character for you. The only way I could see you agreeing to go along was either you didn't know, or he was coercing you somehow. I debated a long time whether I should get involved because, as you said, a gal has a right to make her own choices."

"But . . . ?"

"It felt all wrong. As I said earlier, I know how you were raised. I've met your father. And it got so I couldn't sleep at night. Now I wish I had said something sooner." The razor edge in his voice was like a balm on her heart. He was angry—yes, but not at her. No matter how foolish she had been, Ted hadn't abandoned her as a friend.

"What do I do?" She wished her thoughts weren't so blurred.

"I know you don't want to go back to your apartment, but you're in no shape to be out and about. You're upset, you've had a long day, and you've been drinking."

"Then take me to Charity's—oh, wait, she's probably out."

"What about your roommate?"

"She's out tonight, too. And I'm not sure I want to talk to her right now, because she'll just say 'I told you so.' She's never liked Dick from day one . . ."

*You deserve better . . .* The memory of Lavinia saying those words ripped the air from Genie's lungs. All her friend's veiled warnings took on new meaning. "She knew."

"What was that?" Ted asked sharply, but her brain was working too feverishly to respond.

"Lavinia knew he was married. She's known all along. That's why she never liked him. That's why she was so upset when . . ." She swallowed and glanced up to find Ted watching her intently. She looked away as renewed shame burned her throat. *Please don't let him be able to see into my thoughts.* She would die if he ever found out how far she had gone with Dick.

"Genie," he said evenly, but something dark lurked in his tone. "Did you just say your roommate knew?"

"Maybe . . ."

Kitty's voice joined Lavinia's in Genie's memory. *If you sleep with vipers . . . I wasn't talking about you, Nia, dear.*

Genie shivered despite the heat radiating off the pavement. No, she had been talking about Dick. And if Kitty had known he was married, likely so had Lavinia. Her chest constricted under the double betrayal. "She did."

Ted exhaled and ran his fingers through his short hair. "When do you think your friend Charity will be home again?"

"Late. She had a date with one of your buddies. Some flight lieutenant with dreamy eyes." She hated the bitterness leaking into her voice.

"Okay, so I can't take you to your friend's place just yet, and you won't go back to your apartment, which is fine, considering I have a low opinion of your roommate at the moment. I can't take you back to base with me. And if we show up at Flo's with you looking the way you do, she's likely to shoot me."

She touched her tear-slicked cheeks, suddenly self-conscious of her ruined makeup and sweat-soaked clothes. "I must look awful."

"Like you've been put through a wringer," he agreed grimly.

"Wonderful." She briefly closed her eyes, wishing she could turn back time. "You would think in a town as big as LA there would be somewhere quiet I could go, somewhere away from everyone."

"I'd offer to stay with you, if you wanted. But I don't think that would be such a good idea under the circumstances."

"Because you don't want me to get attached?" She tried to make it sound like a joke, except her emotions were too raw.

A muscle leaped in his jaw as he pulled her gently against his chest. "Genie, I'm sorry. I've obviously hurt you."

"Saved me, you mean." Her voice broke, and it took everything she had not to cling to him. He felt so sturdy beneath her cheek, his heartbeat reassuringly steady and strong.

"I wish . . ." He made a frustrated sound as his arms tightened around her. "Lord, what a mess. No matter what I do, I'm only going to make things worse."

"It's all right. We're still friends, yes?" She struggled not to burst into tears again.

He hesitated, and that brief pause was like a knife in her heart. "Yes. Always."

Cursing herself as being the worst kind of fool, she refused to look at him as she pushed back and out of his arms. She glanced up at the shadowed buildings and drew a deep, shuddering breath. All the blinds were pulled down tight to prevent light from leaking out. Shuttered like her heart, except she was trying to keep pain in. Lord, she felt so alone. "I think I'd best go home."

The drive to her apartment was blessedly short. She couldn't think of anything she could say that wouldn't sound desperate or weak. He seemed to be wrestling with his own thoughts, so the silence lay between them as deep and undisturbed as a winter snow. When he pulled up at the curb, she bounced out of the truck, her satchel over her shoulder and her key already in her hand.

"Thanks for the ride."

"Genie." He leaned across the seat, the low urgency of his voice stopping her. She paused, her heart squeezing in spite of herself. "Take care of yourself."

She forced a smile. "I will."

The truck stayed idling at the curb while she fiddled with the front lock. Once she was inside and the door shut safely behind her, she heard the engine rev and then fade away. She released the breath she hadn't even known she was holding and glanced up the stairwell. No matter what Ted had said, she wasn't staying here any longer than she had to. The familiar scents of dusty carpet and half-faded dinners mocked her. How had she ever thought of this as home?

She hitched the satchel higher on her shoulder and started up the stairs. It wouldn't take her long to pack, and if she couldn't get to Charity's tonight, she would leave first thing in the morning. She had no doubt that once she told Charity the situation, her friend would squeeze her into their apartment. It would be for only a short while, anyway. Just until she could find a new place.

And possibly a new roommate. Depending on the outcome of the conversation that needed to happen, she could very well be out a friend. She could forgive evasiveness and mood swings. She could even forgive the strange obsession with Kitty. But if her hunch was true, and Lavinia had known Dick's marital status, then their friendship was over.

Her battered heart winced at the possibility, but she shoved any regrets aside as she unlocked the door. She was a woman on a mission.

She opened the door, and a flurry of sounds greeted her. The rustling of fabric punctuated by soft profanities had her reaching for the light switch, her pulse racing.

"Lavinia?" She flicked the toggle up, and light flooded out of the kitchen and into the living area.

Lavinia and Sheila were stretched out on the couch, the shock and horror reflected in their faces matching Genie's own reaction. Both girls were half-naked, their shirts missing.

Genie tried to breathe and failed. She tried again. Sheila, her breasts entirely bare, shifted to crouch protectively over Lavinia, who was lying beneath her. Genie was finally able to tear her eyes away, and she stared blindly at the opposite wall. *Oh my Lord.* What she'd seen couldn't be true. Couldn't be actually happening. Her chest squeezed even tighter, her ears buzzing slightly.

"Genie, it's not what you think." Lavinia's voice held a desperate note as more rustling came from the couch, the sound of clothing being put back on.

"Oh, really? And what am I supposed to think when I come home to . . . this?" Genie switched her gaze to the ceiling, not wanting to see any more of the two than she already had. What she had seen was quite enough. "I want her gone. Now."

"We were just messing around. We weren't—aren't . . . It didn't mean anything." Lavinia's voice had become pleading.

Genie hazarded a glance at her roommate. "You do know that what you are doing is illegal, Lavinia. *Illegal* as well as immoral. What if someone had been with me when I walked in? What were you even thinking?"

"I . . ." Lavinia pulled her blouse together more tightly, her blue eyes haunted in her pale face. Her thin body began to tremble. "You won't tell anyone?"

Genie turned on Sheila, who was busy tucking her blouse into her work pants. "I thought I told you to get out. And don't you even think of setting foot in this apartment again."

The woman's expression hardened. "You can't ban me. It's Nia's apartment, too."

Hearing that nickname again hit Genie like a punch to the gut, temporarily robbing her of air. She whirled to Lavinia. "Nia? Is that the name your lovers call you by? Like Kitty?" The burgeoning realization that this wasn't her roommate's first brush with illicit passion left her reeling.

Lavinia licked her lips nervously. Her gaze flicked to Sheila. "It's all right. Genie and I need to talk. I'll call you tomorrow."

Sheila's steely blue gaze locked on Genie. "Nia asked you a question. Are you going to call the police?"

Anger rushed back into the emotional void, and she threw her satchel onto the table. "Just get out. I've got bigger problems to deal with."

"Go," Lavinia said softly in the taut silence that followed.

Genie tried not to react to the slight catch she'd heard in her roommate's voice. She was hurt enough for both of them. No matter what was said now, there was no returning to the way things were.

While Sheila grabbed her things, Lavinia studiously buttoned her blouse, refusing to meet Genie's eyes. She flinched as the front door slammed shut and then bit her lip.

For the second time tonight, Genie found herself at an utter loss for words. Which of tonight's shocks should she address first?

Lavinia drew a shaky breath and looked up. "You look awful. What happened? Did you fail the test?"

"I passed just fine," Genie said tightly, all her pain over Lavinia's betrayal resurfacing. "'What happened' is I found out Dick is married."

Her roommate stilled. "Who told you that?"

"Who told me doesn't matter, because we both know it's true. Right?" Genie searched her friend's face—which seemed more like a stranger's after what she had just witnessed—for any sign of surprise or shock. *Please, please say you didn't know . . .*

Lavinia shivered and began rubbing her arms. "I'm so sorry, Genie. I did warn you to be careful."

Genie's heart shattered for a third time that night, and the pain nearly drove her to her knees. "That's not quite the same as saying, 'Hey, Genie. That fellow who's helping us, who keeps asking you out? Yeah, he's married.'"

"Genie, I . . . I'm sorry. He promised he wouldn't make a pitch with you."

"And you believed him?" Genie practically yelled.

"I didn't have a choice. I did what I could to protect you." Her friend looked on the verge of tears, but Genie was too hurt and angry to care.

"Except tell me the truth," she pointed out hotly, "like any *true* friend."

Li Ming would have told her. Genie was sure of that. And Ted *had* told her, even though he hadn't wanted to.

Lavinia's lips compressed into a distressed line.

Genie closed her eyes, wishing she were somewhere, anywhere, else at this moment. "You said you had no choice. Was Dick blackmailing you?"

A choked laugh escaped Lavinia's lips. "After walking in on this"—she gestured toward the disheveled couch—"what do you think?"

Genie felt ill. "That if Dick knew, there were others before Sheila."

Lavinia opened her mouth and then closed it as she glanced away, the internal battle taking place clear in her face. She sank onto the couch. "Yes."

"Kitty?" The woman's name was bitter on her tongue.

"Does it matter?" Lavinia said, sounding resigned. "If I give you a list, will it make any difference or only compound my sin? If I tried to explain how I've fought this curse my whole life, how I was only ten when I kissed Anna Christina, and how that one act earned my father's eternal hatred, what then? Should I be damned for Liesl, who I fell in love with despite near-constant prayers for divine guidance? What about when I was married off to John with the hope that marriage would fix me, only to fall in love again, this time with a fellow missionary in Thailand?"

"Lavinia—" Genie held out her hands, wanting her friend to stop. This was much more than she wanted to know.

"You might as well know the extent of my depravity if you're going to condemn me," her roommate said bitterly. "And don't worry; the Lord punished me for my sins by taking her away, along with John and the others, in the attack, though how could I have expected anything else? I knew what I was doing was wrong, and yet I didn't stop."

"Why not?" Genie asked, genuinely perplexed. It seemed like it should be so simple . . .

"I don't know!" Lavinia sprang to her feet and went to the window. Pulling back the blackout curtain, she stared out into the night. "I swore I would be good after the attack. I would never love where I shouldn't again. I promised myself I would be as the Lord intended. I tried so very hard to resist—" She stopped abruptly and bit her lip. Her hands closed into fists.

"Kitty." Genie had never despised the vapid socialite as much as she did in that moment. It was clear Lavinia had been hurting and vulnerable after Thailand, and weak—a weakness that Kitty had exploited without thought to the consequences.

"I hated myself afterward. What kind of vile, broken, ungrateful person would throw away the Lord's love like that? And yet I couldn't stay away."

A chill ran up Genie's spine. "Nathan found out, didn't he?"

"He was already suspicious. Marcus had warned him and had given him John's letter. We were arguing because you were right: he was planning on taking me to see my father. He was going to deliver that letter, and I couldn't let him. It would have meant my death."

"Did you kill him?" Genie could barely get the words out, her horror having numbed her lips.

"No!" Lavinia's eyes widened. "I swear it. He was the road to my salvation. I would never . . ."

"No." Genie shook her head as her thoughts whirled in hopeless confusion, the rock of her father's teachings the only guidance she had left after the disasters of the night. "That's not right. The road to salvation is through Christ."

"Who has abandoned me!" Eyes wild, Lavinia thumped her chest. "Do you think I want to be this way? Do you think I haven't prayed every day of my life to have this curse lifted?"

"Christ abandons no sinner who is sincere in his repentance." Genie rubbed her aching temples, no longer sure if she was talking to herself or her friend, her guilt blurring with her friend's. "If anyone was abandoned, it was you who left him by carrying on with Sheila. And worse, you've tried to drag me down to your level by not telling me about Dick."

Lavinia's nostrils flared, and a flush appeared high on her cheeks. "Drag you . . . Oh, let she who is without sin cast the first stone. Who was succumbing to the pleasures of the flesh that night I rescued you? And who kept you from becoming a fallen woman?"

Stung, Genie lashed out. "At least I wasn't indulging in unnatural pleasures."

Lavinia reeled back as if slapped.

Remorse flooded Genie. Horrified by what she had said, she reached out as Lavinia swayed, her fingers digging into her short black hair. "Lavinia—"

"No." Lavinia jerked back, tears sliding down her cheeks. She took a deep, shuddering breath. "Don't say a word. You're justified in your repugnance. Give me a moment, and I'll leave."

Genie shook her head. "No. I'm the one who has to leave."

Lavinia glanced up, her blue eyes clouded with confusion. "But I'm the one at fault."

"Perhaps, but I can't stay here in Dick's apartment, not after all that's happened. It would be an insult to my father's lifework."

"You're leaving me?" The panic in Lavinia's voice tore at Genie's conscience, but she would not, could not, back down on this.

"You don't need me, Lavinia. You have your friends, this apartment, your job. You'll be fine."

"But we're still friends, yes?"

Anger and pain flared within Genie, pushing her to be brutally honest. "I'm not sure we ever were. Not after you willingly chose to keep your lover over my well-being. That's not how friends behave. Not true friends."

Too upset to continue the conversation, Genie whirled toward the bedroom, her heart sick. Never would she have believed that Lavinia and Dick—two of her dearest friends—would betray her like this. Yet both had, neither one caring how badly she would be hurt by their lies. They had thought only of themselves, and that's what hurt the most. Her trust in them had been absolute, and they had played her for an utter fool.

The apartment was eerily silent as she packed. With the passing minutes, her anger slowly faded into a deep sorrow and then a kind of numbness, as if her heart were too exhausted to feel any more. She had just lost her best friend and her boyfriend in one fell swoop, the two anchors of her life turning out to be nothing like she had imagined them to be. It was like a bad dream from which she couldn't wake.

Finally, with nothing left to do but call a cab to take her to Charity's, she lugged her suitcase into the living room.

"Lavinia, I'm . . ."

The room was empty, as was the kitchenette, the closet, and the hallway. Lavinia must have sneaked out while she was packing. Genie returned to the living room, where Lavinia's clothes were still piled on the couch. Likely she was out trying to find Sheila.

Quashing an unexpected pang of hurt, she picked up the telephone receiver to call a cab. Who Lavinia chose to spend her time with was no longer her concern. From now on, only the future mattered. Her future.

Cab ordered, she picked up her suitcase and headed out. She resisted the urge to look back as she closed the door.

# Chapter 38

Genie flipped through the Thursday morning *Los Angeles Times*, past the front-page photo of Clark Gable taking the oath before leaving for basic training, past the news of the raging marine battle in Tulagi and the increased domestic unrest in India, past the depressing news of Japanese reinforcements pouring into China, until she found the classified ads.

Ignoring the chatter around her, she spread the pages out on the breakroom table and began to read over the rooms to let. Caring whether Gloria had been seen going into a motel with Skip over the weekend seemed so petty compared to what the rest of the world was going through.

Of course, maybe that was the point. Worrying about things one had no control over—like whether her village still stood, or if all the people she had met on her journey through Kunming and Calcutta were safe, or if the war would drag on forever until everyone she cared about was gone—was a sure path to madness. She should know, having stared into that dark maw for the past few nights.

She made herself read again and had managed to circle two likely prospects when Charity pulled out the chair next to her and sat. Not feeling up for company, Genie tried to ignore her, too, but Charity didn't seem to catch the hint. The girl continued to stare at her expectantly, her painted fingernails tapping the tabletop.

Genie sighed. "What?"

"I'm trying to figure out why you're so eager to find a new place when you're perfectly welcome to stay with us."

"I'm not so sure your roommates would agree. It's only been four days, and already I feel like I'm wearing out my welcome."

"I disagree. But if you're that worried about it, why not move back to your apartment? I know you're not happy that Mr. Pelton forgot to mention he was married, but that doesn't mean you have to move out. Most landlords are married. Just stop going out with him, and problem solved."

"He didn't forget. It was deliberate."

"So spit on his rent check before you mail it. There's no need to cut off your nose to spite your face."

"He never charged us rent."

A fact that, while it had made affording flight lessons that much easier, left her despondent now. Without knowing it, she had let him turn her into a "kept woman" in appearance, if not in deed. And the latter wasn't for lack of trying on his part.

"Which reminds me, why haven't you invited Lavinia over? She's probably lonely over in that apartment all by herself."

An image of Lavinia and Sheila cuddling together popped into her head, but she immediately brushed it away.

"I doubt it," she said, not wanting to think about her former friend at the moment. Lavinia's betrayal still hurt too much.

"Do you mean you haven't talked to her?" Charity sounded confused. "I thought you two were best friends, travel buddies who had sailed the world together."

Pain slid between her ribs like a knife as a searing wave of grief and anger washed over her. Fighting tears, Genie pushed back from the table. "Drop it, Charity. I don't want to discuss it right now."

"Wow. Someone is in an awful mood."

"I'm sorry." She took a deep steadying breath, aware of the stares from the other girls. If she didn't calm down, questions would be raised, and Lavinia's secret might be exposed. "It's not you. I'm worried about my father, and the war, and finding a place to live, and . . ." *And the fact I trusted the wrong people,* but she didn't say that part aloud.

"Did you and Lavinia have some kind of falling out?" Charity asked, refusing to let it go. Not that Genie was surprised by that. Her friend's doggedness was one of the things that had gotten her through flight training.

"Let's just say we didn't see eye to eye on the landlord issue."

Which was true, in a way. And she hoped it would keep Charity, and everyone else, from speculating too much on the collapse of their friendship. While devastated that Lavinia had lied to her, and shocked by her illicit behavior, Genie still cared about her former friend and didn't wish her any harm. The hard reality was that Lavinia would certainly lose her job, if not be jailed, if her proclivities were exposed. And Genie wouldn't allow that to happen.

She had too many sins of her own to atone for.

She began doodling along the edge of the paper. "I was also thinking I should get serious about finding a church to attend."

"You don't have one?" Charity said in surprise. "I guess I assumed you already . . . I mean, you being raised by missionaries and all."

"No." The lapse haunted her, too. She couldn't quite put her finger on when she had stopped caring about her faith, but her father would be appalled by the result. *She* was appalled. Nathan was likely dancing in spiteful glee, wishing he had an earthly presence with which to say, *I told you so.*

Her pencil stilled as it suddenly occurred to her that she had left something in the apartment. In the front closet, to be exact.

"You can always come with me to my church," Charity was saying. "I go to the Wednesday night services, since the sermon is shorter.

I figured with the war and all, He might forgive me if I spent my Sundays flying instead."

"Likely," Genie said absently, her thoughts more concerned with what to do with Nathan's grave marker. All her extra funds had gone toward flying lessons instead of securing him a memorial plot. Maybe she should reconsider her priorities. Not that she was superstitious or anything.

Charity suddenly smiled. "Hey, I know what will cheer you up. Let's go flying after work. The weather is perfect."

"I can't. I need all my pennies to pay my share of the rent this week." Temptation pulled at her, though, weakening her resolve.

"Come up with me, then. We'll fly around together! It'll be fun."

It would be fun, and it wasn't like the grave marker was going anywhere. She could pick it up later, once she had a place for it. Once she could face Lavinia without remembering a topless Sheila bending over her.

"Break time is over," Skip announced coldly from the door. A flushed and nervous-looking Gloria stood just behind him. She smoothed her skirts, not making eye contact with anyone. It didn't take a genius to decipher what activities had likely just taken place in her boss's office. Genie's jaw tightened with disgust, though not with Gloria. No, her ire was firmly centered on Skip, who, despite his latest conquest hovering nervously behind him, was openly staring at Genie. *The big jerk.*

As soon as she got a new place, she was definitely looking for a new job.

∿

"So I guess you girls are going to have to find a new flight instructor," Flo said cheerfully. "Because there's not a chance of me turning this down. Who would have thunk it? Women flying for the army. Not this gal, that's for sure."

"Not me, either." Charity handed the letter to Genie. "Do you think it's for real, Flo?"

"I certainly intend to show up and find out. What's the worst thing that can happen?"

"You miss two weeks of instructor's pay? It'll take you a week to get to Delaware, at least, with the trains as crowded as they are."

Genie skimmed the letter. It was a personal invitation from a Mrs. Harkness Love to apply for one of twenty-five spots in the Women's Auxiliary Ferrying Squadron. "Too bad you don't have at least five hundred hours of flight time, Charity, or you could apply, too, since you have your commercial license now."

"I'd need to get rated for high-performance engines."

"Which isn't hard to get," Flo said, taking the letter back. "Just expensive, like everything else in flying."

"I can't even imagine having five hundred hours," Genie said glumly. "Let alone nearly a thousand like you do. I'd have to fly ten hours every weekend for almost a year. And that's not even counting all the money it would take."

Flo cuffed her lightly on the shoulder. "That's why you should become a flight instructor, so someone else pays for the plane."

"I call dibs on taking Flo's spot," Charity said, her face alight with excitement. "I think it would be fun to be an instructor."

"As long as you don't mind students trying to kill you," Genie said drily, remembering Ted's story from last Friday. It seemed like a lifetime ago. So much had happened since then. She wondered what he was up to, whether she would ever see him again.

*I don't want any gal getting too attached . . .*

"Aw, you're just sore because you don't have your commercial license yet," Charity said, mistaking the reason for Genie's sigh.

"Speaking of which," Flo interrupted, her expression serious, "I'm not leaving until the first of September. If you can get in here at least a couple more times a week before then, I could have you ready to take the test before I go."

"I wish I could. Oh boy, do I wish it. But I'm not sure I'll be able to afford any lessons for a while."

"Why not?"

Charity rolled her eyes. "Because she had a fight with her roommate *and* her landlord and thus is looking for a new place to live, one that likely requires rent payments."

Flo pinned her with a hard look. "When did this happen? Over the weekend? This isn't because of anything Lieutenant Younan did—"

"No," Genie said, horrified. "He didn't do anything. He was a perfect gentleman."

"Well, that's good. Otherwise I'd have to take him aside and give him a stern what-for."

"Wait." Charity glanced from Genie to Flo and back. "Genie went out with her Flying Tiger, and no one told me?"

Genie held up her hand. "It wasn't a date. He drove me home Friday night, that's all."

"This last Friday night, the one where you showed up on my doorstep, crying and hysterical?"

"I was not hysterical, and it was totally unrelated to Ted. Well, mostly," she amended at Flo's sharp look. "He's the one who told me Mr. Pelton was married, but I'm not mad at him. I'm thankful, if anything."

Flo looked relieved. "Well, good, because I was going to invite him and some of the other army boys to my going-away party, but I'd happily leave him off the list if it'd cause problems."

"No, it's fine. I'm always happy to see Ted."

Which she realized was the absolute truth, even if it meant facing the fact that she would never mean as much to him as he did to her.

Charity's frown didn't fade. "We still have the problem of trying to get Genie her commercial license. It just seems a crying shame that some jerk's marital problems are going to cost her like this."

"It's fine, Charity. It'll give me more time to go to chur—"

"I'll see if I can get her a better rate than the one Vultee's got," Flo said, rubbing her jaw. "I'll see if I can waive my instructor's fee, too."

"And you'll stay with us for another couple of weeks," Charity told Genie sternly. "No arguments allowed. Think of it as your own personal sacrifice for the good of the country. Because this country needs more pilots to support the war effort, and that means female pilots, too. Even if Uncle Sam doesn't realize it yet."

"Though that could be changing," Flo said with a smile even as Genie's eyes filled with tears of gratitude for her two friends. "And we're the start of it."

# Chapter 39

"Genie, phone's for you." The voice of Audrey, one of Charity's three roommates, floated in from the other room.

"If it's Mr. Pelton again, I'm still not here," Genie called back as she rummaged through Audrey's closet for something to wear on her blind date tonight. It would be her first dinner out since that awful night two months before, when Ted had told her about Dick being married and her world had fallen apart.

Not because she missed Dick, the lying rat. It was the fallout of that discovery she regretted, because not only had it destroyed her friendship with Lavinia, it had apparently also swept away Ted, too. She hadn't heard word one from him since he had dropped her off. Not that she was all that surprised. After all, she had cried all over him, thrown up, and generally made an utter fool of herself. Her behavior had all but screamed that she was the kind of girl who would get attached, which was the exact opposite of what he wanted.

Luckily, she had her work and flight lessons to keep her busy, so she couldn't dwell on how she might have handled that night differently. And she had new roommates she adored, which also took up time, since she was bound and determined to do her fair share of chores—as well as pay her part of the expenses—so as never to be a burden.

She pulled out a Hawaiian print skirt and held it up for consideration. Even though it was way past Labor Day, her mood begged for something more summery than her old standby blue dress. It was time to come out of mourning . . .

"It's not. It's some woman," Audrey said.

Genie's heart leaped as she turned around. *Lavinia?* "Did she give a name?"

She hadn't seen or heard from her former friend since their falling out, something that had been weighing on her conscience more and more. In the past two weeks, she had even started varying her arrival and departure times from the plant, hoping to run into the elusive girl, just to make sure she was all right, but it hadn't happened. Perhaps Lavinia had noticed, though, and was finally trying to get in touch?

Genie could only hope. There was so much she wanted to say . . .

"It's not. It's a Mrs. Sharkey. She says she's your aunt?"

"My aunt?" Shock and disbelief raced through her, her sadness over Lavinia temporarily displaced.

"I'm just reporting what she said, but I'd beat feet, chickie. It's long distance."

Genie tossed the garments aside as excitement raced through her. "Coming!"

Flinging open the bedroom door, she dashed over and snatched the receiver from Audrey. "Hello, this is Genie."

"Eugenia Claire?" a woman asked hesitantly, her voice scratchy and thin through the earpiece. "I'm trying to reach the daughter of Reverend Eugene Baker."

Tears filled her eyes. She had waited so long to hear her aunt's voice. Her heart pounded with excitement and even a little fear. "Aunt Hazel?"

"Oh, thank the Lord!" the woman exclaimed. "Yes, child, yes! It's me, your father's sister. I've been trying to find you ever since I saw the article in the newspaper. You could've knocked me down with a feather when it said you were on your way to the States. Eugene was quite remiss in not warning me."

"We didn't have your new address," Genie said, still not quite believing her aunt had found her, and through Dick's article, no less. The Lord truly did move through mysterious ways, though it struck her as ironic that the man who had led her the furthest into sin was also inadvertently responsible for bringing her family back to her.

"My father didn't even know you had married," Genie continued. "I tried to find you. I went up to Bakersfield, but no one knew where you and Uncle Art had moved."

"Didn't Eugene get my letter? Oh, but never mind that now. Long distance is so expensive I should cut right to the chase, as Arthur would say. Though I guess I should say Uncle Arthur." Her aunt's voice warmed in obvious affection that gladdened Genie's heart. "We want to come see you, if that's all right."

"I would love that," Genie said honestly. "When?"

"Thursday? It's the only day your uncle could get tickets on the train."

"Do you know what time? I might have to ask off from work." Which Skip would just love, but she didn't care. She would take her lumps, because family was more important. Her father had taught her that.

There was a pause on the line. "You're employed?" Then her aunt rallied. "Well, of course you are. Well, don't worry, dear. We can talk about that when we see you. That, and when you'll be able to come home with us."

"Wait, what?"

But her aunt was talking again. "Uncle Arthur says we won't arrive until one thirty-five, so maybe we can go out for a late lunch afterward and catch up on all your experiences. Oh, and he says we'll be coming into Union Station."

Genie gave herself a little mental shake. "How about I meet you at the train?"

"Perfect, and don't worry—as long as you still look like your photo, we'll be able to pick you out." The smile in her aunt's voice told Genie that she thought there would be no change at all. Before Genie could say otherwise, her aunt was saying goodbye and promising to see her next Thursday.

Genie hung up the receiver, a little dazed. While thrilled to know her aunt was alive and well, she wasn't sure she knew how she felt about having family so precipitously dropped into her lap. She hadn't missed Aunt Hazel's beat of hesitation when Genie mentioned having a job. Then there was her aunt's assumption that Genie should move in with them, which could be heaven knew where.

Maybe once, when she had first arrived in the States, she would have been relieved by such a proposition. It was what her father had intended all along. But now, after having lived under her own supervision for six months, she wasn't sure she wanted to give that up.

Charity breezed in from the bathroom on a cloud of perfume. "You're not ready yet?" she asked in surprise as she adjusted an earring. "We've only got fifteen minutes until the boys arrive."

"Oh shoot! Just give me two shakes of a lamb's tail." Genie flew back into the bedroom. Tonight she was still Genie Baker, secretary and pilot. Later she would worry about her upcoming family reunion.

"You look swell tonight, Genie. Every fellow here will be green with envy." Tom, her blind date, winked as he held the door to the diner for her.

"Thanks." She gave him a wide smile. "You don't look so shabby yourself."

And he didn't. His army flight cadet uniform was freshly pressed, his cap perched confidently atop his soft-looking, sandy hair. With his thin, foxlike features, he wasn't exactly her type, but his brown eyes were friendly and intelligent. She was even coming to terms with his thin brush of a mustache that he no doubt hoped would make him look older.

He smiled back, and they went inside. Charity and her date were already sliding into a red leather booth. A gum-chewing waitress waited impatiently for Genie and Tom to sit. The Ink Spots crooned in the background, courtesy of a brightly lit jukebox.

Genie scooted into the booth, and Tom sat beside her. Briskly going over the day's specials, the waitress handed menus around.

"I wonder if they have beer here." Charity's date, Jack, flipped the menu over and glanced up. "Anyone else want a drink?"

"Coke is fine with me," Genie said, setting her menu down.

"Are you sure?" Tom asked, his brow furrowing slightly. "No need to be cheap on my account. I just got paid."

"It's not that. I just don't drink," she said, thinking how things always seemed to go wrong whenever she imbibed. "But you can order whatever you like. It won't bother me."

"If you're sure . . ."

"I'm fine." She smiled, giving him her best Charity impression, since everyone loved Charity. Seeing as how this was her first real date since coming to LA, she really didn't want to mess it up. Actually, it might be properly called her first real date ever. Having dinner with Ted in Calcutta didn't really count, nor did her dinner in July with Dick, since neither man had wanted to actually date her.

An appreciative warmth smoldered in Tom's gray eyes as he gazed back. "I can't get over how pretty you are, especially considering you're a pilot."

Her smile faded a bit. "What do you mean?"

"Well, you have to admit it's not the most feminine of pastimes, though I might have to rethink my objections after meeting you and Miss Charity," he said, utterly oblivious to the insult.

She glanced at her roommate in disbelief. Charity gave a small apologetic shrug, and Genie's hopes for the evening dwindled from finding true love to counting the minutes until she could escape.

The waitress came back to take their order. While Tom ordered for the two of them, Genie dug through her purse for spare change. The jukebox had gone silent, spurring her to action. If she hurried, she could at least have decent music to help her endure dinner.

Two dimes and five nickels later, she touched Tom on the sleeve. "Can you get up? I want to go pick out some songs."

"Sure, doll. Do you need some change?" He shifted and reached into his pocket. "I think I've got a quarter."

She hesitated briefly, not wanting to become too indebted to him, lest he expect more than a quick good-night kiss at the end of their date. Still, there was the whole dinner to get through. She took the coin. "Thanks."

He stood and let her out. "Don't get lost."

She smiled through gritted teeth; his teasing condescension reminded her a little too strongly of Nathan. "I won't."

Two hours. She would give him two hours to improve her impression of him. After that, she was going to throw in the towel and plead a savage headache.

The jukebox was ten cents a song, or five songs for forty cents. After a quick calculation, she began selecting the eight songs that appealed to her the most.

"I hear number three is a classic," a voice drawled close to her ear.

Her heart did a little stutter step. Hardly daring to breathe, she tilted her gaze up. No, she wasn't dreaming. Ted was really standing next to her, close enough to touch. Close enough for her to fall into those incredibly beautiful dark eyes.

"What are you doing here?" she managed when she could finally find enough air.

"Grabbing a bite to eat, same as you." His lips curved up ever so slightly, the small movement drawing her attention to his mouth. "Are you going to make a selection or not?"

It took a second, but then she heard the tease in his question. Heat flooded her cheeks as she hurriedly dropped her gaze to the song list. Good gravy, but she could not keep her wits around this man. "So number three, hmm?"

It was "Begin the Beguine." The title instantly transported her back to the 300 Club, to that moment when she had been in his arms as he hummed along to the song while the band played. Little butterflies took flight by the thousands in her veins, and her fingers shook as she fed the coins into the slot.

"Any others you'd suggest?" she asked, praying she didn't sound as breathless as she felt.

"Well . . ." His fingers touched the glass right next to hers, the warmth of his skin making hers burn with anticipation. *Please, please, please* . . . As if hearing her plea, he moved his hand until his fingers rested against hers. Sparks of sensation flooded up her arm and through the rest of her body, leaving her light-headed and weak. "I've always liked this one." His voice deepened as he guided her hand to the right to stop above "Who Wouldn't Love You?" by the Ink Spots.

She shivered as his nearness brushed like fire along every nerve ending. "What are you doing, Ted?"

"Enjoying your company," he drawled in a low voice, his breath feather-soft against her ear. "Hoping you'll join me for dinner."

Her knees felt like they would give way any second now. She cleared her throat. "That would be a little awkward, since I'm on a date right now."

"Really? With whom?" Abruptly, he straightened and looked around, his brows drawn into a harsh line.

"The cadet by the window who's waiting for me."

"Tom Anderson?" He relaxed. "That's all right, then. He's harmless enough."

"Harmless, maybe, but he's also a first-rate ass."

"Genie, such language!" he said, feigning shock even as he laughed.

"You should have heard what he said about female pilots," she said, irritation sparking again. "It took everything I had not to bean him with the menu."

"You probably should have." His amused smile sent her wits scattering again. "Maybe it would have knocked some sense into him."

She turned her attention back to the song list. "I think it might be a hopeless cause in his case, but thanks for the moral support."

"Who's the other gal you're with?"

Her spirits sank. "My roommate, Charity." *And yes, she's beautiful. Just don't fall for her like every other male on the planet.* "If you had come to Flo's going-away dinner, you would have met her there."

His eyebrows climbed a little farther. "That's Frank Short's little niece, the pilot? Wow. She's quite the looker."

"I know." Glumly, she punched a series of numbers with a bit more force than the machine deserved. The number three for "Begin the Beguine" wasn't among them.

"But too blonde for me. I prefer gals with a bit more fire."

Her gaze jerked up to meet his. This time there was no mistaking the warmth in his eyes, and her pulse kicked in response, as did her bruised pride.

"Where have you been?" The words were out before she could stop them. "I thought we were friends."

Apology darkened his gaze. "I'm sorry. I didn't mean to drop off the map like that. I was sent to Texas on a special assignment that kept getting extended, which is why I wasn't at Flo's party, and why I never called you. I actually just got back into town this morning."

"Oh." Further speech was beyond her, even though there was so much more she wanted to say, like she had missed him, and she understood he didn't want to be more than friends, and that it was fine with her, as long as she could still see him once in a while.

He glanced back at the booth containing Charity and the two cadet pilots. "If you're done choosing songs, I think I'll join you all for a bit, just to make sure a certain cadet knows to behave himself."

She noted the single bar pinned to his collar. "Do lieutenants outrank cadets?"

He winked at her. "This one does." He gestured for her to lead the way back to the booth, so she did.

"Did you hear Flo is flying for the WAFS now?" she asked over her shoulder.

"I did. Pretty amazing."

"Charity is going to apply to be a Woof Teddie as soon as she gets a few more hours. You know," she added at his blank look, "a pilot with the Women's Flying Training Detachment. It's a new army program for those of us who don't quite have the five hundred hours to become a WAFS pilot but still want to help fly for our country."

"Try more like a thousand hours to join the WAFS, or so I heard. And are you sure about the army part? I haven't heard a word about it."

"Well, here, ask Charity," she said as they reached the booth. She almost laughed as the two younger pilots scrambled to their feet the second they saw Ted, their eyes wide.

"Good evening, sir," they said almost in unison. Tom's gaze darted to her, and he swallowed uneasily.

Ted smiled easily. "Gentlemen, mind if I join you for a moment? I'd like to speak with Miss Charity about this new training program she's signing up for."

Tom scooted over on the booth bench to make room. Genie took a seat in the middle with Ted next to her, sandwiching her in. It was a little tight between the two men, but she couldn't complain. Not with Ted's thigh pressed against her own, sending delicious thrills of pleasure through her.

A faint sounding of alarm prickled her conscience as she recognized the warmth in her blood for what it was: sexual attraction. She should shift away so their legs no longer touched, but that would mean moving closer to Tom. There just wasn't enough room on the dratted bench.

"The new training division is set to start in November down in Texas," Charity told Ted, her face glowing with excitement. "Right now they're looking for gals with as little as two hundred hours, but there's also talk they might drop it lower if the first class is successful."

Ted frowned slightly. "That's awfully low time to be ferrying military planes around."

"Oh, I don't think so." Charity leaned forward and tapped on the table with a painted nail. "Admit it, you're sending pilots into battle, in these same planes, with a lot fewer hours and with less experience in general."

"True, but that doesn't make it ideal. And they know what the score is when they sign up."

"And we don't?" Charity arched an imperious eyebrow. "Or are you saying that women are somehow incapable of flying military aircraft?"

"No, what I'm saying is it's dangerous work, ferrying untested aircraft around. If I were you, I'd leave it to us men."

"Why?" Genie asked, genuinely curious. "Women do plenty of other dangerous jobs, like working on the assembly line. Should we leave that for men, too?"

His eyebrows lifted at her question. "I hadn't actually thought about it, but . . . yeah. I think women should be treasured, protected. They're what holds society together. They represent everything that's good and right in the world, the heart of the family. What do you think every soldier, sailor, and marine is out there fighting to preserve?"

"Oh, I don't know," Genie said drily. "Maybe our way of life? Democracy and freedom?"

"Well, that, too." He tilted his head, conceding the point. "Still, I'm glad I don't have to worry about you signing up anytime soon."

"Really?" Her temper sparked.

"Really," he said firmly. "Face it. The war will be long over before you get enough hours."

She narrowed her gaze. "And what if it isn't?"

"Then I would tell you to think twice, because I couldn't date a girl who would recklessly endanger her life like that."

"Well, then, I guess it's a good thing we're not dating. Because no one—except the Good Lord and my father—has the right to tell me how to live my life."

"If you want to fly army aircraft, the army gets to tell you *exactly* that. I get told all the time what to do and how to do it, and I listen because they're trying to keep me alive."

"Only until they aren't," she said. "There is a war going on, and you can't tell me the army wouldn't sacrifice you in a heartbeat if it meant the difference between winning and losing."

"As is their right," he said stubbornly.

She tried a different tack. "And if they asked you to give up flying because it was too dangerous, would you do it?"

"That's not what we're arguing here. We're talking about the intrinsic value of women to society. How important it is to keep you all safe and alive." He sat forward, all electric intensity. "Take the case of our mothers. We both know firsthand the damage caused by their untimely deaths."

"Yes, but our mothers also both died without ever setting foot in an aircraft," she said just as passionately, refusing to be intimidated. "Or by doing anything more risky than just living. People die, Ted. No one lives forever."

A muscle in his jaw twitched as he stood. "I'm done with this conversation. Charity, it was nice meeting you."

"Oh, fine. Walk away just because you don't want to hear the truth," Genie said, still incensed. "You're such a coward."

He stiffened, and she abruptly realized she had all but shouted that last part. The other diners had stopped talking and were now staring at her.

He flushed under his tan, and his nostrils flared. "What was that?"

She shifted uncomfortably, but she would not back down. This was too important. "I said you're a coward. Not physically. I know you risk your life every day, without hesitation, in service of this country. But when it comes to your heart, you won't risk a thing.

"You say it's all about protecting women and keeping us safe, but really it's about keeping us locked in gilded little cages so you won't get hurt. *You.* Not us. But life doesn't work that way. Love doesn't work that way. Putting us in a cage will eventually kill us all by itself."

A deafening silence spread over the diner. Ted stood stock still, his dark eyes boring into hers. Heat prickled all over her skin as her anger turned into a kind of desperation. Her chest squeezed so tight, she couldn't breathe. *Please, please understand . . .*

Slowly, he turned his back on her and walked away.

As if an electric cord had been cut, she slumped back in the booth, her mood turning bleak. What kind of fool was she? Ted had met her father, been in her home . . . and now she had driven him away.

She had severed her last link to China.

She felt like she might vomit.

"Genie!" Charity hissed across the table.

"I'm sorry. I think I'd better go." She stood, refusing to meet her friend's eyes. The shocked disapproval in the two flight cadets' faces was awful enough. *This is what comes from speaking one's mind.* How many times had she been counseled to hold her tongue—that it was better to be seen than heard? This was why.

The fact that no one protested as she left the table only made her feel worse. Her hands shook as she lifted the receiver on the pay phone to call a cab. Then she realized she had used all her change in the juke-box and had only bills.

"Here." Charity appeared beside her and held out a dime, her pretty face pinched with worry. "Do you want me to come with you?"

Genie shook her head and wiped her eyes with the back of her hand. "No. I'm so sorry."

"Don't apologize. I was getting pretty steamed toward the end, too. You were just a lot braver than me. So don't worry." Charity gave her a quick hug. "You take care of yourself, and I'll take care of the boys."

Drawing a deep breath while her friend returned to the booth to smooth the waters, Genie turned her back on the diner and inserted the dime to call a cab. Her emotions were too raw to see if Ted was still there. Part of her knew she had done the right thing by speaking up. She had fought too long and too hard for her right to make her own choices to be told she couldn't.

It still hurt, though, that the person she had to tell off was Ted. *Ted*, who, out of all the men gathered there, was the only one who had seemed to care what she thought, had actually seen her as a person.

Or so she had believed. Now she wasn't so sure.

# Chapter 40

By the time Thursday arrived, Genie was a nervous wreck. She had changed her outfit at least five times, trying to decide which one would be the most appropriate for meeting her aunt and uncle for the first time. Was her aunt as conservative as her father, or had living in the States these last twenty years made her more tolerant? Should Genie wear her hair up or down? If she put on a little mascara and lipstick, as was her custom now, would her aunt have a heart attack?

There was so much she wanted to say. So much she wanted to ask. Like what was her father like as a child? What had her mother been like? Her grandparents? She was so hungry for information on her family, she didn't know where to start.

More than anything, though, she wanted to love her aunt and uncle, and to have them love her in return. What worried her was that they wouldn't, because she had strayed so far from her father's teachings. The doubts had started Friday night, after her argument with Ted, on her long cab ride home.

The hard truth was her father would have agreed with Ted: women were to be protected. *She* was to be protected. Even worse, she believed it herself. Wasn't that why she had felt so betrayed by Lavinia, because she had expected Lavinia to risk becoming a pariah to protect Genie? Yet protected meant caged, and she didn't want that. Did she?

Ironically, the more she tried to figure out what she wanted, the more unsure she became. An even greater irony was the fact that it had been Ted who had encouraged her all those months ago to start thinking for herself, and by doing so, she had driven him away.

The only real clarity she had achieved from the weekend's introspection was that she had been too harsh with Lavinia. Even though Genie still hadn't figured out how to reconcile her faith with what Lavinia had been doing with Sheila that night, she recognized her friend had truly been between a rock and a hard place, thanks to Dick's blackmail. Genie couldn't honestly say she would have handled the situation any better than Lavinia had. Pricked by conscience, she had called the apartment over the weekend, not once but three times, hoping to catch Lavinia. But no one had answered.

All week she had kept her eyes open at the plant, hoping to catch at least a glimpse of her former friend, but to no avail. It was getting absurd. If she didn't see Lavinia this morning, tomorrow she would make the trek over to the machine shop tomorrow and hunt her down. Decency demanded that she make every effort to apologize, and the truth was, she missed Lavinia. A lot.

"Genie, we're leaving!" Charity called from the front hall. "Don't miss the bus. Skip is irritated enough you're taking the afternoon off."

"I know, I know!" Genie threw a belt on around her skirt and called it good. By the time she reached the kitchen, her roommates were gone. Grabbing her bag and hat, she flew out the door and down the stairs.

She had no sooner turned left on the sidewalk, heading toward the bus stop, than a sedan pulled up next to the curb. A man jumped out of the driver's side.

"Genie! Genie Baker, wait."

To her dismay, it was Dick. Ducking her head, she walked faster, pretending she didn't see him. *Oh Lord, not today.* She was already late and emotionally on edge.

His fingers clamped around her elbow, drawing her to a stop. "Genie, please. I've been worried sick ever since I came back and found you and Lavinia gone."

Repulsed by his touch, she yanked her arm free. "Well, I'm fine, and what do you mean Lavinia is gone?"

He reached for her again, and she backed away. Comprehension flashed in his hazel eyes, and his expression hardened. "She told you."

"No. She guarded your secret faithfully to the end." Anger at Lavinia's betrayal flared in her blood all over again. "I had to learn from someone else."

Something like regret flickered in his face. He held his hands out to her. "Genie, I'm sorry. I know I should have said something sooner, but I'm getting a divorce—something I should have done a long time ago, I see that now—so we can be together. Genie, please say you forgive me. I love you."

Funny how four months ago, before Ted had told her the truth, she would have been over the moon to hear those three little words from him. Now they only made her sad. And furious. "No, you don't. If you did, you wouldn't have tried to turn me into your mistress. How could you even think I would be all right kissing a married man? You knew my father was a reverend, and that I was raised by missionaries."

"That was never my intent," he said earnestly. "That night was a mistake. My control slipped, but that it did is a testament to how much I want you. Desire you. You brought light back into my life. I have done everything I could to take care of you. Do my other actions count for nothing?"

Her conscience shifted uneasily, because he had done a lot for her. She would have been lost after Nathan's death without Dick's help. If he hadn't been there to lean on during those first dark days and then offered her and Lavinia a place to stay and almost-guaranteed employment, she might have given up and stayed in New York doing heaven knew what to survive. Certainly not learning to fly.

*On the other hand* . . . "You lied to me, Dick."

"And I apologize. Can we at least be friends?"

An echo of a similar question from Lavinia came back to her. Her heart twisted with renewed loss. "It's not that I'm not grateful for everything you've done for me. I am. But you and Lavinia should have trusted me with the truth from the start. Yes, I would've been shocked and likely would've asked for changes, but our friendship would have at least stood a chance of surviving."

"But not now."

"No." Pain lanced through her as reality as well as the rightness of her decision solidified in her soul. "After having been lied to about something so big, I no longer trust you. And without trust, there is no friendship, and certainly not love."

"So we're through."

She nodded. Nothing she could say would make it easier for either of them, so she stayed silent.

He exhaled heavily and looked out over the street. "There were two letters for you at the apartment. I didn't think to bring them. I can drop them by next week."

"No, wait," she said, her heart skipping a beat as she suddenly remembered that Nathan's grave marker was still in Dick's front closet. She had meant to retrieve it weeks ago but had been afraid of running into Lavinia, and the awkwardness that would result from it. "I left something in the apartment, and I was planning on stopping by to pick it up—if you don't mind, that is. I can leave the key on the table after I'm done."

He frowned slightly. "Are you sure? The place was pretty cleaned out when I stopped by last week."

Sudden unease made her heart skip a bit more. She hadn't worried too much about not seeing Lavinia at the plant, since they worked in different areas, but to hear that her friend had also apparently moved made Genie wonder if there was something more to her friend's absence.

She took a deep breath and told herself Lavinia was fine. "I should still check. Better safe than sorry."

"All right." He gave her a small, sad smile. "And if you decide, once you're there, that you want to move back in, that would be all right, too. The rent is paid up for another three months."

She shook her head. "Dick—"

He held up his hands in surrender. "I know, I know." He winked at her, a little of his irrepressible spirit returning. "Can't blame a fellow for trying. But I should let you go, so you won't be late."

She gasped as she remembered the time. "Oh shoot!"

Without even saying goodbye, she sprinted for the corner. To her dismay, her worst fears were confirmed. The bus stop was without its usual crowd of people. She had missed the bus and would now officially be late to work.

Skip would fire her for sure.

She whirled around, hoping against hope Dick would drive her. He wasn't there. His sedan was gone, too. But then why should he hang around after she had turned him down so completely?

Tears of frustration burned in her throat. She could wait for the next bus and throw herself on Skip's nonexistent mercy when she got to work. Either he would fire her on the spot, or he'd spitefully revoke her afternoon leave so she couldn't meet her aunt and uncle, forcing her to quit. Or, more likely, once again try to pressure her into having sex with him, now that he had broken it off with Gloria. *Wonderful.*

Well, she had been thinking of looking for a new job, anyway. Maybe this was the Lord's way of telling her it was time. And maybe it was time for her to start listening to Him again.

She glanced at her watch. Four hours before she had to meet the train. Plenty of time to do all the things she should have done weeks ago.

She realized now that she had been hiding these last few weeks from the pain in her life. Well, she was through with that. Dick had started the ball rolling by showing up this morning, and she had survived. She might as well continue down the path.

Rehearsing what she would say, she ran back up the stairs to the apartment. After throwing her bag on the chair, she picked up the phone and dialed before she could change her mind. Her hands were slick with perspiration as she waited for the Vultee switchboard operator to put her through. She wiped one hand on her cotton skirt, and then the other.

"This is Stuart Winston." The impatient edge in Skip's voice shook her resolve. *What are you doing, Genie? You need this job. You need the money, the character reference for the training program application.* "Hello?"

"Mr. Winston, this is Genie Baker." Hating how breathless she sounded, she tightened her hold on the receiver and continued more forcefully, "I—I'm not coming in today. In fact, I quit. I wanted to give two weeks' notice, but I think we both know that would be ill advised, given your interest in me."

She stopped herself in the nick of time from adding *I'm sorry*, because she wasn't.

Silence greeted her pronouncement, and her knees turned to water as she waited, a million doubts assailing her.

"I see," he said finally. "You sure you want to do this? We're busier than ever. You'll be leaving us shorthanded at a really bad time."

She felt herself weakening. He was right; they were extremely busy recently, with the new government contracts rolling in. The other girls in the office pool would hate her if she quit. Tension coiled in her shoulders, making her feel ill.

*Don't do it, Genie. Don't give in. Skip will make your life miserable. He's already asked you twice this month to meet him at the hotel after work. How much longer do you think you can hold him off? And there's a Help Wanted sign on nearly every corner.*

"You'll be fine," she said before she could change her mind. Again the urge to apologize rose within her, and again she shoved it down. "Goodbye, Mr. Winston."

She hung up, light-headed with relief. There was a lot she would miss about working at the plant, but Skip wasn't among them.

She glanced at the clock on the wall. Still time to catch the number nineteen over to Dick's apartment and deal with the next thing she had been avoiding for too long. Well, two things, really: the ghosts of the dead and the living—Nathan and Lavinia.

Thirty minutes later, she got off the bus at her old stop. She dug through her bag to find her key to her former apartment. Perhaps it was telling she had never gotten around to returning the key. Like this morning, she could have asked Dick to bring her the grave marker, thus avoiding the trip. But she hadn't.

A wave of nostalgia rolled over her as she unlocked the building door. How clearly she could remember lugging her suitcase up the stairs that first day. So much trepidation and hope. And then, after her first flight lesson, she had raced up these same steps, taking them two at a time, eager to share her excitement with Lavinia.

She took a deep breath against the rush of bittersweet pain. How innocent she had been. How green. How trusting.

The familiar odors of the building greeted her as she made her way up the two flights of stairs, releasing more memories. By the time she unlocked the apartment door, she half expected to find Lavinia there, standing by the table, waiting to hear how her day had been.

"Lavinia?" she called as she walked in, even though she knew no one was there. Nor had been for some time. There were no lingering smells of food or soap. Just empty silence.

Feeling like an intruder, she ventured farther into what had been her apartment. It looked the same as the last time she had been there, though someone had put away the dishes and taken out the garbage. On the dinette table were two envelopes, just as Dick had said. Curious, she walked over, wondering who they were from. She hadn't even thought to have her mail forwarded.

Her fingers hovered over the envelopes as she recognized the handwriting. Both were from Lavinia; only one was addressed to Genie, and the other was to Kitty. Kitty's was stamped "Return to sender." Abruptly, Genie fell back in time to that fateful afternoon when Dick had showed up out of the blue. Had Lavinia mailed it then, after Dick had given her the address, or was this a later one?

Perhaps if Lavinia had been brave enough to tell her the truth that day—or the next, when Genie had pressed her on why she didn't like Dick—things would have turned out differently. Instead the widow had chosen to cling to her secrets. *And maybe she had been right to do so, considering how you threw her aside when they came to light.*

She shook her head, denying the thought.

Lavinia's mistake had been in lying to her, not in being attracted to women. Unnatural as it seemed, how Lavinia handled her love life was between her and the Lord. Lavinia's "curse" was not why Genie had pulled away.

*Liar. Dick's lie was even more damning, and yet you sent him away with kindness. Not kicked like an unwanted dog.*

She sucked in her breath at the unfairness of the accusation, but the guilt and despair spilling into her veins told her otherwise. Some of the things she had said that night had been unforgivably cruel. She had not only "kicked" Lavinia; she had kicked her when her friend was down. How many times had she begged her friend to tell her the truth about her curse, promising to understand?

She wanted to sink into the ground, her sorrow and disgust over her failure complete. Lavinia had known her better than she had known herself, and the truth of that was devastating. Despite knowing Genie's limitations as a decent human being, Lavinia had remained her friend. Genie was the one who had thrown their friendship away.

With shaking hands, she took up the letter addressed to her, almost afraid to open it.

Lavinia's spiky, erratic handwriting was difficult to read. Reading the contents, though, was even more difficult.

> *Dear Genie,*
> *I'm leaving town today because I know you never want to see me again, and this will help with that . . .*

Silent recriminations blurred Genie's vision, and she had to blink several times to see the paper again.

> *I hope you keep flying. I tried to help out where I could by covering extra expenses so you would have more money for lessons. And I hope you will forgive me, but I took Nathan's grave marker. I know you paid for it, but it bothered me that we never did anything with it. I know you won't believe me, but I really did care for him.*
> *I replay that last day over and over in my mind, wishing I had thought to say or do something different. I didn't kill him, Genie. After you left the cabin that morning, I went to find him. I couldn't believe what you had said was true, but yes—he was going to take me to my father's. We were standing by the outside stairs, in the midst of a heated argument, when Kitty arrived.*
> *For reasons she never explained, she began to taunt Nathan, until he was beyond furious. Then she turned and kissed me full on the mouth right there in front of him. I pushed her away, but it was too late. He had*

*already gone pale, his horror so clear it is forever imprint-*
*ed on my soul. I reached for him, begging forgiveness. He*
*backed away as if faced with a monster, heedless of the*
*stairs behind him. The rest you know.*
    *The train is leaving soon.*
    *May you live with the Lord's blessing,*
    *Lavinia*

*P.S. One last thing. I'm ashamed to say I was so angry*
*with Kitty those final days aboard ship, I threatened her,*
*which is why she paid for us to fly to California. I'm sorry*
*that you share my guilt in that, even if only by associa-*
*tion. As for Kitty, I find that, with the passing of time,*
*even if I can't forget her role in Nathan's passing, I can*
*forgive her. I hope someday you will forgive me. —L*

Genie stared sightlessly at the cramped letter for she had no idea how long.

Her poor friend.

Genie had utterly failed her. Numbly, she put the letter back into the envelope. The letter to Kitty she would discard somewhere discreet, unopened, and away from prying eyes. Safeguarding her friend's privacy was the least she could do at this point.

Shoving both letters into her purse, she double-checked the front closet. As expected, the grave marker was gone. Aware of the passing minutes, Genie went into the bedroom one last time. Drawn by some unknown impulse, she went to the wardrobe and opened Lavinia's drawers.

To her surprise, her friend's clothes were still there, neatly folded, but perhaps there were fewer items. It was hard to tell. Silently asking Lavinia's forgiveness, she opened the bottom drawer, the one where her friend had kept her most private things. Carefully, she moved aside the familiar pile of sweaters. The faded floral blouse and long skirt were still there, as was the water-stained Bible. However, the journal was gone.

Her gaze caught on a scrap of paper sticking out of the Bible. With shaking fingers, she opened the book to remove the torn remains of a black-and-white photograph. The one from Thailand. Lavinia and Marcus and the other male missionary looked somberly out at her, but the woman was gone. *Only I fell in love again . . .* Lavinia's words swirled like apparitions in the silence, leaving the identity of the woman no longer in question.

Some things were too precious to be left behind.

Genie closed her eyes against a surge of remorse. Who was she to damn Lavinia for finding love wherever she could, especially after all her friend had lived through? Was Genie any different, letting her desire for love initially cloud her judgment with Dick? The need to love and be loved in return was the root of the human condition.

Her father would be appalled by how quickly she had cast Lavinia out. He, who after finding Zhenzhu, had opened his home to the homeless and had served as a friend to the friendless Wu Fang, bringing him back to the village to live. *She* was appalled.

When had she grown so cold? The worst part was that she was never likely going to have a chance to apologize. Wherever Lavinia had gotten off to, the permanence of the ripped photo suggested she was never coming back.

The soft ticking of the wall clock reminded Genie she needed to get going. Unsteadily, she made her way to the door and gave the apartment one last visual sweep. Somehow, she would figure out a way to make things right, even if it took her a lifetime. Lavinia deserved better.

"Forgive me," she whispered to the empty rooms, hoping somehow her friend would hear. "I'm so, so sorry."

With nothing left to hold her there, she placed Dick's key on the kitchen counter and left.

# Chapter 41

Genie rushed into the cavernous waiting room of Union Station and scanned the mass of humanity for any likely older couple who might be her aunt and uncle. Unfortunately, all she had to go on was a twenty-year-old photo in her father's study. Her search wasn't helped by the hundreds of people crowding through the beautiful room. On any other day, she might have stopped to admire the soaring wood-beamed ceiling and floor-to-ceiling windows that filled the airy space with natural light. She might have even taken the time to examine the four enormous chandeliers with their art deco detailing. This afternoon, she only noted them in passing. After reading Lavinia's devastating letter, she didn't have the emotional energy for anything but her immediate mission.

Her gaze snagged on a dark-haired man and a short, rounder woman standing beneath a huge clock jutting from the wall. Both were neatly, if conservatively, attired, much as she would expect her father's family to dress. However, it was the way the woman peered intently at everyone who passed with a worried look on her face that decided it.

Genie's heels clicked on the polished marble as she hurried toward them. Anticipation and excitement fizzed through her veins, scattering the morning's sorrows. Finally, after all this time, she would be face-to-face with an aunt she'd known only through letters and a single photograph. "Aunt Hazel?"

The woman turned, her face lighting up. "Eugenia Claire! Oh, but you look just like your mother. I would know you anywhere."

"I'm so glad to meet you." Genie stepped into her aunt's embrace, all the turmoil in her heart vanishing under a warm tide of love.

Aunt Hazel excitedly pushed her back and inspected her at arm's length. Her blue eyes, so very like her brother's, swept from Genie's curled and pinned hair, down the blue-striped blouse and navy pencil skirt, to the pumps Genie had borrowed from Audrey.

"You look so grown-up in that outfit," her aunt gushed. Then a slight frown narrowed her gaze. "Does your father know you wear lipstick?"

"I haven't mentioned it to him in any of my letters," Genie said, keeping her tone light. "But I can't imagine he would object."

It was like Kunming all over again, except this time it was her father's sister, not his assistant, who was questioning her choices. Her mood slipped a little. *Thank goodness I wore the longer-length skirt.*

"Never mind, Hazel. I think you look pretty as a peach, Miss Eugenia." A kind smile lit the weathered face of the older man. His brown eyes were warm with welcome. "I'm your new uncle, Arthur Sharkey. But you can call me Art, like everyone else."

She liked him at once. "It's nice to meet you both. Do you have any baggage?"

"Just the one case." Uncle Art gestured to the leather valise on the ground. "We only expect to be here one night."

"Unless you think it will take you longer to pack," Aunt Hazel said with sincere concern, seeming to have recovered herself. "We don't want you to feel rushed."

"Pack?" Genie blinked in surprise. She had barely come to terms with meeting them.

"So you can come home with us tomorrow." Aunt Hazel gave her an odd look. "That is why Eugene sent you here to the States, isn't it?"

"Well, yes—"

Aunt Hazel took both of Genie's hands, and again Genie was struck by the uncanny resemblance between her aunt and her father. It was like looking into her father's all-too-perceptive eyes. Her heart twisted with the sudden longing to be with him and Zhenzhu again.

"Don't worry," her aunt said firmly. "We've an extra room in our apartment, so it will be no bother. There's plenty for you to do with all the war activities going on: knitting and collecting and volunteering at drives. You could even help the girls in our church write letters to the boys overseas, to help keep up their morale."

"That all sounds lovely, but—"

"Hazel, dear," Art said gently. "Perhaps we should discuss the particulars over lunch. Eugenia here is looking a little pale."

"Yes, lunch." Pulling herself together, Genie grabbed ahold of the suggestion like a life rope. "There's the Harvey House here, or maybe we could find something close to your hotel. Do you know where you're staying?"

They did. Genie guided them out of the station, and at that point Uncle Art assumed complete control of the situation despite Genie being more familiar with the city. Ten months ago she would have expected nothing less from the lone man in the group. Now it exasperated her when he asked a train conductor, instead of her, the best way to get to the hotel. Still, Uncle Art was now family, and she had been raised to respect her elders.

She turned her attention to her aunt while Uncle Art flagged down a taxi. "How was your trip?"

As she had hoped, her aunt took the bait and began to describe everything they had seen along the way. Loving to talk seemed to be a Baker family trait, and Genie wasn't above using it to her advantage. While her aunt complained about how crowded the train was and all the inconveniences of travel since the start of the war, Genie tried to decide what she wanted to do.

Yesterday, if asked, she would have flatly stated she wasn't moving from LA no matter what. Today she wasn't feeling quite so sure of herself. Being with her aunt was making her face the uncomfortable truth that she had made a lot of decisions since leaving home, many of which her father would have decided differently.

Maybe the failure was his, for never giving her the chance to practice speaking for herself. Or maybe it was hers, because she didn't deserve the right, because women inherently couldn't be trusted to make the right decision. Or—thinking of Dick and Skip and Ted—maybe men sometimes made bad decisions, too, in which case, she was only being human.

The taxi arrived, and the three of them got in. While Aunt Hazel took in the sights, and Uncle Art discussed the war with the taxi driver, Genie refocused on the upcoming discussion.

To be fair, their invitation wasn't wholly unexpected. Family took care of family—that was just how things worked, in her experience. Of course her aunt wanted Genie to move in with them. It was, in fact, what her father had counted on when he had sent Genie to the States. If the situation were reversed, her father would be horrified to find his niece living in Peking on her own, having to find work to pay for food and a roof over her head. And if he had learned that the same niece had also been briefly under the protection of a married man and was still being pressured to sleep with her boss?

She would be on the train bound for Kweilin faster than she could blink.

Which meant if she wanted to stay in LA, her aunt and uncle mustn't find out about Dick or Skip—or Lavinia, for that matter—lest her aunt ask why the girls were no longer friends after all their travels together.

"Hazel was telling me you have a job?" Uncle Art asked, pulling her from her thoughts. "Where are you working?"

*Good question.* Rather than go with the absolute truth, that she would be looking for a new one tomorrow, which might lead to questions of why she had just quit the one she'd had, she chose to answer as if he had asked in past tense, not present. "At Vultee Consolidated, in the secretary pool."

Her uncle's eyebrows rose as if impressed. "So you're involved in the war effort. Do you like it?"

*Another thorny question.* She chose her words carefully. "I like feeling that I'm making a difference and helping our boys win the war. And they have a wonderful employee flight program, which helped me get my pilot's license."

"You fly?" her aunt exclaimed from beside her, clearly aghast. Genie tried not to feel hurt by her aunt's reaction. It wasn't like she had taken up gambling.

"I do," she said, keeping her tone light. "And I'm told I'm a natural at it."

"But it's so . . . unfeminine. Does your father know?"

"I don't know, but I don't think he would mind." On this, she felt like she was on firmer ground. "When he took me to the aviation exposition in Shanghai, he never said anything about women being unsuited for flight."

"Have you heard from your father?" Uncle Art asked suddenly. "Recently, I mean."

A deep-seated sorrow stole over her. "No. I send him a letter every week, but so far I haven't gotten anything in return."

Her aunt sighed. "We haven't, either. That's why I was so happy to finally locate you. You and Eugene are my only family, besides Artie." She reached over the seat and gave his shoulder an affectionate squeeze.

He smiled warmly back at his wife, and the love between them was so clear, Genie felt a pang of envy even as her anxiety for her father's safety increased. It had to be the postal service's fault that nothing was getting through. She refused to allow it to be anything else.

The taxi arrived at the hotel, and Genie got out of the car with the others. Aunt Hazel had started asking her questions about her trip around the world, and Genie did her best to make it sound exciting. It took a lot of self-editing to not mention Lavinia or Dick, which was exhausting. Especially after all the morning's emotional landmines. However, there was no getting around Nathan's death.

"Oh, you poor dear." Aunt Hazel's eyes were bright with unshed tears, having mistaken the cause of Genie's voice breaking when mentioning it. Genie wanted to hug the older woman, who was clearly as empathetic and intrinsically kind as her brother—yet another couple of Baker traits that somehow had skipped her.

Genie sighed inwardly as she reassured her aunt that she was fine. What she didn't add was that it hadn't been her heart broken that day, but Lavinia's.

"Does your father know?" her aunt asked. This was becoming the standard question of the afternoon.

"The captain sent a cable when we reached port, but I don't think he got it. I honestly don't think anything is going through, on account of the war. The Society didn't even know Nathan had left China, even though I'm sure my father had notified them so they could forward Nathan's stipend to the States."

Which only reinforced her belief that something was off with the mail in and out of China, thanks to the war raging within her borders.

Uncle Art shot Genie an uneasy look from the front desk, one that she wasn't sure how to interpret.

Her aunt was talking again, her face alight with excitement. "I can't wait to show you all the things I picked up in San Francisco. They have a Chinatown there, and I wanted you to feel at home, so I bought all sorts of things for your room."

Uncle Art joined them. His smile wasn't quite as easy as it had been. "You beautiful gals ready to head upstairs? The front desk is making a reservation for us. As soon as we drop off the bag, we can eat."

413

"Oh, and I have a surprise for you, too!" Aunt Hazel said as they got into the elevator with the bellhop. "I went through my old family albums and found some wedding photos of your father and mother. I brought a few along because I couldn't wait to show them to you."

"I would love to see them," Genie said, touched by the gesture. The more time she spent with her aunt, the more she wished she didn't have to let her down. Aunt Hazel was so excited by Genie's mere existence, it was humbling.

The elevator operator opened the gate for them when they reached their floor. Genie followed her aunt and uncle into their small hotel room.

"Hazel, love. Why don't you look for those photos while we wait for the front desk to call with our reservations?" Uncle Art asked his wife as he set the valise on the bed.

"Good idea. I think I even threw in one of Eugene as a baby." Aunt Hazel immediately seized the tiny lock and began rolling the tumblers. While she did so, Uncle Art gently took Genie's elbow and pulled her aside.

"You should probably see this," he said in a low voice as he pulled an envelope from his inner jacket pocket. "It came yesterday. I haven't shown it to Hazel yet. I didn't want to spoil her day, but I figured you've a right to know. It sounded like your copy hasn't arrived yet."

Genie hesitated and then took the envelope from him. Turned slightly so her back was to the room, she read the front. It was from the Society. Dread, sharp and cold, swept through her veins, leaving her light-headed and shaky.

Uncle Art touched her arm. With one eye on his wife, he leaned closer and whispered, "The news isn't good, Genie. You might want to wait until you're alone to read it."

Fighting a wave of nausea, she stared at the unopened envelope, the need to know duking it out with the very real possibility of having her worst fear realized. Her aunt prattled on happily behind her as she dug through the suitcase. With crushing certainty, Genie knew what the letter would say and what the news would do to her aunt. What it would do to *her*.

Her breath came quicker, her lungs refusing to expand. The pain was too great.

The floor tilted, and she reached for the wall. She couldn't lose her father. She wasn't ready to be an orphan.

Uncle Art caught her shoulder. "I'm so sorry I had to be the one to tell you, but when you kept saying you hadn't heard anything, I wasn't sure if you were protecting your aunt, or if you really didn't know."

"I didn't know," she said, amazed she could actually speak.

"If you need some time to yourself, I'll make your excuses to Hazel." His brown eyes radiated strength and compassion as their gazes met. She felt the pang of envy again. Her aunt was so lucky to have him to help her through the dark months ahead. Genie had no one.

*That's not true,* her mind whispered. *If you go home with them, you won't be alone. You and your aunt will have each other. And Uncle Art.*

It wasn't like she had to worry anymore about asking for time off from work.

Grief hit her again in an unassailable wave, and her knees almost buckled under the blow. If her father was gone, then likely Zhenzhu . . . *Oh Lord, no. Please. Not Zhenzhu, too.* She had to get out of here.

"Will you tell her soon?" she asked, handing the envelope back to him. Perhaps tomorrow she would ask to read the letter, when she was stronger and not so broken.

"I'll tell her tonight, after you leave. I wanted her to have the joy of meeting you before the news took it all away."

She gave him a small smile, his face blurring with tears. Maybe, someday, if the Lord forgave her, she would find someone as kind and loving for herself.

"What are you two whispering about?" The friendly tease in her aunt's voice made Genie want to sob.

Summoning the last of her emotional reserves, Genie turned around to face her father's sister, her aunt, and smile. "Nothing important. Though, if you don't mind, I think I'll pass on lunch. I've got a lot of packing to do if I'm going to make that train tomorrow."

"Yes, of course." Delight and relief sparked brightly in her aunt's face, making it clear how much Genie coming home with them meant to her. Genie was definitely doing the right thing. "Will we see you tonight for dinner?"

"I'll try, but it depends on how far I get." She hugged her uncle and then her aunt. More tears threatened as she clung to her one last family member. "I'll see you tomorrow, though, for sure."

# Chapter 42

"I can't believe it," Charity said later that evening. Her friend lay on the bedspread, her chin propped in her hands as she watched Genie cram the last of her clothes into her battered suitcase. "I'm so sorry about your father, but it won't be the same without another pilot in the house. Audrey and Janice glaze over whenever I try to talk about flying."

"You'll be with other pilots soon enough." Genie looked dispiritedly around the room for anything she might have missed. She wondered if Uncle Art had broken the news to Aunt Hazel yet. She hoped the grief wouldn't kill her aunt. Genie wanted many, many more years to get to know her relative.

"You're going to keep flying, right?" Charity gave her a stern look. "Because if I hear you've quit, I will personally come to Fresno and drag your little derriere to the airport. And if I can't make it, because I'm in training, I'll be sure to send Mrs. Cochran."

Genie huffed a small laugh at the thought of the feisty Women's Ferrying Division head showing up at Aunt Hazel's house. Her spirits lifted a little. Now, there was someone Genie would love to meet. Jackie Cochran was a legend, having started her own cosmetic empire in her twenties and learning to fly on a whim. Now she was a fearless champion of women being allowed to fly for the military. Something both Ted and Aunt Hazel disapproved of.

Her spirits crashed and burned again. Moving to Fresno would also mean never seeing Ted again, too, even in passing. Still, returning to her father's family and leading the life he would have wanted for her, surely that would provide its own reward. Wouldn't it?

She rearranged her clothes to make them lie smoother in the suitcase. "Speaking of Mrs. Cochran, when do you think you'll hear back on your application?"

"Soon. My acknowledgment letter said I'm being considered for the November class, so I should be finding out any day now."

"You'll make it. Don't worry." Of that, Genie was sure.

With nothing left to pack, she shut the lid, the click of the latches sounding hopelessly final. At least she had dodged the question of whether she would keep flying, because likely she wouldn't. It was something she had wrestled with all afternoon after stopping by the plant to pick up her last paycheck.

Though it depressed her to no end, the bottom line was she couldn't keep doing something if it distressed her aunt. It would be selfish of her, and she had been selfish enough recently to last the rest of her life. Maybe someday, once her aunt had recovered from this latest shock, Genie would consider returning to the air.

Maybe she would even return to China, to see if anything was left of her village.

Tears welled in her eyes, and she struggled to breathe.

Charity hopped off the bed and threw her arms around Genie. "Don't cry, dear heart. Do you know how it happened?"

Genie dragged in a shuddering breath, Charity's familiar perfume comforting her. At least some things didn't change.

*Panta rei, Genie.* Her father's beloved voice echoed in her memories. It was like a knife between her ribs.

She closed her eyes and exhaled. "I don't know. I never actually got a chance to read the letter."

"Wait—you what?" Charity sounded almost angry. "If you didn't read it, then how do you know he's actually . . . you know."

"Uncle Art said it was bad news."

"Yes, but maybe it said he was ill, or missing, or had lost all his money in a bad bet."

"My father doesn't . . . didn't gamble."

"Still, you said the letter was from his employers, right?"

"Yes. It was from the Society. So?"

"Didn't you once say they were hopeless, not even knowing where their own ministers were?"

Genie frowned slightly. Charity had a point. The Society had lost track of Nathan with the chaos reigning in China.

Mentally she kicked herself for not reading the letter. *He might still be alive.* The thought made her giddy and devastated at the same time. Her heart had been so thoroughly shattered thinking he was dead, she couldn't let her hopes get too high. She might not survive having them destroyed again.

Should she call her uncle and ask what the letter said? For that matter, where was her copy? She had corresponded with them several times. They had her address.

No, they had Dick's address. She hadn't remembered to correct it with them, nor had she had her mail forwarded. It was likely in the mailbox at the apartment building, the one she no longer had the key to, or else Dick had picked it up and forgotten to leave it for her. She couldn't believe this.

It was either call her uncle or Dick.

"You're right," Genie said, getting to her feet. "I'll call Uncle Art."

The operator put her through to the hotel, and the clerk at the front desk rang her aunt and uncle's room.

"The line's busy, miss. Would you like to leave a message?"

Genie closed her eyes in frustration. In all likelihood, her uncle had taken the phone off the hook so they wouldn't be disturbed, which meant he wouldn't get her message until tomorrow. She wasn't sure she could wait that long to know whether or not her father was actually dead. "No. I'll try back later."

"Now what?" Charity asked, her eyes wide with concern.

"Now I call Dick and see if he has it."

This call was a little harder to place, and her stomach flip-flopped several times as she waited for the operator to find his home number—was she looking for the Richard Pelton in West Hollywood?—and then put her through.

A woman answered the phone, her voice slurred. "Hello?"

"This is Genie Baker. I'm sorry to call so late, but is Mr. Pelton available?"

The woman cursed and hung up with a decisive click.

Genie inhaled shakily and hung up the receiver. "I guess not."

"Likely that was the very unhappy Mrs. Pelton," Charity observed drily.

Genie collapsed onto one of the kitchen chairs. "This is awful. I don't know how I'll sleep tonight."

Charity sat across from her. She drummed her red-painted finger-nails on the table for a moment and then stopped. "What about the police? They could get into the mailbox, couldn't they? If you tell them it's an emergency, maybe they could still do it tonight."

Genie rolled her eyes. "The police are not going to care if I find out how or if my father died tonight."

"How do you know?" Charity said stubbornly. "Are you just going to give up without even trying?"

The answer was no, she was not. Without much hope, she had the operator put her through to the LAPD.

"This is Detective Joe Vital," a gravelly voice finally said over the line.

She explained about the locked mailbox, and the letter that might or might not say her father was dead in China, and how she really, really wanted to know if he was all right.

The detective cut her off. "We don't open mailboxes without a warrant."

"Wait," she said, trying to keep him on the line, her brain working furiously. It wasn't easy, given all the shocks it had had today. "What if I told you my roommate is missing—which is true, by the way—and she might have left a clue as to her disappearance in the mailbox." Which was also true, if unlikely.

"How long has she been gone?" he asked, sounding more interested.

"Two months, I think."

"You think?" Boredom had crept back into his voice.

"We had a falling out, and I moved out right afterward. No one has seen her since."

"Any chance she might have done herself in? Because I've got an unidentified white female I'm trying to identify." He paused, and Genie, breath held and sick to her stomach, heard what sounded like papers being shuffled. She hadn't even considered the awful possibility that Lavinia might have harmed herself.

"Here it is. Female Caucasian in her early twenties. Found not far from Venice Beach, an apparent drowning victim. It was hard to say how long she was in the water, but coroner guessed at least a month. Long enough to make identification difficult, in any case."

Genie swallowed hard as the kitchen swam before her eyes. "Do you know what color her hair was?"

"Says here, blonde. Does that fit?" Detective Vital continued, sounding almost hopeful.

Relief flooded her so fast, she almost dropped the receiver. "No. Lavinia's hair is dark, almost black."

"Well, I guess this isn't her." Disappointment laced his tired voice. "Shame, too. It would've been nice to get this file off my desk. You would think families would keep better track of their loved ones."

Her heart squeezed as she thought of Lavinia's family, and then of her own father. Was someone, right now, in China lamenting the same problem concerning her father's body?

"I wish I could help you, miss," the detective continued. "But without probable cause, we're not opening that box. My advice is wait for the postman tomorrow."

"And my friend?"

"You could file a report, but if your friend doesn't want to be found, you'd be wasting your time. Unless she turns up in an alley, or washes up on a beach, there's not much we can do. Especially with the war on, and so many people moving around."

The war again. Lord, how she wished it would end. It tore everything apart, scattering entire nations, soldier and civilian alike, to the four winds, with neither care nor concern.

"So?" Charity asked as Genie hung up the receiver.

"The short answer is no, they can't help me."

Charity hesitated. "Is Lavinia really missing?"

"Yes." Rubbing her temples, Genie closed her eyes against the wave of despair, all the fight beaten out of her. She had made so many mistakes, hurt too many people, Lavinia especially; it was time to give up and forget about being independent. "There's one more person I can ask: her friend Sheila. If she doesn't know where Lavinia is, I'm at a loss. I could take out personal ads in different newspapers, hoping she'll see one, though I'll need to wait until I know my aunt's phone number."

Her friend's perfume enveloped her a second before Charity's arms closed around her in a tight hug.

"Don't go, Genie. I know you love your aunt and want to help her, but I think you're making a mistake. Whether your father is alive or not, he wouldn't want you to give up the fight. There's real evil threatening China and the US and the rest of the world, and you are in a unique position, because you can make a real difference in this war.

"You and I both know we've got planes aplenty, with more rolling off the line every minute. What we don't have are enough pilots to move them. Genie, there just aren't enough of us. If you quit, that makes one less."

Genie sighed. "But my father wanted me to—"

"Escape China, which you did. But consider this: What if his survival is depending on that one fighter plane to arrive, that one bomber, that might turn the tide of this war? The one that's stuck on our factory lot because we don't have enough pilots to move them. What then?"

Charity sat back, her gray eyes intent. "Anyone can write letters to the troops, Genie, or help staff scrap material drives. Anyone can work in an office typing letters or on the production line setting rivets. But not everyone can be a pilot."

Genie bit her lip in distress. In her mind's eye she could picture one of their planes zooming over the emerald green of her homeland, on its way to battle the enemy. She could almost feel the controls beneath her fingers, the frame vibrating with the throttle full open.

No. She had made her decision. Aunt Hazel would be devastated if Genie didn't return with them tomorrow, and Genie had been raised to put family first. But her father and Zhenzhu were also family, and what if one or both of them were still alive, waiting for help? She had made so many bad choices since leaving home, she was afraid to make any more.

Going with her aunt and uncle would mean returning to a life with which she was familiar, where she would know her role. Where she wouldn't be expected to think, or speak, or make decisions for herself. Where she wouldn't be able to fly.

Genie no longer knew what to do. If only her father were here . . .

Except what had she learned these past few months if not that she was an independent person, with thoughts and dreams of her own? She wasn't just her father's daughter. She was herself, Eugenia Claire Baker. She was the tree that stood against the wind.

"I would have to find a new job," she said slowly, testing the feel of her decision against her conscience. "Building hours isn't cheap." That her conscience was silent spoke volumes. It convinced her she was doing the right thing.

Charity pushed back and searched Genie's face. "You're not going to go to Fresno?"

"No," she said, her resolve solidifying. "I think winning this war is more important than any one person's sorrow. And what our side needs is more planes, which calls for pilots. Male and female."

"Especially female!" Charity hugged her again. "I'm so glad. Your father would be so proud of you. And your aunt will forgive you. Don't worry."

Genie wasn't so sure on either account, but she had to be true to what she believed.

Her father would at least agree with that.

And in her heart, she believed she was meant to fly.

# Chapter 43

After a sleepless night, Genie sprinted into the train station for the second time in twenty-four hours. The buses had been running late this morning, so she missed an important connection, which had led to her just missing her aunt and uncle at the hotel. Aunt Hazel was likely in a panic. If she had tried to call the apartment, no one would have answered, since Charity and her other roommates were already at work.

Her gaze raced over the crowded platforms, but there was no sign of her aunt or uncle. Her nervousness ratcheted up another notch. She had no illusion the upcoming conversation was going to go well, and—Lord as her witness—she had tried to arrive early enough to have it in private. The train heading to Fresno was starting to load. Genie hurried forward, determined to find her relatives, even if she had to sneak aboard.

"Genie, Genie Baker."

She almost tripped as she recognized the familiar drawl. *Ted?*

She spun around, her heart beating way too fast. Sure enough, Ted was jogging toward her. He was in uniform, or mostly. He had on his battered brown flight jacket, the same one she remembered from China. He had never looked more handsome. "What are you doing here?"

"I might ask you the same." He smiled a little hesitantly, his beautiful eyes luminous with something she couldn't quite decipher, but it wasn't anger. "You're not leaving town, are you?"

"No." But she had been until about twelve hours ago. Urgency gripped her again. She backed away, even as it killed her to do so. "I'm so sorry, but I'm looking for someone."

"I've got a few minutes until the new cadets arrive. Let me help you."

"Oh, I . . ." Two familiar faces appeared down the platform, both clearly searching for her, and both clearly worried. Relief raced through her. "There they are!"

Leaving Ted behind, she hurried toward them. Aunt Hazel saw her first and waved madly.

"Where were you?" her aunt said, tears in her eyes. "I was so worried."

"I'm sorry, Aunt Hazel. The buses were—"

Her aunt's gaze dropped to Genie's empty hands. Her face clouded in confusion. "Did you already leave your bag with the porter?"

"No, see . . . I'll explain in a moment." She turned to her uncle, the need to know her father's status overriding all else. "The letter you showed me yesterday: What did it say exactly? I was so upset, I never actually read it."

Her uncle cast a hesitant glance at his wife, who had paled. "It said they had lost contact with your father, and since it had been more than three years since they had heard from him, they had to presume he was dead, a casualty of the conflict over there."

"They *presume* he's gone," she repeated, wanting to be sure she'd heard correctly, even as relief pounded in her head. "But they don't know for sure?"

"No," he admitted. "But three years is a long time."

Hope surged within her, leaving her dizzy. "I was just with him nine months ago, remember? And I'll attest that we never got Aunt

Hazel's letter announcing your marriage, so it could be the mail isn't getting through in either direction."

She turned back to her aunt, feeling the lightest she had all day. "So there's still hope. But we won't know for sure until the war is over, which is why I have to stay." She glanced pleadingly at her uncle, hoping he would understand. "I'm needed here. The sooner this war is over, the better for everyone. And because I'm a pilot, I can actually do something to help shorten the war."

He nodded, as she hoped he would, though his eyes remained sad. "We've all been called upon to make sacrifices during this time of national peril, you no less than us. We'll miss you, though."

She threw her arms around her new uncle and hugged him. "Thank you. And I'll miss you, too."

"You're not coming?" Her aunt sounded so lost, it broke Genie's heart.

She took the older woman gently into her arms. "No, Aunt Hazel. Not right now. But I'll come visit you as often as I can."

"But what would your father say?" Aunt Hazel's voice trembled.

Genie hugged her tighter. "I think he would understand. After all, he's the one who taught me about duty and being true to one's beliefs." She pulled back slightly to look into her aunt's blue eyes. "Yes?"

A tear slid down her aunt's papery cheek. "But flying is so dangerous."

"A week ago I had the same reaction, ma'am," a bystander interjected gently. "But your niece here set me straight."

Genie glanced up, startled to see Ted standing beside her. He smiled at her, and her heart thumped painfully.

He continued, his dark eyes never leaving hers. "She told me it shouldn't matter if it's dangerous or not—a gal should have a choice in deciding her own destiny. It took a couple of days for the truth of that to sink in, for me to realize my objection had more to do with my fears than her abilities. And to be honest, it wasn't easy for me to admit I'd been wrong."

Genie's mouth dropped open in surprise as he turned to her uncle and held out his hand. "Lieutenant Ted Younan, at your service, sir. Sorry to interrupt a family discussion, but I wanted to tell you that your niece is one smart cookie, brave as heck, and someone I feel honored to know."

"How do you do?" Her uncle smiled and shook Ted's hand. "Arthur Sharkey. And this is my wife, Hazel. Eugenia's aunt."

"I would have guessed," Ted said, his smile broadening. "You look a great deal like Genie's father, but a lot prettier."

Aunt Hazel sniffed as she wiped her cheek. "How would you know?"

"Oh, I'm sorry. I just assumed you would know." Ted's expression turned serious. "Your brother was the man who rescued me after my plane was shot down in China."

Aunt Hazel froze midwipe. "You're the Flying Tiger from the newspaper?"

"I think so, ma'am. I did fly for the AVG. And help Genie here get out of China."

"Oh my," Aunt Hazel said faintly, her tearstained eyes wide. "Did you come to see my Eugenia off?"

"No, ma'am. That I'm here is something of a happy accident." He turned to Genie, his dark gaze becoming hesitant, vulnerable. "I was planning to call this weekend, when I finally got some time off, to see if she would forgive me for being such a blockhead at the diner. My rudeness was uncalled for. I was completely out of line when I said what I did about women and flying. It may have been my honest opinion, but it wasn't fair. And I'm sorry."

Caught off guard, she didn't speak for a few heartbeats. "And your position on women being allowed to ferry airplanes?"

"I still think ferrying is dangerous work, more so than people think. But you've fought for the same rights and privileges as any other pilot, and you proved yourself as worthy as any fellow, or you wouldn't have that license. Which is not to say I wouldn't worry every time you went up. But if the situation were reversed, and someone tried to ground me for my own safety? I would've said something a lot stronger than what you did that night."

She forgot about the audience, her focus entirely on the man in front of her. "So is it just me who gets the pass, or any female pilot?"

"Any and all," he said firmly.

She believed him. Of all the people she knew, he was the only one she trusted to always tell her the truth, even if she didn't want to hear it.

"Then I forgive you." She hoped he could hear the sincerity in her voice.

The flicker of relief she saw in the deep brown depths told her he had.

"All aboard!" the conductor called from down the track.

Genie turned back to her aunt and uncle. "Take care. I love you both."

With a flurry of kisses and hugs, the older couple boarded the train. Genie waited and then waved as the train slowly moved out. It saddened her more than she had expected.

"I'm glad I got to meet them," Ted said from beside her. She glanced up. He was watching the train disappear down the track with a pensive look.

"I'm glad, too. I think they like you," she said with a small laugh.

His dark eyes smiled down at her. "I think they like you, too. And for the record, so do I."

"You do?" She had meant to sound cool and sophisticated, but her voice squeaked.

"I do," he said firmly. "And if you'll let me, I'd like to take you out to dinner."

"I might get attached," she warned, quite seriously.

He took her hand and studied her knuckles. "Yes, well. The same gal who convinced me women should fly ferries also chewed me out for being a coward about that."

She groaned and tried to pull her hand away. "I'm so sorry. Can we forget I said that?"

"No." His grip tightened ever so slightly, refusing to let go. "Because you were right about that, too. I was being a coward, and I didn't even know it."

She finally looked up at him, and her breath caught at the open adoration on his face.

He gave her a small smile. "You're going to think this is crazy, but we have a cadet who is Chinese, and he told me this fable about a princess and a tiger. He said reading about me in the damn paper made him think about it."

"Oh heavens. Not Dick's article again."

He laughed. "The very one. Anyway, I wonder if you know it."

"I do," she said, an eerie chill ghosting up her spine. "It was one of my favorites growing up. The princess was Guan Yin, the goddess of compassion, who was slated to die, except the Great Celestial Tiger swept down from the heavens to save her. Together they journeyed to hell, where he was supposed to leave her, but the tiger fell in love, so he carried her to the Fragrant Mountain instead, where she lived evermore in peace."

"Yes, well. One could say that sounds a lot like us."

"You are a Flying Tiger," she agreed, her heart in her throat. "And you did drop out of the sky. Though more like a meteorite than a celestial being."

"True, and true," he said with a laugh. His gaze turned tender. "So all we need to do is find that Fragrant Mountain, and we're all set. Because somewhere along the way, I fell in love with you, Genie. And

I don't want to lose you. That's something I also thought about this weekend . . . a lot."

"I . . ." Joy, shock, disbelief, and elation all washed over her in a single wave, leaving her light-headed and momentarily speechless. She swallowed hard. "I think I've fallen for you, too. But the war . . ."

He exhaled. "Is still going on, I know. And I wasn't kidding the other night about fighter pilots leading short lives. I'll do my best to come back to you, but I can't promise."

She shushed him with a finger on his lips. "I know. And I appreciate you always telling me the truth. It's one of the things I love about you."

Dark promise entered his eyes as he caught her hand. "Then I will never tell you anything but the truth."

"Then tell me this: Did you like kissing me that night in Calcutta?" Her lips curved at the memory. "It was my first. Did you know that?"

He looked instantly apologetic. "No. If I had, I would've taken my time and done a better job."

"If you want to try again, I wouldn't object."

One dark eyebrow slid up. "Is that so?"

Her smile deepened as she leaned forward, silently daring him to kiss her again. "Why don't you try and find out?"

The blast of a horn had them both jumping. Across the station, another train was steaming up to the platform.

"Shoot," Ted said, glancing over at it. "I've got to go."

Genie's pulse accelerated with alarm. She was not going to miss her chance again. The second he turned back, she seized his face between her hands and kissed him. She felt his surprise, and then his arms enfolded her, clutching her tightly to him as if he would never let her go. In the space of one heartbeat to the next, he turned her rather chaste kiss into something far, far different.

All thought fled as the world receded and left just Ted, his strength, his heat, his courage, his innate goodness. Her heart sang.

The squeal of brakes had her pulling back, breaking the kiss. For a moment she could only stare at him in amazement. That hadn't been a kiss like the ones Dick had given her, of a man overpowering a woman, but a kiss between equals. One that gave as much as it took, and she was utterly and completely hooked.

"Can I call you later?" he said, his gaze touching her face everywhere as if memorizing every detail.

"Yes." She forced herself to step back and was amazed she could. Her legs trembled like reeds in a wind. "But I might be out flying."

"Sounds good." He started backing away, duty calling. "You still going to apply for that ferry training school?"

"I am."

"Good. You'll do great." He gave her a grin and quick two-finger salute, the same one he had in Calcutta, before turning around. As he jogged away, she stared after him. She wondered if he even noticed all the women admiring him as he passed. She doubted it, even though he certainly was every girl's dream with his dark, exotic looks and aviator jacket. And he was hers, if she wanted him.

And she did.

She smiled to herself as she walked back through the station. There were still plenty of challenges to face, the most pressing one being to find another job to pay for hours. She didn't care. Life stretched out in front of her like an open runway.

And this time, no matter where the future took her, she was ready to fly.

# Acknowledgments

This story would never have been born without the encouragement of my wonderful agent, Laura Bradford, who suggested I try writing something a little different. As usual, it was a fantastic idea. Also thank you to my wonderful editors at Lake Union, Chris and Tiffany, for believing in this story and in me.

I would also like to sincerely thank Tami Richey, beta reader extraordinaire. Without your friendship and steadfast patience, I would have given up on writing long ago. You are the absolute best, and I am forever in your debt.

Also, a huge shout-out to my critique partners: Lizbeth Selvig, Laramie Sasseville, and Nancy Holland, all talented writers in their own right. My life and writing are richer for your involvement, and I am beyond happy you allowed me into your clique.

Thank you as well to Sarah Chien, Betty Chien, and Margaret Hung Fong for their cultural feedback on the scenes set in China. Your willingness to read unedited prose was exceedingly brave of you, and greatly appreciated.

Finally, I want to thank my wonderful husband for believing in me even when I didn't. Without you, this book would never have been completed. You are simply the best.

# About the Author

*Photo © 2014 Shelley Anderson Photography*

Always fascinated by history and adventure, Ellen Lindseth received her BA in classics from the University of Colorado, Boulder, with an eye on becoming an archaeologist. When that didn't pan out, she decided to write stories of strong, spirited women eager to embark on adventures of their own.

She studied at Minneapolis's Loft Literary Center and is a member of the Women's Fiction Writers Association and Romance Writers of America. Two of her WWII historical romances were finalists in the prestigious RWA Golden Heart contest, and one of her short stories was chosen for publication in Midwest Fiction Writers' popular anthology.

When not writing about the resourceful women of the 1940s, Ellen, a licensed pilot, flies with her husband (also a pilot), exploring the world and looking for new ideas.